After a successful and varied career in the British Special Forces
and service with the American military and government, Oscar
King now works in the financial sector in London and the
Middle East. When not working or adventuring, King writes.
Having previously written military non-fiction for Bene Factum,
he has now successfully turned his hand to fiction.
Persian Roulette is the first of three novels in the
Harry Linley series.

PERSIAN ROULETTE

OSCAR KING

NINE
ELMS
BOOKS

Persian Roulette

First published in 2015 by
Nine Elms Books
An imprint of Bene Factum Publishing Ltd
PO Box 58122
London
SW8 5WZ
Email: inquiries@bene-factum.co.uk
www.bene-factum.co.uk

ISBN: 978-1-910533-00-0

A CIP catalogue record of this is available from the British Library.

Cover design by Henry Rivers, thatcover.com
Book design by Bene Factum Publishing

Set in Borgia Pro
Printed and bound by ScandinavianBook

For my Minoosh

Contents

Characters

Bunny – a Persian cat

Shaheen Soroush – Iranian expatriate, TV channel owner

Vlad Berezniki – money launderer for Russian cartel

Luka Karchenko – sidekick and partner to Vlad

Alexei Delimkov – member of the Duma, Godfather of cartel

Ilyas Soltegov – member of the Duma, controller of cartel operations

Harry Linley – financial manager, former SAS soldier

Farah Soroush – Shaheen's wife

Maxim – cartel's senior assassin, AKA Bernhard Vorhoelter

Boris – cartel's junior assassin, AKA Jan Sperling

Natella Sultanova – company registrar, Financial Centre

Oleana Katayeva – Russian executive concierge

Mahmoud Abadi – rookie Dubai policeman

Omar Shamoon– CID warrant officer, Dubai Police

Graham Tree – managing director, private security company

Toby Sotheby – SIS, Abu Dhabi

John – CIA station chief, London

Pat – SIS, London

The President of the United States of America

US Secretary of State

Russian Foreign Minister

Iranian Foreign Minister

Abbreviations

ANPR – Automated Number Plate Recognition

BFF – Best Friend Forever

BRIXMIS – British Mission to the Soviet Forces in Germany

CIA – Central Intelligence Agency

CID – Criminal Investigations Division (Dubai Police)

HMG – Her Majesty's Government (UK)

KGB – Committee for State Security (English Translation)

MOE – Methods of Entry

NoK – Next of Kin

PM – Prime Minister

RFID – Radio Frequency Identification

RTA – Road Traffic Accident

SAS – Special Air Service

SF – Special Forces

SIS – Secret Intelligence Service (MI6)

SRR – Special Reconnaissance Regiment

SVR – Foreign Intelligence Service (Russia)

UAE – United Arab Emirates

UKSF – United Kingdom Special Forces

UN – United Nations

VP – Vice President

"The single biggest problem in communication
is the illusion that it has taken place."
George Bernard Shaw

"How often, you wonder,
has the direction of your life been shaped by such misunderstandings?
How many opportunities have you been denied –
or, for that matter, awarded –
because someone failed to see you properly?
How many friends have you lost, how many have you gained,
because they glimpsed some element of your personality that shone through
for only an instant,
and in circumstances you could never reproduce?"
Kevin Brockmeier

PROLOGUE
On The Palm

Shaheen Soroush was a nice man but not necessarily a good man. Life had been kind to him since he had left Iran, supposedly converted to atheism and established a satellite and internet distribution business for pornographic films that were made in 'Tehrangeles', the nickname given to LA by the expatriate Persian community.

He now lived in a luxurious villa on M-Frond on the prestigious Palm Jumeirah in Dubai. He owned a six-month-old Rolls Royce Ghost, had an elegant and immaculate Iranian wife, two Western-educated kids and the most expensive and beautiful, white, pedigree Persian cat that the mind could ever imagine.

Bunny was three years old and in her prime, her fur was white as fresh snow, her huge and perfectly shaped eyes were blue as an Icelandic lagoon, her face was large and flat, her nose small and pink, and she loved people.

In return, everybody adored Bunny; she wore a delicate Louis Vuitton cat collar; her nails were even painted vivid pink, which was a significant subject of amusement for all house visitors. However, in reality, it was for practical purposes that they had this acrylic covering, in order to blunt her nails and protect Shaheen's overpriced furniture. The pink was simply Shaheen's way of playing to Bunny's adoring crowd.

No one had ever pushed Shaheen on the subject of his priorities in life, but if one had to guess their marching order, it would be earning and spending money as fast as life would let him, followed by Bunny, and only then his family. Certainly when he was at home, the outpouring of affection that Shaheen showered on Bunny was inversely proportional to that which he showed his wife and family.

Naturally, not everyone approved of Shaheen's foray into pornography. The Iranian government had pledged that if he ever returned to his country, they would put him in jail for un-Islamic behaviour; this despite the fact that every senior minister had viewed and, in all likelihood, masturbated to his product. Shaheen's defence, in part, was that he was no longer religious; this, however, was not recognised by the Iranian regime, nor was the fact that he did not actually make the films; he just distributed them and took advertising revenues from the sites and channels under his ownership.

Meanwhile, those that socialised and partied with Shaheen were clearly of the opinion that his generosity and lavish hospitality by far outweighed any consideration regarding the origin of the funds that paid for such events.

So it was perhaps ironic that the most controversial and notorious source of income reaped by Shaheen was not the cause of the contract to kill him; rather it was something far more innocuous...

CHAPTER ONE
Good Debt, Bad Debt, Worse Debt

It all began during the pre-meltdown boom years of Dubai when all property was good property and no one could lose. Saudis were sleeping on the beach with briefcases full of money just to put a deposit on an apartment in tower blocks that were more imagination than reality. However, the buyer's intent in many cases was not to see the property achieve delivery. The strategy was to buy and flip the off-plan properties to make a profit of five percent a month on something that did not even exist. When demand became so high in Dubai that buyers could no longer buy off-plan, then the lesser-known Emirates became a popular area of speculation; after all, logic dictated that these were buildings and not a dot-com boom, so how could the bubble burst?

A little known, relatively adjacent Emirate to Dubai, called Ajman, was introduced to Shaheen Soroush as a 'no-lose' opportunity. The *Burj Takseeb* Towers, two blocks to be built to house lower-middle-class workers that could not afford to live in Dubai were designed to push the occupants onto a new level of quality of life. The apartments were cheap to build and even cheaper to equip, with plenty of landlord buyers looking for investment properties. Shaheen bought the development rights, commenced construction and had a scale-model tower built that could be displayed on a sales stand in Dubai's Mall of the Emirates.

The entire deal was a huge mistake but, once again, it was not the core deal that caused a death order to be issued.

Shaheen had known that Ajman was not everyone's cup of tea, so he needed a hook to attract potential buyers to the replica of the *Burj Takseeb* Towers on a stand outside the Mall's Seddiqi Rolex watch shop. The sales slogan was emblazoned across the stand and sales material:

Burj Takseeb – to enrich your living and your life

Shaheen decided to go the route of hiring two stunning Russian women to attract the attention of passing shoppers. However, the unseen hazard was that these tall, perfectly proportioned women attracted male 'birds of a feather'; Russian men who were not so interested in the merits of the Ajman properties than in getting these beauties in-between the sheets. He should have seen it coming, but he did not.

The girls worked on commission, and when a couple of Russian studs turned up at the stand dressed in designer clothing from head to toe, Olga and Elena did their job. They sold multiple apartments to their countrymen who were money laundering funds on behalf of a cartel, led by Alexei Delimkov, who also happened to be a representative of the Russian State Duma. The girls collected their commission for the multiple sales of 144 apartments and also obliged the two buyers by fucking their brains out when called to do so.

Shaheen was elated that he had accrued his 55 percent in cash in the form of deposits totalling $12 million, which was enough to build and deliver. Yet this was the issue that would eventually bring two Moscow hit men into town to snuff Shaheen, because delivery was something Shaheen did not achieve.

To be fair, like everything else that was about to cause an implosion in Shaheen's life, it was not his fault; nor had it been his intent to fail the buyer. However, he really should have checked that water and electricity would be available for the properties being developed in Ajman. The prominent Lebanese businessman had undoubtedly known about this crucial omission when he had sold on the project to Shaheen, but failed to disclose such things because that would surely have killed the deal. Then on top of that, a legendary Wall Street financial institution went bust in the US and caused a worldwide financial meltdown; so even if there had been utilities, Shaheen's *Takseeb* towers were beyond redemption. They were built but undeliverable.

Naturally, the decent thing to do would have been to give the Russians their money back, but this was not going to be easy on a number of counts. Firstly, there was the simple fact that Shaheen had taken the deposits before the introduction of an escrow law, so he had spent most of the money on building the towers themselves. What was left was blown on the best things that money could buy.

Shaheen had repeatedly explained the shortfalls of the Ajman infrastructure to the Russians, and had also pointed out that the deposits were non-refundable. All parties were well aware that only a civil case in the Ajman Arab courts could solve such an issue, but the Russians wanted no such process to bring attention to their money-laundering operation.

Shaheen was unaware that several years previous to his current problems coming to a head, Sulim Yamadayev had been assassinated in Dubai; it had been a perfect hit.

Sulim was the rebel commander during the first Chechen war in the days when young Russian soldiers were being slaughtered in Grozny. He subsequently showed the depth of his loyalty by switching sides to become the commander of the Russian Military Special Battalion Vostok. So by the time of his death, he had pretty much pissed everybody off on both sides.

Following the two and very separate assassinations of both of his brothers, the latter of whom was shot while driving Sulim's car in Moscow, Sulim had understandably and discreetly relocated to Dubai. Here he had lived under a pseudonym and only permitted himself one very inconspicuous bodyguard.

The small two-bedroom apartment in the 44-tower Jumeirah Beach complex should have been enough urban camouflage to protect him, but it was not. When the Russians finally tracked him down, the assassin waited in the underground car park for his quarry to show. As Sulim walked from his car to the lifts, the assassin moved innocuously past him, spun around and shot him twice through the back of the neck with a silenced pistol. It was all over for Sulim. The assassin then pistol-whipped the bodyguard into unconsciousness, picked up the two empty cases that had been ejected from the pistol, and simply disappeared.

In reality he walked out of the car park onto the busy street and turned the corner so as not to be tracked by a camera; he was then driven towards Abu Dhabi, where he was dropped at Raha Beach Hotel; the Russian driver was not aware of his identity or of the job. The assassin went to a prearranged room in the hotel for which the driver had given him a key; he showered before leaving his clothes with the pistol in a sports bag that would be retrieved by the 'Fixer' who had booked and paid for the room. He then left the hotel, walked to the shopping mall next door, got into a taxi to Abu Dhabi Airport and caught a Qatar Airways flight to Doha. From here he flew to South Africa before travelling home via Spain. He would never again return to the United Arab Emirates, even though his real identity would never be compromised.

His ultimate paymasters, the Delimkov cartel, were accused by Dubai's police of ordering the hit, and a warrant was issued for the arrest of the cartel's leader. This, of course, would never happen.

Rather than be deterred, the cartel's godfather was keen to reaffirm the extent of his reach to Interpol and the Dubai police and send an unambiguous 'I'm still a factor' message to other would-be debtors. He was, for these two reasons, unusually eager to send two of the assassin's colleagues to Dubai, but this time to dispatch a Persian who had screwed them out of 12 million US dollars.

CHAPTER TWO
Harry's Game

The precise sequence of events that caused Harry Nicholas Linley and Shaheen Soroush to meet was not clearly recalled by either of them. If anyone had asked, they would have guessed that it was a friend of a friend that had asked Harry to meet her at one of Shaheen's lavish parties in his villa on the Palm.

In any case, the meeting and the acquaintance that followed would result in destiny for one of them and fate for the other.

Harry certainly recalled being dropped off by the taxi outside of Shaheen's villa and being suitably impressed with the super-cars double-parked in the roadway outside, the Rolls Royce in the driveway, and the latest and loudest Iranian chart music booming out from the back garden.

As he walked through the large double front doorway, Harry did not know whether to soak up the lavish decoration, art and furniture or the stunning beauty of the Persian women who were flocking about the hallway and living room entrance. He decided to concentrate on the women, who were amongst the most beautiful he had ever seen in Dubai.

Harry must have been on his second beer when someone offered to introduce him to the host. He noticed straightaway that Shaheen was a man of some style and, while Harry deemed that, had he worn white flannels with a white shirt he would have looked a bit on the gay side, the look somehow suited Shaheen. It also did not hurt that throngs of women were hanging around the man.

As both men made small talk, they became acutely aware of a male chemistry between them, and both knew from experience in life that such events did not happen very often.

Shaheen explained that he ran a number of television channels, conveniently omitting the pornographic distribution element, and Harry explained that he worked in Dubai's financial district, conveniently omitting the multiple tours he had served as a British Special Forces officer in Northern Ireland, Bosnia, Iraq and Afghanistan.

Frankly, they both viewed each other as equals but from worlds and sectors apart. They also recognised that they kind of complemented each other.

Whereas Shaheen was wealthy and carried a small paunch, Harry was upper-middle-class with a concealed but hard-earned six-pack. Where Shaheen was married but unfaithful, Harry was divorced and cautious towards relationships. Where Shaheen longed to be anything except from the country of his birth, Harry could not be prouder of his Queen and country. Finally, where Shaheen was inherently dishonest but had never physically hurt anyone, Harry was inherently honest but had completed a kill-list as per the mandate handed him by Her Majesty's Special Air Service Regiment.

What both men did not realise was that the very differences that separated them would now thrust them together; it would cost a few men their lives and only much later, or possibly never, would either of them ever understand what had really happened.

Shaheen deemed the nightmare of Ajman and *Burj Takseeb* to be a dormant issue and he was happy because the money had funded the Rolls Royce. Harry had resolutely put all his Special Forces work behind him. He was grateful, however, that someone in the financial sector had recognised that if he could manage risk in a world where the blood ran red, then he could sure as hell manage risk in a world where it ran green; they had been right, and Harry planned to buy a property on London's Richmond Hill before he exited Dubai and the hedge fund industry.

Following their conversation, which Shaheen's wife had noted was longer than any exchange her husband had had with a male in her presence, Harry did what all Brits do at parties: he made his way to the kitchen.

Here he was glad to find likeminded loiterers and he managed to get himself a seat at the large kitchen table, where conversations regarding sex, politics and religion were already well into their second round.

It was about this time that he felt something rub his leg. Harry half-hoped it might be the foot of the Persian beauty, Ava, who was sitting beside him; he glanced down, but was bitterly disappointed. Rather than the first covert physical contact that could lead to a night of debauched sex with said beauty, it was, in fact, a cat. Harry hated cats.

However, this was clearly no 'moggy' saved from the dumpsters of Dubai. This was a pristine white ball of perfectly groomed hair. The cat sensed that she (and she was most certainly a 'she') was being looked at, and locked onto his blue eyes with hers. Harry smiled; after all, if he was cool with animals, then that might be cool with Ava too.

"And what's your name?" he asked, knowing and hoping the answer would come from his right.

"*That* is Bunny," Ava said on cue. "And she's a right little slut, she just loves men."

Ava was half-right: Bunny did love men, but only because her instincts told her to keep things sweet with those who exuded the smell of male musk, which she could easily sense.

She also loved to soak up heat, so orientated herself towards any human who pushed out body heat. She did not know it, but the difference between a European and an Aryan Persian body was that the former generated heat to cope with a cold climate; the Persian DNA did the opposite.

So this combination of musk and heat was good enough for Bunny, and it wasn't long before she was up onto Harry's lap with one graceful leap and purring.

Within a couple of minutes this instinct had been mis-interpreted as desire by the ladies present, who concluded that Bunny must be able to recognise nice personalities and that Harry must therefore be a really nice guy. Shaheen's wife was captivated by the sight of her cat, normally so aloof, now purring on Harry's lap, just as if she had known him for years. She was quick to point this out to Shaheen when he came into the kitchen; he liked Harry all the more. For once, Harry's body heat had proved an asset in the heat of Dubai.

Ava also showed Harry her appreciation later that night.

During the ensuing weeks, whenever Shaheen was having a social event, he touched base with Harry to see if he wanted to attend. He liked having the Brit connection; he deemed it gave the impression of respectability, and they chatted about business in a bland but friendly manner. Harry was well aware that doing business with anyone who was Iranian was a nightmare due to international sanctions, and therefore it was not worth the trouble to pitch Shaheen for investment. However, there were no rules about being entertained and it did not hurt that Shaheen's wife, Farah, was a brilliant cook.

Since his divorce, Harry had lived on his own in Marina View Tower in Dubai Marina. He was happy enough, but had come to realise that the inevitable sequence of change and loss that divorced life delivered was forcing him to the periphery of his children's lives. Like so many of his Special Forces mates, his single life was a product of his instinctive quest for adventure adapted to the service of his country. His marriage, although one that had been entered into for truly the right reasons, eventually revealed his and his wife's steadfast refusal to adapt to the inconvenient situation that it had come to represent.

Its conclusion had always been inevitable; Harry's ex-wife even admitted that she had married him because he was different, but that now she needed him to be like everyone else. She had sadly come to realise that most men, and especially Harry, could not do that. So she had instinctively selected her alpha-male to provide her with a couple of kids and then turned her attraction towards softer beta-males. Hence her affair and eventual marriage to a young Hereford bank manager, who thought that all his fantasies had come together when he was able to boast he was screwing the wife of an SAS man. Of course, by the time he realised what he had got himself into with two teenage kids and a pre-menopausal woman, the vows had already been sealed.

Despite the fact that Harry should have seen the divorce coming, he did not, and it had been anything but easy to cope with the break-up; leaving the Army had also proved a bitch. In truth, he missed his kids and he was lonely. The whole event of post-divorce had taught him that loneliness is not about having someone to do something with but much more about having someone to do nothing with. However, he had to be grateful for a well-paid job and the occasional experiences with the likes of Ava. Life could be worse, but he so wanted something to happen, something exciting. Or would life just be this dull for the rest of his days?

He often reflected that his situation was much akin to the poster of three vultures sitting on a branch with one of them saying: "*Patience my arse, I'm going to kill something*". Of course, it did not have to be that extreme; to be honest, any excitement would do. These musings would transpire to be a regretful case of 'be careful what you wish for'.

While Harry got on with his life as a relative hermit with very few close friends, Shaheen's life of social interaction and dodgy deals continued. The demand for pornography was predictably global and served as a foot in the door for further TV channels and advertising in far-flung places, including Singapore.

Shaheen was discovering a whole new market in this beautiful country that he viewed as Thailand's back yard. He quickly concluded that if he could achieve a foothold there, then Indonesia would be his next venture. His experience in the Middle East had taught him that he could make much more money in countries where pornography was blocked, and he silently thanked the United States Navy for developing the Tor browser that enabled internet users to download his films despite the most ardent attempts of religious zealots to block them.

Much to his surprise, Shaheen had discovered that the freedoms and climate of Singapore were preferable to those of the Middle East and, even with his life of privilege in Dubai, he was acutely aware that no taxes also meant no rights; so with Singapore discovered, he decided it was time to transition his home and business out there. However, he had to convince his wife before that could happen, especially as her entire social life and family were either in Dubai or an hour's flight away in Tehran.

His plan was simple enough: let her visit, smell and see the country. She would fall in love with it like any other visitor, and with that approval he could unwind his operation in Dubai and start anew, free from the shadow of debtors' prison that loomed in the event that a real-estate debt claim were made against him, which would prevent him from leaving the country.

Shaheen's wife did not leap at the thought of a week in Singapore, but she also thought, what the heck. It would at least be a decent break in a five-star hotel and if she did not like the place, she could simply veto the whole idea.

They tried to find some dates when the kids were off school and when Shaheen's business contacts were in town; they also needed to ensure Farah's social calendar was not full and when the mother-in-law could come from Tehran to housesit, mostly for the purpose of looking after Bunny. The matter was so complicated because Farah refused to have a live-in maid as a result of previous theft problems.

As it transpired, just when most of the jigsaw pieces had fitted into place, there was, as ever, one that did not. Shaheen had been getting increasingly frustrated, before finally they found a good 10-day stretch; only then did his mother-in-law make some lame excuse as to why she could not come to Dubai at the required time. A huge family row erupted. From Shaheen's point of view, he supported his in-laws' life-style for 52 weeks of the year and now the bitch could not even bother her arse to come and help when called? The ensuing domestic explosion resulted in his wife threatening not to go at all, which would dash his entire relocation plan.

Shaheen needed to find someone who could be relied upon to stay at the villa and look after Bunny without throwing parties every night. These parameters actually excluded most of his parasitic friends, who he had no doubt would bring in the white powder as well as everything else. He scrolled through his phone contacts to prompt an idea of whom to ask.

He got to 'H' and stopped at Harry Linley. He did not know the guy that well, but from what he did know, it would work. Sure, he was not part of their inner social set; but that was the perfect way to keep his Iranian friends at arm's length, because he was a Brit. He certainly was not a party animal and it seemed his biggest flaw was that he was honest (or so Shaheen assessed). However, the ace in the pack was that Bunny loved him and Shaheen's wife knew it.

Shaheen picked his moment to pitch the idea to Farah and, to his amazement, she actually agreed. If he could persuade Harry to cat-sit, then his future in the Far East could begin.

CHAPTER THREE
Don't Mess With The Duma

For the Delimkov cartel, which, in addition to its money laundering and other mafia activities, authorised the odd hit here and there, the decision to dispatch Shaheen Soroush in Dubai was not complicated. It would send a clear message to their debtors and show their disdain to credible law enforcement; so they called in another Duma member, their trusted Controller in such matters, to order the hit.

Former KGB Colonel Ilyas Soltegov's link to the Delimkov was well known in dubious circles, but he had always remained clean from a legal perspective. He explained to the Godfather that it would be "money for old rope" and that they would even get a chance to give one of their new boys a "bit of a run" to get him blooded.

Ilyas explained that he could make it all cost-efficient, from the labyrinth of flights, to the false but entirely authentic identification material, and the payment to the Fixer in Dubai. The cost would be about eight million roubles (about 250,000 US dollars); he would need 50 percent, plus logistic costs up front.

The subsequent planning process was procedural and, for a man with Soltegov's experience, second nature.

It ran: selection of the striker team (so named because of his love of football), entry route to country, reception team and equipment in country, linking of strikers to equipment, route to target, method of entry, method of dispatch, extraction to detach from equipment, sanitise, exfil from the country, route home. Nothing to it.

The striker team was an easy decision, the only restriction being that neither must have previously been in the UAE. This was in light of the facial recognition technology that had been installed after 2010, when Israel's Mossad had inadvertently blown their cover following their successful assassination of Hamas's Mahmoud Al-Mabhouh in his hotel room. That operation had gone brilliantly with regard to all of the above phases; it had been assumed that Al-Mabhouh simply died of a heart attack since his body was discovered as if he had been sleeping peacefully in his bed; there had even been heart medicine sitting on his bedside cabinet. His hotel room was tidy and his body showed no signs of struggle, with no bruising or wounds of any sort.

Had it not been for the keen, young and highly skilled Emirati pathologist who was on duty the day after the death, Mossad would have totally got away with it. However, knowing what he knew about the man on the slab, the pathologist had paused before signing the death off as 'Natural Causes' and looked at his watch. He had 30 minutes left on his shift, so decided to just take one more look, and this was when he noticed what looked like two little birthmarks just five centimetres under the deceased's left armpit. Probably nothing, but he asked his assistant to pass the magnifying glass and light.

As he peered at the two marks, he felt the blood drain from his face. These cells were not this colour because they were birthmarks but because they had been burned very shortly before death. Al-Mabhouh had been tasered!

The Mossad team were long gone and the humiliation they had inflicted on the entire security mechanism of Dubai was complete.

They had, however, underestimated the tracking ability of the Dubai authorities, and every surveillance tape was re-run. The painstaking detective work of the Dubai Police quickly identified the entire compilation of the Mossad team; they also ascertained that all had left the country and all had false (but real) passports. Ten days after the hit the faces of the Mossad agents were plastered over every newspaper. Yet none of them were ever publicly identified, let alone captured.

In a pledge that such matters would never again happen, the UAE spent well over $100 million on the best facial recognition technology money could buy. Everyone who entered the country was to be digitised for a match to their own passport, which was, of course, a vain attempt to seek out any of the Mossad team should they ever set foot back in the UAE – which, of course, would never happen.

With all this in mind, the Godfather agreed with the Controller that Maxim and Boris would be perfect for the job and that they should replicate Mossad's killing technique in order to cover their tracks. The Controller knew that this would probably be Maxim's last job. He was fit enough, but any man in his fifties got a little slower and, although no one would suspect Maxim's tradecraft, he had learned that knowing when to get out of such a business was a lot more important than knowing when to get in.

For Boris, this would be his first blood-job for the cartel. He had fallen into organised crime shortly after leaving the SpN PDSS, or Naval Spetsnaz as it was better known. Life out of the military had been a difficult transition with no job or prospects, so when he was asked to start driving and delivery for the cartel, he took it. He was then trained to help them with 'Methods of Entry', called MOE in the trade, but lock-picking by everyone else. In the back of his mind he recognised that each job they gave him was more complex (and more criminal), but the payouts were good and their network was as secure as any. Even so, Boris was surprised when they contacted him and subsequently explained that they had an elimination job abroad for which he had been selected as the 'number two'. Would he take it?

Even though the information was understandably scant, he knew that there was only one response. To turn down a job would effectively mean no consideration for 'promotion' and ejection from the inner circle.

From here the process was simple: behind closed doors Maxim was told that the target was an individual living in a single-family, luxury villa on the Palm Jumeirah. He would put his plan together and present it to the Controller. If the latter agreed with the plan, then he would quickly open the logistic support links. The key to the entire operation was the tight circle of knowledge; just one controller in Russia and one fixer in the UAE. No one except the Controller would be aware of all the elements involved. The UAE Fixer would not know the where, the who, or the what. Her job was to obey instructions to the letter and ensure that all the requested components were ready at the given time and place.

Even the *ab initio* Boris would not be briefed until it was time to go, and neither he nor Maxim would know the identities of anyone they met in Dubai, except Shaheen.

Maxim had his plan together within 24 hours, and the following day he met with the Controller at the State Duma offices, which, ironically, were considered entirely secure for the purpose of discussing such matters.

Maxim explained that they would enter the country from Germany and carry German passports. Maxim knew that these were easy to procure due to the old East German/ Soviet network; he emphasised to the Controller that the actual holders of the passports should be of similar age to the two-man team (he did not yet know the identity of Boris) and they needed to make damn sure that neither assumed nor real individual had set foot in Dubai since 2010. The Controller nodded: no problem.

"We'll be there to attend a convention, there's always one going on in Dubai; we'll pick one that's on at the time. The Fixer will need to organise the reservation of a white Toyota Camry from one of the large car rental companies. Whoever books the car should say they need it in white because the driver is very particular about having a white car that helps reflect the heat." Maxim paused to give the Controller the opportunity to interrupt. He need not have done so.

"Concurrently, prior to our arrival, the Fixer in Dubai should have identified a separate, recent-model, white Toyota Camry, and will need to steal the rear number plate off the car and have a similar copy made for the front of the car. He should also reserve a room at a hotel that is popular with Germans so that we have a reservation form to show immigration – but we won't use the room, so he can cancel the reservation as soon as we're in the country." Evidently, Maxim did not know that the Fixer was a woman.

"We need to rendezvous at a safe house with the equipment and the number plates. It needs to be a discreet private residence, preferably with a garage or driveway that can't be viewed from the road. The place should also be equipped with a decent washing machine, plenty of bottled water, a gas-fired barbecue grill and a kettle."

Here, the Controller did interrupt: "A kettle?"

"Yes, I like to drink tea," Maxim said simply before continuing.

"We also need two sets of surgical gloves, two bottles of spray-bleach, a local mobile phone, a pack of bin liners, two bottles of unscented Dettol soap and shampoo, washing powder, two ski-masks." He paused for a moment. "He can buy those from that indoor ski-slope they have there; I'll also need two roles of quality clingfilm and a Taser gun." He handed the Controller the shopping list.

The Controller smiled; he had been wondering if Maxim would agree to the method that Mossad had used to dispatch their victim. He would stun the target with the Taser, then wrap clingfilm around his head until he was asphyxiated. They would then remove the clingfilm, place the body in a natural position and exit the house. If there were any problems with Shaheen's family, they would presumably get the same treatment. The Taser and clingfilm combination was also an easy option in terms of procurement because there was little chance of such equipment being compromised, unlike firearms, which were more likely to be ratted out on by someone down the chain.

Maxim explained that once they had arrived at the safe house he would SMS "*thank you*" to the only number to be found in the local phone's memory. This would indicate to the Fixer that they were in the country and that he was to book their Etihad flight out any time after 6 am on the day after the text was sent. The Fixer should be instructed to text back the booking number and time of the flight. While at the safe house, they would detail-brief each other and prepare their equipment, and drive a dry-run if there was time.

Maxim then set out the details of the 'neutralisation' itself. It was just how the Controller had envisaged and he ever so slightly smiled as he listened to the assassin.

"We then return to the safe house to forensically cleanse. Strip our clothes and stick them in the washing machine, bleach down the surgical gloves and the ski-masks, before burning them on the barbecue. We bleach the Taser and clingfilm and put the clingfilm back in the car. Then we shower, bleach down the showers after use, and change into our exfil clothes, switch the number plates back to the correct ones and depart. We drive up to Abu Dhabi and stop briefly on the roadside in the middle of the desert to destroy the Taser by crushing it under the car. Finally we exfil by catching an Etihad Airlines flight back to Germany."

The Controller instinctively interrupted: "You don't want a filter country?"

"No need", responded Maxim. "We'll head back from where we came so that it looks as if we just cut our trip short. The Fixer should book the flights after we are in country," he added. "I reiterate, his should be the only saved number on the mobile phone. I'll simply text '*see you*' to the Fixer when we're clear of the safe house. If I don't send that text three hours before the flight, the Fixer needs to call me; if I don't answer, the Fixer needs to come to the safe house, because it'll mean there's been a change of plans that I can't discuss on the phone." Maxim paused. "Where was I?"

"No filter country," the Controller prompted, glad at this juncture to be asked anything by Maxim.

"Right, we'll throw the clingfilm out of the car on our way to Abu Dhabi, I'll text '*thank you*' to the Fixer when we're close to the airport. We'll then dismantle the phone, soak the pieces in the drinking water and let the desert consume them. We then board the flight and return via Munich."

The Controller leant back in his chair; if Maxim truly were going to retire after this job, he would miss him. He so hated getting young dispatchers coming in with ever increasingly fancy plans. This one exuded all the tradecraft that Maxim had learned over the years and was elegantly simple. So much so that he thought it worth the target's life just to see it happen. The only flaw was the family, but he knew how well and silently Maxim did his work, so it would only get complicated if they were all in the same room when the team entered the house. He assumed that Maxim would mitigate against such risk, so he was happy.

Maxim stayed silent, waiting for the verdict.

The Controller broke the silence. "It is approved."

"How soon?" asked Maxim.

"As soon as the passports and IDs are complete and the Fixer is ready to receive you." The Controller smiled. "You are my favourite employee, Maxim; I hope you won't hang up your boots after this one."

Maxim did not know what to say so instead made a 'let's see' expression.

The Controller continued: "You will meet and brief your number two 24 hours before you leave for Germany. This is his first dispatch for us but he's what you were 20 years ago; he won't let you down."

CHAPTER FOUR
The Love Affair Begins

It had been a crap day in the Dubai International Financial Centre, and had anyone told Harry that he would one day be worried about the facial expression made by the Chairman of the US Federal Reserve whenever she made a speech, he would have told them they were nuts.

However, such had been the ride on free money issued by the 'Fed' since the financial crash that everyone was shitting themselves about when the quantitative easing tap would be turned down or off. Traders were once again in a state of denial with regard to the real value of the markets and everyone knew a correction was coming; the only snag was that only the Chair of the Fed had the power to know when. Hence any negative expression by her could signal the end of the recent big-bonus era.

On this particular day, she had not ticked the boxes and the 'All Seasons Fund', which was the name of the fund that Harry's employer managed, had experienced a major thunderstorm. Harry knew that the following day he would have investor after investor calling him for updates and predictions. God, how life had been so simple in the Special Forces; at that time he had never realised how much fun he had been having.

It must have been about 7 pm as he flowed with the traffic on Dubai's Sheikh Zayed Road towards home. His iPhone rang and he hesitated before answering it, being well aware of the lethality of this stretch of road. He glanced at the display – it was Shaheen. This could be another party so he slipped in his earpiece and accepted the call.

"Harry, how are you? It's Shaheen." Harry reflected that it was a generational thing to tell the person on the end of the line who was calling. Most kids these days knew who you were through caller ID so did not bother with such courtesies.

"I'm fine, thank you for asking, Shaheen." It was an exaggeration but Shaheen would never know. Harry continued: "I'm just on my way home from work."

"Oh, okay, Harry, I'll keep this short then." Harry enjoyed listening to the Persian accent on Shaheen's English. "My family and I have been called away next week and sadly my in-laws cannot come to look after Bunny."

"Bunny?" Harry's mind was racing. 'Ah yes, the fucking cat,' he thought.

"Well, anyway," Shaheen went on, not realising that Harry would even have to think about who Bunny was. "My wife and I were just wondering if you would be willing to housesit, to look after Bunny for a week or so?" He continued before Harry had a chance to answer: "You would have the full run of the villa, the gardens and pool; my wife will make sure she's stocked up on food for you and Bunny, I have plenty of booze, and if you would like to entertain, that's fine too; I'll even leave the keys for the Rolls Royce!"

'Blimey,' Harry was thinking. That would be sweet, rolling up to the Financial Centre in a Roller.

"Well, I'm in town next week, Shaheen, what day do you leave?"

"On Sunday afternoon," Shaheen replied, "so we would need you there for one week from Sunday evening; if you could pop round on Saturday so my wife can tell you how to feed Bunny and everything else, that would be great. We'd be so grateful if you could help us with this one, Harry."

To be honest, Harry was a bit gobsmacked that they would let a comparative stranger occupy their house for a week just for the sake of a cat, but what the hell. If they were happy, he would be happy to stretch out beyond the one-bedroom apartment in Marina that he currently called home.

"That's fine, Shaheen. How about I pop round at about 3 pm on Saturday to get the brief from your wife?"

"That's perfect, Harry, and we'll grab a beer and have a chat then too. Thank you so much for doing this." Harry had no idea of the weight he had just lifted off Shaheen's shoulders.

Harry hung up the phone thinking about the beer. Shaheen clearly did not know or did not care about Dubai's zero-tolerance alcohol policy when driving. Get caught with a fraction of a milligram in your bloodstream and it was off to jail for a month followed by deportation. So, although he doubted he would have the beer, a week in a luxury villa on the Palm would go down very nicely, thank you. He was still wondering about a certain babe that he wanted to entice there during his stay as he pulled into the underground parking of his apartment block.

Saturday came round quickly. As Harry drove along onto the Palm, he reflected that he was always surprised by the size of the place. Someone had once told him that the amount of sand it had taken to create this manmade peninsula was the equivalent of what it would take to wrap a two-foot-high and two-foot-wide wall around the world twice. All he knew was that the escape route was crap: it only had one road on and one road off; it was overpopulated with apartments on the 'trunk'; and, ultimately, it was a sandbank, and sandbanks moved. For those reasons he would never live on it, but for one week he was willing to take his chances.

He followed the signs to M-Frond and, once through the token security at the frond's entrance, he entered the territory of the privileged. The street that gently curved like the flimsy branch of a palm tree was tightly lined with huge villas. In the driveways were samples from just about every supercar manufacturer that he could readily think of; the gardens were all immaculate, and the only pedestrians were the occasional maids walking their employers' dogs.

As he pulled up outside of Villa 132 on M-Frond, he knew that he had got the right house; he recognised the Rolls Royce and Maserati parked in the driveway.

The visit took about an hour, with Shaheen's wife explaining every light switch and emphasising that she had stocked up on beer for him. The American-size fridge had a full shelf allocated to Heineken.

She explained that Bunny liked soft, luxury cat food out of a sachet, and that he should leave dry food each morning before he left for work. She had an automatic water feeder so he need not ever worry about that.

The wife emphasised that Bunny was an "inside cat" and was not to be let outside under any circumstance. If she got ill or anything like that, she had a bespoke cat-carrying bag, so he could use that to take her to the vet whose details were stuck to the fridge door.

Harry was being shown the contents of every drawer and cupboard in the kitchen when Shaheen came downstairs, having clearly just woken from a nap. He asked if Harry would like a beer and, despite the risk, he took one. They wandered out into the garden by the small pool overlooking the private beach and blue seas. Harry reflected that this really was a micro-paradise; he would enjoy his week.

CHAPTER FIVE
Date Night

Two days before Harry had been briefed on Bunny's feeding habits, the Controller had called Maxim to let him know that the passports were ready and that the Fixer would be ready for reception any day after Monday evening.

"Any bumps in the road or changes to instructions?" asked Maxim. There were none, and in any case, he did not need to know any additional details until the face-to-face brief.

In truth, the only real challenge had been the Taser, import and possession of which were illegal in the UAE, but the Controller had used his political pull to ensure that one of the diplomatic pouches being sent to the Russian Embassy contained a two-layered package. The address on the outer packaging was the receiving diplomat; the mobile number on the inner packaging was that of the Fixer. The diplomat had not been briefed on the contents of the package, nor would he ever be. He had simply received it, unwrapped the first layer and called the number to let the recipient know that their "passport was ready for collection". He had then left the package at the Embassy reception with instructions that whoever was carrying the mobile that answered his call was authorised to collect it. The delivery had worked perfectly.

Maxim turned up at the Controller's office on Sunday morning. It was quiet; all the secretaries and assistants had the day off. He simply said that he was Maxim and he had an appointment with Mr Soltegov; he was told the floor and let through.

As he entered the Controller's office, he was not surprised to see a man in his thirties was already seated at the coffee table, but he was surprised at his ethnicity. He smiled as the Controller broke off the conversation and came forward to greet him.

"Bernhard, welcome," he said loudly.

Maxim knew straight away that this was his identity for the journey.

The Controller quickly went on: "Let me introduce Jan; he will be your number two and MOE for this one."

The men shook hands as they sized each other up. Part of their tradecraft was to be able to work with complete strangers, so this was no big deal. Maxim was trying to figure out where Jan was from, but he could not, so he asked.

Boris, codename Jan, explained that he was from Moscow but his parents were from Tajikistan. Maxim was content to leave it at that, but he would bet his bottom rouble that this guy was a Muslim. He hoped that this would not be an issue at any juncture.

The Controller ushered them to the table where German passports, driving licences and credit cards were neatly laid out.

"You'll fly into Munich on these passports," he instructed. "Everything's in order, with a phantom departure two days ago from Germany to Moscow in both systems. When you arrive, Bernhard here" – he looked at Maxim – "will do the talking, as he speaks fluent German. Jan" – he looked at Boris – "you're his travel companion at that stage. You should then go separately to check in with Emirates Airlines; Bernhard is in business class, Jan you're in economy; sorry. We don't want you to appear connected in the airport. If asked by Dubai immigration, you're both separately booked at the Habtoor Grand Hotel in the Dubai Marina and are in town for the Dubai International Motor Show; you both work in business development for Audi; here are five business cards each in case you're asked for one on entry. The numbers and emails on them will reach this office."

Both men looked at the cards: '*Bernhard Vorhoelter*' and '*Jan Sperling*'; each also featured the subtitle '*Director, International Business Development*'.

'If only,' thought Boris.

The Controller continued: "Once clear of customs, go directly to the Avis office, which is in the car park across the road from the terminal on the same level. You'll see the signs. Rendezvous with each other there. Jan, if you see Bernhard already at the counter, just wait outside for him." Jan nodded.

"Here are your instructions and directions from the Fixer. Do not accept any car except a white Toyota Camry. They're as common as shit so it shouldn't be an issue. If it is an issue, you also have a reservation at Hertz as a back-up. Their office is the next one along from Avis."

He pulled out a large road map of Dubai and proceeded to trace their route across the city to the safe house with his pen. "The safe house is number 54; everything that Bernhard requested is in place there."

He moved to another sheet and a photograph.

"Your target is Shaheen Soroush; he's 44 years old of Iranian extraction. He has no military or police training and is considered the softest of targets. From what we know, he does no physical exercise whatsoever and he's described as having a small paunch. He lives with his wife and two children in this villa on the Palm Island, on M-Frond, number

132. His kids are both school-age, so I'm guessing they'll be in bed when you go calling. If you can establish that his wife is not with him, so much the better; if not, do what you have to do." He looked at Jan. "Bernhard will brief you on the method and tactics, follow his lead." Jan nodded again. "Soroush has a Rolls Royce Ghost with this registration and a Maserati with this one." He indicated them on the briefing sheet before pausing. "Usual procedure, memorise what you can, keep notes of anything you can't, but *these* notes do not leave this place. You can take the map. Any questions so far?" There were none.

"Okay, Bernhard, you will brief the extraction and clean up on the hoof. Happy?"

Both men nodded.

"There's a car parked in slot 42 outside; here are the keys. Take it to the airport, park it in short-term parking, leave the keys in it." He held out his hand. "Now, go rid the world of that robbing bastard."

"Can I just ask when we get paid on a job like this?" Boris asked nervously.

The Controller and Maxim looked at each other and laughed. "Shit, I'd forgotten you didn't know the procedure. Fifty percent is already in your account; I assumed you'd checked it. The rest will be wired on your return. Is that not right, Bernhard?" The Controller looked at Maxim who simply smiled and nodded.

Just a few hours after Bernhard and Jan had received their instructions, Harry was letting himself into the villa. He was so ready for a week of luxury that he had even booked a couple of days off work during the coming week.

Bunny, who had been alone for about half the day, was pleased to see some company and came trotting up to rub her scent on his legs. He stroked her and said hello, wondering if she even understood greetings in English instead of the family's Farsi; he really knew so little about cats.

He found his perfectly prepared bedroom upstairs and unpacked his clothes and toilet bag. Bunny stuck with him.

He then went downstairs with her leading the way, through the kitchen and into the garage to feed her. There was a note on the large fridge reading:

> *Hi Harry,*
>   *Please help yourself to anything. I have left car in the driveway because it is a tight squeeze in and out of the garage. Thank you again for helping us with this.*
>   *Shaheen*

'You're welcome,' Harry thought. He pulled a beer from the fridge, changed into his trunks and went to take a soak in the pool. This was going to be a tough week.

Before turning in, he ensured all the doors were locked and the outside security lights were left on. He noted that the lock on the front door was normally on a single latch and needed two turns of the key to throw the bolt; he also noticed that these double doors were not a good fit; there was a significant gap between them where they should have met snugly.

Upstairs, he pulled the duvet cover over him on the sumptuous bed; just before dozing off, he felt a furry presence alongside him.

She purred and pawed the duvet into the desired shape. During the course of the night, this turned out to be insufficient comfort for Bunny, so she settled for the heat between Harry's legs. In his slumber he vaguely recalled thinking, 'If it's good enough for her, it's good enough for me.'

★   ★   ★

Harry and Bunny did not wake up until 7 am.

He went downstairs, made his tea, and emptied one of her sachets of food into her bowl while she meandered in and out of his legs. He was beginning to understand why Shaheen loved this cat. By 8.30, Harry was out of the door and driving his Peugeot 207 to his office in the Financial Centre. He had decided against taking the Roller; he had already promised himself not to rip the arse out of driving it, just in case he dinged it.

His priority plan today was to invite Natella Sultanova for some sushi at lunch. She was a ridiculously elegant woman from Azerbaijan who worked in the centre's registrar of companies, and she was Harry's 'Miss Dubai'. He would judge her mood at lunch; if she seemed receptive, he would invite her for dinner on Thursday evening in the villa. He had already schemed to pick her up in the Rolls Royce, have the dinner catered, soak with her in the pool, then spend the rest of the night in bed romping until her eyeballs swivelled in their sockets. He had it all planned.

In the office there was significant relief when the European markets opened and rebounded from the knee-jerk response to the Federal Reserve's comments at the close of the previous week. Harry had already learned that in the world's stock exchanges, the giant traders could now cause the good news to be good news, no news to be good news and bad news to be good news. It was a 'heads they win, tails you lose' world, where any dip in the market for any reason was always followed by a new high. It was simply left to the traders to ride each minor and major bubble in order to secure their massive bonuses.

Harry went to the toilets and rehearsed his call to Natella; she was so hot, he did not want to fall at the first fence. He went back to the office, took a deep breath, and then called her – she sounded happy to hear from him and said yes to the sushi. 'Bingo,' thought Harry as he put down the phone.

At 1 pm, Harry was taking a seat at the sushi bar of YO! Sushi with Natella. She looked great: auburn hair, unblemished skin and fit as a butcher's dog. He reflected that all the best-looking humans came from the gene-mixing that had occurred in the crossroads of the world, and Natella was no exception.

At the very same moment, in the same time zone, Maxim and Boris, knowing each other only as Bernhard and Jan, were leaving Moscow in separate rows of Air Munich flight 5903 inbound to Munich.

Following the Controller's brief, Maxim had gone through the entire plan with Boris, not least because the notes from the Fixer only included details up to the use of the safe house. No one in Dubai was aware of the target.

Both men realised that there were a few imponderables and gaps in aspects of the villa, but they also knew that such omission was almost always the way when there was a trade-off with maintaining operational security. In any case, nothing was ever completely the way you expected it to be. Once you learned that, you were well on your way to being able to deal with whatever came at you.

They both agreed that the Fixer's notes to the Controller had been comprehensive and, whoever this sleeper was, he had his act together. So far as Maxim could make out, the Fixer had missed just one vital element. He had included the system of electronic tollgates in Dubai (called Salik) and mentioned that these would cost a driver $1.10 every time their car passed under one. What the Fixer had not realised, or briefed, was that these were also the Dubai Government's way of passively tracking the movements of every car that drove through the city.

Maxim had pored over the map and figured out that the gates on the bridge could not be avoided but, thereafter, by staying off Sheikh Zayed Road, they would not show up on the toll system, thereby avoiding at least that element of detection, should anything go awry.

Maxim checked his dual-zone watch; he set the 24-hour sweep to German time and left the 12-hour hand on UAE/Moscow time. They would land in Munich at 1.20 pm and connect with the Emirates flight leaving at 3.20 pm. They were off to a good start.

That evening Shaheen called Harry from Singapore for a Bunny update. Harry reassured Shaheen that everything was in good order and that Bunny had not missed a beat with regard to feeding habits or anything else. He omitted the bit about her sleeping with him; he figured that, even though she was only a cat, Shaheen would not want to hear that.

Just before the call ended, Shaheen said that his wife had bought a load of fruit for him and that it was in the bottom drawers of the fridge; he should please eat it or it would go to waste. Harry looked in the drawers as Shaheen was speaking. She certainly had stocked up – there must have been at least half a dozen types of fruit in there, including a honey melon, Harry's favourite. He figured that he would devour that tomorrow, not least because he had just eaten one of the ready meals that Farah had also left for him.

Following the call, Harry cracked a beer and settled down in the TV room to chuckle at an episode of Seinfeld. Bunny jumped onto his lap and they both woke up at about 1 am, having dozed off in front of the TV. It was Monday evening; Harry had already booked days off on Wednesday and Thursday, so he would be glad to get the following day over and done with and turn his attention to his preparations for Natella. As he dozily transitioned into bed, Bunny once again found the warm part of the bed. Harry's final thought before lulling back into sleep was: 'I wish I could find the human equivalent of this cat.'

CHAPTER SIX
Russian Roulette

Entry into Germany was seamless. Maxim deemed the whole EU open-border policy a joke, but in this case it played in his favour and, as they both walked through the 'EU Passports' channel, the German immigration officer gave neither man a second glance.

From here they would separate until they met again at the Avis rent-a-car office in Dubai. Maxim headed for the Emirates business lounge, which was his entitlement as a business-class passenger; Boris, meanwhile, found the Il Mondo restaurant and settled there for a small pizza and a large glass of Chianti.

The six-and-a-half-hour flight went by comfortably for Maxim as he lounged and slept in his business-class seat. For Boris, in 'cattle-class', it was a different story. He found himself next to a pair of obnoxious Germans who frankly did not give a shit about anyone around them. They talked loudly through their dinner, even though it was blatantly obvious that Boris next to them just wanted to sleep. Worse still, the German next to Boris was a 'nudger' – the type of despicable human being that (either consciously or unconsciously) was constantly brushing up or nudging the complete stranger next to them, whether in a bar, aeroplane or any other confined space.

Boris reflected that, had he been in a Moscow bar, he would have dragged this obnoxious git out by his balls and punched his lights out. However, he was acutely aware that he could not draw any attention to himself, so he would just have to passively sit this one out. It really did not help that he still loathed the Germans for the carnage they had inflicted on his grandparents' generation during the Second World War. Boris's political irritations ensured that he did not get a wink of sleep and arrived at Dubai's Terminal 3 about as grumpy and tired as he could be.

It also did not help that the lines through passport control were huge and the immigration officers laconic. He became further irritated when he noticed the fast-track lane for business- and first-class passengers; he knew that his companion would have breezed through this route by now.

By the time he had arrived at the Avis office, it was over an hour after their arrival. Boris was so pissed off that he could not see straight, but he tried to conceal his irritation from Maxim who was patiently waiting by the Avis office in a white Toyota Camry, engine running.

"Where the fuck have you been?" asked Maxim.

"Don't ask, but that's the last time in my life I want to travel economy," sighed Boris.

Maxim did not like to remind him that he would also be returning by economy, so instead said, "Yes, it's shit, but look on the bright side – it's over...for now. Here, take the map; you have the navigation. The signs we need are Garhoud Bridge, World Trade Centre, Jumeirah, and Dubai Dry Docks to Jumeirah Beach Road – got it?

"Got it," replied Boris; he was feeling better already falling back into role.

It must have been about 1.15 am when they identified the safe house. Maxim did not stop outside but moved to the second available parking space beyond it. He did not want the car associated with the address if anything were to go wrong at this stage. He reached up and switched the car's internal lights to completely off so they would not turn on when the doors opened.

"Let's go check it out. We'll bring the car in afterwards."

Both men knew the procedure. They opened the car doors, then leant against them to close them. Boris locked the car using the key so as not to set off any lights or signals; they then walked back to the gate and gently unlatched it.

The house key was exactly where the Fixer had said it would be, not by the door, where anyone could see, but by the gate under a triangular piece of paving.

They let themselves in; there was a light on in the back room.

"Hello?" Maxim called. There was no answer.

The living room was sparsely furnished; if anyone did live here, they liked things austere. On the dining room table there were all the items that has been on Maxim's shopping list, including a brown package with a scribbled number on it.

"Looks like it's all here. Go bring the car in." Maxim threw Boris the keys. "We'll do a recce tomorrow afternoon, so we won't change the plates until the real run." Boris caught the keys and nodded.

Upstairs they found two beds and agreed that they would get up late in the morning. Now it was Boris's turn to sleep and for Maxim to regret the quality rest that he had already had on the flight.

The following morning found Harry as happy as a sand-boy. With regard to his Thursday plans for Natella, he was like a kid waiting for Christmas. The prospect of getting between those perfectly shaped legs was driving him to distraction and the sooner he got his Tuesday over and done with, the better. He could then spend the next two days in preparation for her: squeeze out a couple of gym workouts, a massage or two (with no happy ending, of course), and organise a caterer, because he was, after all, a shit cook.

Sadly, his intentions to get off work early were not fulfilled. Investor relations had had one of their US clients calling in, who was concerned about market events. He had requested a video-conference at 11 am Eastern Time. The punter was a big client; Harry would need to be in the room, even if only to give the investor the impression that they cared. In truth, Harry's presence was pretty superfluous, and the portfolio managers and analyst would carry on in 'financialese', just so everyone listening in could be convinced of how smart they all really were.

Harry was resigned to the fact that he would have to stay for the call and wondered whether he ought to pop back to the villa in the afternoon, just to make sure that Bunny was okay. He decided that if he had time to break away for an hour, he would do just that.

Maxim was up first that morning and made some tea, before picking up the mobile phone that had been left for him and texting *"thank you"*. Boris emerged at about 10.30. They prepared the equipment and checked the Taser for charge; it was good. The clingfilm was of a thicker variety and would not tear easily.

Boris peeled back the lining of his bag and pulled out some fine strips of metal that were taped to the frame; these were his lock 'bypass tools', or lock-picks. He also had flexible plastic card cut into various shapes. With a combination of the two, he could happily get through most domestic locks.

Maxim went into the small backyard and uncovered the grill; it was new. He checked the false coals were in place and turned on the gas bottle. The igniter worked; he had fire. He smiled and actually wished that he knew the Fixer – though in reality, if he had known what she actually looked like, he would have wished for a lot more than that.

He turned off the gas and walked into the living room. Boris was eating one of the fibre bars that had been left in the kitchen.

Maxim sat down opposite him. "We'll leave here at 1410 for the recce," he said, referring to the 24-hour clock and reinforcing his habit of never leaving at a cardinal point of the clock. "If anyone asks, we're just a couple of Germans exploring Dubai, so don't wear anything sinister." He need not have told Boris, but figured it would not do any harm. "Once we've had a look-see, we'll decide the precise order of march for tonight."

Boris was happy with this military vernacular; Maxim had just given him a hint of his background, though Boris guessed that he had been out of the military for some time now – he was right.

Maxim's phone beeped to indicate a message; it read: "FZB8DB, EY3, 0855". Maxim smiled; once again, the Fixer had delivered a perfect service.

"Freedom flight on Etihad is booked," he exclaimed.

Harry looked at his watch; it was 1.45 pm. He had worked through his lunch hour and figured that he could probably just slip away. He jumped into the Peugeot and headed for the Palm. He would ensure that Bunny had enough food and, if he pushed it, he could be back in the office in just over an hour.

At 2.20 pm, the white Toyota was obeying the 70kmh speed limit on the Jumeirah Beach Road. The route was a piece of cake, but because of the slow speed, the road seemed longer than the assassins had expected. They eventually came to the turn-off for the Palm and stayed right, passing between the multiple apartment buildings "Fuck me," Boris commented, "this place is huge."

Maxim agreed; he had had no idea, either that it was this big, or this populated. He noted the speed bumps along the way, not that he had any intention of speeding at any juncture during his stay; from this desert country there was nowhere to run to if anything went wrong.

They obeyed the signs towards M-Frond, which turned out to be very confusing, eventually leading them onto a slip road, then onto a roundabout, where they found themselves having to U-turn back again towards the frond entrance. "We'll just drive by the turning," Maxim said in a state of distraction; "we can figure the rest out later."

Harry had fed Bunny; she had been fine, but he felt happier now that he knew she had been taken care of. However, now he was running behind as a result of the almost traditional 'daily accident' on Sheikh Zayed Road that had held him up on his way over to her.

He leapt into the car to get back to work and sped along the frond, not really caring about the speed bumps. On reaching the exit, he glanced up the road; it was never an easy view but he could have sworn that it was clear...

Maxim and Boris were eyes-right, checking out the barrier, when Maxim's peripheral vision picked out a blue movement in front of him. The Peugeot had come from nowhere. Maxim hit the brakes and the tyres screeched.

★　★　★

Harry suddenly saw the white Toyota. Jesus, he had fucked this up.

Had it not been for the progressive driving training Harry had received in the Special Forces, he would have probably hit the brakes and been T-boned by the Toyota; instead, he instinctively hit the accelerator and manoeuvred the car to the right, which pulled him away from the Toyota that was almost upon him.

Neither knew it, but both drivers felt and said the same expression of relief at the same time: "Jesus Christ, that was close."

Harry felt guilty; it was his fuck-up, and although his driving skills had got him out of the fix, the other guy had certainly been on the ball to brake the way he did. Harry took the entrance onto the main thoroughfare and pulled over; he brought his window down.

The Toyota pulled up alongside him; the passenger lowered his window and was about to let loose, but Harry interjected first.

"I'm so sorry, mate," he said, looking at both men and noticing that one was darker-skinned than the other. "I just didn't see you. I'm really sorry."

"No problem," the driver replied. "No damage done, have a nice day." His deep voice, combined with his Russian accent, was firm but fair.

Boris studied the other guy's face. It looked well-travelled and rugged, yet refined; perhaps this guy was former military. The fact that he had said "mate" indicated that he was probably from England or Australia. Either way, if he had been military, Boris was vaguely surprised that a guy like him did not have his shit more together.

Maxim drove on. "Wanker," he said to Boris. "Let's get back to the safe house before some other fucking idiot tries to blow the operation – or, worse still, kill us."

* * *

As the Toyota moved off, Harry was just relieved that he had got away with his carelessness; dealing with the police and insurance company would have been a nightmare, but he reflected concurrently that life was like that – a miss was as good as a mile. He was more vigilant with his driving on the way back to the Financial Centre.

At the safe house, Maxim and Boris went through their final preparations. They ensured that their dark clothes for the operation were purged of any ID; each checked that they had a pair of surgical gloves in one trouser pocket. The ski-mask would be stuffed into the back of the belt. They spray-bleached the bottom of their black training shoes. The clingfilm and bleach were put into the glove compartment of the car, the Avis sticker was peeled from the back window, and the 'ringer' number plates fixed into place.

After some discussion, Boris had persuaded Maxim to let him control the Taser for the hit. Boris would bypass the easiest door of entry they could find; they would start with the front door. Maxim would cover the street to ensure that they were not observed. Once Boris had cracked the lock, he would take the lead through the door; they would quietly clear the ground floor first, listening for any indication of movement. Once they had located Shaheen, Boris would hit him with the Taser, rapidly muffle any screams, and Maxim would wrap the clingfilm around Shaheen's head and leave it sealed until he was dead. They would remove the clingfilm, prop the body up on the nearest chair, exit the house, and drive back to the safe house to forensically cleanse before heading up to Abu Dhabi.

If they had to taser any of the family, they would give them each two or three really good shots to keep them down.

They would then dispatch them after Shaheen was dead.

Boris studied Shaheen's picture. The glasses, the baldness; he looked like a soft fucker. He could already imagine himself overpowering this piece of shit. This was his first hit for the Controller and he was going to make it a good one; he also wanted to impress Maxim, even though they would in all likelihood never see each other again once this job was done.

Maxim was satisfied that all the preparations were complete. He decided that they would make entry at 2256, which would hopefully mean that everyone was in bed except the man of the house, who would probably decide to go to bed just after a cardinal point of the clock once a TV programme had finished. It was a wild guess but one that was well grounded on the commonality of people's habits. He told Boris to get some rest. It was going to be a long night.

The conference call in Harry's office had dragged on. Initially the call had been delayed because, for all the investor's self-importance, the idiot could not get his WebEx to work. Harry so often wondered how such idiots could be worth tens of millions of dollars. Surely it had to be luck or a kick-start with a serious trust fund. Such experiences always depressed him.

By the time the investor's ego had been sufficiently stroked, the clock was passing 9.20 pm. Harry was relieved that he had popped away earlier to feed Bunny. He rolled out of the office, tired, hungry and on a caffeine-high. If the traffic were kind to him, he would be home by about 10.

Bunny ran towards him and weaved in and out between his legs as he walked to the kitchen; it was the greeting that he was now used to; Harry was almost starting to feel like the villa was his home. He put his tablet on the kitchen table and filled up Bunny's bowl in the garage. While she was making the most of her food, he grabbed a shower upstairs before putting on a clean pair of boxers and his T-shirt that just happened to have a tongue-in-cheek slogan on the back of it reading: *'Really Really Bad Guys'*.

He wandered back downstairs, pulled a beer from the fridge and slugged it. He scanned the fridge for something to eat and pulled out a microwaveable ready-meal, the honey melon and another beer.

At the same junction where earlier in the day they had almost hit the Peugeot, Maxim swung into the M-Frond turning towards the security barrier. As they approached the checkpoint, Maxim did what he always did in such situations: he kept his window up and waved at the guard like he had known him for years. The guard, earning only $275 a month, was looking for any excuse not to come out of his gate lodge, so he simply pressed the button and raised the barrier.

"Nearly always works," said Maxim with a smile.

Along the well-lit frond there was no activity on the street. The even-numbered houses were on the right and Boris counted them down and checked his watch; it indicated 10.47 pm; they were on time. After what seemed like a mile, they passed by Villa 130 and saw the target house for the first time. 'Perfect,' thought Boris. Set back from the road and plenty of vegetation and cover from view in the front yard.

Maxim continued past the target and found a parking space a respectable distance beyond the neighbouring villa. He turned the car around and parked on the opposite side of the street facing in the direction of their escape route.

They both pulled on their surgical gloves. Boris tapped the side pocket of his black trousers to check for the lock bypass rods and cards. Maxim unfurled the clingfilm and made sure that the end was on the outside of the box. Boris pulled the Taser out of the glove compartment.

"Ready?" asked Boris.

"Let's get it done and get the fuck out of here," replied Maxim.

Both men got out of the car; this time they did not lock it. They walked across the road and the 50 metres to the driveway containing the Rolls Royce and Maserati; their heads were steady but eyes busy left and right; there was no one else on the street. The only thing they did not notice was the blue Peugeot 207 that they had nearly hit earlier in the day parked on the other side of the street. They turned casually into the driveway and were immediately concealed in the shadows of the vegetation.

"The window," Maxim whispered; "let's see if we can see anyone in the rooms."

They peered through the ground floor window into the room next to the front door. It was a TV room or something. They then went down the side of the house. They could see into part of the hallway and beyond that the large living room at the back. There were lights on in the hallway that illuminated the adjoining rooms, but they could not see any signs of life.

"Do you think he's in?" whispered Boris.

"Must be," answered Maxim. "Both his cars are here and the fucking lights are on. Let's get in there."

They pulled out the ski-masks and put them on as knitted hats.

Boris moved to the front door and knelt down to examine the lock. Maxim sat on the corner of the step looking out for any passers-by.

Boris could not believe his luck: the doorway was badly fitted and the gap between the double doors was nearly five millimetres wide. He slipped his card from his pocket, selected the appropriately shaped edge and, holding the door with his right hand, pushed the card forward onto the bevelled latch, easing it out of its bolthole. He felt the door give – he was in.

In the kitchen Harry had finished his ready-meal and was slicing the honey melon into eighths so that he could devour it in bite-sized portions in front of the TV. He had his back to the open double doors of the kitchen. Bunny was sitting on the table facing him, watching him prepare the melon, when suddenly they both felt a change in the air pressure from the AC. Harry looked at the ceiling, wondering if the fan and vent had a fancy setting.

Bunny heard the noise from the hallway; she registered it but did not move. She had no idea that Harry could not hear the same audible frequencies as her, and if he, as the alpha-male, was not bothered, then neither was she.

At the front door both Boris and Maxim pulled the ski-masks full-length down over their faces. Boris changed grip on the door from his right to his left hand and pulled the Taser out of his belt. The picture of Shaheen was engrained in his mind; every nerve end in his body was now alive as adrenaline was released into his system. He looked at Maxim, who had the clingfilm ready.

Maxim nodded.

Boris pushed the door gently open; Maxim slipped in and stayed completely still and silent just on the inside. Boris slipped in after him and silently eased the door shut. It had been the perfect entry.

In the front room the TV was off, as were the lights upstairs. The floor was marble with three Persian rugs equidistantly spaced the length of the hallway. Boris knew that these would provide him with silent footfall.

They could hear a man's voice, which seemed to be coming from the open double door on the left at the end of the hall. There did not seem to be anybody answering him.

Boris edged forward towards the voice.

Bunny was now locked onto the kitchen doorway; not only could she hear footsteps crunching on the carpet but she could also smell male musk and the scent of human fear. She wondered why Harry was not reacting.

Harry was chatting away, telling her, "We'll just clean these last seeds out, baby, and then let's go watch TV." All of a sudden, she startled him by leaping into an arch-back stance, showing her teeth and hissing in the direction of the kitchen doorway.

Harry looked at her. "What the fu...?" He turned around to check what she was fussing about, about half a second before he saw the Taser being held by a black arm come into view, followed by the rest of the man dressed entirely in black, including a face mask. Harry's mind went into overdrive; his Special Forces instincts from years spent fighting the Irish Republican Army were instantly relit. Grab a weapon, any weapon...not that that was necessary – he had a huge knife in his right hand already.

Boris did not expect to see a cat hissing at him and he especially did not expect to see the idiot from the blue Peugeot standing there in a pair of striped boxer shorts. What the fuck was he doing here? Had they got the wrong house?

This microsecond of thought and the hesitation it represented were all that Harry needed. He had already spun the knife in his hand through 180 degrees without even thinking, his eyes riveted on the intruder's chest. He felt his right hand holding the blade flick back beyond the side of his head before his right arm rocketed forwards, propelling the knife two metres through the air whilst aiming precisely at the intruder's chest. Unfortunately, Harry was out of practice.

Boris, in the moment it took his adversary to react, had decided to taser the fucker and get out of there. He was about a quarter of a second too late.

As Boris brought the Taser to bear, Harry's knife missed the point of aim; he was about 20 centimetres too high. It was an atrocious throw at such short range – Harry's lack of practice had made him forsake accuracy for speed and power.

The tip of the knife found Boris's left thyroid gland, then forged its way into his throat, piercing the windpipe. Though the blade was by now slowing rapidly, as it hit the tracheal cartilage, it tilted anticlockwise, and the back end of the blade sliced through the internal jugular vein like a knife through a melon. Boris was a dead man breathing and he knew it. He dropped the Taser and reached for the knife embedded in his throat.

Had Harry had the opportunity, he would have told him to leave it where it was, but the intruder instinctively pulled it out, unwittingly ensuring that he would die from lack of blood to the brain within seven seconds.

Any of this was far from Harry's concern. His previous training now told him only one thing: eliminate the danger. He rushed forward and scooped up the Taser, when suddenly he felt as if a freight train had hit him from his right. Jesus Christ, there were two of them and this guy was now on top of him, close to getting him in a terminal straight-arm stranglehold.

Harry knew that the next part would hurt but he had no choice; he pressed the Taser up against the attacker's side and squeezed. Harry felt the shock pass through his own body; fuck, that felt nasty. However, the strength of the stranglehold instantly weakened and the guy was screaming. Harry let him have another dose. Another scream and a curse, this time in Russian. Harry broke free and let him have another one.

As the third wave of shock hit Maxim, paralysing his whole body, the very furthest thing from the Russian's mind was his smoking, drinking and dietary habits of the last twenty years. He was not aware that it was coronary artery disease that had made him so tired of late. Unbeknownst to him, his heart had been working overtime for some months; these electric shocks were the last straw. It simply stopped.

His body arched in agony as he rolled over, gasping his last breath and watching his killer stagger to his feet. He looked at the man. His final mortal thought on earth was: 'Is that the Peugeot guy?'

Harry stood in the hallway in utter disbelief. Had this really just happened to him? Why the fuck did these guys want to kill him? His mind raced to former dodgy operations he had done in Northern Ireland, Bosnia and Afghanistan. Perhaps this was some sort of revenge squad.

He went forward and pulled up the second man's ski-mask, just enough to check his pulse; there was none.

He stepped over to his other victim lying in the doorway of the kitchen; there was blood everywhere; this guy was dead too. Harry noticed the clingfilm between them. He picked it up. Clingfilm? What the fuck was going on? None of it made any sense.

He looked for Bunny. She was nowhere to be seen and had taken cover in the garage when the fight had started. Harry glanced at the front door; it was closed. He wondered if that was how they had got in. He checked the back door and side door before double-locking the front door. He then ran upstairs to look out onto the road; did they have a driver? It all looked normal and peaceful down there. He needed to call the police.

He picked up the house phone and got as far as dialling a single nine; then he stopped.

If he called the police, this could open up a whole can of worms. He knew only too well that in Dubai it was a guilty-until-proven-innocent legal system, so he would very likely be thrown in jail as a matter of procedure and stay there as a suspected double murderer until found innocent. Ludicrously, given the severity of his current situation, he was even concerned that he had had a couple of beers, so he could additionally get charged with alcohol consumption.

He needed to think this through before calling anyone. Who were these guys? He went over to one of the bodies, pulled off the ski-mask and did a double-take. This was the guy who was in the Toyota he had nearly hit earlier on; he looked a bit like a northern Afghan. He went to the second body, pulled off its mask completely, and any doubts about whether these were the men from the Toyota were completely dispelled.

He could not believe it. Would these thugs really track him down and try to kill him for a simple driving mistake – what the fuck was Dubai coming to? The white guy had spoken in what sounded like a Russian accent, so that was probably where he was from, but what about the young guy? Perhaps one was Bosnian and one a Serb; Harry had certainly done some harm out there, all in the name of good.

Whatever it all meant, he finally decided that he could not call the police. He would have to clean this mess up himself.

CHAPTER SEVEN
The Cleaning Lady

Harry decided to have a cup of tea. It would help him clear his thoughts and, anyway, these two bodies were not going anywhere until he had made up his mind what to do with them.

He ran through the possibilities. If they were thugs working alone because he had nearly hit them with his car, then the chances were that they would not have told anyone they were coming to 'do' him. He wondered whether they had just planned to hurt him or whether they were actually going to kill him. He sipped his tea and picked up the roll of cling-film; whatever was this for?

He went over to the bodies and went through their pockets to check for ID. There was nothing but plastic card and some lock-picks in the young guy's side pocket. He found a bottle of spray-bleach and a set of Avis keys on the older guy.

If these guys were sent from the Taliban or IRA, why would they just want to taser him? Surely they would have wanted to kill him outright, and in any case, if they *were* hit men and they *were* missed, could it be reported? Of course not.

He had subconsciously already deduced that he needed to dispose of the bodies. One of them was simple enough, but it was the bleeder that was going to be tiresome. Harry tied the older guy's feet together using the laces on his training shoes and used a strip of the clingfilm to tie the dead man's hands together. He did the same to the bleeder but also wrapped a sheet around his neck before pulling a bin liner over his head and shoulders to stop the oozing blood from causing any more mess. He grabbed a sheet out of the laundry room, soaked it in water, then wrung it out and spread it over the blood on the floor.

Harry dragged both bodies into the empty maid's room, which was between the kitchen and the garage. He ensured that the window in the room was firmly locked and turned the air conditioning to its fullest and coldest setting. He then closed the door of this temporary morgue.

For the next hour he cleaned up the young man's blood and used the bottle of bleach to ensure that the area was totally clean. He put all the cleaning materials into a bin liner and then thought to spray the bodies with bleach, just to keep the possibility of smell down. Experience had taught him about oozing body fluids.

From here his plan was simple. He would take the Peugeot back to his place and in the morning buy a large roll of plastic sheeting, some rope and some masking tape. He would then return to the villa, line the boot of the Rolls Royce with the plastic, load the bodies into the ample trunk, and drive out into the desert towards the area called the Empty Quarter. Here he would find a place to dump the bodies where the heat would, in no time, decompose them, and where it was unlikely that anyone would ever find them, let alone trace them. Although he realised that the Rolls Royce was conspicuous, he also knew that the police in Dubai never pulled over such cars.

He thanked goodness that he had taken the rest of the week off; this would permit him to get this mess sorted over the Wednesday and perhaps still bag Natella at the end of the working week.

He grabbed Bunny's travelling bag from the garage and some of her food. He found her upstairs, still nervous from all the events of the evening. He gently placed her in the bag before grabbing his toilet bag, the Taser gun and the keys to the Rolls Royce. Outside he checked for a car bearing the registration number on the Avis key fob, but none that he could see on the street matched. He would have to figure that one out later.

Back at his apartment, Harry could hardly sleep as he mapped out the task ahead; he eventually got out of bed at 6 am. However, he was constrained by store opening times meaning that this phase of his plan did not go well. He had hoped to be sitting outside the Ace Hardware store at 9 am when it opened, but he misjudged rush hour. He made it to the store 20 minutes behind his schedule, loaded his trolley top to bottom with plastic sheeting, bin liners, disinfectant, a pair of washing-up gloves, paint fume masks, a couple of cheap rugs and a Stanley knife. He also decided on a petrol container, just in case he found that he needed to scorch the bodies.

He was understandably apprehensive as he drove below the speed limit back onto the Palm, thinking, 'I really don't want to get back to the house.' Who could blame him? The corpses would almost certainly have juiced out by now, so the task was not going to be pleasant.

Harry followed a garden-centre van onto M-Frond. As they turned in towards the barrier, he saw a white van come off the frond and pause at the junction; he could not help but notice the two well-built white guys travelling in the plain vehicle.

He continued to follow the gardening van through the frond's security checkpoint, his mind structuring out the task and day ahead. He kept reassuring himself that this was the right thing to do. Any other action would see him stuck in an Arab jail for months and he could only imagine the slackening effect that that would have on his rectal virginity. Halfway along the frond he did notice a green Mini flash past him in the opposite direction, for the sole reason that he had a passion for those cars; he thought nothing of it beyond that.

Arriving at the villa, he opened the garage, carefully reversed the Rolls into it and closed the door behind him. He had decided that he would do all the preparation possible before tackling the bodies. He took Bunny inside but left her in her travelling bag for now. Harry opened the boot of the car and got to work lining it with the plastic sheet, being careful not to mark the interior with the tape in any way. Within 15 minutes he was content that no body fluids would penetrate the plastic covering. He would also be able to fold the sheeting over the bodies, which he would wrap further inside the house before placing the rugs over the top of them.

He pulled off more sheeting from the roll and calculated enough to adequately wrap around the girth of each body. He figured that he would get the messy one out of the way first. He changed into some old clothes that he would later throw away, pulled on the bright yellow washing-up gloves and pulled one of the fume masks across his face. He went to the door of the maid's room and took a deep breath.

'Here we go,' he thought.

He gingerly opened the door and felt the cold from the blast of air conditioning hit his forehead. There was no smell; these masks worked well, he thought, as he opened the door wide and stared at the floor where he had left the bodies. Stared but did not move or blink – he was trying to assimilate what his eyes were telling him.

The room was in half-darkness so Harry reached over to the light switch for more illumination and flicked it on. He stood there taking in the scene on the floor in front of him before reaching up and pulling his mask down around his neck.

"What the fuck?" he said out loud, looking at the empty floor. "Where are they?" He walked around the end of the bed and checked the far side too. He then dropped to all fours and checked under the maid's bed. Nothing.

He opened the adjoining en-suite bathroom door; there was nothing there. Was he dreaming? Had they both been dead? Had the entire event even happened? Perhaps the older guy had only been unconscious? No way, he reassured himself. The young guy had had a knife through his neck and had completely bled out, and the older guy had been as dead as a dodo; he had checked the pulse and his pupils had been dilated. Also, neither man had shown any sign of life when he had bound them up and moved them. They were dead, 100 percent – but where had they gone? There was no smell, no mess, nothing.

He checked the kitchen, every large cupboard and every room in the house, just in case by some freak of nature the old guy had come back to life and tried to carry the young guy out of there. However, that would not explain why the sheets he had laid down had also disappeared. He checked under every bed, inside every wardrobe and all over the garden outside. He even checked into each of the neighbours' gardens.

The two bodies had simply disappeared. Harry sat down at the kitchen table; he was completely bewildered. There had to be a logical explanation as to why, firstly, these guys had tried to kill him, and now, after they had appeared to be completely dead, they had managed to simply vanish. Perhaps it was a practical joke? If it was, it was a fucking good one. What about the knife in the neck thing? That was sure as hell not fake. Also the older guy had tried to throttle the life out of him – that had been real enough.

Harry's mind struggled to make sense of any of it. What should he do now? Did this mean his body-disposal plan was solved or would friends of these fuckers turn up again at some inconvenient juncture? Perhaps there was such a thing as miracles. He made himself a cup of tea, let Bunny out of her travelling bag and thought through the entire incident from start to finish to find the flaw in what appeared to be reality.

He then searched the entire house and garden from top to bottom again and found nothing.

Like Harry, the Fixer had also taken the day off work. She had set her alarm for 6 that morning and left the pay-as-you-go mobile phone next to her personal Blackberry on her bedside table.

When the alarm went off at 6 am, it was the one sound she really did not want to hear first thing on that particular day. As soon as her conscious thought kicked in she immediately reached for the cheap mobile phone and looked at the messages. There should have been an incoming text prior to 0555, three hours before the visitor's departure from Abu Dhabi, but there was nothing except the outgoing message from her, giving the booking reference and flight time of 0855.

"Shit," she said out loud. "Why can't these fucking people just obey instructions? Stupid bastards." She was betting that whoever the visitors were, they had gone out on the town, enjoyed too much vodka and a couple of cheap hookers, and right now they were still snoring in the transit accommodation. Now she would have to follow her instructions and go around there to wake up the stupid shits so that they could drive at breakneck speed to Abu Dhabi to catch their flight. She called the number – there was no reply. She was livid as she threw on her Juicy-brand sweatpants and top.

It was about 6.20 am when she arrived at the door of the transit accommodation and rang the doorbell three times before letting herself in. She called out but there was no reply. She noticed a set of number plates on the table that were different from the ones she had stolen, and that the other items she had left for them had been moved around in the kitchen. So they had been there.

She went upstairs, calling out "Hello?" as she went. In one of the bedrooms she found a bag with a set of men's clothes and a German passport. It matched the name of one of the passengers. In the other bedroom she found more of the same.

"Shit!" she exclaimed, looking at Bernhard Vorhoelter's passport. "Where the fuck are you?"

She hated to call it in, not least because, whatever these guys were doing or delivering in Dubai, they would be in deep shit with the Controller for not sticking to procedure. To step outside it was to be expelled from the organisation, and she knew that, for some, the repercussions involved more than just a lay-off notice. She also knew that if she did not call it in, she would be included in whatever retribution was forthcoming.

She sat at the dining room table looking at the unused packet of washing powder, when she noticed the phone that she had picked up from the consulate under the empty package; suddenly she felt less bad about making the call to the Controller. This situation did not feel right and she needed to shelve the responsibility.

The Controller was an early riser; when his 'incoming only' phone rang at 6.45 am and he looked at the number on it, he knew this could not be good news.

She had no real clue of the Controller's real identity, but he, of course, knew hers.

"Sorry to call you," she said, "but they've missed their check-in. I'm at the house, their belongings are here but there's no sign of them. I have no way to contact them because they didn't take the phone that I got for them. Is there anything you need me to do?"

The Controller's mind raced. If Maxim was not back by now, then there was a good reason for that, and it was not good. Something must have gone wrong. "Maybe the rental car has broken down or something," he said. "You're going to have to see if you can locate them. There's a man on the Palm who's been very ill of late. They were going to have a vodka with him for old times' sakes and give him a message from me. Perhaps they got paralytic together." He gave her the address.

"Drive out there now and see if they're anywhere on the route with a broken-down car. Use the beach road and when you get to the address, ring the doorbell; if anyone answers the door, assess whether everything seems normal. If it does, pretend you're looking for Villa 142 but you've come to the wrong house." He paused. "If there's no answer, see if you can gain entry. If you get in and anyone responds when you call out, make out the door was open and you have the wrong house. If no one responds, check all the rooms and report back to me with whatever you find. Understood?"

She did.

The Fixer pulled up outside of the target's house. She noticed the Toyota with the plates that she had stolen was parked some way up the road. She found it unlocked but nothing in it. There was no response to the doorbell. She walked around the house to see if there was any activity at all; she tried all the doors and windows for a loose latch.

She went back to her Mini and pulled her Emirates Skyward Miles card from her purse. If this got ruined, it would not matter. She rang the doorbell again and as she did so, she pushed the card into the latch area of the door and worked it up and down. She pulled the door towards her to try to relieve the pressure; the card slipped in and the door opened.

She called out, "Hello? Anyone home? Hello?" There was no answer, thank God, and no sign of any pets – especially dogs.

Harry had only forgotten one thing the previous evening: to double-lock the front door on the way out. He would unwittingly be ever grateful for the lapse.

The Fixer would have likely been impressed by the décor if she had not been so tense. She quickly worked from room to room, being careful where possible to tread on the Persian carpets to minimise the chance of leaving footprints on the marble floor, until she got to the kitchen, where she froze. There was a used roll of clingfilm on the huge table; it was the same brand that she had bought for the German visitors. Nothing else seemed out of place. She went into the large living-cum-dining room where there was no sign of any recent living or dining. The large glass dining room table was bare. On her way back to the kitchen she noticed a painting of a woman and wondered if it was the lady of the house. She noted that it was signed by Fabian Perez; she did not know the name.

She walked through the kitchen and laundry room into the garage. It was empty expect for the normal crap and a watering station for birds or something; she did not notice the cat litterbox that had been placed discreetly behind some boxes to preserve a certain pet's dignity. She walked back towards the kitchen and almost straight past the door on her left but stopped. There was a whiff, as if someone had shit himself or herself – this was weird.

She gently eased the door open to see if anyone was inside the room, and the rush of cold air and the smell of human excrement hit her senses hard. The bed was empty, but as she opened the door wider, the two figures of men dressed in black lying on the floor registered in her mind for what they were: dead bodies.

"Oh shit!" she said, matching her expression to the environmentals. She instinctively went forward and dropped to one knee in order to check for a pulse. As she did so, she recognised the uncovered body as Herr Vorhoelter. She assumed that the other was that of Herr Sperling, but he had a bin liner over his head. She peeled it back and grimaced as she saw the extent of his neck injury and the spread of blood. It was really sticky and she was not sure which one of these poor bastards had shit himself, but somewhere between the sight and the smell that confronted her she gagged.

She examined the massive knife wound in Sperling's throat. Neither of these guys was small. Whoever had killed them must have known what he was doing.

She pulled the phone from her pocket and called the number again.

"They're in that place," she said, avoiding saying the address. "The clock has beaten them." It was a Spetsnaz expression; the Controller knew what she meant.

"How?"

"Not sure for one, but a knife for the younger."

"Any sign of anyone else?"

"No, they were hidden in a room. No sign of anything else at all."

"Are there any cars there?"

"Theirs is outside but there are no keys; my plates. A sports car and Rolls Royce in the driveway."

"Okay." The Controller sounded calm. This was not the first time that a job had gone this pear-shaped. "I think I know what's happened here and we need to beat the opposition to the punch. I need you to get them out of there."

"What?" she snapped back. "I couldn't do that." Her voice was half-panicked. "I can't even lift them! One of them has lost his jugular," she added in almost a whisper; "the accuracy is astounding. The other hasn't got so much as a mark on him; this was the work of a professional. I don't want to be here when whoever did this comes back."

"Listen to me," the Controller said. "You have done a great job so far, but we need to clean this up before the opposition gets them identified. We cannot run the risk of organisational compromise."

She understood.

He continued: "Go outside and wait in your car. I'll have a team out there to help you shortly." He put down the phone.

The Controller thanked his god that this Fixer was one of his best. She was as reliable as she was discreet.

He called his contact in the Russian Embassy over the encrypted net: "Fastball. I have two broken victors for immediate disposal, repeat immediate." He gave the address. "Disposal imperative; one friend on site. You'll need a team of two men with bags."

The key words were 'fastball', 'broken victors' and 'disposal'. The Embassy knew exactly what needed to be done. Disappearing people and bodies was not quite a Russian pastime but it was not far off.

The mechanism swung into action and the vehicle with no other markings except 'Private Ambulance' and manned by larger-than-usual paramedics wearing white coats was quietly backing into the driveway of Villa 132 within 55 minutes of the call, at which point the magnetic ambulance markings were peeled off. The bodies were placed in body bags. The garage door was lifted and the stretcher used to put the bodies in the back of the ambulance. Thanks to the fact that the bodies were already laid out on sheets and tied up, the removal took 10 minutes from time of arrival. The privacy of the driveway and garage ensured that the loading process was not observed. The clean-up took another 15 minutes. The cremation later that day at the Russian Medical Hospital in the Emirate of Sharjah took just a fraction longer; the mafia-organised disposal activity was well practiced and paid for.

The Fixer did one final check for cleanliness in the maid's room, left via the front door and walked briskly to her car. She drove her Mini away at speed and, meanwhile, called

Avis to report that Herr Vorhoelter had had to unexpectedly leave Dubai and inadvertently taken the rental car key with him. She explained that she would pay for the replacement and ensure the car was returned the same day; she would come to their office to pick up the keys. Had she not been speeding or so distracted by her mind moving at similar speed, all the while holding her phone, she might have noticed the blue Peugeot behind a garden services van driving in the opposite direction – but she did not.

She drove to the transit accommodation to pick up the real plates for the rental car and on to the Avis office to pay for the replacement key. From there she would have to get a taxi to the Palm, recover the car, get it to a place where she could switch the plates and then return it to Avis.

Her predominant thought was: 'I do not get paid enough for this shit.'

CHAPTER EIGHT
Sex Driver

The Controller was relieved and livid at the same time. The SVR agents from the Russian Embassy had performed in their usual seamless and 'ask questions later' manner to dispose of the bodies. He was not sure how many times they had done this before but he was grateful that they had unwound this one with such proficiency.

Of course he knew it would only be a matter of time, probably hours, before questions were asked from on high. He would have to come up with some explanation for how a supposedly soft target with purportedly no training or inclination to violence had managed to so efficiently kill one of their most experienced dispatchers and be expert enough in the use of a knife to finish off one of their prodigies.

He called the two money launderers that had originally got themselves involved with Shaheen Soroush. He told them to be at his office in one hour. The tone of his voice let each of the men know that all was not well.

As the Controller waited for their arrival he paced his office, contemplating his options for completion of the job, revenge or to simply cut bait. What would be Shaheen's next move? He wondered if Maxim and Boris had had any identification on them. After all, they had fucked up the job enough to get themselves killed, what other loopholes had they left open? At least by cleaning the bodies out he had denied Shaheen the opportunity to identify them, and he was sure that this event would unhinge Shaheen's initial pride at having come out on top of his two visitors. Their disappearance should be enough to have the killer extremely worried.

In Shaheen's kitchen it was Harry who was pacing, still trying to get his head around the events of the last 12 or so hours. He examined the front door – there were no signs of forced entry, but he now realised that the lock on the $2 million villa was so cheap, it would only keep honest people out.

He got down on his hands and knees where the guy had been hit with the knife. He found a couple of blood spots up against the skirting board. He reflected on how badly he had thrown the knife and put it down to decreased strength in his forearm given that he no longer trained for combat. He relived the shock in the dark eyes of his attacker when the knife had hurtled into his throat; he could not understand why his attacker had hesitated. All Harry knew was that if he had been given that split second, it would be him that was dead or missing right now.

While he was looking at the blood spots, Bunny took advantage of his being on all fours and purred by rubbing up against him. She also sniffed the skirting board. As a carnivore she was instinctively drawn to the smell of iron in the blood.

Harry then went into the maid's room. He could not find any blood spots or traces in there. He did not bother looking for hairs because both men had had it cut so short that none would be obvious. He put his nose against the grouting in-between the floor-tiles. There was the smell of bleach, but a very faint smell of excrement still lingered too.

He concluded that there must have been a back-up team outside that saw him leave the house; they must have then come in to recover their colleagues. If this was the case, he wondered how many more were in the team and whether they would come back seeking revenge.

Surely the house had been under some sort of surveillance when the mobsters had come to sort him out; he would need to ascertain whether it was still the case before he brought Natella there for dinner...and sex.

Harry decided to kill two birds with one stone. He would take a drive to grab a coffee and, if his tail was clear, he would go to his apartment to pick up his toilet bag that he had stupidly forgotten.

He had decided to leave the Rolls in the garage, so instead picked up the keys to the Peugeot. This time he ensured that the front door was double-locked. He then used the side door and went to the back of the garden where he crossed over into next-door's back yard. This villa was empty, so he was able to use its path and driveway to get to his car. If the house was under surveillance, this might at least cause the watchers to miss him, but enable him to observe them.

As he walked out of Villa 130's driveway and crossed the road, he noticed a tall, slim, attractive, yet slightly dishevelled woman about to get into the Toyota that was parked at least 50 metres up the road. He reflected that she looked as if she had just got out of bed. She had her long blonde hair in a loose bun and held up by a clip. She was wearing black Juicy sweatpants with a matching top, and a pair of Aviators sunglasses.

'Nice arse,' Harry thought to himself as she momentarily glanced back at him. She probably cleaned up really well.

He got into the Peugeot and noted that there was no other movement on the street. As he manoeuvred the car out of its roadside parking space, he noticed in his mirror that the woman in the Toyota was doing the same, before proceeding to follow him along the frond. He felt in his pocket for the keys that he had found on the body of the older guy and read off the registration from the key fob. He compared it with the car that was following him. It did not match, but he noted that she was still behind him on the main exit road of the Palm. He told himself not to jump to any quick con-clusions. This was the only road off the peninsula, so she her only choice was to pass him or follow him. He just hoped that she would choose the former.

He decided to take the slip road that would loop him back to the only Costa Coffee on the Palm, and so flicked his indicator to see if she would match his lane – she did not. As he pulled off, she continued along the main road.

Harry took one more look at her as she passed – she was very attractive, which might have explained why she did not bother to give him a second look.

The Fixer had been relieved that the Rolls Royce had not moved from its position in the driveway of Villa 132. For some reason she deemed no change as a good sign. Perhaps it had been her alert state, focus on the target house, and eagerness to get the Toyota back to the transit house that had caused her surprise as she had looked over her shoulder before getting into the car and suddenly noticed the guy crossing the road. She thanked goodness that the angle of his route over to his pathetic little car had not brought him from the target house. It would have been ironic to have had a morning like hers and now be compromised at this stage.

When their eyes had met briefly she had quickly averted her gaze, so registered only that the man was quite a good-looking guy; the glance had been so momentary, however, that it was doubtful she would recognise his face if she ever saw it again.

As she was starting the engine, she saw him pull away, and when she came up behind his Peugeot she assumed that he was driving slowly because he was a respectful resident; but she also noted that the driver was paying a lot of attention to *her* in his rear-view mirror. She hoped that it was because she was a dishevelled blonde, and not for any other reason.

Once they were on the main road, she made the decision not to pass him; she did not want to be noticed by him any more than was necessary, and he had already taken a good look at her face. 'Thank God for that,' she thought, when he indicated to move into a slip road, and she accelerated into the left-hand lane.

Her sole task now was to get back to the safe house and switch out the number plates with the ones that belonged to the car. She would purge the house and put all the belongings and moveable items into her Mini, return the Avis car, catch a taxi back to the Mercato shopping centre, walk back to her Mini and drive home. She could then contact the Controller on Blackberry Messenger for further instructions.

She reflected that she *really* did not get paid enough for this shit.

In Moscow the Godfather arrived in the Controller's office. He sat down in shock when he learned of Maxim's demise. "It was his last fucking job, for Christ's sake!" He sighed. "The poor bastard, he did not deserve this."

The Controller reflected silently that, actually, Maxim probably did deserve it. He had, after all, killed a lot of people in the passage of his duty. It was young Boris that deserved a higher level of sympathy.

The two playboy punks at the heart of all this turned up to interrupt his thoughts. They almost shit themselves when they saw that Delimkov was in the room as well.

The four men sat down and backtracked. Had there ever been anything in Shaheen Soroush's background that could have given them any indication that this guy could not only physically handle himself but, moreover, kill efficiently?

The money-laundering playboys described Shaheen's persona; the Controller went over the personal background notes that they had had compiled on Shaheen when a hit looked likely. There was nothing. He has no military or police training, and there was no indication that he had anything to do with the Iranian covert services. He was, after all, meant to be despised by the regime and was, by all accounts, a wanted man in his own country.

He had never been seen with a bodyguard or any form of physical protection. His oldest son was just 14, so even combined they would not have been able to overpower Maxim and Boris.

They had clearly missed something about Shaheen and they needed to identify just how he had developed close-quarter combat skills. The Controller reiterated that the knife wound, if inflicted by stabbing, had been reported as being perfectly placed, so as to ensure that there could be no survival from the penetration. If the knife had been thrown, then the precision was frightening. Conversely, there had not been a mark on Maxim, so in order to achieve these sorts of results, Shaheen must have been trained by the best. He pointed out that not only had they completely missed a key element of Shaheen's background but that they had also grossly miscalculated his personality as one that was averse to violence.

It was probable that he worked for someone — the Pasdaran, or maybe even Mossad — and they really needed to find out who in order to predict his next move. Their biggest fear for now was that he had some form of DNA or lead that could identify Boris and Maxim for who they really were and link them back to the people in this room.

The Controller's Blackberry vibrated on the table. He read the Fixer's message out loud: " '*Transit accommodation cleaned, rental car returned, no problems. Rolls Royce still home at 1130 am. Standing down until further instructed.*' "

"We're just very lucky to have that girl in Dubai," he said. "The combination of her and the SVR team really saved our skin on this one. If the Dubai police had got hold of this, Maxim's face would have been plastered all over tomorrow's edition of the *Gulf News*, and someone out there would've surely recognised him."

The Godfather and the Controller agreed that they should cool off for a couple of weeks. Delimkov concluded, "Let's see how Mr Soroush decides to play it. He knows the bodies have disappeared – that will send a 'we know who you are and what you've done' message to him. If we hear nothing after two weeks, then I think we can assume that we're not in his ring of suspicion. Either way, we also need to think about laying a false trail."

Harry realised that by now he should be in a dilemma as to whether to continue his date night with Natella or call it off. Every sensible nerve in his body told him that he ought to either postpone or arrange another venue. His testosterone, however, was telling him something else: to go ahead as planned and pretend that the events of the last 24 hours had simply never happened.

He was reassuring himself that, so far as he could make out, he was not under any form of surveillance, unless it was highly technical. This could, after all, simply be the most extreme case of road rage the world had ever witnessed. Perhaps these guys had never meant to kill him; after all, surely they would have carried more than a Taser if they had intended to finish him off. Harry had still not figured out why the older guy had been carrying clingfilm, but he guessed that it was either for some sort of forensic protection, or perhaps they were going to tie him up with it while they beat the shit out of him.

Of course the colossal fly in the ointment was the disappearance of the bodies. This too should have dictated that Harry follow the inclination of his brain rather than his penis; the thought of sweeping Natella off her feet, however, was just too much of an influence. He was just going to have to go through with it and ensure that nothing disturbed them. After all, when would he get another chance with the villa and the Rolls Royce?

Harry texted Natella to confirm the timings, saying he would pick her up around 8 pm on Thursday evening. He added, in hope, that there was a swimming pool in case she would like to bring her swimming costume.

Natella was delighted to receive the text. It broke up the monotony of the dull atmospherics in the Financial Centre's registrar's office. She reflected that there was seldom any laughter in her workplace, due mainly to the dynamics and forbidden fruits that existed between the local Arab men and women. If there was any hanky-panky going on, it was all kept under the radar and there was no open flirting or fun permitted.

She had liked Harry from the moment she had met him at one of their corporate sweetener meetings. At the time she had been trapped in a pretty miserable relationship and recalled having thought that this guy was just like someone out of an action movie. She had even commented on him to Oleana, her best friend. So now that she was 'single' again, Harry's invitation to dinner could not have been better timed. It did not hurt in any case that she was absolutely dying for sex.

No sooner had Natella received the text than she called Oleana to ask her advice – should she take the swimsuit or not?

Oleana took longer than normal to pick up the phone and her voice sounded gravelly as she said, "Hey, girl."

"Were you sleeping?" Natella asked.

"I had to work an early one this morning," grunted Oleana. "I thought I'd grab a quick nap so thanks for ruining my beauty sleep," She half-meant it.

Natella apologised, but went ahead in any case and asked for advice, excitedly explaining that Harry had just texted her.

"Just go for it," Oleana instructed. "Hell, you know you want to anyway. Take your swimsuit – it'll throw out all the right signals. Just don't let him see your toothbrush until after you've had your way with him!" They both laughed.

Natella had heard what she wanted to hear; she apologised again for waking Oleana and went back to the drudgery of her work in the registry, thinking about what she was going to let Harry do to her the following evening.

It was early on Friday evening the next time Oleana's phone rang, displaying Natella as the caller.

"So, you little slut. How did it go?" she asked with a laugh.

Natella could hardly wait to spill all the sordid details but Oleana immediately slowed her down. "Hang on while I sit down," she said. "I want every intricate detail. Did you have fun, is he good?"

She then had to increasingly resist the temptation to interrupt as Natella described the whole "unbelievable evening".

"Yes and yes," Natella said, in answer to the first two questions. "He picked me up at eight and was driving a brand new Rolls Royce! He then drove me out to the Palm and we went onto one of the fronds with all the big mansions." She paused. "It was M- or N-frond, I think... Anyway, when we arrived the house was beautiful, with a huge entrance hall and the floor covered in Persian carpets."

"Go on," urged Oleana.

"Well, he had champagne on ice on the massive kitchen table and when we walked into the living room, the glass dining room table was laid for two and all the food was there on warmers. We sat and talked for a while, then we ate and switched to red wine. He said it was special. Opus One, I think he said."

Oleana remained silent – she was now asking herself who this guy could be?

"Anyway, after dinner," Natella continued, "which must have taken about an hour, he asked if I fancied a dip in the pool; which I did, so we did, and while we were there he kissed me for the first time. It was perfect and I actually thought we were going to do it right there and then because our hands were all over each other, but he was concerned about the neighbours, so we went inside. He grabbed another bottle of bubbly and took me upstairs to the bedroom."

"There you go!" Oleana laughed, pretending she did not care that her friend had managed to snag this guy first.

"I have no idea how many times we did it or for how long but I can hardly walk today. We even did it twice before he drove me home after lunch; he said he had some business to sort out this evening."

"Will he call you?" Oleana had just asked the $64,000 question.

"I reckon he will. He seems pretty keen and very genuine. You'll be the first to know if he does." Natella paused. "Oh, there was one more thing. He has this beautiful white Persian cat that just adores him; although he says it's not his and he's just looking after it." Another pause. "Hey, look, I need to get some sleep; are you still on for coffee tomorrow?"

Oleana said that she was. When the call ended, she sat back in her chair and did not move. She was deep in thought. Rolls Royce, villa on the Palm, great rugs, great booze and great sex? She needed to take a closer look at this guy – he could be a much better fit for her than for Natella, for more than a host of reasons. It was a dog-eat-dog world and she would do what she had to do in order to make it happen.

CHAPTER NINE
The Master Returns

Harry spent his entire Saturday cleansing the villa of any evidence that could compromise his evening of debauchery with Natella. He would hate for Shaheen's little girl to find a used condom or the like floating in one of the toilets, so he systematically checked every flush in the house. He also crawled under beds to make sure there were no empty packets.

The sheets were stripped off the bed and pushed in the washing machine, and he ensured that all remnants of the catering and all empty booze bottles were thrown out.

He then called in the maid who cleaned his apartment once a week to clean the villa throughout as well. He asked her to bleach and disinfect the maid's room in the house; she did not know why, but she obeyed and did a good job in anticipation of Harry's usual excessive tipping.

That night he slept in the guest room, and before leaving for work he checked all the rooms once more. They seemed as good as at the beginning of the week and, with the exception of the two small blood spots on the skirting board (which he would leave just in case the evidence was ever needed), he figured that it would pass any inspection by Shaheen's wife.

He fed and made a fuss of Bunny for what he thought would be their last exclusive time together, and left for work.

It was about 2 pm when Harry's phone rang and he heard Shaheen's voice. He thanked Harry profusely and said that he and his family had had a phenomenally successful week in Singapore but that they were pleased to be back home, and Shaheen's wife was elated that the house was so tidy. He was also happy that Bunny seemed unmoved by her master's week away.

Over the course of the following week Harry fell back into his old routine, and the event with the thugs and their disappearance almost seemed as if it had not happened. Bizarrely, his mind kept flicking back to the perfect form of Natella's body, either underneath him or on top, rather than the trussed-up bodies of the wankers that had attacked him.

He managed to grab some time with Natella in the Financial Centre's Caribou Coffee. The place was very public so he figured that if she did not mind being seen with him there, then she was truly making herself available for him. Natella invited him to a Friday brunch with her and a couple of her friends together at the Fairmont Hotel. Naturally Harry agreed, hoping 'brunch' was Natella's subtext for more sex.

By Wednesday, Shaheen was sitting with his lawyers discussing the transition of his TV and porn distribution companies to Singapore. The extraction was not going to be easy. If they were going to close the companies in Dubai, the lawyers informed him that they would have to go through a solvent liquidation.

Part of the process was the government stipulation that all such companies must make three separate announcements in the classified advertisements of at least two local prominent newspapers.

As Shaheen listened to the various requirements, he realised that such public announcements would make him vulnerable to the outstanding claims against him in the form the *Burj Takseeb* deal in Ajman. He almost phased out from what the lawyer was saying while he tried to think. Should he run the advertisements and hope that the Russians would not pick up on them? The problem was, it would be an all-or-nothing gamble. If the Russians realised that he was leaving, they could push a claim against him into the Ajman courts – once that was registered, his passport might well have an 'Emcheck' stop put against it, which would result in his arrest if he tried to leave the country. If that happened, the entire Singapore move would be thrown into jeopardy.

He was brought back to the reality of the meeting when his conscious thought picked up his lawyer saying, "So are you okay with all that, Shaheen? Do you want us to start the transfer of assets, relinquish the leases, arrange redundancy gratuities and commence the wind down? It could be a six-month process, worst case."

Six months? Shit, thought Shaheen. If he was going to make the move to the Far East, he had hoped that it could be sooner than that. The oriental porn market for US product was opening up so quickly that he would have to split his time to beat the competition in any case. The lawyers would just have to go for it and he would need to see what could be sorted with the Russians. He did not want to elaborate for the lawyers; what they did not know about, they would not worry about – or charge him for. He would just have to see if he could find a compromise with the Russians in order to effect his exit.

That evening, he sat down with his wife to discuss the options. Bunny purred on his lap as he pontificated. The Ajman project was an anchor around his neck. He doubted that it would ever be sorted unless the UAE bounced back to hay-day property market prices, so if he could just get the Russian monkeys off his back, then the problem would be solved. His wife agreed that they should just give the property away and cut their losses. At least then they could be assured a trouble-free exit from Dubai.

The following day Shaheen planned his call to the Russian playboy; this was not going to be an easy conversation but it had to be done.

He recognised that the ringtone was not local so assumed the Russian was not in the UAE. There was no answer.

In Moscow, the Russian punk was enjoying a late-morning coffee. When his phone rang and he looked at the number, the hairs stood up on the back of his neck. Shit, it was Soroush! What to do? Was this brute now coming for him? He let it ring while he thought about what to do.

As soon as his phone had stopped ringing, he called the Controller. His voice half-panicked, he did not even bother with niceties.

"The bastard just tried to call me!"

"Which bastard?" The Controller was giving himself time to think.

"Soroush; he's avoided us for months and now he calls me. What the fuck's his game?"

The Controller felt irritated on two counts. Firstly, why did he have to sort out everything himself? Also, he was now going to be on the back foot with this bastard Soroush until the guy made clear his next move. This fucker had killed two of his best guys and he was doubtless now going to try and extract something from them in terms of power or money. The Controller knew that he would do the same himself if he were in Soroush's shoes, so he would simply have to play him at his own game – but first he needed to know Soroush's next move.

"Call him back, find out what he wants. Don't commit to anything, not even a meeting; just find out what he wants and tell him you'll get back to him."

The Russian punk was not comfortable. Spending laundered money and running around Dubai like a hotshot was one thing; dealing with an Iranian killer was entirely another. He knew, however, that disobeying the Controller could not only curtail his role within the organisation, but also very likely cost him a couple of fingers, or, worse still, a thumb.

He selected the number on his mobile and pressed the call button.

"Hello, this is Shaheen."

The punk listened to the familiar voice on the phone that had avoided him so efficiently over the previous months.

"Shaheen, it's Vlad. I saw you called, how are you?"

"Thank you for calling back, Vlad." Shaheen sounded so polite, he was making the Russian cringe. "Are you in Dubai? It's time for us to settle our differences once and for all."

Jesus Christ, thought Vlad. Settle differences? He already knew what that had meant for the Controller's assassins. "No, I'm not in Dubai," he blurted, his mind now racing. "I'm travelling at the moment. Perhaps if you tell me what you have in mind, we can arrange a meeting."

Shaheen was surprised at the lack of hostility. Given that he had given these guys such a complete run around, the Russian was being pretty amicable.

"Look, Vlad, I'm not sure if you're aware, but there have been a couple of recent developments and I feel like matters between us should be brought to a close." He paused to see if the Russian wanted to say anything but was greeted by silence, so he continued. "I know we've had our disagreements in the past, but I honestly feel that you bought a deal that was fairly represented and I'm sorry if you feel so aggrieved. I also believe that the time has now passed for us to sort this out legally in the Arab courts, and recent events have taken a turn whereby both sides should accept matters for what they have become and end this thing once and for all. To that end, I'd like to meet you and your partner here in Dubai so we can sort this out man-to-man." Shaheen paused again. "I do believe that if you agree with what I have in mind, there'll be no more harm done and we can all get on with living our lives. But I need to meet you in person to discuss the matter in full."

Vlad knew exactly what Shaheen meant – the bastard was going to lure them in, put a deal on the table, and if they did not go for it, he would kill or seriously hurt them both. He would need to play for time and report back. This was the Controller's show, not his.

"Okay, Shaheen," he said, trying to sound casual. "We do realise we're living in a changing world and I'm on your wavelength with this one. However, I do need to check with my partner when we can come to Dubai. How about I call you back within a week?"

"A week would be fine, Vlad, but let me be frank." Shaheen was gaining strength from the Russian's cooperation. "I'd like to get this issue over with before matters go any further – if you can't come to me, I can come to you, wherever you are."

He had Vlad's full attention. Come where he was? Fuck, this guy was on a mission. He wished that they had done their homework a lot better on Shaheen before they had entered into a deal with him. The bastard probably knew that he would never pay them back and kill them if they ever pushed their luck. He had never realised that the Iranian mafia had such reach...or balls.

"I will definitely sort it and get back to you." Vlad hung up the phone. He knew the Controller was not going to like this at all and he hoped he did not choose to shoot the messenger.

★   ★   ★

Shaheen stared at his phone; he was feeling stunned. What did these guys know about Ajman that he did not? He had thought that the guy would be screaming down the phone for his money. Perhaps they had caught wind of something going on around the property, which was why they were not more desperate to meet him. He would check the latest developments down there. Perhaps there was still some money to be made. His greed was once again overtaking his instincts, causing the pendulum to swing from self-made to self-destruct.

The Controller could feel the anger rising in him as Vlad described the call. This Shaheen Soroush clearly now believed himself to be completely in control, and, who knew, he could be right. The quotes from the call – *'a couple of developments'*, *'end this thing'*, *'no more harm'*, *'if you can't come to me, I can come to you'*. Shit, these were not even veiled messages – they amounted to blatant threats.

If this Iranian had been Russian, the Controller would have had him ground up in a fertiliser machine. This, however, was not the case, and they had already learned a lesson – he had turned their brutal world upside-down. Maxim had not only been one of the Controller's most trusted men, he was also about as much of a friend as the Controller would ever have. If this guy could do such a hatchet job on Maxim and Boris, he could slaughter the two young punks in a heartbeat.

Now, there was an idea...

Vlad was instructed to call Shaheen and meet him the following week in Dubai. They were to find out what Shaheen had to say and refuse his first offer, unless he was offering to pay them back all his money plus 20 percent, which the

Controller knew would never happen.

Vlad called Luka Karchenko, his sidekick of a partner, and told him that they had to go to Dubai, before feebly adding, "We should take some Mace spray."

Neither man was happy, but they were in-between a rock and a hard place with this one. They would just need to make sure that they were never alone with Shaheen, somewhere where there were always witnesses.

CHAPTER TEN
Brunch And Bait

Harry spent his Friday morning preparing for Friday brunch. The event had just about become a weekly tradition for many expats in Dubai. To them it seemed like a great deal and a good excuse to get hammered; to the Arab-owned hotels it represented a significant opportunity to reap significant profit.

As Harry slapped on his Tom Ford aftershave and gave himself the mirror test to check out his Ralph Lauren chinos and Massimo Dutti shirt, he reflected that the Fairmont would not have been his first choice of venue.

They had recently shortened the hours of brunch by one hour but kept the prices the same. He might have been one of the few individuals about to attend that realised that the hotel had cut their consumption time by 25 percent but maintained the same cash flows as before. He concluded cynically that this was probably just one of the reasons that the hotel's owner, a certain prince of Saudi Arabia, had purportedly become one of the world's most affluent men.

By the time he had emerged from the taxi and made his way to the Spectrum-on-One Restaurant, Harry was genuinely excited about seeing Natella again. She was, after all, gorgeous, and he reflected that he had yet to see her in trousers, which suited him fine – her legs were spectacular. Harry was a legs man. She did not seem to have realised this yet, though it was clear that she knew she had great legs and liked the looks they attracted.

As Harry entered the restaurant on the first floor, the place was already packed with young female expats dressed to get laid, and equally vulgar guys ready to meet their needs. It was a pretty cheap scene against a classy backdrop.

The polite Filipino *maître d'* directed him to the table where his hostess was already seated with two of her friends. As he approached, Harry thought that all of his Christmases had come at once. They were all stunners, though he immediately picked up that one was wearing a wedding ring.

Natella was all smiles and embraced him like she meant it. She then introduced a dark-haired and voluptuously figured woman, Ikram, and a lithe blonde, "her BFF", Oleana.

Harry noted how all three women were dressed elegantly but respectfully. He felt a tinge of shame to be the same nationality as those other women in the room wearing their skirts nearly up to their clitorises.

He tried hard to concentrate on the names of Natella's friends (having long ago realised that the only name you heard during an introduction was your own), and was about to dwell on a particular naming connection with Ikram when the piercing blue eyes of Oleana cut into the back of his brain.

Her face looked familiar – he wanted to ask her if they had met before, but that might compromise some of his previous extracurricular activities with the pay-and-play variant of Russian women in Dubai. His mind was working overtime as they sat down and the waiter topped up three of the four glasses with Moët champagne. He just could not place her. Ikram quickly interjected to say that she did not drink. She had married a man who let her come out without a scarf but forbade her to drink alcohol. They all laughed when she said that it was a good enough deal for her.

As the brunch progressed, Natella may have sensed Oleana's attraction to Harry, but it was not obvious. Natella did, however, put her hand on Harry's leg and give it a gentle squeeze whenever the opportunity presented itself.

Harry dug deep into his memory as the brunch, booze and conversation flowed. He was sure that he knew Oleana from somewhere, but he was damned if he could remember where. Perhaps she was just one of the hot babes that he had seen in the Financial Centre?

Oleana, meanwhile, concentrated on keeping plenty of eye contact with Harry. She ensured that she never lost his attention, but cleverly manipulated the conversation so that he continued to interact with Natella and Ikram at the same time. She revealed that she was an executive concierge in Dubai and essentially arranged all events for her company's high net-worth clients that came to town. She then kept the entire table captivated with tales of her hometown, Saint Petersburg, its grandeur and undulating fortunes in history.

As the conversation inevitably transitioned into the arena of local politics, Oleana became concerned that her charm offensive on Harry was failing – which made her all the more determined to snag this man.

What she had not realised was that, like most Englishmen, Harry was pretty oblivious to women's pick-up signals. At one stage Oleana actually felt like headbutting him just to get his recognition, but she was aware that Natella was most likely attuned to her use of evocative syllables and body movement. She needed to change her plan.

Oleana decided to wait for her moment and rely on the fact that women always went to the toilet in twos. She made sure not to drink any water and sipped her Moët just enough to ensure that she got a top-up whenever Harry and Natella got one too. Her immediate and simple plan relied on the bladder strength, or lack thereof, of either Natella or Ikram.

Ikram's husband would have been shocked to find out how grateful this Russian was for the reduced strength that childbirth coupled with his teetotal edict had inflicted on his wife's bladder. As far as he could tell, the vodka-swilling, godless Russians would never derive any advantage from his own moral superiority. However, when the weakened involuntary muscle in Ikram's bladder opened, sending a *"Pee!"* message to her brain, there could be no one in the world more grateful or at an advantage than Oleana.

Natella, not wanting to miss her chance to get Ikram's opinion of Harry, jumped at the chance to get the 'by the sink' low-down on her man, and excused herself in order to escort Ikram.

Oleana knew that she had to move fast and come in head on.

"How long have you been seeing Natella?" she asked, already knowing the answer.

"Oh, only a week, but we kind of knew each other before in the Financial Centre," replied Harry, trying to legitimise their relationship but almost dreading what was coming next.

"I didn't know; I thought you were a long-term item." She had laid the trap.

"No, no, no." He had no idea why he had said it three times or why he felt like Saint Peter denying Jesus as he heard himself saying, "This is only our second date."

She recalled the expression 'find, fix, strike'. She had efficiently completed the first two, now it was shit or bust. She figured she had about a minute.

"Look, I hope you don't think me forward, but if it's not a big deal between you and Natella, I have two tickets to the Bolshoi Ballet who are visiting Dubai next week. I would far prefer to go with a man than a woman and I was wondering if you like the ballet?"

Harry had never been to the ballet. He had no idea if he liked it, but it did involve a lot of very hot, fit women prancing around in short skirts. His layman's interpretation was that ballet was sexiness dressed up in layers of art as a way of deriving respectability for those who frequented it. His overriding thought, however, was: 'I'm on roll; go for it.'

"Absolutely," he blurted, thinking his apparent love of culture would turn Oleana's knickers into ankle warmers. "I like the classics – *Swan Lake*, *Nutcracker* and all that." He had actually just exposed the full extent of his ballet-knowledge repertoire. Would it be enough to get it done?

"Perfect," Oleana said, concentrating on staying calm and charming. "Here's my card – give me a call or text and I'll let you know where and when." She paused for effect, smiled and leaned towards him, knowing that the angle would let him view adequate cleavage. "But we'd better keep this between us two. After all, we don't want to ruin someone else's plans for you this evening."

It was mission accomplished. She had all but recruited her man on the Palm and would be glad to get laid in the process.

Harry, meanwhile, was starting to wish he had discovered Tom Ford aftershave 10 years earlier – this stuff really worked!

Natella returned to the table and her night with Harry ensued just as she had planned. Oleana would wait her turn.

CHAPTER ELEVEN
The Killer's Angel

In the Bur Dubai police station, the receiving officer was exploring new depths of boredom. Every single day he had to deal with stupid infidels and foreigners bothering him for advice or a service ticket for some bullshit letter or report, for which his government could charge 200 dirhams.

He invariably chuckled to himself as he handed out tickets and barked orders for the complainant to go to a particular counter. These people thought Dubai did not have taxes, but of course it did. Whereas in other countries police services and certificates might be free, here they were not. But it was not his concern – such invisible taxes were what paid for his job-for-life and funded things like Lamborghinis and Bentleys for the Dubai Police car force.

He looked up; there was what looked like a westernised Arab woman in front of him. "*Naam*," he spouted. She simply and vulnerably said, "Someone has stolen the number plate from my car."

"Are you Moroccan?" he asked in Arabic.

"Of course," she replied, knowing that flirtation and her smile would get her everywhere.

They continued the conversation in Arabic and he revealed that his mother had been Moroccan. She described how her rear number plate had disappeared and explained that it would have been impossible for it to have fallen off. Her Toyota Camry was almost new and she had only had it cleaned the day before the plate went missing, so the cleaners would have noticed if it had been loose. She gave him her best puppy-dog eyes as she explained how she had gone to get another plate made, but the Road Traffic Authority had said that she must obtain a police permission certificate first.

He decided that there might be a date for him in all of this, so he announced that he would handle this matter himself. He called over a junior policeman to take his place on the reception desk.

The trace on the plate – M201187 – revealed nothing; but nor had it been handed in, which was nearly always the case if a plate simply dropped off.

He filed a report onto the system for a 'plate alert', meaning that if the plate was electronically surveilled, it would automatically register, and the data collection system would compare it with the automated Salik toll movements of the car to which it belonged. If there was a 'ringer' out there bearing false plates, it would only have to be driven through one of the tollgates in order for it to be photographed and traced.

He gave his business card and the police certificate to the Moroccan beauty and told her to call him if she had any problems, or if she would like a coffee. She said that she would and exited the police station, certificate in hand, knowing full well that she would never dial the number unless some improvement in her life depended on it.

It was Thursday lunchtime when Vlad and Luka sat in the Caramel Restaurant in the Dubai International Financial Centre waiting nervously for Shaheen.

They had been surprised, but somewhat relieved, when Shaheen had set the venue for the meeting at the restaurant. It was a public place – the Centre and the restaurant were subject to heavy camera surveillance. Every single vehicle arriving and leaving was recorded and there was no quick or easy getaway. It would be impossible for Shaheen to use one of his killer moves here without getting caught. On arrival they picked a table in the corner that would give them room domination (i.e. be able to see anyone who came in or out), and their seat position would force Shaheen to have his back to the door so that he would not be able to pass signals to anyone coming in or out.

Had they known the real reasons for Shaheen's selection they would have either kicked themselves or fallen off their chairs laughing. He too knew that it would be impossible for physical violence to go unnoticed or for an unrecorded escape to be successful, hence why he would be safe from the beating which he was sure the Russians would like to give him. However, the second element was, to Shaheen's mind, far more important and stealthy. If he could get them to agree to his proposal and sign while still in the restaurant, the Russians would unwittingly subject themselves to the laws of the Financial Centre, which operated a court system that enjoyed legal privileges on a par with those of the Vatican.

Ostensibly based on English law and set apart from the Arab courts, anything signed within the Centre's zone – including the coffee shops – had the potential to fall under the jurisdiction of the Financial Centre, and any document deemed signed therein was enforceable in its courts. This fact that had been overlooked by the majority of visitors there placing their signature on documents and agreements, but not by Shaheen since Harry had once explained to him how a contract was only as good as the law that underpinned it. This was the biggest advantage of operating in the Centre – it had its very own laws and jurisdiction.

If Shaheen could persuade the Russians to agree to his proposal and sign the term sheet, he could enforce it without the involvement of the Arabic courts. It would be quick and decisive. He recalled Harry saying that the law of signing was nicknamed 'The Coffee Shop Law', so-called because, when previously tested in court, it had been established that a defendant had signed a contract in Caribou Coffee within the confines of the centre, and that therefore their courts had jurisdiction. Shaheen would entrap the Russians with this law if they signed in the restaurant.

When Shaheen entered the restaurant, the first thing that he forced himself not to do was get distracted by the hostess, who was tall, Asian and elegantly muscled. He saw the two Russians sitting at a corner table and assumed that they had picked it in order to be tucked out of the way. He was grateful that he would have his back to the door, so no one would see him if they passed or entered the restaurant. The less anyone knew about his planned capitulation to the Russians, the better.

The Russians stood as he approached the table. Shaheen knew that these people interpreted joviality or kindness as a weakness, so he fought off the urge to smile as he shook hands with them.

The waiter poured water and asked if they would like the menus. Vlad cut in quickly. "No thanks, we'll just have a drink." He ordered two Zyr vodkas and looked at Shaheen. "What would you like?"

Shaheen told him that he would stick with water, which made Vlad wish he had not ordered first. It appeared that Shaheen was not in a good mood – Vlad was just glad that they were protected by their location.

Shaheen would have loved a vodka, but he did not want to be seen drinking at lunchtime in public. People did still assume that he was a Muslim, so he would play the game by their abstinent rules.

The drinks were served and the small talk ceased.

Vlad took a first sip of his vodka, which tasted smooth over ice – just the way he liked it. "Well, Shaheen, you called the meeting; what can we do for you?"

Shaheen was staggered – he was expecting them to threaten to nail his hands to the table if he did not pay them, but these guys were being nice. His instinct was still telling him that they knew something about this deal that he did not. He did not care – he just needed to get rid of it.

"Quite frankly, gentlemen," Shaheen started, trying to sound firm but fair, "we've both got ourselves into a situation that neither of us would have wished for."

'No shit,' thought Vlad as he glanced at his partner, who he wished would not look so unnerved.

"And in my mind there are only two solutions," continued Shaheen, so engrossed in delivering his deal that he did not even vaguely pick up the unsettled body language on the other side of the table. "We can either continue as we are and descend into additional loss; or we can accept what has happened, agree about the disappearance of the deal and move on without further loss and antagonism."

Both Russians were staring at him with total concentration, trying to unwind the threat that this man had just delivered across the table. He had acknowledged the disappearance of the bodies and referred to additional loss. They both knew that, unless they could unravel this Iranian, the situation could turn into a turf war, and if that happened, the Controller would have the birds of their homeland feeding on their entrails before either of their next birthdays.

"So what do you need?" Luka blurted, knowing it was a slip-up before the word 'need' had even left his lips. Vlad would have liked to punch him in the face but remained calm. Silence would be golden until Shaheen had said want he wanted.

"Need?" Shaheen asked. "I don't need anything." Now he was lying through his teeth, but he knew that he needed to appear tough in front of these Russian bastards. "I can continue with this for as long as it takes. I do, after all, have the title to the building and I live here. Whereas you do not, and I think you know that visiting this place can end up being very costly indeed." He was thinking of the expensive flights and hotel bills.

Vlad could not believe his ears – Shaheen had just admitted that coming here had cost two men their lives. The Russian said nothing and kicked his partner under the table to also stay quiet.

"So here's the deal I propose," said Shaheen. "I'll sign over the title to you. You'll sign this indemnity document. And we'll all walk away. No more fuss, no more visits, no more loss. It's as simple as that."

Vlad had no idea what Shaheen was up to, and if the decision had been his own he would have just signed the papers and got the fuck out of there. However, he had to bring the deal around to the refusal that the Controller had instructed.

"We can't do that," Vlad explained. Shaheen felt his heart sink as he heard the words. Vlad continued. "You see, we were hoping you would offer us our money back and we would sign back our ownership to you."

This could not have been worse for Shaheen; he would have to come somewhat clean with them.

"Gentlemen, let me be honest." Which unwittingly implied that he had not been so thus far. "Even if I wanted to return your original amount, time and events have forced that moment to disappear. The two factors now driving the offer on the table don't leave either of us much choice." He was thinking of the solvent liquidation and Singapore, the Russians were thinking of the bodies. "If you refuse, I'll continue along the path I've been forced upon; you'll have to stand on and watch what happens to your assets, over which you ultimately have no control. I believe the offer on the table is the only one that makes sense for the preservation of you and your people." Shaheen was thinking wealth preservation.

Vlad was now shitting himself; he could feel the sweat dripping under his armpits. This fucking Iranian had just told them that if they wanted to preserve themselves, they had better take the deal. He knew, however, that he was under direct orders to turn down the first deal.

"I'm sorry, Mr Soroush," he said, trying not to sound nervous. "We can't accept the deal you suggest at this time – however," he quickly inserted, "we will present your proposal to our board of directors and seek their agreement."

Shaheen was gutted but knew that he could not show it. He had so wanted them to just sign the indemnity so that he could be off the hook. He reflected that it might have been too much too soon.

Shaheen left the restaurant and was already out of earshot by the time the Russians had ordered another vodka. They needed it.

He wandered down the escalators towards visitor parking, and as he passed the Subway sandwich shop, he heard a familiar voice call his name.

He looked round to see Harry coming from the cash-desk, sandwich bag and drink in hand. He was happy to see a friendly face.

"Hey Shaheen, how are you, mate? What are you doing here? How's Bunny?"

"I'm fine; she's fine; it's a long story," Shaheen answered, ignoring the order of the questions.

"Do you have time for a coffee?" Harry coaxed. Shaheen said that he did and they wandered back upstairs to the discreetly located Costa Coffee.

Shaheen told him all about the Singapore trip and Harry could sense his excitement. Harry recalled having been told by an old friend who had been imprisoned abroad after a sudden change of regime that all expats were temporary guests in any country, and that all should be ready with a debt-free exit plan from these foreign lands; however, few ever did. Harry admired Shaheen for putting his own exit plan into action.

After the coffee, as he walked back to the office, Harry felt relieved that Shaheen had not said anything about the house. Clearly all the cleaning had done the trick, and there seemed to be no fallout from those stupid bastards who had tried to kill him. Whatever it was all about, whoever had cleaned up had done him a huge favour by disposing of the bodies. The entire event was now starting to feel like it had never happened, and as he walked into the office his mind meandered to the impending ballet night with Oleana, now only two days away.

CHAPTER TWELVE
The Black Swan

The Controller leant back in his chair as Vlad and his sidekick explained how they had taken control of the meeting with Shaheen and had refused the cash and ensuing offer of the title deed to the Ajman *Burj Takseeb* towers.

From their description of Shaheen's demeanour and his constant references to the deaths of Boris and Maxim, the Controller knew what would happen next. He has seen it all before – this was 'big boy rules'. They had refused Shaheen's deal, so it would be up to them to come back quickly with a counter-offer or the son of a bitch would send an ineffaceable message forcing the terms of his deal.

Either way, it did not much matter to the Controller. He knew that Shaheen could only deliver his message via a conduit that was known to him, and that would have to be Vlad or Luka; both of their days were likely numbered in any case.

Vlad was told to reject Shaheen's offer and demand the money. The Controller would now send his own message separately to Shaheen. He placed a call to the Fixer.

★　★　★

Natella had been repeatedly checking her phone for missed calls and battery strength all week. She was sure that Harry must have a good reason for not calling but just could not understand why he had not. They had met twice and slept with each other on both occasions. The company had been good, they had shared a lot of laughs and the sex was great – he clearly liked her. As she stared at her phone, willing Harry to call, she reflected that it was not the catching of a man that was difficult – it was the keeping of him. The power with which women were endowed by nature guaranteed that they would be able to attract a man up until the moment in which he planted his seed but, thereafter, all bets were off. She recalled her father's wise words to her when she turned 16: "*Women want everything in one man; men want one thing from every woman.*"

She had thought that Harry was different from the rest; he had an honourable aura about him; he would surely call. But she also knew that after his first ejaculation into her, there had been a significant transfer of power. It was now up to her to play it cool and not to chase. She turned her phone on its face and carried on processing the next corporate application into the Financial Centre.

Harry had thought about calling Natella but decided against it because she would surely ask him to do something over the weekend – and that could seriously disrupt his ballet rendezvous with Oleana. He felt bad about not calling but told himself that it was better than weaving a lie. Instead, he would leave it until Friday morning and call when Natella's weekend was, hopefully, fully booked up; that would avoid any embarrassment.

Natella was pleased and irritated with Harry when the call eventually came. She knew that he would have been busy at work; she had been watching the news regarding the uncertain US markets, so had assumed that Harry must have had to work nights because of the time difference between Dubai and New York. Even if she was wrong, it was the excuse she wanted to believe. When the phone call ended, she knew that she wanted to see Harry all the more, simply because he was going "out with the boys" for the weekend. She knew that she was falling for him.

Dubai World Trade Centre's exhibition hall was a huge place and on Saturday evening, even Harry could not be unimpressed by the number of beautifully dressed human beings loitering in its lobbies. Local Emiratis – the men in their pristine, white, collarless *kanduras*, and their ladies, creating 'desire out of discreet' in their fashioned, figure-hugging, black *abayas*.

They mingled with the majority crowd of Westerners, who were all dressed to impress. Harry could tell that there was a preponderance of Russians by the number of men who looked out of place in designer dinner suits alongside women who were stunning in comparison. Dubai's other elite, the Indians, were making their presence felt by the number of Rolls Royces dropping them at the main doors, the light skin of their women and the gaudy jewels accompanying their captivating saris.

In amongst this mêlée of Dubai's one percent, Harry searched for Oleana. He so wanted to find her just to prove his competence in seeking her out, but eventually he capitulated to technology and called her; within 30 seconds he was trying to catch his breath and stay cool.

Oleana looked absolutely stunning. Her strapless dress in black lace on white satin came to just below her knees, her legs looked immaculate in black stockings (or at least Harry hoped they were stockings), and her shoes were high with black straps. She was a vision.

"You look beautiful," Harry told her as they greeted with a kiss on each cheek. Oleana thanked him and suggested that they grab a drink before the performance. As they sipped Prosecco, Oleana's phone rang. She looked at the number and thanked God it was not Natella; it was a Russian number with which she was very familiar.

Harry heard the conversation in Russian but could not understand it. He did, however, pick up the word "*Bolshoi*", so assumed that she had told whomever was calling that she was at the ballet.

"My boss," explained Oleana, even though she did not have to. "We have some more clients coming into town that I need to breastfeed." She smiled cheekily and winked at Harry adding, "Not literally, of course."

Harry knew he would not mind trying. His mind was soon distracted from that thought, however, as he and Oleana were escorted to their seats and the brass section opened the first scene of *Swan Lake*. He then sat transfixed as the story unfolded with the sheer beauty and the flowing skill of the dancers. He would forever recall the Black Swan's *pas de deux*, not for the beauty of the dance itself, but because it was at that moment that Oleana slipped her hand against his. He gave it a gentle squeeze and she squeezed back.

They remained hand in hand for the rest of the show and in the taxi back to Harry's apartment. They fell into bed together and although Harry had been around the block a few times in terms of sexual encounters, this was different. This was mutual passion and it really felt like she meant it.

From Oleana's side, what had started as the entrapment of a man that could be useful to her had rapidly become something else. At the ballet she had found herself proud to be at Harry's side, she had wanted to hold his hand, she had wanted him to desire her. She felt safe with him – this was a man that she could really try to make it with.

"*If love comes, let it come fast,*" her grandmother had once told her.

The first thing that she woke to on Sunday morning was Harry kissing her shoulder from behind. She rolled over to face him and smiled, hoping that she did not look too dishevelled. Harry looked at her; she was gorgeous, even after sleeping on her face.

He suddenly experienced a flash of recognition – he had seen her before and the event was almost at the surface of his memory. But then it sunk back down again as she kissed him on the lips. "It's a workday," he told her, "and I have to go the office. But please, stay as long as you want, just let yourself out. I'll leave towels and everything out for you."

He showered, prepared the coffee for her and gave her a kiss goodbye, wishing that he could stay in bed with her. He told her softly that he would call her later.

She knew he would; she could feel that this was special. Harry left for work.

Oleana dozed in Harry's bed until just after 9 am; she would have slept longer had it not been for her mobile ringing. She reached for the phone and glanced at the number. Shit, it was Moscow – she had forgotten to call her boss back.

The familiar voice on the other end did not bother with greetings, nor did he mention the fact that she should have called him back. He viewed her as such a good employee that she must have had a good enough reason not to be able to do so.

"We need to revisit our man on the Palm," he said calmly. "Nothing obtrusive, I just need to find out what he cares most about apart from his children."

Oleana knew the voice at the other end was that of a grandfather who adored children; he would never bring their innocent lives into the repercussions of adult cock-ups.

"Is there anything in particular you have in mind?" she asked.

"Nothing specific, and I expect your answer is going to be money, but perhaps there's something else. Be subtle, I don't want him knowing that we're looking. See what you can trawl up in a week. No later." The call ended.

Oleana sat on the edge of Harry's bed. She reflected on how she had just spent the night with someone who had truly swept her off her feet; he was kind, charming, manly and strong. However, she knew from his date with Natella that he must have at least some friends on M-Frond, which was why she had initially selected him as a target for her attention. In the past few hours, however, emotional reasons had overtaken her rational strategy, which was clearly more advanced than that of her Controller's. She vowed to herself that she would have to use Harry just this once and then never again. In any case, he would never know.

The Controller hung up the phone and looked at the Godfather. "She's going to find out for us, hopefully within a week; we should have something to make the Iranian motherfucker come to the table and, more importantly, make him realise that he's not the one in control."

"Does she know to be careful?" the Godfather asked.

"Are you kidding me, boss?" responded the Controller. "She cleared the two bodies of our best eliminators out of his house! She's the best Fixer we have."

"Point taken." This was all the Godfather needed to say.

Oleana stretched next to Harry's bed and looked at the framed photo on the bedside table. It was of two children hugging Harry. She reflected that he looked younger then but better now. Perhaps he was less stressed now.

She wandered into his kitchen and smiled when she saw the mug that he had put out for her morning coffee, and that the coffee maker was primed and ready to go. She pressed the button and the machine gurgled as it percolated her brew. She looked around at the paraphernalia in Harry's kitchen: the beer opener on the fridge, the half-dozen cereal boxes lined up by the kettle and the tea mugs bearing military badges and logos. She recognised clearly that no woman had any influence here, and hoped that she might have a chance to change that.

While she sipped her coffee she walked out of the kitchen, vaguely noticing the row of small hooks on the wall for Harry's keys. She had almost passed by this innocuous display when suddenly she stopped dead in her tracks. She backed up and lifted a bright red key fob bearing the word 'AVIS' in large white print; the fob was attached to a key with a Toyota logo.

She lifted the key from the hook and turned the fob over. From top to bottom it read:

Vehicle Registration Number
DXB O 60599
Colour
White
Vehicle Description
Toyota Camry

The hairs stood up on the back of her neck. What the hell was this doing in Harry's apartment? She had seen an identical car registration plate to this number before. It was the one that she had delivered back to Avis when she was recovering the car for those idiots that had got themselves killed, and for whom she was still cleaning up. 60599 was the original number of the plates that she had switched back onto the white Toyota when she had cleansed it and returned it to

Avis. She had no record of any of this, but she knew for certain that these keys matched that car.

Oleana now had multiple questions running concurrently through her mind. What was Harry doing with these keys? Had Soroush given them to him for some reason? Why would he keep them? Was the villa in which Natella met Harry the same house as that from which she had recovered the bodies? If it was, then it was just 36 hours after the bodies had been removed. Harry could not have known about it. No one would be so foolish as to have a dinner party the evening after two bodies had just disappeared from the same house.

Her conclusion was that Harry must be a lot closer to Shaheen than she had ever envisaged, but why had he been at the Palm villa with Natella in the first place?

Perhaps Harry worked for a foreign government. She hoped like hell that none of this was the case but knew now that she had no choice but to stay close in order to figure out the depth of his involvement. If he was playing her, she would need to expose him.

As she pulled on her dress and wrapped a shawl from her handbag around her, she calmed herself down with some self-reason. If Harry had known anything, then he was certainly being a pretty cool character; nevertheless, she checked his drawers and cupboards, but found nothing untoward. She would have liked to crack his little safe but reflected that he had trusted her enough to leave her alone in his house; he therefore presumably had nothing to hide from her – at least here. Oleana reasoned that if Harry had known she was a fixer in Dubai for a controller in the Duma, then he probably would have done a lot more to cover his arse, including disposing of the Toyota keys.

How Harry would act and treat her over the next week or two would not just decide whether their burgeoning love would flourish or die – it could very well determine the same destiny or fate for Harry.

CHAPTER THIRTEEN
From Party To Pussy

Mahmoud Abadi had only been a year out of police training and had served his penance as a Dubai Metro station guard. Now he had been attached to 'traffic' for six months' orientation.

He had worked hard for his degree in law enforcement and did not want to believe that his future included being a traffic cop, but if he wanted to get into one of Dubai Police's special units, he knew that he had to do well during his rookie years. He had arrived for his shift early and was scouring the computer for incidents or theft reports.

As he scrolled through the data, he probably would not have noticed the report of a stolen number plate, except for one twist of coincidence. His birthday was 20 November 1987 and his first initial was M. The stolen plate was M201187. He thought that it would be cool to have it for himself so he printed out the report with the name and address of the owner who had reported it lost or stolen. Perhaps he would pay her a visit to see if she would sell him the plate.

★ ★ ★

Elsewhere, Natella was frustrated; her weekend had been boring. Harry had been "busy" and even Oleana had apparently been out with Russian friends. Sunday, a workday in Dubai, always put her in a bad mood. It just did not seem right to be working on a Sunday; she was a Christian after all, even if not a very good one.

By the afternoon she could not stand it anymore; she texted Harry one word – "*Coffee?*" – and to Oleana three words – "*Fancy a shop?*"

Within a few minutes she was sitting with Harry in Caribou Coffee, arranging a date for Monday night, and confirming an after-work shopping spree with Oleana the following evening. One day she would regret not having scheduled the events the other way around, but by 8 pm on Tuesday she was sitting drinking green tea with Oleana in Dubai Mall's Fashion Avenue, describing her previous evening with Harry.

As Natella spoke, Oleana felt a tinge of anger but was also quite turned on that Harry had been so attentive with her at the ballet and in his bed, but, when given the opportunity, had promptly slept with Natella just two nights later.

She was acutely aware that she was, in effect, the mistress within the threesome, but she had hoped that Harry would gently fade out of Natella's life and into hers. Clearly that was not going to happen quickly, so she would have to up her game to ensure that he was well and truly snagged. She could not stop thinking of him with Natella and tried to block that image from her mind.

Oleana's mind wandered on to the Toyota keys as Natella rattled on about how much she thought that Harry liked her.

Perhaps Soroush had given him the keys, but why? It did not make any sense. Surely the killer would have just thrown them from one of Dubai's many bridges, or even in the creek of the Palm. The fact that Harry had them hanging in his house meant that he could not be aware of their significance. She would just have to find out why.

Natella and Oleana left the Armani Caffè being eyed up by the many young Emiratis who were there to see and be seen. These two beautiful women, even if only dressed for shopping, would do very nicely until it was time to take an Emirati wife. The vying studs would have been wholly pissed off had they known that both women were only interested in getting laid by the same infidel Englisher in his forties.

As the two women walked towards the exit, Oleana asked Natella how she had got to the mall. "Taxi," Natella replied.

Oleana instinctively offered her a ride home and they made their way into the maze that was the mall's car park. As they approached Oleana's Mini Cooper S, Natella commented on how cute the car was, and without thinking, Oleana opened the boot into which they could put their shopping bags.

As soon as she had done so she felt the hairs stand up on the back of her neck. 'Shit,' she thought. She had forgotten to dispose of the ringer plate and its copy. It was there in plain sight.

Natella saw the plates but did not say anything. As she placed her bags on top of them she noticed the number 201187. Her favourite number was 11 and her sister had been born in 1987. She thought nothing more of it.

Oleana was relieved that Natella had not commented on the plate – it had saved her from telling a lie. When they arrived at Natella's apartment complex Oleana was quick to unload, peck Natella a goodbye kiss and drive back to her own little villa, all the while wondering where to dump the ringer plates.

Shaheen was having a shit week. He was really concerned that he had made a mistake reaching out to the Russians, and now, on top of all his work commitments, his wife had just announced that they were going to have a party on Saturday afternoon. He needed this distraction like he needed toothache, but at the end of the day, he knew that for the most part he was just a passenger in his wife's lavish social calendar. She was oblivious to expenditure, pressures of work or anything else, so far as he could make out. All he did know was that he seldom saw her in the same dress twice and that most of the shoes that she owned had either red or pink soles, and amounted to over a hundred pairs.

As he looked over the lawyer's papers regarding his extraction from Dubai, he decided to have one more round with the Russians. If they did not take the deal, or make a decent counter, they could go fuck themselves. He had tried to find an 'easy out'; if it was not to be, then he would just have to take it as it came.

He tapped out a text message on his Samsung – "*Party, my place 2 pm Saturday, bring swimsuit, dancing shoes and a friend*" – and sent it out to about 20 privileged recipients.

The Pakistani labourer on the mosque building site on Jumeirah Beach Road could not have been more miserable. He tried to take solace in the fact that his task of sweeping up dust as an unskilled labourer on a new mosque project might have some value for him in the afterlife, but right now it was this life that he hated. He worked 12 hours a day on the site and each evening travelled in a non-air-conditioned bus to a labour camp, where he shared a small bunk room with five other labourers. The conditions were so cramped and austere that all he prayed for was the love of his family and his flight home.

Sadly, even praying five times a day was not going to retrieve his passport from the developer, his employer who had seized it as soon as he had entered the country. He would perhaps see it again at the end of his two-year contract if he was lucky, and even then, only after at least 50 percent of his meagre $300 per month had been paid to the agent in Pakistan – the same man who had promised him a great job and great conditions during his employment in Dubai.

As usual, he swept the sands of the desert from the area of work while his colleagues shaped the structure using steel-reinforced concrete. It was close to the end of the day when he emptied his last bin full of garbage into the dumpster and noticed a car registration plate amongst the litter. He picked it up and noticed that there were actually two plates held together by a rubber band – one of the plates, with road tax stickers, was of good quality; the other looked like a photo had been stuck onto a metal plate. He did not so much wonder where they had come from as how much they might be worth. He looked behind him to see whether anyone had seen his find; they had not. He tucked them under his arm and then under some planking while he figured out how to monetise it.

If Harry had been elated to receive Shaheen's party invitation text, it was little compared to Oleana's satisfaction when she got the invitation in turn from Harry. She would finally get to meet the murderer, Mr Soroush. She placed a call to the Controller, just to check that a legitimate meeting at the "scene of the crime" was okay.

Soltegov could hardly conceal his joy. It had only been a matter of days and his Fixer was already into the lion's den.

"Be very careful," he warned her, "but we do need to find his vulnerability. We've underestimated Mr Soroush before; we cannot make that same mistake again. I'll also ensure I have our two men in town who have done business with Soroush; we can then hopefully link whatever you find out about him with the negotiations we need to conclude."

His tone made Oleana nervous. Her craft was to organise and stay in the background – she was comfortable with that. Stepping into a direct contact arena with a blooded murderer was not something she had ever bargained for. She felt glad that Harry would be with her; she could cling to his arm and give the appearance of a quiet woman. She would have to decide what to wear.

The Controller hung up the phone and told himself that he was going to have to promote the Fixer – she was so efficient at everything that she was clearly wasted in her current capacity. The only issue was replacement; it was a process that had to be painstaking and it slowed everything down. The individual had to be spotted, recruited, trained and deployed – and everything had to be discreet, without them knowing the other pieces of the jigsaw.

He knew that the Fixer had no clue as to why Maxim and Boris had been in town, nor did she know his current plan, nor would she ever. But that was just the way.

He called Vlad and told him to get his partner and go to Dubai. "Be there by Friday – await my instructions. There'll be a meeting with Soroush any time from Saturday onwards. Be ready."

When Harry and Oleana met on Saturday, he was just happy about the event, she about everything. They were the consummate cool couple if ever there was one, and Harry reflected on how he wished that his kids could see the way his image had softened.

As the couple enjoyed the taxi ride to the Palm, several miles away on the road on which they had just been travelling, a labourer disclosed to his friend that he had found some car number plates, and wondered if there was a lost value that could be claimed.

His friend asked him if he was crazy. If he tried to sell the plates and was caught, then he would be turned into the police and then goodness knows what would happen. Besides, who the hell was he going to sell it to? "Get rid of them," he advised. "Just throw both of them on a road so it looks like they fell off a car." Without hesitation, the labourer walked over to the planking and retrieved one of the number plates; he walked out to the road, which was adjacent to a junction, and dropped it into the gutter; the other he would dump close to his labour camp. At least now his involvement in all of this would not cause any trouble, or risk delay to his long-awaited flight home. He resumed sweeping dust in the desert.

The party was everything Harry had expected, and surreal for Oleana. As they stepped out of the taxi, music could be heard blaring from the back garden. The front door that Oleana recalled so well was open. The host clearly did not give a shit about his security; she surmised that his ability to snuff people was security enough.

Harry was welcomed like an old friend. Shaheen's wife hugged him and told him that Bunny was upstairs. Oleana immediately wanted to know who Bunny was, but did not ask; she just stayed graceful and polite, and scoped out the competition and men at the party. It was a beautiful crowd and the party was already in full swing.

Farah, Shaheen's wife, immediately warmed to Oleana and guided her by the arm to the drinks table with Harry in tow. She handed Harry a beer and poured a vodka for Oleana. "We adore Harry," she explained. "You see, I used to live in London before I was married, so he reminds me of those carefree days." Oleana could sense sadness in Farah's tone. After chatting for just a few minutes, Farah suggested that they meet for a coffee sometime; they exchanged mobile numbers with a dropped call.

As they walked out onto the patio overlooking the blue sea inlet between the fronds, Oleana noticed an expensive but casually dressed man in his forties surrounded by people; she guessed it was Soroush.

Shaheen spotted Harry and came over to greet him. He could not help but be impressed with Oleana – she was stunning. Somehow blonde women were like a magnet, a forbidden fruit, to Middle Eastern men.

Shaheen noticed her shoes straight away; the stunningly high heels were always a giveaway. He had learned long ago that the height of a woman's heel is directly proportional to how much she wants to be desired. He only had to figure out by whom; in this case, however, it was obvious that Harry was her target, and she certainly did want to be desired.

He asked Harry if he had shown Oleana around the house, and having learned that he had not, Shaheen took it upon himself to give her the guided tour. Harry took no chances and accompanied them; he was surprised to feel a tinge of jealousy when Shaheen offered his arm for her to hold as they walked around the villa.

She pretended that the house was completely new to her and that she was, of course, impressed with the Rolls Royce.

Upstairs they viewed the four bedrooms, and, ironically in the one where Harry had previously ridden Natella rigid, Oleana was introduced to the love of Shaheen's life – Bunny.

He gave Oleana the full rundown on Bunny's pedigree and handed her to Harry, saying, "But I do have competition for her affections." All three of them laughed as Bunny instantly nestled against Harry's chest, recognising his smell and the heat being generated by his body.

They left Bunny in the bedroom and walked back out into the garden, where Shaheen was distracted by his next guests.

"I swear he loves that cat more than anything in the world," Harry commented with a smile; he failed to mention that Bunny was also one of his own top-five favourite entities with a pulse.

Oleana smiled wordlessly. She was now content that she had probably found her leverage over Shaheen, but for the time being she was much more interested in locking in Harry for herself.

CHAPTER FOURTEEN
Speakeasy Rules

Vlad and Luka were not at all happy. They had been perfectly content running around Dubai acting like hotshots, buying up property for the Godfather. No one had ever mentioned that they would end up becoming a collection agency for whatever they bought if it did not work out.

They had been educated of the fact that it cost the cartel 27 cents on the dollar to launder a dollar, and that, in any criminal's mind, would be a fair 'loss'. Seventy-three cents multiplied by a lot of millions mounted up, especially when the money had been gifted or derived for zero in the first place.

Now both men were back in Dubai with insufficient budget to live it up in the crude opulence of the Cavalli Club, or the stunningly contemporary décor of the Armani Hotel. They were, therefore, bored and irritable.

In short, they wanted to cut this deal with Shaheen Soroush and get the hell out of town. However, both had agreed that they needed to obey the Controller, even though neither was at all comfortable about turning down Soroush's next offer, whatever it may be.

★　　★　　★

They called Shaheen on Sunday and told him that they were in town and wanted another meeting to discuss the counter-offer. Counter-offer? thought Shaheen. What the fuck did that mean? He had already offered them the property deed title, for Christ's sakes! If they did not want that, then they must clearly want the money he had already spent. He would have to figure out another way.

He sat in his kitchen staring at the empty booze bottles from the party and his mind wandered – he hoped that Harry had nailed that sexy Russian chick; of course, he need not have wasted concern on that count.

His wife asking him if he could pop to the local convenience store to get her some tampons interrupted his thoughts. He knew he could not refuse; to do so would have got him the 'after all I do for you' lecture. So he reluctantly picked up the car keys, wondering if he was even sober enough to drive in his morning-after state, given Dubai's zero-tolerance alcohol policy on being behind the wheel, even if only with a hangover.

He suddenly stopped in his tracks. The solution had just become completely obvious to him and he reflected that the clearest solution was sometimes the least visible. Was it any wonder that man had stood on the moon long before somebody had thought of putting wheels on a suitcase and pulling it by a handle? Shaheen reflected on the hundreds of years that people had carried their bags instead of pulling them along. His solution for the Russians was almost as obvious.

Having bought the tampons, he made a call to his favourite Indian errand-courier. He was whistling as he re-entered his house.

By Tuesday evening Shaheen was standing outside the main entrance door of the J.W. Marriott Hotel in the Deira area of Dubai. He had chosen this venue for two reasons, and one of them was that they serve exceptional steak in their world-famous steakhouse.

He assumed that Vlad and the other punk, Luka, would not be suspicious that he had met them at the entrance of the hotel, but he had honestly been unable to think of a better way for his plan to work.

The hustle and bustle was fervent on 2B Street, from which the hotel's cramped vehicle drop-off point and valet-parking was operated; the area was busy and as congested as ever. Most hotel guests would be unaware that the stark walls of the bland building on the opposite side of the street confined prisoners being held in the overpopulated jail cells of Al Muraqqabat Police Station. As Shaheen looked at the windowless structure and thought of the miserable souls therein, he smiled and glanced at his Breguet watch. It was unusual for Shaheen to be on time for a meeting, but this one was different – it could be life changing.

The silver Mazda 6 pulled up onto the Marriot ramp; Shaheen recognised that Vlad was in the driver's seat. He also noted the Hertz sticker on the rear screen.

As Vlad got out of the car and accepted his valet-parking ticket from the attendant, Shaheen shook hands with Luka. He then walked towards the back of the car to greet Vlad.

On the opposite side of the road, a skinny Indian, leaning against the wall on the corner of the alleyway and the police station, noted the rental car's registration number and the clothes being worn by the two men that emerged from it.

Shaheen explained that the hotel's steak restaurant was a bit difficult to find, so he had decided to wait for them at the hotel entrance. As they descended the stairs to the restaurant, neither Russian considered anything to be out of the ordinary.

The décor of the steakhouse was as traditional as the cuisine, and Shaheen took delight in being seated at a table with a number of small brass platelets screwed into it. One of them bore his name, which was the privilege of a regular customer.

Shaheen explained to the Russians the process of attaining brass-plate status, and asked the waiter to please bring the "master wine list"; even the Russians realised that this would display only the vintage and most expensive wines held by the house. He asked if red would be okay. "It is a steakhouse, after all," he quipped.

Neither of the Russians would have even suspected that Shaheen had arrived early specifically to check out the wine list, and he just hoped that they would appreciate the fuss he made of ordering a rare bottle of Paul Hobbs Viña Cobos. The waiter congratulated him on his choice and asked if he would like the wine decanted. Shaheen wanted to preface his response by saying "This is such an occasion", but simply answered, "Why not?", and let the waiter go through his theatrics in serving the wine and describing the menu.

It did not surprise Shaheen that the Russians ordered the most expensive cuts of Wagyu beef or that they liked the wine. Both were genuinely impressed, but were also waiting for Shaheen's punchline. If Shaheen had gone to this much trouble, then he must be looking to settle. They were hoping that he would not put anything too enticing on the table; it was the Controller, after all, who wanted to be firmly back in the driving seat.

As they finished the small talk and the steaks were served, Vlad watched Shaheen's handling of the steak knife. He noticed from the way that he cut his meat that this man could handle a knife, and pictured him sticking it in a guy's throat.

As Shaheen let the first bite of his massaged steak melt in his mouth, he decided that it was time to deal.

"Gentlemen." He paused as the waiter topped up their wine glasses. "I'm very glad that we're here today, because

I'd like to resolve this matter once and for all." He had their full attention as they sipped their wine. "I've already offered you the full transfer of deed for the Ajman tower and you've refused. So I'm left to assume that something or someone in your organisation does not appreciate the full situation."

Vlad was sure that they did but knew better than to interrupt and chance irritating Shaheen.

"So I have a deal for you." Shaheen looked at each of the Russians in turn. "And I do mean *you* and *you.*" He could see their interest being piqued. "If you can persuade your investors to accept the deed of the building as full settlement of our differences, I will give you each 75,000 dollars in cash for your involvement, no questions asked."

This was a new angle that neither Vlad nor Luka had expected. Shaheen was not threatening them, but rather he was attempting to buy them off against their own people. Both men felt the threat of physical harm lift from their shoulders, and if it had been solely up to them, they would have immediately jumped on the offer. However, they *would* have to persuade the Controller to accept the deal as it was, and that might not be easy.

Vlad asked, "If you can put some cash on top of your offer for the investors, then we can probably push the deal through."

Shaheen smiled. "My friend, I'm sorry to say that my position in all of this won't permit that. It must be one or the other. Either you keep the cash for yourselves or pass it to others. That's the best I can do."

Shaheen honestly did not care whether they took the offer. He knew that these punks had no real loyalty to anyone except themselves; that said, he really did hate the necessary evil that he had lined up for them if they did not accept.

Vlad took a deep breath. "It's not that simple, Mr Soroush. You see, we'd like to make it happen the way you suggest, and perhaps we can; we are, after all, the individual signatories. But it would help us to help you if you put some additional money on the table. If you say that you can, then we can take the message back, but if you say you can't, then that kind of shortens the odds for us." Luka nodded in agreement, then leant across the table.

"We all know what you're capable of, Mr Soroush," he said in a low tone, "and we'd really like to see this matter closed so that no one else gets hurt."

He had intended for his few words to let Shaheen know that he would not need to take the risk of murdering more men over a debt, hoping that he would stump up the additional money. Instead Shaheen only heard the words "no one else gets hurt". As a consummate coward, Shaheen had heard enough – these Russians clearly intended to hurt him; even if they accepted the deal on the table, he would be living scared. He would simply have to implement the plan, the very reason that they were sitting in this particular hotel.

The atmosphere became stilted and all three men sensed that the dinner was, for all intents and purposes, over. Shaheen asked that they consider the offer and get back to him. To Shaheen's satisfaction, both Russians finished their second glass of wine; they had not noticed that Shaheen had merely wet his tongue rather than drink his.

As the Russians rose to leave, Shaheen was glad they had assumed that he would pay the bill. The moment they left the restaurant, he made his call to the skinny Indian who by now was on 2B Street, sitting on a dilapidated moped right outside the hotel, halfway between the entrance and the exit to the ramp that made up the hotel's private driveway and valet-parking service point.

Vlad and Luka strolled towards the lobby, both agreeing that they should try to get the Controller to take the deal. It was a shame that they had been under instructions to play for time – both could have used the $75,000.

Vlad handed the valet-parking ticket to the attendant out-side the hotel, unaware that the moped rider in the full-face helmet had recognised his target. About two minutes passed before the skinny Indian youth saw the silver Mazda 6 in his handlebar mirror; the number matched the one that he had scribbled on his hand about an hour earlier. The valet-park-ing attendant drove the car around to the hotel entrance.

The Indian saw the two Russians get into the car and noted the hotel driver receiving his tip as he got out. He saw the brake lights come on, indicating that his target had shifted the car into 'drive', and as the car rolled slowly for-wards down the exit ramp, the moped driver took a deep breath.

Vlad stopped the car at the driveway exit to make way for a car transiting 2B Street; he also noted a rider on a moped waiting by the pavement. The visor of the helmet concealed the rider's face.

The road was clear, so he gently released the pressure on the brake and eased the car into the street.

Seemingly out of nowhere there was a crashing 'BANG'. Vlad instinctively hit the brake while his brain tried to slow down time and comprehend what was happening.

He saw the moped rider being projected across the front of the car and immediately assimilated that the crashing noise had been from the moped hitting their front wing; he then watched helplessly as the rider rolled off the bonnet and out of sight onto the road.

"Shit!" was about the only word spoken by either Russian.

"Where the fuck did he come from?" asked Luka after a moment's silence.

"He was fucking parked!" shouted Vlad. "The stupid bastard drove straight into me."

They got out of the car to see the moped on its side, the front wheel completely crumpled and petrol leaking onto the road. At the front of the car, the rider was writhing on the road, crying out something in Hindi. Vlad did not understand the language but assumed that the rider had broken his ribs.

As the rider went through his agony-acting, hugging his ribcage, his right thumb rubbed his left hand, erasing the Mazda's plate number into an illegible smudge.

Almost instantly there was a crowd around the scene and an off-duty Filipina nurse tended to the rider, making sure that he was not in any immediate danger from his injuries. The Dubai police were there within a minute from just across the road.

The two policemen immediately took control of the situation. They had seen this scene so many times before and they were mildly relieved that the rider was not a bloody mess. They had already initiated the signal for an ambulance; it would be there in moments.

One of the men identified himself as the driver and blurted that the rider had just driven straight into him. The policeman told him "No problem" in order to keep him calm and asked him to stand by the car with the passenger until they had got the rider off into an ambulance.

The second policeman assisted the nurse until the ambulance arrived.

With the casualty safely on his way to hospital, both policemen turned their attention to their post-RTA immediate action procedure. The second policeman ran the registrations through the on-board computer. The moped was properly registered and insured by a small courier service, with named riders, one of whom matched the identity of the injured driver. The Mazda belonged to Hertz and had been rented out to a Vladimir Berezniki, a Russian national.

He walked over to his partner who was clearly letting the driver have his say. They listened patiently to the Russian's continued protestation that the moped had simply driven straight into him.

The lead policeman remained totally calm, knowing he should do nothing to excite the culprit. "But you do realise the moped had the right of way?" he asked eventually. "You should have given way to him according to the road layout. I'm sorry, but this accident would appear to be your fault from an insurance point of view."

Vlad was relieved that the policeman was only thinking from an insurance perspective. He was wrong to be so.

The policeman turned to his colleague and asked in Arabic, "Do you smell what I smell?" The response was a nod. He turned back to the driver and reverted to English.

"Have you consumed any alcohol, sir?"

Vlad replied that he had, but added that he had only sipped two glasses of wine with dinner.

The second policeman reached for his radio and called for back-up in Arabic.

"And you?" The policeman looked at the passenger.

"The same," he said with a shrug of the shoulder, having no idea of what was unfolding.

"I'll need to breathalyse you both," the policeman said calmly. "It's just procedure."

Vlad blew into the Alcometer; it beeped. He was not worried – he had only sipped two glasses of wine. He saw the red light glow on top of the box, confusing him, but little did he know that the Alcometer was set to zero to detect *any* trace of alcohol.

The policeman remained placid, replaced the blow tube and asked the passenger to follow the same procedure; again, a red light, but Luka did not give a shit – they knew he was only the passenger. And in any case Vlad was not even close to drunk.

A further police car arrived; the initial team now had the back-up they needed.

The policeman looked at Vlad. "Sir, you are under arrest for driving a vehicle after consuming alcohol. That is illegal in this country. You are further charged with causing an accident while driving with alcohol in your blood." He paused. "Do you have a licence to consume alcohol?"

"A what?" asked Vlad, as the fact that he was in deep shit was becoming gradually apparent.

"In order to legally consume alcohol in this country, you must possess a licence. Do you have one?"

"But I'm a visitor here," protested Vlad. "A businessman. I don't live here."

"That is not my concern, sir. If you don't have a licence to consume alcohol, then you're breaking the law; you'll be charged with that too. Please turn around." He handcuffed Vlad, who was then led to the back-up car.

The policeman then asked the passenger the same question and got the same answer.

"You are under arrest as well," he explained. "You are not permitted to consume alcohol in this country without a licence to do so."

"But everybody does it!" Luka protested.

"Everybody is not my concern," the policeman answered. "Just the people that cause trouble or accidents that I catch. Unlike your friend, who's in a lot of trouble, you'll likely only be deported. Now, please turn around and face the car."

Behind the crowd of onlookers, Shaheen stood on the mound that was the hotel lobby entrance. As he watched the second Russian being led to the police car, he could not help but smile. His plan had worked like clockwork. He praised himself for his genius.

These two Russian punks would now spend some time in an Arab jail before getting deported and probably banned from the UAE. They would never be able to bother him again over the Ajman deal, and so far as the world knew, they had both messed up in a foreign country by not respecting its laws.

Upon the skinny Indian's discharge from hospital — ultimately with no broken ribs — Shaheen would pay him the remainder of the 10,000 dirhams ($2,725) that he had promised, a far cry from the $150,000 that he had offered those stupid Russian bastards. He hoped that they would get violated in jail. As white-skinned playboys, it was highly likely that they would.

CHAPTER FIFTEEN
The Mountain Comes To Mahmoud

It was just another day of toil for the street cleaner on Jumeirah Beach Road. The irony had never occurred to him that the only reason he had his godforsaken job was that his labour costs were less than an efficient mechanical sweeper. His was not to reason why; he was just grateful that the winter had brought cooler weather.

He spent his day hoping to find valuables or money that had been dropped or discarded, and even though he was under strict instructions to hand in such items, he had soon realised that to do so was for the sole benefit of his supervisor. His self-imposed rule was simple – if he found it, he owned it.

There was only one exception to finders-keepers and that was if he came across a part of a car or a number plate. In such cases there were strict rules for reporting to the police. So as he picked up the battered number plate from the gutter and read the numbers 201187, he was merely sorry that it was not something of saleable or saveable value. However, for the rest of the day he would keep a look-out for the car with one matching number plate; perhaps if he found it, the owner would give him a reward for its return.

It did not happen.

★　★　★

It was Tuesday before Oleana decided to call the Controller. She had spent the entire weekend with Harry. The day after Shaheen's party they had driven out to Bab Al Shams, the desert hotel retreat; here they had dined on the roof of the hotel in relative solitude and enjoyed the silence offered by the desert. She was growing to adore everything about Harry. He was worldly in his views and found amusement in most aspects of life. She had not realised that he had been a soldier; she smiled, recalling their laughter when he had explained that he had been an infantryman in the British Royal Anglian Regiment – she had mistaken Anglian for Anglican and asked Harry with some bewilderment if he had been a religious policeman.

The Controller picked up on the third ring, which was just as well, since he knew that his Fixer only ever let the phone ring four times before hanging up, and she never left messages.

He heard Oleana's dulcet voice at the other end of the phone, instantly recognising her Saint Petersburg accent. She described the party and her interaction with Shaheen Soroush; she commented that he was a very cool character and that he seemed to go out of his way to appear harmless. She added that he has obviously been trained by a professional organisation to be inconspicuous regarding his ability to look after himself. He had a nice house and an attractive wife and family. She summarised by saying, "He's got his shit together. He keeps a nice circle of friends, including the one that invited me to his house." She purposely omitted the gender of her 'friend'; she did not want the Controller to know about or jeopardise her relationship with Harry.

"Any chinks in the armour apart from his family?" the Controller asked.

"Don't laugh, but there are two things" she responded. "First, his Rolls Royce, he just loves it; but he also has the most beautiful, white, pedigree Persian cat. I mean, this thing is fabulous and must be worth a fortune. He absolutely adores it."

The Controller instinctively thought that if they needed leverage, such a cat might just work. It was a lot easier to steal and hide a cat than a car. However, he said nothing in that regard.

He moved the conversation along, informing the Fixer that he had a couple of his financial guys in town but that they were self-supporting, before adding that she had done a good job over the past few weeks. He would ensure a bonus in her pay-check. "Just sit on your hands for now," he instructed. "We'll reach out if we need you."

These were words that Oleana loved to hear; her life of shopping, sunbathing, the gym, and of course, catching Harry, could resume.

The Controller put down the phone at his end, and walked down the row of Duma offices. He stopped at the door labelled '*A. Delimkov*', entered and took a seat opposite the Godfather.

"You are not going to believe this," he chuckled. "We might be able to get our money and our revenge on this Soroush bastard, all because he loves his fucking cat!"

The Godfather sat in disbelief as he listened to the description of this creature. He hated cats and for the life of him could not understand why a human being would put the interests of any animal beyond its monetary value. "So are you thinking of taking the cat?" he asked.

"It can't do any harm, and it might bring the bastard to the table. But it won't be me taking it – the idiots who got us involved with Soroush in the first place can do that." He reached for one of his mobile phones and called Vlad. There was no reply, so he tried again; he then tried to call Luka. Neither phone could be reached. He cursed loudly, took a breath and told himself that he would simply call later.

He would not have to.

It was about two hours later when his assistant told him that she had the Russian consular officer from Dubai on the phone. It was his old friend from the Economic and Trade Department, a fellow money launderer and facilitator who was also an employee of the Russian government, their common source of illicit funds.

He asked the name of the men that had been involved in the Ajman property deal, which the Controller promptly reminded him of.

"Shit," the officer said. "We've just received an arrest notification for both of them. "Apparently one of them was drunk when driving and hit a motorcyclist; the other was arrested as an accessory."

"Jesus Christ," came the response. "These two idiots have fucked up everything they've touched."

The consular officer continued and explained that the procedure would be for an Embassy legal officer to visit them and that perhaps there was the possibility of making a penalty payment that could bypass the legal process to obtain an early deportation. But he added that this would depend on the handling officer and judge; that was as good as it could get under these circumstances. He was shocked by the Controller's response.

"Let them rot."

Those three simple words meant that it would be a full year before Vlad tasted the cold Moscow air again, 11 whole months more than Luka, his more fortunate partner. When they arrived home, the best they could expect was to become outcasts from the 'organisation'; the worst, to meet an untimely demise. Either way, their life of privilege was over.

Following the call, the Controller pursed his lips and thought, 'If you need something done properly you have to do it yourself.' He would have to go to Dubai in order to sort this mess out once and for all. In the meantime, he would have to use the Fixer to shape the impending battlefield. If Shaheen Soroush did not capitulate and give him his money back, he would kill the cat and strangle the man with its skin.

Natella had just about given up on Harry; he had not called for over a week and this was becoming a pattern. Maybe he was not the nice guy that she had taken him for. Perhaps he was just like all the other men out there, after all. However, whenever she thought about what had happened between them, she reverted to telling herself once more what she wanted to believe: that he was a really busy guy with a hectic social life and he simply did not have enough time to fit her in in-between his innocent commitments. Natella was good at ignoring negative evidence if it gave her hope of a meaningful relationship.

Over the past few weeks she had got to know Harry's haunts in the Financial Centre. If it was coffee, he went to Caribou; if it was a snack, he went to the Freshii sandwich and salad bar; if it was alcohol, he favoured the bar in Caramel. He was a creature of habit and these were his favourite places. She had also noted his preference, more often than not, for picking up a salad from Freshii after work, and he normally finished around 6.30 pm. She decided that she would have to make sure that their paths crossed, but it had to look like a chance meeting.

Natella inevitably decided that Oleana was her best cover so she invited her to the aerobics class at the centre's Fitness First gym. The session started at 5.15 pm and ran for an hour. She figured that they could complete the class, then go to Freshii for a fruit-shake. With luck, they would bump into Harry and the chance meeting would remind him to call her.

The timing worked out perfectly. When the class ended, Oleana pulled on her black Juicy-brand sweatsuit and adjusted her hair with a large black clip in order to hold her hair off her face. Natella reflected that Oleana still looked damn good without make-up – but then again, so did she.

As they sat in Freshii sipping their healthy shakes, Oleana still had no idea that she was Natella's alibi. She had her back to Harry when he breezed in to make his order, but saw Natella's face light up and say, "Hi"; instinctively she gave a sideways glance to see whom it was that Natella was greeting. She was shocked and pleasantly surprised to see Harry, but it took her brain a moment to register him before she broke into a smile. It was not soon enough.

Harry had seen Natella almost as soon as he walked in, but had also noted the blonde with the hair clipped up and the Juicy-brand suit. It looked familiar. As the woman glanced around and he saw that it was Oleana, he suddenly realised where he had seen her before, in the same attire, the same clip, the same dishevelled but not unattractive look. She had been the woman who had got into the Toyota when he had emerged from Shaheen's villa on the day that the bodies had gone missing, and the very same woman that had followed him off the frond.

As the hairs on the back of his neck stood on end, he caught his composure and greeted both ladies. He and Oleana pretended that they had not met each other since the brunch. Natella was all smiles and asked him to join them. His instinct was to get the hell out of there but he agreed to sit with them while he was waiting for his salad. Small talk about the gym ensued.

When Harry's name was called by the salad maker, he excused himself and said that he needed to get home in order to pay his cleaner. Natella took the only chance she had and pounced. She explained that she had an invitation for two to a jazz evening in the centre's Capital Club on Thursday – would he care to join her?

He could sense Oleana's amusement, knowing full well that she would be scrutinising every word of his response.

He stammered as his mind raced. "Uh, sure, I think so, I'll have to check with work in case I'm liaising with the US markets then. I'll call you." And with that, he made good his escape.

On his drive home, Harry tried to analyse why he had not recognised Oleana earlier, but then he thought about how she always had her hair down and she always wore make-up. Additionally, he had never seen her surprised sideways glance; the only missing component from that first sighting had been her sunglasses.

What the hell had she been doing on the frond that morning? Perhaps she had one of her clients out there, but why would she not have told him that she had been out there before? Had she even recognised him from that day? She had certainly got a good look at him as he had emerged from the neighbour's driveway and crossed the road.

Those bodies had disappeared overnight – someone must have been watching the property and seen the two guys enter but not emerge. Was she part of a surveillance team? If so, and she knew of his involvement, why had she permitted herself to form a relationship with him? The most basic rule of surveillance is that you can never effectively follow anyone who knows you.

She had been driving a white Toyota but she owned a Mini? The Avis keys he had found on the old dude's body were for a Toyota but the number plate did not match the key tab. He wished that he had used the remote key to see which car locked or unlocked, but he had just been too distracted by events. Where did those bodies go and who knew about their deaths? Surely if anyone had seen him leave the night of the killings, they would have intercepted him in some shape or form. The only logical answer that Harry could come up with was that their back-up team had retrieved them, but how could Oleana be a part of that? The bodies must have been long gone by the time he had seen her getting into the Toyota, so it made no sense for her to have hung around for so long after they had been moved. None of it made sense except for the fact that she was drop-dead gorgeous and that she was all he could think about all day long.

No sooner was Harry out of sight from Freshii than he became the subject of conversation between Natella and Oleana.

Natella explained that she was confused. Harry was always so nice to her when they were together, but after each date he became distant just as quickly as they had become intimate.

"Perhaps that's your answer," Oleana responded in a philosophical tone. "Perhaps you let him make his move too quickly."

"But it was the whole event," Natella responded. "The Rolls Royce, the villa, the meal, the pool." She paused. "Shit, even the way the cat loved this guy made him seem like a nice guy. I mean, animals can sense that stuff right?"

"Cat? There was a cat at the villa you went to?"

Natella proceeded to describe the one-and-only Bunny and Oleana was forced to ask a question to which she did not really want the answer.

"How long was Harry a guest at the villa?"

Natella was not sure, but she recalled that he had told her how he had not stayed there the whole week and that he had slept in his own apartment until the night before their liaison. Oleana gave a mental sigh of relief and reflected that Harry was one lucky man. Had he been there that Tuesday night, he would have witnessed Shaheen murdering the

Controller's visitors – and God only knew what Shaheen would have done to Harry in order to cover his own tracks.

She needed to double check. "Do you know when the owner left Harry the house?"

Natella had no idea but asked why Oleana was being so inquisitive; hence, the subject was immediately dropped. Oleana then advised Natella to "back off; let Harry do the chasing and give him space."

"I was always told," Natella retorted in a resigned tone, "that when a man needs space, she's normally got a name."

Oleana nodded. 'Yes, girl, and she's looking right at you.'

They finished their healthy shakes and went separately to their cars. On her way home, Oleana called Harry and quipped, "So what are *we* doing on Thursday?" It was a deliberate blocking manoeuvre and he was happy that she was doing it.

"Anything you like," responded Harry. He wanted to get to the bottom of the Toyota mystery on Thursday evening and then work on Oleana's actual bottom for the reminder of the weekend.

Across town, Mahmoud, the young policeman, was delighted when he logged on to the police report network to find that there was an alert specifically for him. The case that he had flagged regarding the missing number plate was reporting an update and he eagerly pulled up the message. The plate bearing his birth date had been found, handed in by road cleaners. The retrieval location was given as the junction of Jumeirah Beach Road and Umm Al Sheif Road. This was at the other end of town from the owner's registered address in Mirdif, but at least he now had an excuse to visit the driver – perhaps she would sell or swap the registration with him.

He climbed into the patrol car to join the seasoned sergeant and asked if they could make a house call on the Mirdif address to find out if the plate could have been lost in the location that it had been found. The sergeant sighed to himself and reflected on how he himself had long ago lost the eagerness of youth, but he did not want to dampen the youngster's mood; he agreed and tried to sound enthusiastic about it.

The Moroccan Toyota-owner was surprised to open the door and see this young, good-looking policeman; he was certainly a lot easier on the eye than the station officer to whom she had reported the loss.

She was all smiles as she told him that she had not driven on the Beach Road in months and added that she had no need to go to that end of town. She was amused that the young policeman was taking notes.

He explained that the plate could have been stolen, and that if she wanted to swap out the plate for a new registration, it might prevent problems and complications in case someone else had used the original for criminal purposes.

He mentally smiled when she said that *that* seemed like good advice; he reassured her that he would sort out all the paperwork for a replacement registration himself, and then call her. She gave him her mobile number and half-hoped that he would call for more reasons than just the plate.

As Mahmoud sprung back into the police car, the sergeant was once again amused at the rookie's enthusiasm. 'Roll on retirement,' was his only thought as they rejoined the traffic back towards the airport. In the passenger seat, the young policeman had already decided that he would work late to ensure that the plate was clean, and complete the paperwork for the transfer.

* * *

On the Palm, Shaheen was as happy as he could recall having been for a very long time. His plan to dispose so subtly of the Russian punks had been a masterstroke and worked flawlessly; he was now free from any implications. The Singapore initiative was looking good, his wife was excited about the move, the kids might learn a fourth language and he had instructed his lawyer to take the fast track with regard to the solvent liquidation of his Dubai Company. Concurrently, all his assets could be moved offshore to his Virgin Islands and Jebel Ali Free-Zone company's holding accounts.

Additionally, with the Russians in jail and destined to be deported, he could likely sell the deed to the Ajman project at some future juncture. No matter the selling price, he would get out at profit thanks to the Russian 'subsidy'.

The Controller's morale was the opposite of Shaheen's. He was so pissed off that he could not see straight, let alone think in his usual scheming and methodical style. This guy Soroush had really got under his skin – two men dead, two men in prison, no deed, no money, and for now no prospect thereof. He had to turn the tables.

The only readily apparent vulnerability that Shaheen Soroush seemed to have was his fucking cat. The Controller even googled '*Persian cat*' to see what one looked like. He concluded it was a breed that would likely be most popular with women and gays. His mind wandered for a moment, questioning if Soroush might be gay. If he was, then that would make him easier to entrap and snuff, but two kids, wife *et al.* – it seemed pretty unlikely.

He looked at his clock – it was approaching 6 pm. He pulled the bottle of Absolut vodka from his desk drawer. When he was short on ideas, the clear liquid helped produce clear thoughts. He slugged a shot and poured himself another. He was feeling better already; he would find a way to sort this out and sort it quickly.

Back in Dubai, if Natella could have slugged some vodka, she would have done the same, but instead she was sat in front of the TV watching some diatribe on the *E!* channel. Wallowing in self-pity, she hoped that crap TV was not what her life would become, so reached for the phone and called her BFF for some solace.

Oleana was at Harry's apartment but decided to take the call in any case. Harry was in the bedroom getting changed; she was relaxing on his couch with a green tea and was ready for a snuggle, a film, a pizza, and then sex.

"I'm so pissed off," Natella whined as soon as Oleana picked up. "The bastard hasn't called. I think I'm just about done with him."

Oleana noted that Natella had left herself an out by using words like 'think' and 'just about'. These meant she was likely not done with Harry just yet.

"I think it's becoming obvious, my darling." Oleana tried to sound sympathetic. "Maybe he's just not into you."

Oleana listened as Natella started on her list of how Harry had been so nice to her, when Harry suddenly walked back into the lounge from the bathroom.

"More tea?" he asked above the noise of the TV, not realising that Oleana was on the phone.

Oleana pushed her hand over the mouthpiece of the phone, but it was too late. Natella had heard the voice and stopped what she was saying in mid-sentence.

"Where are you? Are you with someone?" Natella asked indignantly.

"I'm with one of my work clients," Oleana quickly lied.

Natella's mind was racing; it has been an English accent. To date Oleana had only ever talked about her Russian concierge clients – they would not be making *her* tea. Should she question further or leave it? She should have done the latter but could not help herself.

"He's English?"

"No, no, Irish." It was the best Oleana could think of. "Hey, look, I really have to go, can I call you a bit later?"

They said a brief goodbye and as Oleana pressed the red button on her phone, she looked at Harry. "Fuck, Natella just heard you ask if I wanted tea! I hope to God she didn't recognise your voice."

Harry shrugged his shoulders thinking, 'Problem solved.'

He had still not assimilated that hell hath no fury like a woman scorned.

Alone in her apartment, Natella muted the TV. She tried to replay the voice she had just heard in her head: "*More tea? More tea? More tea?*" Was it Irish? It sounded like it was English but she was not sure. She *was* sure that the accent was similar to Harry's and *he* was definitely not Irish. She turned off her phone, decided that she was doomed to be the world's most attractive spinster and opted to take an early night in bed with her vibrator.

The Controller flew first class into Dubai International Airport. He was acutely aware that every single mobile call made in the Emirate was likely recorded and retained in case it was needed for future evidence. His tradecraft, however, had been learned during the days of strict 'Moscow Rules'.

These rules had nothing to do with communism or actually anything related to the city. It was simply a convenient label given by Western intelligence services to the rudimentary, but totally effective, communication techniques used by Soviet agents during the Cold War.

Messages would be passed by exchange of a note or a few spoken words outdoors, leaving no chance for electronic intercept or recording. It was based on the KGB's realistic paranoia that any conversation on a phone or in a room could and would be listened to.

The Controller reflected that, since those days, the world had advanced so much that a solitary modern iPhone contained more technology than the entire Sputnik space programme. To him, those who took advantage of the convenience with which information could now be passed deserved to have their communications collected by the Americans' eavesdropping capabilities. He also knew that similar data collection capabilities had been bought and paid for by allied Middle Eastern governments. This increasing reliance on electronic intercept had caused almost total detriment to the ability of 'the system' to detect and monitor Moscow Rules operators, who, like the Controller, maintained the lowest of technology profiles in order to covertly achieve their tradecraft.

He purchased two pay-as-you-go SIM-cards at the airport and caught a taxi to the two-star Beach Resort Hotel – the quietest and most discreet down-market hotel in Dubai. Over the following two days, he shopped for a designer suit at the Dubai Mall and visited several local bars in order to scope out an unsurveilled meeting place. He was simply viewed as another Russian shopper who was in town to escape their brutal winters and blow some illicit money.

On the third day he called the Fixer. He explained that he was in town and that "her father had asked him to check if she was okay". He named the Sho Cho bar at the Dubai Marine Beach Resort; it was an open-air bar.

★   ★   ★

Oleana was shocked to learn that the Controller was in town; she had never known him to come to the UAE before, but reflected that he would be unlikely to tell her unless there was a need for her to know. This time there was.

She sat in her kitchen and reflected that, while she was comfortable working for this man when he was thousands of miles away, she was distinctly nervous when he was close-by, and especially at no notice. She had heard tales of his brutality, and working for him was either a big win or a big lose, with nothing in-between. Oleana reassured herself that, to date, she had done a good job for the cartel – hopefully she had nothing to fear.

The Controller had just one rule when it came to female employees – never have sex with them. Experience in his younger days had taught him that, if as a boss he had sex with an attractive junior employee, he would eventually have to fire her, marry her, or both. He had paid such a price with 15 years of his second marriage and he was still doing the penance.

He had actually picked Oleana for her job because of her looks, but he had thought that he could be disciplined enough never to be drawn in by them.

The Sho Cho bar was packed with a preponderance of Lebanese partiers. These people lived life like every day was their last. Beirut had surely taught them that one day they would be right.

When Oleana arrived, the Controller was already up at the bar, drinking a large vodka with a clear view of all entering the immediate area. The music was pulsing; they would not be overheard.

He instantly recognised her and waved; this was the first time he had met her in person.

They greeted each other with a handshake. "Ilyas Soltegov," he said. "We meet at last."

She spoke in Russian: "Welcome to Dubai."

He ordered her a Dirty Martini and looked around him before exclaiming with irony, "Tough life!"

She responded by saying that it had not exactly been a bed of roses just lately, and he thanked her for all she had done. "Did you get the bonus?" He wanted to reinforce that she had just been well paid for her efforts. She thanked him, knowing in all likelihood that he had actually paid her for what she was about to do rather than what she had done.

He cut to the chase. "I need to bring Soroush to the table." She nodded and he continued. "He has caused us a lot of problems and cost us a lot of money. We cannot let him get away with this, as a matter of principle."

Oleana sensed that her boss was about as serious on this matter as he could get. She asked the very question that he wanted to hear: "What do want me to do?"

"The cat," he replied. "We'll start there; I need you to get me the cat." He paused briefly. "Once I have the cat, I can do something, but you know the ground. Work it out and get back to me within five days. Leave a subtle note at my hotel reception when you've worked out a way." He handed her the hotel's business card.

Oleana nodded again; her mind was now spinning as to how to do it. The Controller broke the ice: "Okay, now let's look relaxed and chat about anything else." He waved to the barman for another round of drinks.

By the time Oleana had finished the second Martini she had had an idea. "I'll need a week." She was not sure whether it was a question or a demand.

The Controller smiled; he knew she could deliver. "You've got it."

$\star$ $\star$ $\star$

The following day, Shaheen's mobile rang; he did not recognise the number and reflected that his hesitation to answer was probably not justified.

As it turned out, it was.

The Controller introduced himself in his gruff voice, explaining that he was Vlad's boss and passing through Dubai. "I believe we have some unfinished business and we need to talk."

By the time the call was over, Shaheen felt like the bottom had dropped out of his world. He had so believed that the Russians were done and dusted, but now he had to deal with this arsehole. He realised, though, that he had choices. All the titles to the Ajman property were in Vlad's name and he, currently, was indisposed, having his sphincter stretched in a local jail. Unless there was some power of attorney document that Shaheen did not know about, he was still in the driver's seat. However, he would have to meet this man; hence why he had agreed to meet him in the Starbucks opposite the Jumeirah Mosque.

The following day, as he walked into the small, confined coffee shop, he did not need to guess which occupant was the Controller. By appearance, the burly man in his early sixties could be nothing if not of Russian descent.

The coffees were ordered but there were to be no niceties from the Russian. "Mr Soroush, I am Ilyas Soltegov. I'm not sure where you were taught to do the things you do, but I do know that you should know better than to fuck with us."

"I have no idea who 'us' is." Shaheen's response was genuine. "In fact, I don't even know why I'm here. The property title is in Vlad's name, but I haven't seen him for some time. I have no idea of your relationship to Vlad or why you think you have an interest in the property."

The Controller tried to control his short temper. "Vlad works for me, that's all you need to know. If you rob Vlad, you rob me; if you fuck him, you fuck me, and you need to understand a couple of things." His temper was starting to get the better of him. "You see, I know exactly what you've done – the property deal is only one matter, Soroush." He had dropped the 'Mister' as he leant across the table. "When you get rid of two of our men, we cannot simply let sleeping dogs lie, and certain debts have to be settled in full as a matter of principle."

Shaheen nearly shit himself. How the fuck did Soltegov know about his getting rid of Vlad and Luka? Shaheen had told no one. That fucking skinny Indian must have sold him out! He could have kicked himself for disobeying one of life's lessons that had been passed to him several years ago by another Indian: "*Never trust an Indian; don't even trust me.*" He would find the little bastard and punish him; but now his mind commutated a response in line with any inherently dishonest mind: deny, deny, deny. "I have no idea what you mean, but if you can't keep tabs on your employees, that's truly none of my concern. I didn't seek an altercation, and I've always been willing to sort all of this out amicably, but your people made it very clear that that wasn't on the cards."

'He's right about that at least,' thought the Controller, wishing that he had known this guy was a killer – he would have better prepared Maxim and Boris. "Look," he said, locking onto Shaheen's eyes. "Just because you've got rid of two of our men, don't imagine it's over; this matter has to be settled or we will finish it. You pay me the fucking money you took from us or else we'll extract the debt as we see fit."

Shaheen somehow drew strength from the fact that the Russian knew he had stitched up Vlad; he needed to be warned that he could do such things to all comers. "There's no debt to pay as far as I'm concerned – the title is in Vlad's name, and you and your employees should know that what I've done already, I can do again in many different ways."

The Controller balked; he was now starting to understand just how much his entire team had underestimated this man. "Mr Soroush, you owe my organisation 12 million dollars and two men. At this point, I'll be content with your agreement to return me the money; however, if you refuse, be assured, I will revert to Plan B."

"Plan B?" Shaheen smiled. "You have no title, no rights and you've lost the only two men who could have made it happen. I'm the one in the driving seat now, so there's no deal unless you can bring me something that tells me you have right of claim." He put on his serious face. "So I think Plan B should be go back to your Bolshevik home. Are we done?" Shaheen stood up.

"It looks that way." The Controller took a sip of his coffee. "For now, Mr Soroush."

Shaheen left Starbucks as scared as he had ever been but hellbent on retribution against someone that he *could* bully. He pulled his phone from his pocket and called the skinny Indian.

The Controller felt shellshocked. That Shaheen had all but admitted to the murder of Maxim and Boris with such nonchalance had taken him quite aback. The 10 minutes spent with Soroush had not gone at all the way he had anticipated, and now he regretted having called the meeting. It was time to take from Mr Soroush what he most cared about.

CHAPTER SIXTEEN
Bun In The Oven

Natella was not sure whether it was a matter of infatuation with Harry, or that her pride needed the last word in the rejection process, but her call to Oleana the night before had been bugging the shit out of her. She had started to think that she would spend the rest of her life peering down the bottom of a glass of wine unless she did something about it.

She texted Harry while she was at work, asking him out for a coffee, and when he replied yes, suggested that they meet at 11 am.

Natella had thought this through. She knew that Harry was always on time, so she arrived at Caffè Nero 10 minutes early and ordered herself a small tea. She had specifically chosen the Nero brand because their cups were smaller than those of their competitors.

At the sugar station she removed the lid from the cup and poured two-thirds of the tea away, but was careful to leave the teabag on its string in the cup. She chose her table carefully, sitting down at one that was away from the noise and bustle near the counter, and sipped the remainder of her tea.

As Harry breezed in, he immediately saw Natella and could not help but notice that she was so bloody beautiful.

He also reflected that, of late, beautiful women had a lot in common with London buses – none turn up for ages, then too many all at once.

He kissed her on both cheeks as she quickly explained how she had arrived early to chat to one of her friends, who had just left. He glanced down at the table and saw the almost empty cup with the teabag still in it.

"More tea?" he asked.

To which Natella replied, "Yes, please."

Harry walked off to join the queue at the counter while Natella inwardly fumed.

There was no mistake – the "More tea?" had been identical in every way. The overriding thought in her mind was not to blame Harry but 'that fucking Russian bitch, Oleana'. She was supposed to be a friend, but had instead been with the very man that Natella had been obsessing to her about. The cow had used this additional inside knowledge to snag him.

As Natella watched Harry interact with the bar staff, her anger was turning to thoughts of revenge; she would make the Russian slut pay for this and deal with Harry too, the bastard playboy. But for now, she had to act cool.

By the time Harry left Caffè Nero, he was convinced that Natella was as on-tap to him as she had ever been. He would need to keep her sweet with another date in the very near future.

The young policeman, Mahmoud, had diligently completed all the details necessary for transferring the number plate into his name, as well as the application for a replacement plate for the Moroccan lady. He then looked at the paperwork in front of him and pondered. The plate had been reported missing nearly three weeks before it had turned up in the gutter of a road, a road on which the Moroccan had claimed she had not been in months. There were no traffic-camera violations for the plate during this period. He could not understand how or why it had turned up where it had, unless someone had either thrown it from a vehicle or it had fallen off the car on which it had been fixed. He pulled up the departmental directory onto his screen and called the static surveillance unit. He asked if they would accept an unusual activity request regarding a stolen number plate, from the cameras covering the junction of Umm Al Sheif Road/Jumeirah Beach Road, from the date of recovery and back 10 days.

The analyst at the other end fed in the camera coordinates and the giant data collection centre spewed him information. He confirmed to the policeman that they did have that coverage but that he would also need a collation request. Mahmoud told him that he would have it within the hour and decided that he would hold off on the plate transfer request until he had received the results.

The Controller was still fuming about the exchange with Shaheen and now he needed to get out of Dubai. Compared to Moscow, it was just too restricting and he was well aware that the privileges his status afforded him at home meant nothing in the Arab world. He walked from his hotel to the small mall adjacent to the Mercato shopping centre, rearranged a flight in the Emirates office using 'Moscow Rules', checked out of the hotel, and returned to Moscow, knowing that he would come back to Dubai when he had adequately shaped the battlefield upon which Shaheen Soroush would be defeated.

Oleana had thought long and hard about how to obtain the cat for the Controller, and she was somewhat relieved when she returned from her morning jog to see a text from his

Moscow number, simply saying: "*It is cold here and I am with your father*". He had left town.

She had been focussing on Harry as the conduit that could get her one step closer to the cat. From there she could figure out a way of snatching Bunny, but for the life of her she could not see a way to do so without making it obvious. That she worked alone had significant advantages, but right now she was having difficulty appreciating them.

She was about to put her mobile back on the table after reading the Controller's message when she noticed that she had a missed call from a number she did not recognise. She compared it with a previous missed call from the date of Shaheen's house party and realised who it must be. She pressed the call button and smiled as she heard the voice on the other end.

"Farah, how are you? It's Oleana, Harry's girlfriend; I was just wondering when you and I were going to grab that coffee we talked about?"

The plan to deliver Bunny to the Controller was in motion.

When the call was over, Farah hung up the phone and felt a wave of contentment. She was excited about getting to know Oleana because, for all her life of privilege, for all she had in terms of material possessions, she had a void in her life. Her husband was almost permanently at work or distracted with some other event in his life. She was almost certain that he had had multiple affairs with other women, but she had long since learned not to ask questions to which she did not want to hear the answers.

Then there was the cat. When Shaheen was at home he would invariably show more affection to Bunny than to Farah, and stupid as she knew it was, she had come to resent the animal that she had once loved. Little had she ever thought that this ball of white fluff would be the main competition in her life for her husband's attention. She was determined that the cat would not accompany them to Singapore, but knew that she would have to use the woman's intuition so deeply entrenched in her Aryan race. She looked in the mirror while she was thinking.

Her pure Persian genes had blessed her with a combination of features that resulted in stunning, exotic beauty. Long, thick, jet-black hair, olive skin, a petite but perfectly proportioned body, lips that just asked to be kissed, and finally her ultimate man-alluring weapon – eyes so black that her irises could not be distinguished from her pupils. There was, however, just one aspect of her that no one would have ever guessed, and it was the one reason that Shaheen had never suspected her of cheating on him with another man. Farah had had several affairs across the years; these made her enjoy her marriage all the more and if Shaheen had ever bothered to look for another man in her life, he would have found none. All of Farah's extramarital affairs had been with other women.

She could feel the excitement tingle inside her at the anticipation of her *coffee* with Oleana.

It had been a long week for the Controller, and even though there was no time difference between Moscow and Dubai, he was feeling his age.

He sat in his boss's Duma office in silence, awaiting the arrival of their 10.30 appointment. The Godfather reflected that the Controller was not looking well, and he could not understand why this particular matter, which was one of many, was eating into him so badly. Stress, he thought, was a killer, and he did not want to see his comrade in crime and politics succumb. They had too many other things to do and too much money to distribute to their own globally dispersed accounts. If anything were to happen to the Controller, the flow of governmental monies into their accounts could be disrupted. He so wanted to tell the Controller to drop this case, but he knew such a comment would be interpreted as weakness.

The Controller looked at the large clock on the office wall. "Where is the little punk?"

They had heard earlier that, contrary to the non-involvement policy of the Russian Consulate in Dubai, Luka had been scheduled for deportation following his unlicensed consumption of alcohol as a visitor in the Emirate.

Even though the humiliation of being taken to the door of the aircraft by two policemen and having his handcuffs removed in front of rubbernecking passengers had been particularly bad, Luka had never been so glad to get on a plane. The immigration control officers had told him that they would remain at the aircraft door until it was closed, just in case he tried to escape. He had wanted to laugh and tell them, "This *is* my fucking escape!" However, his short time in prison had taught him that the less interaction with those in authority the better. In their eyes, he had broken the laws of their land and their religion; he had foregone all rights. He was just glad to be out of that hellhole of a jail.

As Luka entered the Controller's office, he should have been shitting himself, but after all he had been through for merely drinking two glasses of wine, he thought he was ready for anything.

He immediately noticed the smell of coffee in the room and that he was not offered any.

The Controller stayed calm; he recalled that they had recruited Luka Karchenko because he was a follower, a non-decision maker, someone clean who would sign his name to anything on their behalf and not rip them off. This punk had no ambition and was rewarded for that weakness. "So tell me..." the Controller said in a tired tone.

Luka described the meeting and meal with Soroush and the efforts of the man to cut a deal. They had stuck to instructions and refused the offer. Soroush had remained amicable throughout, paid for the meal and they had left before him. He described the accident and how he had not even seen the guy on the moped until he was flying across the front of the car. Luka then recounted the breathalyser and how he had thought that it was just procedural until the extra police had turned up and they had been arrested. He had not even realised that it was actually illegal to drink alcohol in Dubai – "All the foreigners drink," he proffered as a last remark.

As the punk was talking, the Controller reflected that even he had not appreciated the law in Dubai as it pertained to alcohol, that it was illegal to consume without a licence but that the law was largely ignored until the police chose to enforce it. He would be more careful during his next visit. "And Vlad?" he asked.

"I only saw him on the night of the arrest and two times after in passing. He told me he was being transferred; he was nearly in tears when he told me." Luka went on to describe the crowded cells and mixture of prisoners. "The really bad men are mixed in there with guys like me who've just messed up in a foreign country."

The Controller felt a tinge of sympathy, not least because he could well imagine the stinking conditions in an Arab jail, and Luka had just confessed to "messing up"; but he had to ask the next question. "Why did it happen – do you think it was just bad luck?"

"I really don't know," came the reply. "One moment we were just doing our job, the next we were arrested. Vlad's crime is serious; I don't know how long they'll keep him – a year I was told. I got lucky because at this time of year, they have a lot of tourists on holiday and a lot of arrests for drinking, so unless there's another crime connected, they just caution and deport. "I've been banned," he added. "I can't return for five years." He lowered his head and tone. "But I never ever want to go back there."

"But was it an accident?" The Controller broke through the man's self-pity.

"I've thought a lot about it. It was either an accident, or maybe we were under surveillance from the authorities from the start, I'm just not sure." He paused. "Perhaps we were being watched because of our business activities, but the police never mentioned anything and we've never been questioned by any bank about deposits because we've always stayed below their Central Bank's alarm threshold." Luka was referring to the alert triggered by any single transfer into the country of more than $500,000.

The Controller looked at the Godfather for an indication of opinion.

The Godfather looked at Luka and took his chance to keep the atmosphere calm. "I think we got unlucky this time, and it's a shame that we still haven't finished with Mr Soroush. I think you should take a couple of months off, but let us know where you are. Your signature is on the property deed so we might need to sort that out if Vlad can't sign; however, it'll be difficult now that you're banned from the country. We'll call you when we need you."

Luka did not need to be given any additional cue to leave so he stood up. "I'm sorry this happened," he said. "Both Vlad and I had nothing but loyal intentions."

The Controller could see that the ball of fire this play-boy punk had once been had now been reduced to a pile of ashes. Perhaps he would become a better man for it. "Shit happens, my friend; but put your passport on my desk and go get some rest."

If staying in Russia was to be his punishment, then Luka would gladly take it, although he knew that this ordeal might not be over for him just yet. He placed the maroon passport on the desk and left the room.

"Poor bastard," muttered the Godfather.

"Poor bastard he may be," replied the Controller, "but there goes any chance of getting our money back unless we can force Soroush's hand; and he was a lot luckier than Maxim or Boris." He knew it was stating the obvious, but he needed to remind his sympathetic boss of the fact. "If we can't kill Soroush to force an insurance payment on the property, then we must force him to pay us. As soon as the Fixer has the cat I'll go back there; if that doesn't work, then perhaps we'll have to threaten his wife." He looked at the clock and wondered how his beautiful Fixer was progressing.

"Even so," replied the Godfather. "He has a point about them maybe being under state surveillance – we should be wary."

Mahmoud had been off duty for a couple of days, so he was pleased to receive a message on his return saying that the time-lapse video from the area where the plate had been retrieved had been collated. He was prematurely disappointed, however, when he read the comment stating that there were only three movements of interest; but he pressed the play arrow anyway, and smiled as the black and white images came up in front of him.

He noted the date-time group as he watched a Mini pull up just past the junction. A blonde woman got out of the driver's seat and went to the boot; she looked around her, opened the boot and pulled out what appeared to be a car number plate. She walked over to the dumpster on the site and pushed the plate into its contents. She then got back into the car and drove off.

The video collator had anticipated the requirement and pasted an enlarged still of the Mini's number plate. Mahmoud noted it down. The second date-time group showed a man in labourer's overalls walk from the site and drop the number plate in the gutter; the third showed the roadsweeper pick it up and put it on top of his dust cart. "Bingo," the policeman said out loud; he had proudly solved his first live crime and walked towards the lieutenant's office to give him the news.

Within 10 minutes the plain-clothed and scruffy, but legendary Omar Shamoon strolled into the room to join the lieutenant and the rookie, who eyed him with discreet envy. This was the policeman that Mahmoud wanted to become: totally cool, fit, nonchalant and whose appearance looked like anything other than a policeman. Omar was the epitome of clever calmness and went out of his way not to look or dress like an Arab.

He listened to the description of the case and viewed the video; he was confused about one thing and looked directly at the rookie. "How did you get onto this? What was the lead?"

Mahmoud had not expected a question instead of praise, and he certainly did not want to admit that the only reason he had pursued the matter was because the number plate matched his birth date. He stammered and blushed slightly as he answered, "I was bored between shifts and just noticed the report – it just didn't feel right."

Since joining the plain-clothed division of the Criminal Investigations Division (CID), Omar had been lied to more times than he had been told the truth; he knew that the youngster was lying but he would not call him out on it just yet. Omar always played the long game; he knew that the truth would reveal itself if it was forced to do so, and finding out why the rookie had chosen to lie to the first question he was asked would eventually become a priority, but not just yet.

Omar asked for the file and said that the CID would accept the case; he added that neither the lieutenant nor the rookie need take any further action, but asked the young policeman for his mobile number. "I may have some more questions for you." As he left the room, he turned back. "Good job, by the way; it looks as if you have a real instinct for sniffing out crimes."

Mahmoud was elated, believing that this could be his big break, and in some ways he was right, because concurrently Omar was thinking: 'I will break his fucking legs when I find out why he lied.'

Back in the confines of the CID section, Omar used his access to the various databases in order to build a landscape around the potential crime.

The Road Transport Authority database displayed the Mini registration as belonging to Oleana Katayeva; he linked the information from her driving licences to her UAE National ID Card, and from there he pulled up her visa and passport details. It all looked in order; the woman did not even have so much as a parking fine. A Russian national, she had lived in the UAE for over two years, had a Jumeirah address, and her visa was tied to Dacha Property Brokers, where her status was simply 'broker'. Omar reflected that the picture on the passport was a nice one. She was a good-looking woman; perhaps she was also a hooker. There were a lot of them in Dubai and not only the professional 'working girls' that had been shipped in by the Chinese, Arab and Russian cartels. Perhaps Ms Katayeva was one of the 'soft' variants – a broker by day and an escort by night. He brought his mind back from his internal pontifications. Nothing on his screen indicated that she was part of the sex trade, even the self-employed kind.

He pulled up the passive electronic surveillance commands menu. The first one was linked to her national ID card and he activated monitoring of its Radio Frequency Identification Device (RFID). This would track the chip in her card to give him information about her movements around the city and, if necessary, internationally, if she left the country. He placed a passive watch on her passport, which would alert him if she did just that. He placed a facial recognition tag on the system, which would additionally track her movements whenever the range of cameras linked to that database detected a match. He then placed an 'alert' status on the Salik tag in her car; this would help him get an automated report of her vehicle whenever it passed through the numerous electronic tollgates that were dotted around the city.

He moved on to her bank account and mobile phone details, and smiled when he saw that she banked locally and held an Etisalat number. He filed a monitoring request for her banking activity and one for active monitoring of her phone. The latter would enable him to see all calls sent and received; each would be attached to a tag number that could pull the entire conversation if required.

Finally, he entered her car registration number into the Automatic Number Plate Recognition (ANPR) system. The plethora of cameras around the city were programmed to recognise a required plate within their field of view and report the car's movements in real time. The recorded information would then be automatically collated and fed back to him.

Omar leant back in his chair, smiled and put his hands behind his head. "Now, Ms Katayeva," he said to himself. "Let's see what kind of game you're playing." He figured that he would know for sure within a couple of weeks.

Inside the registry of the Financial Centre, Natella had not been thinking at all about the pile of corporate applications, renewals or amendments in front of her, but rather about how she could drive a wedge between Oleana and Harry.

She was sensible enough to realise that Harry's deceit was a clear indication that he currently preferred Oleana to her, but she reassured herself that that was only because he did not really know the bitch. Her plan was almost schoolgirl in its simplicity. She would back off from Harry, hoping that that alone would make him come back to her. Concurrently, she would pour on the friendship with Oleana, along with lots of temptation, which would lead to the Russian slut getting laid by someone else; she would then compromise the entire event to Harry. It could hardly fail.

Oleana knew that she had to pick up the pace in order to gain the upper hand for the Controller. There had been no communication between them since their last call, but she instinctively sensed the urgency of the situation. She called Farah in order to establish a time and a place for them to have coffee and become friends. She was delighted when Farah suggested that they use her VIP invitation to a fashion show that was being held by designer brands the very next evening in Dubai Mall. "We can use the Rolls Royce," Farah added, "so we get lots of attention, and we can go for a drink afterwards. It should be fun."

Oleana was genuinely excited – this had all the ingredients of a good night and, even better, she could leave the car at home.

Farah was careful with her selection of clothes and shoes. She needed to dress to either be desired or envied, but did not want to make it too obvious until the timing was right to explore Oleana's interest. She settled for a Diane von Furstenberg wrap dress and Jimmy Choo heels. The Agent Provocateur underwear was just in case things went better than expected.

She was not disappointed when Oleana slid into the passenger seat of the Rolls Royce; she reflected that Russian women just oozed sexiness.

They took their seats at the fashion show and proceeded to sip Prosecco, admiring the clothes and the models. Both women were keen to continue the evening after the show and the patio bar at the Address Hotel was both appropriate and convenient. They both enjoyed the attention of the men as they entered the patio area and were seated on one of the loungers.

Oleana got to work straight away, asking questions about Shaheen and how they had met, how long had they been married, and so on. Her sole objective was to get into the house so as to be able to snatch the cat. If she could just find out when the house was going to be empty, then that would at least be mission accomplished for this night.

Farah ensured that she maintained eye contact with Oleana at all times; she knew that women loved to be listened to and complimented. Frankly, if Oleana had said that she cleaned toilets with her bare hands for a living, then Farah would have pretended to be impressed. As it was, Oleana explained about her executive concierge service that was tailored to Russians; she was thrilled that Farah was so interested, but she needed to get Farah to do the talking. She brought the conversation back to Shaheen. "Has he always been in TV?"

Farah assumed that Harry had told Oleana what he knew, but she explained how they were in the process of relocating to Singapore and that she had mixed feelings. "Shaheen can be a very ruthless man when it comes to getting his own way," she added. Oleana wondered if Farah knew about the double killing.

They had been through three glasses of bubbly each before Farah dropped the 'hook', hoping that Oleana would bite on it. "Shaheen's in London on business for two nights." She was nervously excited but did not show it. "We have some really good champagne at home and it'll save me drinking and driving – shall we go back there?"

Oleana could not believe her luck. This was being served up on a plate. She smiled. "Now that sounds like a lovely idea."

If ever there was a signal for Farah, then that was it; she was starting to feel glad that she had so carefully chosen her underwear. As they walked out to the lobby, Oleana thought it merely cultural that Farah looped her arm through hers. She was now thinking solely of the improvisation that she would need to surreptitiously remove Bunny.

Back at the house, Farah poured the Salon champagne while Oleana looked on. Bunny joined them, being primarily driven by her pride-instinct for safety in numbers. Oleana was intent on somehow smuggling the cat clear of the house, but had yet to figure out how she would achieve it. She was genuinely concerned that this window of opportunity might come and go and that it would be weeks before she would get another chance.

She sat down on the large couch in the lounge and did not feel uncomfortable when Farah chose to sit next to her rather than in the large armchair, which was at a right-angle to her.

They clinked their champagne flutes and Oleana got her first taste of what Shaheen deemed to be the best bubbly in the world; she could not disagree. Farah thought that she would leave it until the second glass to make her next move. She kept the conversation flowing and jovial, but was careful not to bring up the subject of Harry or Shaheen. She did not want Oleana distracted by the subject of men.

Halfway into the second glass, she could sense that Oleana was a little tipsy; she hoped that it was to an inhibition-lowering level. She made her move.

"You know, you're welcome to stay the night here with me." She wondered if Oleana would pick up the key words.

"There's always another bottle if we want it."

Oleana knew that if she could encourage Farah to get drunk, then getting Bunny out of there would be easier. "Why not?" she replied. "I can think of worse ways to spend an evening." She raised her champagne flute.

Farah leant over and put her hand on Oleana's knee. "I do mean *with* me..." She smiled and paused. "If you like."

The moment took Oleana by complete surprise; she had not seen this coming. She immediately wondered if Farah was the most feminine bisexual she had ever come across.

Farah could not let silence ensue, so she quickly stepped in. "I like having a husband, but I also like to relax with beautiful women. It's just so much nicer and cleaner than any alternative." She smiled again and stopped talking. She had to hear the Russian beauty's decision.

Oleana's mind was spinning; she had never tried same-sex except for fooling around with kissing when she was a schoolgirl. Given a choice right now, she would turn it down, but she had suddenly seen her window of opportunity open. The time afforded by this extracurricular activity would allow her to figure out a way to get Bunny out of there. She said nothing, but leaned in towards Farah and kissed her full on the mouth. Before she knew it, they were in full embrace and Farah's hands were exploring every part of her body. She responded in kind.

"Let's go upstairs," Farah suggested.

Oleana stood up and smiled; they kissed again and went up to the master bedroom, taking the second bottle of champagne with them. Throughout their love-making, Oleana ensured that Farah's glass was kept full. At one point, just as they were bringing each other to orgasm, Oleana could not help but reflect that she was enjoying the heck out of this. Farah was right – it was gentle and cleaner, and this woman certainly knew precisely where and how to touch another woman.

*   *   *

Afterwards, Oleana dozed off, but her human alarm and sense of needing to get something done woke her at about 3.30 am. She slid out of bed and collected her clothes from the floor where they had fallen. She eased the bedroom door open and closed it behind her with equal caution. She went downstairs, hoping that Bunny would be easy to find and was relieved to see her asleep on the cushioned bench by the kitchen door.

Bunny liked sleeping there, not least because there were a couple of spots on the wall that still retained an interesting smell.

Oleana did not notice these, however, and wandered around the kitchen and garage to figure out how she should carry Bunny. In the empty maid's room she found a pillow-slip and hoped that no one would notice it missing; it was a risk she would have to take. She returned to the bench and picked up the cat, all the while whispering and stroking her. Bunny loved the attention and purred as Oleana slid her into the pillowslip, where Bunny felt warm and secure.

Oleana gently opened the side door of the house, which led out to the garden; she slipped out and left the door about 15 centimetres ajar. She walked barefoot along the pavement and called a taxi on her mobile, asking it to pick her up by the barrier on M-Frond. She returned home and sent a text to the Controller: "*Cat is in the bag.*"

The following morning Oleana's phone rang; it was Farah.

"What time did you leave?" she asked.

"About five," Oleana replied. "I had to be at work this morning, but look, I had a great time; I'd like to do it again soon." She had lied twice in one sentence and could have predicted Farah's next sentence.

"I'd like to do it again soon too, but listen, which door did you use to leave last night?"

"The side door." Oleana knew this was going to script.

"Oh my God." Farah sounded genuinely concerned. "I don't think you closed the door properly and Bunny's escaped. She's an indoor cat and I've looked all over and around the neighbourhood – I just can't find her anywhere."

"Oh shit," Oleana was sticking to her rehearsed script. "I could have sworn I closed it. Do you want me to come over and help you look?"

"No, no, the kids and Shaheen can't know you were here. That bloody door has slipped open a couple of times, you weren't to know." She paused and switched subjects. "I really did have a lovely time last night; do you think we can make a habit of this?"

"I think we should." Oleana could hardly believe that she had been absolved so quickly. The call ended with her assessing that she would have to have at least one more session with Farah to ensure that Shaheen would never know that she was there the night Bunny disappeared.

At the villa, Farah made certain that all evidence of Oleana's presence in the house was purged, including the blonde hair in the bedroom, the lipstick stains on her bra and panties, and the smell of her perfume on the pillow.

She popped downstairs to get a replacement pillowslip from the maid's room, which was where she kept all the clean laundry. There was only one of the set there. She called the laundry to tell them that she was one pillowslip short, adding, "It has mine and my husband's names embroidered on the corner." They had been a wedding present. She was confident that they would find it.

CHAPTER SEVENTEEN
Moscow Island Rules

When the Controller read Oleana's text he smiled for two reasons. The first was that the Fixer had once again proved her worth; he was beginning to ask himself if there was anything that this woman could not do? The second reason was that he would again be escaping Moscow's brutal weather for the seasonally amicable heat of Dubai.

He booked his flight at the close of the week. He would arrive in Dubai on the Sunday and deal with Shaheen Soroush before the following Arab working week ended. It would take 10 days maximum; this time it would be 'all in', and Soroush would pay, one way or the other.

Oleana was pleased when Natella called to inform her that it was all over with Harry; apparently she had met a wealthy and, more importantly, keen hedge fund manager in the Financial Centre. Natella claimed that the guy was calling her everyday and that Harry was "history".

"Does Harry know?" asked Oleana.

"Shit, no! He hasn't called me so I'm hardly going to call him to say it's off." Natella laughed as she lied.

It all made sense to Oleana and she was just glad that this particular complication was done and dusted; she had more than enough moving parts in her life right now. Natella suggested that they go out at the weekend, Oleana agreed.

By the time Shaheen had returned to Dubai from London, Farah had already broken the news to him that Bunny had escaped. He had angrily wanted an explanation but it was clear that Farah was either protecting one of the kids who must have left the door open, or that she was being nice, not blaming him for failing to repair the door that had a habit of not closing properly.

He hoped like hell that Bunny would find her way back home; he put cat food in the garden, knowing, however, that most of it would be devoured by strays, but there was little else he could do beside hope that she could survive and use her homing instinct.

As the days passed, however, he began to realise that Bunny was probably not going to appear. Over breakfast on Sunday he discussed the matter with Farah and asked if there was anything else that she thought they could do. They had notified all the neighbours and the security company that manned the barriers and conducted mobile patrols. There had been no sightings of Bunny and Shaheen thought it most likely that she had wandered into someone's garden and been taken in. Any new keeper would know that she was a pedigree and was treasured by someone – the pink nail varnish would surely give that away. Sadly, he concluded, the new keeper was by now probably attached to Bunny's affection and likely considered their emotional need to be greater than that of the rightful owner.

Farah pointed out that if Bunny did not turn up, they could always get another cat when they moved to Singapore. Shaheen reflected that she was correct. Perhaps if Bunny had found an alternative home, then that would save them the trouble of moving her to the Far East, where, if she repeated her escape, she might conceivably end up as a menu item.

It was mid-morning when Shaheen's phone rang and he answered to hear the dreaded Controller's voice on the other end. "I'm in Dubai, Mr Soroush; there's been a new development and it is imperative for you that we meet. I propose Zuma restaurant in the Financial Centre at 1 pm."

The Controller had not actually checked with the Fixer that the cat was secure; he wholly trusted her simple text. He arrived in Zuma, aware that his every move was on one of many surveillance cameras, but he was pleased that the place was as busy as it had been described to him.

Shaheen arrived about 15 minutes late, in keeping with his Persian culture of timekeeping. The Controller reflected that the Iranians might have had a better chance of winning the wars that they had most recently lost if they had only bothered to turn up on time for the battles; his train of thought was broken, however, when he saw Shaheen enter the seated refreshment area.

They shook hands and the Controller started the conversation with a lie. "Mr Soroush, I never wanted this to get messy; I need you to know that. However, it's you who decided to dispose of two of our men, so it's you who's pushed us to a level that we didn't wish to explore."

Shaheen still did not have a clue how this man had figured out that he was behind the two Russians being thrown into jail, but it was clear that somehow he had. "Look..." He paused. "If the cat's out of the bag with these two characters, then it's hardly my fault. They come to this country, they drink and they pay the price."

'Fuck,' thought the Russian. 'Cat out of the bag? Does he know what I'm going to say next? Drinking? Is that why Boris and Maxim died, because they had been on the booze before they went to his house?'

Shaheen continued. "You send two men to threaten me, I dealt with it, you should have no complaint. The Ajman deal was fair – I offered, your people bought. If the value's fallen, then I'm sorry, but it's not my fault or my responsibility."

"Look, you fucker." The Controller was livid now. "You sold us a functional building, not one without water or power; do you think we'd have bought on that basis? I'm done fucking about with this." He paused for effect. "Have you seen your cat lately?"

Shaheen was now really confused – how did the Russian know that his cat had run away. "What the hell has that got to do with anything?"

"I'll tell you what," came the reply. "I have your fucking cat and I will skin it alive and turn it into a pair of gloves for your wife if you don't settle with us."

"You have my cat?" Shaheen was bewildered. "How the fuck did you find her?"

"Let's call it a coincidence," replied the Controller. "How she came to me isn't your concern. Rather, it's in what state she's brought back to you. She'll be left on your doorstep either with her fur and a pulse, or with neither. It's up to you."

Shaheen was about to answer when the two men were interrupted.

"Shaheen, how are you? What are you doing here?"

They both looked up. Shaheen had never been so glad to see Harry. He stood up and shook his hand. "Harry, how are you? I'd forgotten this was one of your haunts."

"My office is just 50 metres away," Harry confirmed, "so this is a good place to entertain for lunch." He turned to the small but powerfully built man standing beside him. "This is Graham Tree – he's an old friend of mine from the military; he works in the security business now."

While Shaheen and Graham shook hands and exchanged greetings, Harry looked at the Controller. Shaheen realised that Harry was waiting to be introduced.

"Oh, I'm sorry," Shaheen interjected. "This is Mr Soltegov from Moscow."

The Controller reluctantly shook hands with Harry and Graham; in truth, he just wanted both of them to fuck off so he could get back to the subject of skinning the cat.

Shaheen sensed the Controller's discomfort and decided to play on it. "Mr Soltegov and I have a mutual interest in cats and real estate, which is why he's here."

Harry was confused as to why Shaheen would offer such an explanation but responded to the power of suggestion by replying, "Well, Bunny is one cool cat, that's for sure." Shaheen gave an awkward chuckle, but said nothing.

Harry and Graham sensed their cue to leave and did so.

Now alone, Shaheen and the Controller resumed their discussion. "I'll hand over the title of the building to you," Shaheen said, though aware that in reality he was offering nothing.

"No," the Controller replied. "You'll hand over the title and 12 million US dollars."

"I don't have that sort of money to hand." Shaheen was, for once, telling the truth, but also acutely aware that he needed to play for time, if only to think.

"Get it." The Controller leant forward across the table. "I need your response within seven days, or else the gloves and carcass will be delivered." He paused. "Oh and by the way – the cat will be skinned alive."

Shaheen pictured the bloody scene and cat screams; Bunny did not deserve this sort of end. He stood up and said that he would do what he could, before walking off, leaving the Controller to pick up the bill for the soft drinks.

★   ★   ★

About 50 metres down from Zuma, Harry and Graham were in deep conversation.

Graham Tree had served in the British Army's Intelligence Corps and had specialised in counter-Soviet intelligence before carrying out selection for the Special Reconnaissance Regiment, where he been on joint operations with Harry. He now worked for the World Advisory Group, a company that provided common-sense security advice and services to just about anyone who was willing to pay through the nose for it. Graham was also fluent in Russian.

Since they had left the restaurant, the name Soltegov had been bugging the shit out of Graham; he knew it from somewhere but could not place it. He googled it on his Samsung.

"Holy shit." He had Harry's attention. "That bastard's not Russian, he's originally Chechen." He showed the picture to Harry – it was the same man. "He's a member of the Russian Duma and get this." He paused for effect. "His fellow party member and business associate is Alexei Delimkov, the guy who was implicated in arranging the assassination of that Chechen who got whacked in Jumeirah Beach Residence a few years ago. Interpol and Dubai Police issued an arrest warrant for Delimkov, but there's no mention of evidence against Soltegov."

Harry felt the hairs stand up on the back of his neck and his blood rush as his body released adrenaline into his system. Shaheen was sitting with a man associated with an assassination in Dubai? A Chechen? This could be no coincidence and the jigsaw of why those two men had come to Shaheen's house that night to kill him was becoming clearer. It had had nothing to do with road rage.

Shaheen must have placed Harry in the villa in order to deliver Harry to the assassins. When it did not go the assassins' way and Harry had left the house, Shaheen must have known and had the bodies removed so as not to implicate himself on his own property.

Graham could see that Harry was miles away. "Are you okay, mate?"

"Er, yeah, sure," Harry stilted. "But I've got to go." They shook hands and Harry walked into his office tower; Graham watched him go. He had known Harry for many years and considered him unflappable, but he had just seen the face of a worried man. Graham knew that there was something about the Soltegov name that had got to Harry. He would need to find out what that something was.

Harry sat in his office and stared out of the window. Why would Shaheen want him dead? It must be something to do with his past. He had fought Chechens in Afghanistan; perhaps it was something to do with that. His mind drifted back to the prisoners that they had taken while on a covert cross-border patrol into Pakistan. There had been no choice but to kill them. He still did not feel good about it, but to have released them would have been to compromise their position and it had been impossible to take them back through the mountains. Two of them had been from Chechnya. Perhaps one of the members of his patrol had squealed to a journalist and the Chechens had tracked him to Dubai and set him up via Shaheen.

His mind flashed to Oleana. Why had she been getting into that Toyota close to Shaheen's house? Perhaps it was not a coincidence that she was there, and, worse still, perhaps she was sleeping with him solely to deliver him to the next set of assassins. He had avoided confronting her about the Toyota but he now came to the conclusion that he needed to blow the plot wide open. If she was associated with the ongoing attempt to kill him, then he would need to drop some hints in order to see if she would withdraw or change her pattern of behaviour. He picked up his mobile and selected her number.

★   ★   ★

Oleana had just completed a session at the gym when her phone rang; she was pleased to see it was Harry. "My darling," she greeted him, milking the sexiness of her accent.

'Yeah, right,' thought Harry before he spoke. "Hey, you'll never guess who I just bumped into in Zuma."

"Natella?" Oleana thought that in the end Natella might have caved and told him it was over between them.

"No, Shaheen with a Russian politician." He paused before pouncing. "A Mr Ilyas Soltegov. Have you ever come across him?"

Now it was Oleana's turn to have the hairs stand up on the back of her neck. The Controller was in town and he had not told her. She wondered why. "Um, no I don't think so – what does he do?"

"I'm not precisely sure, he's in the Duma or something, but that's not the point." He paused for effect. "Do you recall the Chechen general that was assassinated in Dubai a few years ago?"

"I think so." She wanted to sound vague.

"Well, this guy is a friend of the boss that apparently ordered the killing. Does that ring any bells for you?" he asked again.

'Plenty,' she thought, but it was something that she would only admit under threat of death or imprisonment – the Controller did not pay her enough to endure either of those. "No bells here," she lied. "I don't know any Chechens; I'm from Saint Petersburg." She hoped that this would give weight to her denial.

Harry figured that he would leave it at that for now; he would get around to asking her about the Toyota later on the Palm. He changed the subject and asked when they could see each other again.

Oleana was relieved that he had not continued and told him whenever suited him, adding that she was not busy.

"I was thinking we should try some shashlik," Harry said, revealing that he had been reading up on Russian kebab cuisine. "Do you fancy eating in or out?"

Oleana was impressed and ordinarily would have invited Harry to her home, but with Bunny as a houseguest, that was just not possible. "In," she replied. "I'll come to you and bring the ingredients; you sort out the booze. Shall we do it this evening?"

Harry was pleased; he really did want to see her, yet his guard was now well and truly up.

Oleana drove to Spinney's supermarket in the Mercato shopping centre, where she bought lamb for grilling, bell peppers, onions, mushrooms and tomatoes; she also stocked up on luxury cat food and a bag of cat litter to complement the full cat-care kit that she had bought earlier in the week in Carrefour. She paid with her local credit card.

Her evening with Harry went well – she really did adore him and enjoyed cooking for him. After the meal, however, she was not sure whether their love-making felt different because her last orgasm had been with a woman, or whether there was something different in Harry's passion. In any case, she stayed the night.

The following morning, she was a bit surprised to find Harry waking her, strongly hinting that she should leave his apartment at the same time as him. As they left, she noticed the Avis keys to the Toyota were no longer on Harry's door-side hook.

As she drove down Sheikh Zayed Road in amongst the congestion and madness of the commuter drivers, her car passed through two Salik toll points. Her phone rang; it was a new number and the Controller's voice came through over her Mini's Bluetooth speaker – "I'm in town."

"I know," she blurted, immediately realising her mistake.

"You know?" he asked indignantly.

"No, no." She tried to correct herself. "I meant I knew you would be here very soon."

He continued, appearing to accept her explanation. "Is everything okay with the cat?"

"She's fine," Oleana said with some relief. "I've bought a litterbox and plenty of food, so she's very happy." She continued quickly in the hope that it would brush over her error. "You know cats, they're total mercenaries, they attach themselves to anyone who feeds them or offers them comfort."

"Well, don't get too attached," the Controller interrupted. "You won't need cat food for longer than a week. I'm not prepared to let this thing drag on. If the message needs to be sent, then it'll be done." He paused. "You might have to do it for me."

Oleana was mortified – he wanted her to kill the cat? 'Fuck him,' she thought; there was no way that she could kill Bunny. She hated the thought of the cat being hurt in any case, and had assumed that Shaheen would just pay up. She had already cleaned up two human bodies, but they had already been dead; she knew that killing the cat was beyond her. "I don't want to do that." It was a request as much as a statement.

"You will do as you are told," the Controller said firmly, before pressing his point home. "You are paid well to do very little, never forget that."

She knew that he had a point, but she was also complicit in a murder, a receiver of contraband from the Russian Embassy, and God only knew what else. She reasoned that it would take him years to replace her with someone with her streetwise efficiency. "I'm just not sure I can." She was surreptitiously pleading.

The Controller went ballistic: "If I tell you to kill the fucking cat you kill the fucking cat! I don't give a shit if you have to stick a pound of butter down its throat to kill the fucking thing, but if we need you to do it, then that's precisely what you'll do. And I'll be needing its skin, too."

As soon as he had finished his rant, he realised that he had probably said too much over the phone; but it was just about a cat, so technically no crime had been discussed. He did, however, instinctively want to get off the phone.

"For now, keep it healthy; I'll get back to you."

As he hung up, he felt his affection for the Fixer slip away. If she could not even kill a cat, how could he possibly use her in more elaborate rackets? Also, her instant "I know" on hearing that he was in the country could not have been a lie. She had not known that he was calling on a new number, so she must have known for sure that he was in town and slipped up. It seemed that he had a security breach in his organisation – he would need to root it out and eliminate it.

Oleana arrived home to be greeted by Bunny, who purred as she rubbed herself against Oleana's leg. Oleana reflected that the cat must have a sixth sense regarding the conversation that had just occurred; either that or Bunny was becoming attached to her. Regardless, she enjoyed Bunny's affection and reflected that she really did not want to hurt the cat.

Had she known the real reason for Bunny's affection, Oleana would not have felt so flattered – the cat could smell the musk of her alpha–male of choice on Oleana's legs. Unbeknownst to Bunny, humans called her favourite alpha-male 'Harry'.

Across town Shaheen sat in his lawyers' offices as they wittered on about any tiny detail that would keep their clock running over at $600 per hour. He took hardly notice of anything they were discussing. He was too busy thinking about the skinned carcass of a cat on his doorstep along with two bloodstained white fur mittens.

He loved the cat, but whether she was worth saving for the additional money was truly debatable; he knew, however, that this would be the thin end of the wedge with the Russians. They would not stop at the cat; this was just one brutal message and there would surely be something more serious to follow – perhaps his kids. He would have to strike a deal, skip town or figure out a way to get rid of this Russian – one of the three.

The lawyer interrupted his meandering train of thoughts. "Mr Soroush, are you okay with that?"

Shaheen apologised and asked the lawyer to repeat what he had just said. The lawyer smiled; he was happy to do so. Along with his other four on-the-clock colleagues in the room, he knew that a repeat explanation would take 10 minutes and permit him to bill Shaheen an additional $300.

The past few days had gone quickly for Omar. Proper crime in Dubai was rare and cases were normally completely trivial and non-investigative, like those involving bad expatriate cheque-writers trying to leave via the airport, or ones necessitating constant vigilance of suspects of terrorism, human trafficking or narcotics. Fortunately for Omar, he had recently been occupied with a narcotics case against an Afghan gang. It had gone well and earned him a couple of days' well-earned rest. He was now staring at his case file and had plenty of time to see what the tracking systems had thrown up on the car-plate thief, Oleana Katayeva.

He reviewed the RFID tracking information from her UAE National ID Card and compared it with the Salik reports and ANPR hits. There was nothing particularly unusual – just one trip that did not tie in with the car and that looked like a trip to Dubai Mall and the Address Hotel, followed by a night on M-Frond on the Palm. She had left the frond at 3.30 am. "Naughty girl," he muttered to himself. "Who were you screwing out there?" He smiled as he tapped in the real-estate coordinates of the villas towards the end of the Frond, which would provide him with the power and water billing information. Number 132 displayed a Mr Shaheen Soroush, national of Saint Kitts and Nevis, but originally from Iran. The man had plenty of speeding fines and owned a Rolls Royce. "Got yourself some Russian pussy while the wife and kids were away, didn't you, Mr Soroush?"

Omar then noted the overnight stay that she had spent in Marina Terrace – perhaps she was a soft hooker of some sort after all. He pulled her phone records and tapped in the numbers on the in- and outgoing call list. Two calls with Mrs Farah Soroush; he thought that perhaps the husband had used his wife's phone but quickly discounted this theory on the basis of risk. The suspect had called a gym several times and had had a call from a Natella Sultanova, who held an Azerbaijani passport. The day she had stayed at Marina Terrace, she had taken a call from one Harry Linley, a UK national. Finally, there were two calls from separate SIM-cards purchased at Dubai Airport three days ago; he would need to listen to all of these. He entered the times, numbers and dates into the audio retrieval database and put on his headphones.

Over the next half-hour, he was able to piece together what he believed was a snapshot of the circumstances and relationships in Oleana Katayeva's life. He scribbled down notes and lines linking the various characters. He picked up the phone to get a name on the anonymous SIM-card. There was nothing to give him a clue as to why Ms Katayeva had had the stolen plate, but there was plenty to indicate that she had a complicated life, and was a liar, especially when it came to her relationships. His notes read:

- **Farah Soroush** – *friend, but suspect seems to have taken her cat.*

- **Natella Sultanova** – *friend, who has some sort of relationship with Harry Linley. Probably innocent party.*

- **Harry Linley** – *probable lover, knows a Shaheen, probably Soroush. He asked her about a Mr Soltegov.*

- **Russian Male ID TBD** – *speaks and shouts at her like employer, he wants the stolen cat dead? Reason unknown.*

He checked the name Soltegov in the passport entry records and located an Ilyas Soltegov who had arrived in Dubai on the day that the unattributed SIM-cards had been purchased.

He then trawled the records for all four characters; they all came up clean with the exception of Soltegov with his links to Delimkov and his unproven but probable connection to the Yamadayev assassination. He also noted the immigration control tags regarding political sensitivity. He held a Russian diplomatic passport, but for some reason had not used it to enter Dubai.

Omar thought about reporting Soltegov's presence in the country and the bizarre events surrounding the transcripts of the monitored calls, but concluded that he should give it one more week. He really needed to know why Soltegov was in town and if it was he who was calling Oleana – and why he required the sacrifice of a cat.

Omar could see nothing to explain why Oleana Katayeva was in possession of that stolen plate. He filed a request to have Harry Linley and Soltegov's mobile numbers added to the audio collation list. The process would take at least two days.

Harry's friend Graham sat in his office in Jumeirah Lake Towers and called a former Intelligence Corps colleague in the UK to see if he had heard of Ilyas Soltegov.

Graham's interest was a matter of professional pride, because during the last three years of the Cold War, he had been a corporal in the British Mission to the Soviet Forces in Germany (BRIXMIS). His role had been an overt presence as part of a supposedly covert observation mission in East Germany, where the Soviets and the West played cat-and-mouse by authorising entry of observation teams due to an outdated but still valid post-World War II agreement.

The UK contact immediately jogged Graham's memory, reminding him that just prior to the fall of the Berlin Wall, two of the British team had gone missing. The Soviets had claimed that the men had been involved in a road traffic accident, but when the bodies had been returned, an autopsy revealed that they had died of injuries not consistent with the Mercedes G-Wagon that they had been driving. It appeared to have been a staged death.

Some years after the break-up of the Soviet Union, a former junior KGB agent had confessed that the two soldiers had been captured, interrogated and killed, and that the officer running the operation had been a Major Ilyas Soltegov. Graham called Harry to give him the news.

At the other end of the phone, all of Harry's worst fears seemed to be coming true. He could have kicked himself for having so readily explained away his two attackers with the excuse of road rage, thereby lulling himself into a false sense of security; furthermore, he should have realised that the only person who could have coordinated the deadly visit by the two assassins, and their subsequent disappearance, was Shaheen. The bloke must be part of a Russian or Chechen plot that had somehow compromised Harry's background. He was aghast at the fact that Shaheen had managed to play it all so cool, and concluded that he must be one ruthless bastard.

On the way home, Harry called into Ace Hardware – it was a veritable Aladdin's cave of lethal weapons. He was going to buy and secrete chisels and Stanley knives in his car and his apartment; if the police stopped him, they were merely DIY implements; if Soltegov's men came calling again, they would get a first-hand lesson in the use of improvised weapons.

By Thursday evening Oleana had succumbed to Natella's insistence that they have a girls' night out, but was at least pleasantly shocked when Natella gifted her with a Carolina Herrera scarf, in its trademark gift box and distinctive over-sized red bag, emblazoned with 'CH'. Oleana had decided that they should go to the Sho Cho bar; she reasoned that the Controller was unlikely to visit the same bar twice. She had also really enjoyed the atmosphere and so suggested that they go and scope out the men there.

On arrival, they managed to get a couple of seats on the perimeter of the outside deck and Natella got right down to the girl-talk.

She described her new imaginary lover from the world of hedge funds and how he was young, fashionable and wealthy – the perfect toyboy after the Harry experience. She then quickly brought the conversation around to Oleana and asked her a direct question. "So who are you seeing? I know you have someone."

"Actually, I have met someone." Oleana knew a lie was better if it stayed close to the truth. "We went out on a first date earlier this week, to a fashion show." She leant towards Natella and smiled. "We had way too much champagne and, what can I say? One thing led to another."

"You slut," said Natella with a laugh. "On the first night? When was this? Where does he live?"

"The show was Monday at Fashion Avenue in Dubai Mall, then we went to the Address, then back to his place on the Palm. But I have known this person for some time," she added defensively, "so it wasn't like a first night thing." Oleana looked over towards the bar and instantly realised that she should not have used someone else's haunt as a place to patronise Natella. The grey-haired man smiled at her; he seemed to have noticed that she was with a shapely woman with beautiful auburn hair and this had piqued his interest. Oleana could feel herself thinking, 'Please don't do this.' But it was too late – he was already making his way towards her.

The Controller reached her table and began speaking in Russian. "How are you? I didn't know you frequented this place. Does your friend speak Russian?" He figured that Natella would respond if she could – she remained silent but was looking at him as if expecting an introduction. "I'm Ilyas," he said in English. "Oleana has provided an excellent concierge service for me."

They shook hands and Natella told him her name.

"Where are you from?" he asked.

"Azerbaijan. Baku," she responded.

"Lovely place," he said. "But I won't detain you ladies any longer." He broke back into Russian and looked at Oleana. "How's our little friend at home?"

"She's good," Oleana replied simply.

"Excellent; make sure you look after her and that you're available over the weekend into Tuesday. We need to finish this matter once and for all." He turned his attention to Natella and switched back into English. "It was very nice to meet you; I hope it can happen again." He walked back to the bar, sent over two Dirty Martinis, finished his own drink and returned to the convenient and inconspicuous Regent Beach Resort Hotel, half-wondering if the Fixer would be able to fix him up with the beauty from Azerbaijan.

"He's your client?" Natella asked.

"One of them." Oleana gave her the only answer that made any sense. "I've known him for years. I used to arrange business trips for him."

"Does he live here?" Natella persisted.

"I don't know and I don't care." Oleana was dismissive.

Natella sensed Oleana's disdain for the man; there seemed to be something dark about the relationship, so she dropped the subject. She was intrigued by the exchange, however, because, although she had told the truth about coming from Baku, she had omitted to ever mention that her mother was from Khudat, on the border with Dagestan – Natella therefore had a fluent understanding of Russian, even though she seldom had the confidence to speak in it.

Natella was dying to know what Ilyas meant by "little friend" and what it was that they needed to finish. Perhaps she would learn more as the evening progressed, but for the time being she already had more than enough material to better educate Harry about this Russian slut.

This occurred the following morning when she called Harry, using the excuse of a short-notice invitation to brunch for which she assumed he would be too busy.

Harry predictably declined but was riveted when Natella mentioned that she had been out with Oleana the previous evening. She innocently recounted how Oleana now had a new boyfriend who had taken her to a fashion show on Monday, and how she had spent the night on the Palm with him. She then mentioned the Russian guy coming over, but did not mention that he spoke or that she understood Russian. "She has a friend staying with her at the moment, and she must be doing business with the Russian guy, because he definitely wants to finish whatever it is off."

Harry wanted to ask his name and get a description but he knew that that would be too obvious. So he simply said, "Hey, I've changed my mind – can I accept your brunch invitation?"

By 4 pm the next day, Natella was well and truly drunk from the bottomless champagne-brunch served by the Grosvenor House Hotel's Tora Tora restaurant, during which Harry had ably extracted the name 'Ilyas' out of her. She would not recall the conversation when she woke up alongside Harry the next day. So far as she was concerned, her schoolgirl plan had worked perfectly – she had won back her man.

The confirmation of Oleana's association with Soltegov and that the bitch was cheating with someone on the Palm repulsed Harry. He wanted nothing more to do with Oleana and realised that he had wronged Natella; she was clearly the good and innocent party in all of this. However, he was well aware that he needed to stay on his toes until he could confirm whether or not he was still a target for Soltegov or Shaheen, at least until the Russian left the country. He would have to keep his friends close, but his enemies closer, and he was under no illusions about the fact that he needed to keep Oleana, and Shaheen in particular, very close indeed.

He called Oleana and asked her if she was available for dinner with a couple of his friends that evening; she was. He then called Shaheen and asked if he and his wife would like to go out as a foursome that evening. Shaheen said that he would be delighted and Harry heard him shout, "Farah, are you free to go out to dinner tonight?" before coming back on the phone and confirming that she was. Harry said that he would reserve something for about 8 pm and text him the booking.

Harry hung up the phone and decided that Shaheen was one cool bastard. He reflected that he would probably not be so cool if he had known that his part in trying to kill Harry had been compromised. To avoid the risk of a 'no-show', Harry decided that he would not identify the couple to Oleana until they had arrived at the restaurant. "Let's see how all you shits handle this," he muttered to himself.

As Shaheen got off the phone, Farah came downstairs. "Who are we going out with?" She smiled to herself when Shaheen told her. She had not planned to see Oleana in this circumstance, but this would be fun. She would wear something flirty.

Graham had spent the entire weekend simmering about Soltegov and his involvement in the demise of the two BRIXMIS soldiers. Graham had known one of them personally – Jay had had two young children; the autopsy had shown that he had died of a broken neck. Graham reasoned that this would probably be the singular moment in time when revenge could be served up on his old friend's behalf, but he had no clue as to how to track Soltegov down in Dubai. The thug could be staying in any one of the city's thousands of hotels. Graham deduced that there was only one way to find him – he would have to ask Harry to act as a conduit to the man through his friend, Shaheen. Between two former UK Special Forces soldiers, they would surely be able to find and fix Soltegov.

He called Harry. "Mate, I need to talk to you about something that's time-sensitive and it needs to be face-to-face."

Harry knew straight away not to push the subject over the phone and simply replied, "Okay, mate, but I'm out to dinner tonight so it'll have to be tomorrow. 10.30 at the Capital Club work?" He knew that they were both members.

"See you there."

The 101 Restaurant was spectacular; perched at the very end of the Palm Crescent island, it was a convenient drive for Shaheen and Farah and a romantic, luxury ferry-ride from the One-and-Only Hotel for Harry and Oleana.

When Oleana arrived, she looked stunning. "So who are we dining with?" she asked.

"It's a surprise." Harry put on his naughty smile. "But I'll tell you what," he teased. "If you guess, I'll tell you."

"If I'm with you, baby," she replied, "that's enough for me." She meant it.

'Yeah, right,' thought Harry. 'You cheating, lying, deceptive bitch.' But instead he just smiled and said, "That's nice. Likewise."

Predictably, Harry and Oleana arrived before the Persians, who remained firmly in their own world so far as timekeeping was concerned. They sat at the bar, where Harry broke his cardinal rule of always facing the entrance to see trouble if it was coming. He wanted to see Oleana's face when Shaheen walked through the door – it was 20 minutes before he noticed a change in her relaxed expression.

As she saw Farah coming into the restaurant, Oleana did not even notice Shaheen following her. Embarrassment overwhelmed her and she felt the blood rushing to her capillaries, her eyes flickered from side to side, and she smiled nervously as the ravishing Farah advanced towards her, Shaheen now by her side.

Harry noted her expression and awkward body language, and it all added up to her discomfort at seeing Shaheen. The bitch was as guilty of collusion with Shaheen as the day was long. The two of them had clearly worked together to set him up for the Chechen hit. As the two couples greeted each other, Harry was amazed at Shaheen's calmness in Oleana's presence; he had to admit, this guy was one cool operator.

As Farah gave Oleana a peck of greeting on each cheek, she subtly touched her waist and whispered, "I've been dying to see you again."

Oleana managed to squeeze out a "me too".

As the dinner progressed, Oleana reflected that Farah was an expert in putting her at ease and keeping conversation flowing. The ladies had sat down opposite each other and Harry was facing Shaheen, who by now was unwittingly convincing Harry that he was a great actor.

The highlight below the table was that Farah had positioned her leg alongside Oleana's and was keeping the movement so slight that it could not be noticed by anyone but its intended recipient, who found herself genuinely turned on by the event.

Above the table, Shaheen dropped a bombshell that shocked Harry and immediately quelled Oleana's arousal – "We've lost Bunny."

"What?" said Harry. "Where?"

"Well, if I knew that," said Shaheen with a sad smile, "she wouldn't be lost."

Farah then explained how earlier in the week the side door had come open and Bunny had slipped out, and she had not been seen since.

"We've checked everywhere," Farah sighed, looking directly at Oleana. "We think someone must have found her, recognised her breeding value, and adopted her."

"So that's it?" Harry asked. "Isn't she chipped or anything?"

Oleana looked up from her meal; she had not considered that the cat might have an identity chip under her skin.

"No," said Shaheen. "We didn't bother because she was an indoor cat."

'Thank God,' thought Oleana.

"So what's the plan?" asked Harry.

"It is what it is," replied Shaheen. "Now that she's gone, it's upsetting for us both, but there's probably no way to find her or get her back unless someone hands her back."

Farah nodded as Shaheen spoke.

Oleana was astounded – Shaheen was going to let the cat be killed and was not going to complete a deal to effectively pay the ransom. The Controller would go ballistic if he found out. Worse still, Oleana knew that he would make her do the dirty deed on the cat. The thought of killing Bunny put her off her food, which, ironically, was fish.

"That is a shame," Harry mused. "I'm not normally fond of cats, but in Bunny's case I make an exception. I really got quite attached to her. She even made me consider getting my own Persian."

The evening could not pass quickly enough for Oleana; she needed to get home and think about how she was going to handle this. She toyed with her food and was not her normal gregarious self. Harry noticed her withdrawal and knew it was because of her guilty association with Shaheen. Farah saw Oleana's behaviour for what she knew it was – Oleana was embarrassed to be aroused by the leg-rubbing and could not concentrate on anything else.

By the end of the evening, only Shaheen would sleep soundly. The other three individuals all lay awake thinking, each sure about the motives of one or more members of the party.

At 10.30 the following day, Harry was sipping coffee with Graham on the fifth floor of Dubai's Capital Club. They each reflected that it would be unusual for most people to chat so casually about a revenge plot, but their background could be summed up by George Orwell's quote: "*People sleep peaceably in their beds at night only because rough men stand ready to do violence on their behalf.*"

They were part of a select group of men who were trained in controlled but complete violence, and each had 100 per-cent trust in the other. They would take with them to the grave much of the operational detail that had given them their most adventurous moments.

Graham was no diplomat and knew that he would get an honest appraisal of his idea from Harry. He explained the demise of the BRIXMIS soldiers and Soltegov's involve-ment. There should have been some excitement in his voice, but there was none. "This is probably our only chance to get this fucker. We need to take it, mate. For Queen and country – and for Jay." He paused, looking for an indication of rejection or enthusiasm from Harry; there was no sign of either, so he persisted. "The key is your man, Shaheen – if he can deliver us to Soltegov, then we can work out a way to right some wrongs."

Harry wanted to leap into the air with enthusiasm, but remained passive. Graham was asking him to help dispatch at least one of the bastards that were part of the plot to kill him. This was perfect, especially if Graham was willing to do the 'vinegar stroke'. He just had one question.

"Do you want to hurt him or snuff him?"

Graham knew that Harry's asking was a positive sign – he had not dismissed it out of hand. "I think we should go all the way," he replied. "If we were to just hurt him, we could end up with a bunch of Russian thugs on our tail. We can make it look like an accident. I've got a plan. Do have time to hear it now?"

Harry did, so for the next 45 minutes, the two men applied all their guile to a plan of which Her Majesty herself would have been proud. Her government had, after all, spent millions of British pounds on making these men the best in the world at rough deeds and, more importantly, covering their tracks.

While Harry was deep in discussion with Graham, Oleana wandered into the massive Carrefour in the Mall of the Emirates; she loitered around the household furnishing section and reflected that most of the items were of ridiculously low quality and taste, and left a lot to be desired. She located the rug section and found what she was looking for. The rug was cheap but authentic, and looked good enough for her purposes; she placed it in her shopping cart, then made her way across the aisles to the meat department. She selected a leg of lamb for the quality of its skin and bought a kilo of mincemeat; she paid at the check-out with her credit card.

As she drove out of the mall car park, the ANPR camera registered her number plate onto the system, simultaneously triggering another camera, positioned specifically to capture the driver's face, to send an alert to Omar's CID terminal.

On her arrival at home, Oleana put the rug upside-down onto some newspaper that she had laid on the non-air-conditioned garage floor, and went to the kitchen. Bunny watched her as she unwrapped the mince and the leg of lamb and carefully removed its skin.

It was about two hours later when her phone rang, showing the Controller's latest Dubai number. She sighed when she realised that it was not Harry – she had expected him to call. She answered and the Controller issued her instructions. "I'll give Soroush until Tuesday. If he doesn't deliver by then, we have to use the cat. I want you to dispatch it and dump the skin at Soroush's address."

Oleana was disgusted; this pig of a man really was going to make her do his dirty work. "I'm not sure I can kill the cat." She was pleading now. "How am I supposed to do it?"

In truth, the Controller did not want to kill it either; his life had been spent manipulating others into doing the gruesome stuff – he had merely derived his reputation off the back of the brutality of others. "I suggest you get a couple of heavy-duty bin liners, one within the other. Put the cat in them and tie off the top to make it airtight. Then go out to the gym, or whatever it is you do, while nature takes its course. You'll then need to skin it. You can do that, right?"

She half-lied in response. "I suppose I can. I used to skin rabbits with my father when I was a girl."

"Good enough," the Controller replied; he was relieved that she had seemingly accepted the task. "If you don't hear from me on Tuesday by 7 pm, kill the fucking thing and deliver the skin to the Iranian's house."

He ended the call, knowing that he needed one more meeting with Soroush to see if the thief would capitulate to his demands with the cash. He decided to wait another 24 hours before following up, in the hope that Soroush would initiate the meeting himself.

Harry finished his day at work and called Natella on his way home. He felt abject guilt that he had made the wrong choice between her and that duplicitous Russian bitch. They agreed to get together the following evening; Natella remained elated that her plan to undermine Oleana was working.

Content that he still had Natella in the bag, Harry called Shaheen. "Something has come up Shaheen," he explained. "I think it'll be a once-in-a-lifetime opportunity and I thought of you because of your Russian friend. It's time-sensitive and I can't talk over the phone. Can we meet?"

Shaheen's answer was not the one he wanted to hear. "Come round to my house now."

Harry hoped to hell that he was not being set up, but he agreed and took the slip road to the Palm. He reached across to his car's glove compartment, retrieved the box-cutter knife and slid it into his right trouser pocket.

At Shaheen's villa it became quickly apparent that there was no immediate threat. Farah and the kids were in the middle of the usual family turmoil, which included sound from at least two different TVs showing different programmes, and teenage food-trails leading from the kitchen to the TV room and various bedrooms. Harry had never seen Farah in a state of relative dishevelment; he reflected that she still looked hot.

Shaheen guided Harry to the living room, where Farah brought them some green tea. Alcohol was neither wanted nor offered.

Shaheen genuinely liked and respected Harry – if he could help the man he would.

Harry was just relieved that this deceptive bastard was not trying to set him up to have him killed on this particular occasion.

"So tell me," Shaheen opened.

"Something's come up, Shaheen, and I believe that it'll be an opportunity of significant interest to any Russian who has an ego."

"Is that not all of them?" Shaheen smiled.

"It is indeed, Shaheen." Harry smiled back, but then immediately continued. "A deal came into our office today – it was an offering to our distressed assets fund, but I figured that perhaps you and I might make some money out of it." Harry had piqued Shaheen's interest; now it was time to give him the detail. "Several years ago, just before the Lehman Brothers debacle and Dubai's real-estate market went into freefall, this government-owned developer sold two Pakistani property speculators the 13-acre, manmade 'Moscow' island, one of the largest of the World Islands off Dubai. The purchase price for Moscow was 58 million dollars, and shortly afterwards the pair acquired the 11-acre Great Britain island for an additional 43 million dollars. A few months later the global economy crashes and batters Dubai's property market; the funding bank panics and pulls the loan, and that's how the two owners end up in debtors' prison for bouncing the guarantee cheques that'd been written on the two transactions." Harry paused and took a sip of his tea; he could see that he had Shaheen's full attention.

"Anyway," continued Harry, "it seems that, to get out of jail the two men have struck a deal with the original development company to hand over title to their bank, which in turn will release their frozen assets back to the same developer. We've been approached by the developer to take title by assuming the outstanding note on the island."

"How much is the note?" interjected Shaheen.

"That's just it. It looks as if the entire amount is being applied to the Moscow island in order to shift the debt off the short-term balance sheet, and the bank'll retain the UK island for itself. The rumour is the Virgin guy's looking at that one, hence why they're not offering it." He paused for effect. "Because the islands are still undeveloped it looks like we can snag the entire island for five million US dollars on a five-year note. So it occurred to me that, for ego reasons alone, many a Russian would leap on this, and I thought of your connections because of the Russian guy you were with the other day in Zuma."

Shaheen could not believe his ears – this could be perfect. He structured the deal in his mind. He could sign over the Ajman property, no cash. Take the title for the Moscow island for $5 million over five years and sign the property over to Soltegov. Once he was clear of Dubai and safely in

Singapore, he could decide whether he would continue to pay the note, in the hope that Soltegov would bear liability if he took the note on the island. It was brilliant.

"This sounds very good Harry – it could just work. What do we do to make it happen?"

"Well," explained Harry. "Do you remember the British guy I was with in Zuma?" Shaheen nodded. "He's the man who has the inside track on the deal for the original developer. He brought the deal to me because he saw it as a win-win for our fund. I knew our fund doesn't do this sort of thing, so I immediately started thinking of alternatives. Do you think your Russian will be interested?"

"There's only one way to find out," Shaheen said reaching for his phone.

"Wait," instructed Harry. "My friend has a survey by boat planned for tomorrow afternoon; they're going out to view the island. Check whether your man would like to come."

Shaheen made the call; Harry listened on. He noticed that Shaheen's tone of voice changed as he spoke to Soltegov, perhaps because this Russian was his partner in crime. "Ilyas? Shaheen." He paused for the acknowledgement. "I think I have an offering that will satisfy you."

"Do you have the money?" the Controller asked.

"Better, Ilyas. Do you know the World Islands?" The Controller confirmed that he did. "Well, how about I bring you Moscow as part of our deal?"

The Controller thought for a moment and decided that his cartel masters would love this – it would be a real demonstration of one-upmanship against those who had issued their arrest warrants in Dubai.

"This could work," the Controller grunted, not wanting to seem too enthusiastic.

"We are viewing the island tomorrow; can you come?" asked Shaheen, whispering over to Harry, "What time?"

"Three pm prompt, Dubai Marina Yacht Club, but we'll need copies of both your passports to register the passengers on the boat. Graham and I have to dive to check the shelf of the island." It was too much detail, but Harry needed to say it.

"I heard it," the Controller told Shaheen before he had had a chance to relay Harry's information. "I'll be there by three."

Shaheen was elated – this could be the 'out' that he had been waiting for. No sooner had Harry left than Shaheen was googling the information on the island. It all stacked up. The historic news reports aligned with what Harry had just told him; little did he realise that this was exactly as Harry had planned it.

CHAPTER EIGHTEEN
Dive, Deal, Deliver

As he drove off the Palm, Harry called Graham. Fifteen minutes later they sat in the lobby of Graham's apartment block and finalised the plan. They had already decided that Shaheen was the only difficulty, but Graham assured Harry that he could make the appropriate preparations before they all arrived at the marina. As Harry walked away, he reflected that it felt good to be on an operation again, even if it was one for which they would get a life sentence should they fuck it up.

The next day was Tuesday. Omar sat at his computer having looked at all the surveillance reports and tagged the necessary mobile phone conversations. It still made no sense to him that the only crime beyond the theft of the number plate was an apparent plot to kill Shaheen Soroush's cat. He reflected that the animal-cruelty laws of the region were not quite developed enough for cat-killer prosecutions.

He noted that Oleana's movements were all 'domestic', and the conversations – with the exception of the one about the cat and the one where she deceived her lover – gave no lead to anything else.

He listened attentively to the 'World' conversation between Shaheen and Soltegov. He checked the information and noted that two men had indeed been recently released from jail, presumably for clearing the cheque, but he was not sure how Shaheen planned to deliver. However, there were so many deals happening in order to restructure government-owned real-estate development companies that Omar was not surprised.

He thought about notifying the maritime patrols regarding the planned boat trip but decided that, ultimately, it looked entirely routine. He concluded that he needed a pivotal event to move on any of this. Unbeknownst to him, he would not have to wait long.

Harry had taken the afternoon off work and would arrive at the Marina Yacht Club about two hours before Shaheen. He was in his car when Oleana called him; he pretended that he was pleased to hear from her.

She asked him what he was doing. "Same old, same old," Harry replied – which, ironically, was absolutely true. "Just trying to close a deal," he elaborated duplicitously.

"I've been thinking about the cat," she said, changing the subject. "I just can't believe they don't care whether or not it comes back." She was fishing for his opinion.

"I saw Shaheen and Farah briefly last night," Harry replied. "Neither of them even mentioned the cat. I think they've both accepted that she's run away and that someone's taken her in. Let's face it," he added, "no one's going to mistake Bunny for a stray."

This was not what Oleana wanted to hear. She looked at her watch and then at Bunny, thinking about how the cat had only another six hours to live. "When can I see you?" she asked, trying not to think of the task ahead.

"We should shoot for Thursday evening," Harry replied, knowing full well that he would let her down.

As he walked through the Marina Yacht Club and out onto the pontoons, he looked for Graham's Azimut 45 boat, *Luke's Lady* – a name that only men from a specialist unit would appreciate. The vessel was not big but it was functional. Graham had bought it for a pittance following the global meltdown, and in doing so he had broken his cardinal rule of '*if it flies, floats or fucks – rent it*'. At that time, however, banks were literally giving boats away; this had also happened for Graham, who had found himself relatively affluent at the back end of a security contract in Iraq.

As he went on board, Harry noticed that the two sets of diving equipment, three weight-belts and the roll of masking tape had all been prepared. Graham showed Harry the receipt from the dive shop showing both sets had been recharged that morning. He then showed Harry the gauges on the bottles. They smiled at each other. "The pressure differential is identical for the lifejacket bottles," Graham added.

He showed Harry the ice bucket containing cans of Pepsi in the forward compartment, one of which was open; he then pointed out the adjustments that he had made to the compartment's door and to that of the head (or toilet).

"Did you bring your kit?" Graham asked. Harry opened the carrier bag so that Graham could peek inside. "That ought to do it." Graham smiled again and placed it in the fridge.

"I reckon so," Harry concurred.

They then sat in the rear of the boat and went over the plan one more time, covering the detail of their roles and the equipment.

Shaheen arrived about five minutes before the Russian. Harry was surprised but elated that he was on time for this particular event. Both Englishmen were already sipping a Pepsi, so Harry dipped into the cabin and handed Shaheen a can on which he had already pulled the ring. Graham looked on contentedly as Shaheen sipped the high sugar content drink. When the Russian arrived, Shaheen went to greet him and brought him onto the boat. Shaheen reminded Ilyas of their previous meeting with Graham and Harry in Zuma, and explained that Graham was the broker of the deal and Harry was along to help crew the boat and do the inspection dive.

Graham confirmed that everyone had their passports before slipping the hawsers, and gently manoeuvring the boat out of the berth and towards the southern exit of Dubai Marina.

Once clear of the channel, he opened the throttle and three out of the four men enjoyed the movement of the boat as it chopped up and down through the small swell. The views and magnitude of the Palm were impressive, and were the subject of conversation for Harry and Soltegov as they rounded the peninsula's crescent island, on which stood the Atlantis Hotel.

Graham adjusted the vessel's heading in the direction of the distant sandbanks that formed 'The World', and the relative angle of the sea's swell changed the boat's motion from pitch to include roll. Graham looked over his shoulder at Shaheen, now sitting down, his face as green as was humanly possible. He suddenly spun around and retched over the side of the boat to partially empty the contents of his stomach.

The other two men turned around when they heard Shaheen's vomiting strains. "Good grief, seasick in this?" Soltegov commented with a smile to Harry. "Not much of a sailor."

"Clearly not," answered Harry. "He'll probably settle down when we get close to the breakwater around the World. This is our one chance to take a look at how the barrier sands are holding out below water," he added, "so we need to get it done, just to check that Shaheen's financing's equally firm."

Shaheen gave another stomach heave as Soltegov assured him, "He'll be okay." The Russian was quite enjoying Shaheen's discomfort.

Shaheen, meanwhile, felt awful; he had not experienced motion sickness like this since his childhood days on the Caspian Sea. In those days, however, he did not use to drink a full can of Pepsi laced with ipecac syrup to induce vomiting while he was out on the water.

Graham shouted at Harry to take the wheel of the boat and instructed him to stay on the heading. He then went into the cabin and emerged with some water and two tablets. He sat down by Shaheen. "Here, take these, they'll settle you down."

Shaheen was in the second stage of seasickness by now – he just wanted to get off. His shaking hand grabbed the tablets and he slugged them down with the water.

"You'll feel better in no time," Graham assured him, before returning to take the helm of the boat from Harry. They smiled at each other, knowing so far, so good.

As they pulled up level with the breakwater that surrounded the World Islands, they were all surprised by the height of the rock and sand pile that formed this substantial barrier. Graham explained that they were not permitted to go all the way inside the breakwater, but they could "take a peep" at one of the entrance channels – which they did before returning to the permitted zone.

Soltegov liked what he saw. The kudos of owning this Moscow island without any debt, and getting the title for the Ajman property at the same time, would be good enough for his master; he knew that they would be happy with this result. He looked at Shaheen, who was still sitting down and looking a total mess, with vomit splash stains down the front of his white polo shirt. It served the Iranian bastard right, he reflected, and in hindsight, he now mused that Boris and Maxim should have tried to kill him on a boat rather than in his house – they might have prevailed. "So this is it?" Soltegov pressed the point with Shaheen; he needed to make sure that he understood the deal. "I get title and no debt to this Moscow island, and *Burj Takseeb*?"

Shaheen was ready to agree to just about anything right now; he just wanted to get off the boat or go to sleep. He nodded. "Yes, that's the deal."

"Accepted," Soltegov snapped. "You have a deal."

Neither Harry nor Graham had a clue as to why Soltegov had mentioned *Takseeb*, but, whatever it was, they did not care. They could see that the ipecac had done its job, and now the Zolpidem Tartrate sleeping pills that had just been administered in the guise of seasickness tablets were also kicking in. Graham looked at Shaheen. "Do you need go down below and lie down while Harry checks the sand banks?"

"I think so," replied Shaheen; he was feeling very drowsy.

"Come on, I'll show you where." Graham led him to the forward cabin and showed Shaheen where he could lie down. Shaheen did not notice the adjustment that had been made to the outside of the door. Graham gently made his way back outside and slid the bolts top and bottom to ensure that Shaheen was locked in. He then retrieved the equipment from the fridge that Harry had brought especially for Soltegov.

At the stern of the boat Harry had stripped down to his swimming trunks and was preparing his diving equipment. Soltegov looked on – he had his back to Graham as the latter emerged from the cabin.

The first time Soltegov realised that anything was wrong was when the paralysing electric shock of the Taser penetrated every nerve end in his body – the pain was about as intense as anything he had ever known.

As he screamed out and fell paralysed to the deck, his noise was cut short by Harry jumping on top of him to muffle the cry. Graham, Taser still in hand, was on him at the same time. He took the pre-prepared tie-straps from his back pocket and slipped them over Soltegov's wrists, pulling them tightly enough so that the Russian would not be able to slip them, but still loose enough so that they would not cut into his skin. He then carried out the same procedure on Soltegov's ankles.

Meanwhile, Harry had retrieved the masking tape which had been lying by the diving equipment and wrapped it around Soltegov's head, covering his mouth. He ensured that the Russian could still breathe through his nose. He then pulled a pair of scissors from his pocket and began to cut Soltegov's T-shirt from his body, leaving only his shorts.

Harry grabbed two of the weight-belts and slid them towards Graham, who put his arm under Soltegov's body and pulled and secured them, one after the other, around the Russian.

By this time, Harry had pulled out a thin length of cord and looped it under one of Soltegov's arms to tie a bowline. The makeshift plasticuffs made escape impossible. Graham, meanwhile, emptied the victim's pockets.

The paralysing pain of the Taser was subsiding and Soltegov's senses were trying to make sense of the speed and reason of the attack. He recognised that whoever was attacking him knew exactly what they were doing, but he had no clue as to why.

The answer would be the last thing he would ever learn.

Graham leant in close to his ear as Harry ensured that he was fully restrained. "Do you remember the BRIXMIS soldiers you murdered in East Germany?" the Englishman said menacingly. "Well, one of them was my friend, you motherfucker." Graham turned his attention to Harry and simply said, "Clear."

Harry let go of the Russian. "Clear." Graham gave Soltegov another burst from the very Taser that the Russian had sent to Dubai in order to kill Shaheen.

He was still dizzy with pain and disorientation when the two Englishmen picked him up and dropped him off the back of the boat. The two weight-belts did their job and took him down to the shelf of the breakwater, about 10 metres below the surface of the sea. Harry immediately grabbed the cord that he had tied around the Russian, and let it feed out as Soltegov descended.

When the rope stopped, he knew that the Russian had reached the bottom.

Harry tied off the cord on one of the boat's tie-downs and turned to his diving equipment. Graham helped him don the lifejacket, breathing apparatus, weight-belt and fins. Harry sucked in a couple of breaths to ensure that the demand valve was working, then sat on the stern of the boat, adjusted his mask and entered the water.

Graham handed him the spare set of fins and the life-jacket with the small hole in it, as well as the bottle with the expended charge. Harry submerged himself and followed the cord down to find the Russian, predictably dead by drowning. He pushed the spare fins onto the victim's bare feet and slipped the lifejacket around his body. He used the scissors to gently cut the tape from Soltegov's head, before re-knotting the cord through the loop on one of the weight-belts.

Harry returned to the surface, where Graham handed him the second set of breathing apparatus, which had also had its air expended. He passed Harry the spare diving-mask. Harry went below again, following the cord, and pulled the mask over the Russian's head; he then cut the plasticuff straps from the dead man's wrists and used the weightlessness underwater to gently fit the diving set onto the lifeless body.

He made sure that the valve on the set was open and tried to breathe the air from Soltegov's demand valve. Content that there was none to be had, he took one last look at the Russian, cut the ties from his ankles and undid the bowline on the cord, pulling it free. He then reached down to release one of the weight-belts around Soltegov's body and let the belt, along with the cord, settle on the seabed.

Harry dragged the Russian's body to the edge of the sand shelf and let it go. He watched as the body drifted down towards the dark blue depths. He turned, looked up at the light of the sun above him and the dark shape made by *Luke's Lady*'s hull. He swam up towards it, breathing out as he did.

On the surface, the cord and the weight-belt were retrieved and stowed. Harry bled out the rest of the air in his diving bottle and they waited 20 minutes before gently moving the boat further along the breakwater.

Graham was relieved that they had not run into any coastal patrol boats – clearly his information regarding their shift-change at 4 pm had been correct.

The 20 minutes seemed to take an age, but the time allowed Harry and Graham to ensure that all evidence of struggle or equipment had been cleaned up. The Taser and the torn clothes were placed in a bin liner, along with the tape, the spare cuffs and the spare weight-belt. They tied off the bag and pushed it into the locker by the helm.

Meanwhile, the boat drifted subtly away from the point where they had disposed of the Russian.

On regaining consciousness, the first thing that Shaheen experienced was Harry shaking him vigorously. "Wake up, Shaheen, wake up for fuck's sake. We can't find Ilyas. We've lost him."

Shaheen was as confused as anyone could be, but first he had to figure out where he was and fight off the effects of the sleeping tablets. As he realised that he was on a boat and pieced together the reason that he was there, he tried to understand what Harry was telling him. "Lost Ilyas? What do you mean, lost Ilyas?"

Harry quickly explained that Ilyas had wanted to dive with him, so they had reluctantly agreed to let him do so. They had both been swimming along the sandbank for several minutes when Harry had looked behind him to find that Ilyas had vanished. Harry described how he had swum back and forth trying to find him, but there had been nothing. They now needed Shaheen as an extra pair of eyes to see if Ilyas was on the surface or whether perhaps he had made it to one of the World Islands.

Shaheen was now as awake as he could be under the circumstances, and as he reached the deck area where Graham was standing at the helm of the boat, he heard the man say, "We need to call the authorities, we need to get help."

Shaheen's mind was now racing. Had Ilyas really disappeared? If he had, this would be perfect. "Let's wait before we panic," he suggested. "We should see if we can find him ourselves."

Harry looked at Graham; they had expected Shaheen to go into a tailspin once he realised that his partner was missing, but instead he was calm. Both men simultaneously concluded that it must be the effect of the drugs.

"We can take one more look," Graham said, looking at his watch. "But if we haven't found him in 10 minutes, we need to report him missing." He looked over at Harry. "Will he be out of air yet?"

"I reckon," pretended Harry, "but he has his lifejacket, so if he was in trouble you'd think he'd have inflated that and be on the surface by now."

"Do you think a shark got him?" Shaheen asked.

"I have no idea," responded Harry. "One moment he was there, the next he was gone."

The 10 minutes passed while Harry and Graham play-acted as if they wanted to find the Russian. Of course they would have shit their pants if he had floated to the surface, but both knew the weight of the belt and the diving equipment would be enough to keep Ilyas on the bottom, and the deeper the better.

Graham put out a call on Channel 16 from his maritime radio. The transmission was immediately picked up by the Dubai Coastguard, who instructed Graham to stay where they were.

Within another 10 minutes, the coastguard patrol boat had pulled up alongside them and two officers boarded Graham's boat.

Graham immediately explained what had happened – Harry and Ilyas had dived and Ilyas had simply disappeared. Graham had remained on the surface as safety; Shaheen had been below because he was not feeling well – the vomit stains on his shirt were proof enough that this part of the account was true.

The officers had already checked the registration and trip filings for Graham's boat. All was in order. Even the boat's registration sticker was clearly visible.

One of the officers went below and checked for anything suspicious, including booze. There was none – these men seemed like good guys who were clearly shaken because they had just lost a friend.

The officer noticed a shirt folded on one of the seats, along with some money, a pair of sandals, a phone, and various other personal accessories. "Whose are these?" he asked.

"They belonged to the missing guy," Graham replied. "He left them there before he went diving. He was only wearing shorts because the sea's so warm."

The officer thought about these Westerners liking water at 28°C – he knew that he would find it cold. "How much air did he have?"

"The same as me," Harry replied. "I used all of mine looking for him; I'm guessing he would've run out by now."

The officer looked at the T-shirt and sandals, before picking up the credit cards, cash, Soltegov's passport, a hotel keycard and his mobile phone, which was still turned on. "We'll have to keep these."

"No problem," Graham replied, before mentioning that he had the recharging receipt stipulating the air pressure that had been in the bottles if the officer would like to see it. The officer said that he would. The cooperation and distraction process being pushed out by Harry and Graham seemed to be working.

"He's out here somewhere!" Harry blurted. "We have to find him."

The officers looked at each other. They had seen it too many times before. A couple of amateurs thinking they were Jacques Cousteau, lured by the good visibility and the lack of tides or currents. They knew only too well that if the friend had not made it to shore, then he would likely have been the first course for some fish right now. It did not take too long for them to clean a body in these waters.

They explained to Graham that they would escort him back to Dubai Marina and that a sea and air search would ensue, but that they were also running short of daylight. Harry and Graham both protested that they should remain for the search but the officers told them that there was nothing more either of them could usefully do.

As they followed the coastguard vessel, Shaheen sat in the open air and stared at the folded T-shirt inside the cabin. "Was that Ilyas's shirt? I thought he was wearing something dark blue not light blue." He directed the question at Graham.

Graham turned round and dismissed the question as casually as he could. "No, no, the shirt was his."

Shaheen wanted to debate the fact but still felt very groggy and figured that he might be mistaken.

Harry sat next to Shaheen and put his arm around him. "Shaheen, I'm bloody sorry this happened. I'm sorry you lost your friend."

"He's not my fucking friend." Shaheen's teeth were gritted together but he was almost crying. "I hated the fucker. I hope a fucking shark's chewed him to bits – balls first."

Harry was astounded. "What? But I thought you were his friend?"

"Oh, Harry, you have no idea." Shaheen spoke with a little less hate in his voice. "The man was a bully, a gangster, an extortionist. I got trapped in the *Burj Takseeb* deal with them and they wanted payback. I was only interested in the deal you offered because it would help me get rid of him." He paused and looked at Harry. "The fucker kidnapped Bunny and said he'd skin her alive if I didn't settle a deal with him."

"He has Bunny?" Harry was really confused now. "I thought she escaped?"

"I had to tell everyone that." Shaheen's eyes were brimming with tears. "I couldn't tell my wife and kids the real story, they'd have been mortified. At least, as it is, they think she's being looked after by whoever found her."

"So how did Ilyas get his hands on her?"

"I have no idea, but he said he had her and that I only had until 7 pm to seal the deal; I really thought I'd done it." He had a moment of thought. "The only bad thing about that Russian bastard being fish food is that now we'll probably never find Bunny."

Harry's jigsaw had just been blown apart and goodness knew where Shaheen fitted into it anymore, but it was way too early to think about trusting him in any shape or form. Too much bad shit had happened and it all led to Shaheen; Harry still needed to test him.

"Look, Shaheen, I don't have a fucking clue what's going on, but I think we ought to agree on one thing." He needed Shaheen to will him to say it.

"What's that?"

"When we get into harbour and they take our statements, then I think it'd be best if we didn't mention anything bad about Ilyas. We don't want to start a hare running, and if you have other shit going on, then that might not be good." Harry knew that there must be stuff attached to this deal that Shaheen would not want discovered – including the murder of two Russians in his house.

Shaheen thought about how he had set up Vlad and tricked his way out of the warrant for his own arrest issued by the Iranian government so long ago. Harry was right – it would be best not to add a complication. "I agree, Harry, it was a boys' day out and a diving trip that went wrong. Which it was, really," he reassured himself out loud.

Harry smiled – at least one potential bump in the road had been flattened. Apart from the public facts, the island deal had been a complete fabrication that he and Graham had made up by using factual background information. The only flaw in the entire plan to snuff Soltegov had been that Shaheen might elaborate when questioned. With that element calmed, any cursory investigation by the coastguard would generate a genuine source of false information, not least because there was always a preponderance of such deals being bandied around Dubai. This one would have appeared to be nothing more than yet another couple of white guys being duped into buying something that was perhaps not the seller's to sell.

As the light faded and they crossed the open water towards the marina, neither the lead coastguard vessel nor Shaheen noticed Graham take a weighted bin liner from the footlocker closest to the helm and let it slide off the side of the boat and into the depths.

Back in the marina, two additional coastguard officers took individual statements from the three men. Each man's story matched – this really did appear to be nothing more than a tragic diving accident. Ilyas Soltegov had entered Dubai on a visitor visa using an ordinary Russian passport. He had the profile of a tourist businessman. The only flag against his name was that he also possessed a diplomatic passport, but he had not used it. Either way, the Russian Embassy in Abu Dhabi would need to be notified of the demise of one of their citizens.

It was 10 pm by the time everything had been tidied up in the marina. The coastguard officer and the policeman from Jebel Ali police station were both content that nothing was out of order. The search for the Russian diver would start in the morning, although everyone concerned knew that the effort would in all likelihood be futile.

As Harry drove home, he called Oleana. He needed to get to the bottom of her relationship with Soltegov, but there was no reply. For good reason.

Oleana grimaced as she cut the white, soft fur into shape. The congealed blood on the inside of the skin was already starting to smell and she wondered if this was normal. She pushed a hole into the pelt and threaded Bunny's Louis Vuitton cat collar through it. She then took what remained of the pink cat-nails and superglued them onto the collar. She hated what she was doing and the impact that it would have on the family, but, to use an airline metaphor, she had to put her own life-saving mask on before anyone else's.

She placed the gruesome contents into a bag that would not squash the contents together before putting on her exercising clothes and running shoes, and drove her car to the marina area. She then caught a taxi to the Palm and once again used her looks and charm to bluff her way onto M-Frond.

She exited the taxi at the very end of the frond and pretended to fumble for her keys in the bag that she was carrying. When the rear lights of the taxi had disappeared around the bend, she walked casually down the road, scanning for any activity; as usual, thanks to the low population density around here, there was none.

She walked assuredly to Shaheen's doorstep, put the bag up against the front door and made her way back onto the street. She walked a further 40 metres, then broke into a jog. At the barrier-end of the frond she simply continued jogging past the gate-guard – he took no notice of another crazy Westerner exercising at night. Once clear, she hailed a taxi back to the marina, picked up her car and returned home. She cursed the Controller for making her do what she had just done and that he had not called her before the 7 pm cut-off. She texted him a message saying:

It is done.

By 6.45 the following morning, the noise and turmoil of Shaheen's children readying themselves for school was as shambolic as ever. Farah was constantly barking out the time with an almost minute-by-minute countdown of when the schoolbus was due.

Their son was the eldest and would leave first, but the biggest challenge was getting him out of bed. Their daughter was less of a lie-in, but her vanity over what to wear would invariably make her late. In-between it all, Farah shouted and cajoled. Shaheen did his own thing, which pretty much extended to shit, shower and shave. He aimed to have the three completed before the kids came to kiss him goodbye.

Shaheen was one kid down and one to go that morning, when suddenly he heard Farah's shrill scream downstairs.

He dashed down the stairs to see her standing with one arm around her son, both clearly distraught; she was holding a Carolina Herrera shopping bag in her hand.

She looked up at Shaheen. "Someone killed Bunny." With her arm she gestured that he should take the bag from her. "Somebody killed Bunny," she repeated.

Shaheen's face was one of genuine surprise. He had somehow assumed that, with Ilyas now missing, the deadline to meet the deal in order to save his cat had been null and void. It seemed that he had been terribly wrong.

As he came forward, Farah held up the bag and cried. "It's awful. I think they skinned her. Her collar's in there."

Shaheen took the bag and looked inside. The smell of rotten flesh hit his nose and he could see the white fur congealed with blood and the collar too. He was fixated in disbelief – the bastards had even glued Bunny's painted nails onto her collar.

"Who would do this?" Farah asked. "Why?"

"I have no idea," lied Shaheen, "but I'll fucking well find out and make them pay." He regretted swearing in front of his son, especially since he knew that Soltegov had already paid in full with his life. However, the bastard must have had an accomplice in order to deliver Bunny. He reflected that he would actually rather avoid them than find out whoever it was that had done *that*.

There were only two people outside the family who knew how Bunny had gone missing. He decided to call one of them.

Harry had long ago learnt that if his telephone rang between 10.30 at night and 7.30 in the morning, then the caller would most likely be a bearer of bad news. It was only 7 am – this was not going to be good.

Shaheen was clearly distraught; he was asking Harry to come round. "Bunny's here but it's not good. Please, come and see."

Harry knew instantly what he meant. "I can't come this morning. I'll come after work today, but enough said, I have to dash."

The last phrase was said to quickly shut Shaheen up. Harry was well aware that he and Graham were ahead of the game with Soltegov; the last thing they needed was Shaheen spilling his guts on the phone.

Shaheen realised instantly what Harry had just done and why. Now that Soltegov was gone, they should not tempt fate by linking his name and Bunny's demise with any third party, especially on the phone.

Harry was livid as he hung up. Oleana had denied that she knew Soltegov, when clearly she did. Natella had told him that the Russian had told the bitch to make sure that the job was done by Tuesday. It had all happened on Tuesday. Harry did not believe in coincidences, though in this case he really should have.

He somehow doubted that Oleana was the type to kill Bunny, but she surely knew people who would, and he would be damned sure to get to the bottom of it. He was tempted to call her, but decided that he would wait until he had seen the evidence.

Graham appeared at Harry's office around 2 pm.

"Have you heard anything?" Harry asked, as soon as they were in one of the meeting rooms.

"Mate, I called the coastguard first thing this morning and called them again every two hours to check if they'd found anything. I'm trying to give the impression that we're really concerned. They've scanned all the islands for him; he's not on any of them." He paused and smiled. "But then we already knew that."

"Do we know what they're using to find him?" Harry asked.

"Not sure, but most likely they'll use sonar, divers or drag hooks, and, let's face it – even if they do find him, the fucker's a fully equipped, drowned diver with a spent bottle and no functional lifejacket. We're in the clear, mate."

"I know," replied Harry. "I'll just be a lot happier when they either call off the search or find the bastard. I actually hope it's not the latter." Harry then briefed Graham on Bunny's demise; although he did not disclose the connection to Oleana, he pointed out the obvious in that they should be careful, since Soltegov clearly had one or more accomplices in town.

That evening in Shaheen's garage, Harry viewed the now chilled remains of Bunny. "Have you taken it out of the bag?"

Shaheen shook his head. "No, I couldn't face it."

Harry turned to face him before giving him an out. "You don't have to look at this if you don't want to." Shaheen asked Harry to look first; then perhaps he would come back and see the skin for himself. He left Harry alone in the garage.

Harry gently lifted the white pelt from the bag; it smelt of rotten meat. He figured that either Bunny had been dead for a few days, or else the night that the package had been left on Shaheen's doorstep had been warm enough to accelerate the decomposition process.

He spread the small fur out over the bag, laying it on the floor; it felt slightly thicker, cold and laid flat, than when it had been warm, attached and wrapped around Bunny's little body. He looked at the familiar collar with the nail endings glued to them. He reflected that at least the bastard who had done this had not cut the paws off to get to the nails.

He turned the fur over and looked at the skin. Whoever had done the job had known what they were doing, although there was still loose bits of tissue left on it. They had not bothered to scrape it off.

He peered in the bag and noticed that there was one more item; he pulled it out and took a good look at it before stuffing it in his pocket and returning to the kitchen. He told Shaheen to keep the pelt somewhere safe and chilled.

Harry left and drove to the Mall of the Emirates where he located the Carolina Herrera boutique on level two.

The polite young Filipina sales assistant was welcoming and eager to please Harry. He handed over the gift receipt that purposely didn't show the price of the purchase, and explained that his wife had been bought a gift from the store but she was not sure if she wanted to keep it. Would the value of the gift receipt cover an exchange for the cost of one of their designer 'CH' ties?

Harry waited patiently as the sales assistant tapped the reference numbers into her keyboard. She looked up and smiled. "The gift was 600 dirhams, sir. You could exchange it for a tie."

Harry nodded and smiled. "I'll have a quick look and if I like one, I'll let my wife know I'd like to do that." He leant forward over the counter and in a lowered voice asked, "Can you tell me which friend gave the gift to my wife? She didn't tell me."

The shop assistant smiled back – she loved the politeness of Western men. "Of course, sir. It was a Miss Natella."

'Holy shit,' thought Harry – why the fuck would she be messed up in this? He thanked the assistant, retrieved the gift receipt and headed back to his car.

Natella was delighted when Harry called her and said that he had to see her straight away. She frantically changed into something attractive but super-casual so as to give him the impression that she also dressed in cool attire at home. By the time her doorbell rang, she had managed to put on a trace of make-up and brush her hair.

As soon as Harry sat down, it dawned on her that this was not a romantic call. He was clearly tense, so there had to be another reason. He waited until she had made tea to ask her about the gift receipt.

Natella's heart dropped – he must have been with that Russian bitch again in order to retrieve the gift receipt, so why would he come around and flaunt it. Tears welled up in her eyes. "Why are you doing this Harry? Why would you ask me questions like this? That Russian bitch stole you and I only did what I had to do to get you back."

Harry was astounded. "So you helped kill the fucking cat? How the fuck would that get me back?"

"Cat, what cat? I don't know what you mean." The confusion was now suppressing Natella's emotions. "I only bought Oleana a present so that she'd relax around me. She stole you away from me and I wanted to show you that if she cheated on her friend, then she'd cheat on you too. That's all. I haven't seen any cat. What cat?"

As Natella spoke, Harry was not sure whether all or any of what she said was true, but he did know it was unlikely that she would have retained the CH bag and left the gift certificate in it for herself. Certainly if she was lying about Bunny, she was putting on a hell of an act. He also realised that she had not actually named Bunny at any juncture. He asked when she had given Oleana the gift and Natella told him that it was the night when they had seen the Russian man in Sho Cho.

It was all starting to add up for Harry. All roads led to Oleana.

The exhausted policeman in Jebel Ali had traced the hotel key to the Beach Resort Hotel and confirmed with the hotel that Soltegov had been a guest. He told the hotel to contact him if anyone either called or asked for Mr Soltegov. He posted a missing persons report on Soltegov with an explanation of the apparent diving accident, before placing a call to the Russian Embassy to notify them of the death. Afterwards, he picked up Soltegov's mobile phone and saw the message – "*It is done*". He noted that the text had been sent long after the suspected time of death. He would wait until the morning to process the rest of the file, just in case the body turned up.

Omar was at the other end of town and about to review his suspects' movements and calls, when he noticed the flag against Soltegov's name. He nearly fell off his chair as he read the missing persons report. He made a note of the name of the boat and pulled up the records; its most recent owner was Graham Tree, a British national. The name had no record or blemish against it. The report said that there had been three persons on board in addition to the missing male, and that all maritime registrations and diving equipment test certificates were in order. He noted the comment:

> *Appears to be a diving accident. Search for victim continues. Russian Embassy informed. Media withheld until NoK informed.*

Omar wondered who the other men on the boat had been; he would call for the records in the morning. He then pulled Soltegov's phone records and noted the message from Oleana Katayeva – "*It is done.*" He wondered whether it was some sort of gloating message to the dead man, or if in fact she had gone through with the threat to the cat. There were no other significant calls, except the one from Soroush to Linley. Surely he would have said something if they had snuffed his cat; perhaps it had come back, but was all dishevelled. Omar decided that tomorrow would be a good day to make a visit to Ms Katayeva. Before he finished work at midnight, he placed a CID tag on the file – this would ensure that all the information on the missing persons report would come to him as an alert.

The following morning around 11, Harry found himself surprised to see Graham arrive unannounced at his office. The grim look on Graham's face made his words almost needless. "They've found the body."

"What?" Harry was astounded. "How? Where?"

"I'm not exactly sure," Graham explained, "but they've found it with all the diving kit on."

"Shit," was about the only word that Harry could think of to say. "I hope to fuck we didn't miss anything."

Graham ignored this statement of the obvious. "They want us to go up to Jebel Ali to talk to the policeman again, but I thought we should have a face-to-face first. The guy that called me was the same copper we spoke to yesterday. He reckons he's due to hand the case off but he's asked us to go up there just to clear up a couple of points." Graham paused. "Let's get it over and done with."

Harry nodded gravely.

As the two men were driving south towards Jebel Ali, Omar was on his way to the morgue.

He had printed off the report on the retrieval of the body and wanted to see it first hand before the pathologist started destroying any evidence. He was waiting by the morgue when the van transporting Soltegov arrived.

The duty pathologist was one of the most experienced that they had; he was, however, also one of the most lethargic. As he uncovered Soltegov's body, he nodded at the flesh already hanging off the corpse's legs and face. "It looks like the reef sharks have had a go at this one. Give me a hand."

Omar did not really want to help him remove the diving set, but he figured that he would get the best answers by cooperating. While the pathologist went to work on the body, Omar checked the pressure gauge on the diving set – it was empty. He checked the lifejacket and noted that there was a small rip in it, as well as no pressure in the bottle. The poor bastard must have tried to inflate a leaking jacket.

He turned to the morgue van driver who had come in to see what was going on. "Was there a weight-belt?"

"Yes, it's in the van. The coastguard reckoned the buckle had slipped around his back, so he might not have been able to reach it."

"And what about a knife?" asked Omar.

"I haven't seen a knife." replied the driver. "You'll have to ask the coastguard."

The pathologist looked up at Omar. "This looks straight forward so far but just give me half an hour to check him over and perhaps cut him open. I should be able to give you a cause of death pretty quickly."

'What a genius,' thought Omar; the guy had been pulled out of the sea after two days in diving equipment; he did not need a dead persons doctor to tell him how the man had died. However, the only words from Omar's mouth were: "I'll go get a coffee."

Harry and Graham sat quietly in Jebel Ali police station. They were not sure why precisely they had been asked to come in, but they knew that theirs was not to reason why. As the time passed, both started to feel steadily more uncomfortable.

In truth, the only reason why the policeman had asked them to come in for questioning was because he knew that the morgue would call as soon as they produced an initial report. He figured that if both men were already sitting in reception, then it would make for an easy arrest. He loved that Westerners were so compliant.

It was an hour and a half before he emerged and asked Harry and Graham to come into the interview room.

"Gentlemen," he said in a broad regional accent. "The morgue has inspected the body of your friend; it is apparently not a very pretty sight, but he is recognisable from his passport picture."

'Get on with it,' thought Graham.

"I'm sad to inform you that your friend died of drowning. There's no sign of a large predator injury, although his skin has sustained some fish damage." He paused again. "I'm very sorry this has happened, but you need to know the sea is a dangerous place in our Gulf. You're free to go, and we'll call if there is any change of news."

The relief felt by Harry and Graham was only overcome by their need to suppress any sign of it. Both men stood up together.

"Just two questions."

They both stopped in their tracks, waiting for the policeman to ask.

"Was your friend wearing a diving knife?"

They looked at each other both thinking, 'Shit, we forgot to put a knife on him.'

"Yes." Harry took the initiative. "He had one on his right leg." He was taking a bet that Soltegov was right-handed.

"It's missing; I suppose it must have fallen off," the policeman replied before asking, "Do you know anyone by the name of 'Fixer'?"

Both men shook their heads.

"Only, someone that your friend had named 'Fixer' in his contacts sent him a message late last night."

"What was the message?" Harry had to ask.

"It only said, '*It is done*'," replied the policeman. "Do you know what this could mean?"

They both shook their heads again and Graham answered truthfully, "Not a clue, sorry."

As they drove back up the Sheikh Zayed Road, Graham crowed the merits of their plan and that they had pulled it off. Harry pretended to be pleased, but he had only one thing on his mind – get to Oleana and find out once and for all the depth of her involvement. Why had the bitch lied about her connection to Soltegov, and why were Bunny's remains in the gift bag that Natella had given to her? She had some explaining to do and he was determined that no charm offensive on her part would throw him this time. He decided to make an unannounced visit.

CHAPTER NINETEEN
The Cat's Out Of The Bag

It was the end of the workweek when Harry drove to Oleana's house, just stopping short of it as soon as the small villa came into view. Parked directly outside was a green and white Toyota Land Cruiser that bore the livery of the Dubai Police.

"Shit," Harry said out loud, as he concentrated on driving past the house as if he were local traffic. Once out of sight, he parked two streets down. He thought perhaps that the police car might not be there for Oleana, but given the recentness of the Soltegov accident, he just could not risk it. Perhaps the police had linked her to the drowned Russian; perhaps it was something else entirely; or perhaps it was nothing at all. Either way, he was not going to knock on that door for as long as there was a police car parked outside.

Oleana had almost shit herself when she had opened the door to be greeted by an attractive, uniformed female police officer and a male plain-clothes officer; the latter had showed her his identification and introduced himself as Warrant Officer Omar Shamoon.

He explained that there had been a recent accident involving a Russian citizen with whom they believed she was acquainted, and that they were just making standard enquiries in order to ensure his next of kin were informed.

Oleana did not have a clue what he was talking about, but she had lived in Dubai long enough to know that if the police bothered themselves to make a house call, then it was not for the sake of community relations, or, for that matter, 'standard enquiries'.

As she showed the police into her living room, she was unaware that both officers were CID. The policewoman wore the two-stripe insignia of a corporal on her arm. She had worn her uniform at the request of Omar, in order to provide Oleana with the comfort that a woman of recognisable police status was in the room. Her presence was as much for cultural as procedural reasons.

Omar calmly scanned the room, trying to absorb the clues and character of the home. He quickly noticed that there were no photographs of family members or loved ones. The paintings on the wall were contemporary and the furnishing much sparser than he would have expected of a single white woman. He reflected that this might be a Russian trait; he was not sure. He glanced across at her desk and noted the orthodox crucifix – she was a Christian, but he also saw that all her books were related to travel and reference. It seemed that Ms Katayeva was a no-frills kind of woman, except, perhaps, for her dress sense.

Oleana's mind was buzzing. She wanted to know what they wanted, but was dreading the impending conversation. She offered water or tea; both police visitors refused. Oleana sat on her couch; the policewoman and Omar sat opposite her in separate armchairs.

"Do you know Ilyas Soltegov?" Omar asked directly; he wanted yes or no answers so as to establish quickly whether she was lying.

"Yes, I do, he's one of my concierge clients." Oleana's answer was steady and she purposely wanted to qualify her familiarity with him.

"When did you last see him?" the Arab asked.

"I'm not sure exactly...last week, I think. I know he's in town at the moment." Oleana was wondering what the stupid bastard had done and why; whatever it was, it had led the police straight to her.

"What is your relationship with him?" The policewoman now took up the questioning. Omar liked his colleague's instinct; she was one of the best young women in the CID; he could see that she was already reading the interview and planning several questions ahead in the process.

"Entirely professional – I assist him with his business activities in Dubai...but why are you asking these things?" Oleana needed them to give her a clue.

Omar responded by showing her Soltegov's passport photo.

"Is this Mr Soltegov?" He needed to confirm the identity and waited for her to nod. "We have some bad news, Ms Katayeva." He paused for effect. "Your client is dead." Now he would study her response.

"Dead? Ilyas Soltegov, dead? How can that be? When?" She felt the fear of Moscow's reprisal hit her, and in response the blood drained from her face. She knew that the shit would really hit the fan when the big boys in Moscow got this news. They would go berserk, and might, God forbid, blame her.

Fortunately for her, her reaction was in keeping with what Omar had been trained to recognise in terms of response and body language. Her instant need for confirmation and the instinctive, inquisitive questions, together with the blood draining from her face, rather than blushing. The combination was indicative that the news had been a complete surprise to her. The blood flow was an impossible act to imitate because its response to fear or shock was involuntary. "It was a diving accident, off the World Islands. He was with an experienced diver but got lost and fell into difficulty at some point. We've recovered the body; he ran out of air, most likely panicked, and drowned." He watched her face carefully; he could see the blood returning to replenish her healthy glow. He reflected that she was a stunningly beautiful woman. "We think he had a few things go wrong all at once, and his apparent inexperience caused him to panic."

"What things went wrong?" Oleana needed to know – she would have to tell her Russian masters.

"It looks as if his weight-belt buckle-release slipped around his back and he couldn't reach it. If he was wearing a knife, he must have dropped it, so he couldn't cut the weights free. He was wearing a lifejacket, but it appears to have been defective thanks to a leak, so he used up all his air but had no flotation." He paused. "We've had one of our coastguard divers check his equipment and the charging records. It does look as if it just wasn't a good day for him to dive – if something could go wrong, it did. Had he ever mentioned an interest in diving to you?"

Oleana shook her head. "No, but then again, he would have no reason to unless he wanted me to organise it for him. When did this happen?"

"Tuesday afternoon; we recovered his body the next day." The policewoman once again made her presence felt.

Oleana wanted to squirm but remained composed. She had just been informed why the call to save Bunny had not arrived before 7 pm on Tuesday. She felt a pang of regret as the sad realisation dawned on her that she had gone through the cat's entire demise for nothing.

Omar resumed. "He was with some friends and I was wondering if you knew any of these men." He read aloud from his notebook: "Shaheen Soroush, Harry Linley and Graham Tree?" As he finished the question, he smiled to himself – she would now surely lie and entrap herself.

"I know the first two men but not the last." She had unwittingly shocked Omar with her honesty, but he quickly regained control.

"Did you know that they were friends with Soltegov?" He was enjoying this cat-and-mouse questioning; she would surely mess up soon.

"I know that Soroush does – I mean *did* – business with Mr Soltegov. The second guy is a friend of Soroush, he's a nice guy, very athletic," she qualified. "I've never heard of the last name."

Everything she had said matched with what the men in the boat had told the investigating officer. He would need to up the odds if he was ever going to get to the bottom of why she had been tasked to kill the cat and thrown the number plate in the dumpster.

"We have Mr Soltegov's mobile phone. It doesn't have many local numbers on it because he bought the SIM at the airport. He was a very careful man – his messages had been purged." Omar had opened his own lying stakes, but he could now pounce: "You texted him on Tuesday evening the words, '*It is done*', no?"

Oleana knew that she could not deny this so she nodded.

Omar continued. "What does this mean? What is '*done*'?"

"I used to arrange many things for Mr Soltegov. He was a member of the Duma, you know?" She was playing for time while she dreamt up a credible response.

"Yes, we know," Omar responded, knowing that he had her cornered.

"I'm hesitant to tell you why I texted him that message." Oleana switched her glance between her two questioners. "You see, what I did for him might not be termed legal, but in my defence, I would add that, given the circumstances, no crime was actually committed."

Omar was stunned. Was she actually going to confess to the cat abduction and killing? She was right, he thought – it wasn't nice, but it certainly wasn't illegal either."

"We cannot give you immunity, Ms Katayeva," warned the policewoman; it was the first time that she had made Omar resent her presence.

"I'm, aware of that." Oleana had bought the time she needed to formulate a credible response. She got up and walked to the kitchen cabinet and pulled out a bottle of Absolut vodka. "I have an alcohol licence," she explained. "This is Mr Soltegov's favourite brand of vodka..." She went to correct herself again, but this time the mistake was deliberate: "I mean, *was* his favourite vodka." She had their full attention. "He'd asked me to get him a bottle because he couldn't buy booze except by the glass in his hotel. I know my licence doesn't permit me to give alcohol to someone else, but he was a high-paying client." She paused. "So I guess I might have had intent to break the law, but because he died I didn't get the opportunity to actually go through with it." She looked at the policewoman. "Does that amount to confession of a crime?"

Omar sat in awe. One way or another, whether by luck or judgement, this beautiful Russian was running rings around them. She had just confessed to a trivial intent to break the law, something no right-minded person would do, but she had doubtless done so in order to cover up her real activities. She had made it practically impossible for them to contradict her story and he and the policewoman knew it. Oleana had, however, made a mistake, and Omar was quick to seize on it. "Do you have a cat, Ms Katayeva?"

Oleana was blindsided. "Er...what do you mean?" she stammered. She had no idea what had generated the question; how the fuck could he know that the vodka story was a cover for the Bunny disposal plan?

Omar pointed up to the cupboard from where she had taken the vodka. "Cat food. I see you have tins of cat food in your cupboard – I'm a cat lover," he qualified, "and I just wondered what kind of cat you have."

Oleana was livid with herself; this guy was clearly a very smart detective and trained to notice every detail. How could she have let herself mess up like that? Now the guy wanted to talk cats and would force a second lie; she would have to make it a half-lie. "Not my own cat." She quickly re-gathered her composure. "I often look after another client's cat when they're travelling, so I keep a decent supply of cat food just in case."

"Do you have one at the moment?" Omar pushed.

"No, not at the moment." She smiled and closed the cupboard, hoping that it would also close the line of questioning. "I'm very sad about Mr Soltegov. Does his family know?"

She had changed the subject perfectly. Omar was once again smiling to himself – she was exceptional.

"The Embassy's been notified, that's the extent of what we can do. His hotel room's been emptied. We'll go through his belongings and repatriate them to the Embassy within a day or two." He and the policewoman got up to leave. "Thank you for your help, Ms Katayeva." They moved towards the door. It was all part of Omar's questioning theatrics that he used in order to pounce, the first of two questions to which he needed to study the response. As they reached the door and opened it, he turned around and looked at the gorgeous Russian. "Did he have any enemies?"

"Who?" She was playing for time.

"Soltegov, of course." He was irritated that she had chosen to ask. It had broken the momentum. He knew that he should have included the name in the question. She had seen the weakness in his phrasing and exploited it.

"No, I can't think of any off the top of my head." She said the sentence slowly and deliberately. She was consciously displaying an unconscious expression of recollection by casting her blue eyes upwards.

Both police visitors thanked her and Omar gave her his business card. As they walked back to the police Land

Cruiser, he looked at the Mini and then back to Oleana. "Is this your car?" He smiled; she did the same and nodded. He stood by the Mini for a moment. "It's a nice little car, very distinctive."

She thanked him for the compliment and closed her front door.

"Jesus Christ," she said aloud to herself. "That murdering little bastard has done it again." She poured herself a generous glass of Absolut and quickly concluded that coincidences like this could not happen. Shaheen Soroush must have sabotaged the Controller's diving gear. He was, after all, the only guy in Dubai who had good reason for wanting Soltegov dead. The Iranian bastard must have used Harry in some shape or form to set Soltegov up, and she just hoped that Harry was not the next guy on Soroush's death list.

She reflected that Shaheen Soroush was taking on the Russians at their own game and beating them. For their part, three of the Moscow cartel were dead, local business deals were falling apart, and one of their best launderers was in jail. It was one holy mess. She knew that Harry did not know of Soltegov's involvement in any of this. She also knew Harry well enough to know that he would certainly never be party to the murder of a stranger, not least for the sake of some Iranian. Harry was a banker not a killer; he would be way out of his depth, she thought, not paying heed to her accidental diving metaphor. Poor Harry, she reflected; he would not have a clue what was going on. Her doorbell rang.

She opened the front door and was astounded to be faced by a grim-looking Harry, who immediately blurted, "What the fuck is going on?" His expression was agitated.

"I wish I knew. You'd better come in," she said.

She picked up her glass. "Vodka?"

"Fuck it, why not?" Harry responded with a resigned expression. They sat down opposite each other as she poured.

Oleana raised her glass. "*Za zdorovie!*"

"Cheers," responded Harry. He knew that Oleana's beauty and elegance were working on him again. He needed to get to the truth, but if he could also get in-between her legs, that would be a nice bonus. There were a few seconds of awkward silence, while he thought about the firmness of her body and Oleana waited for him to speak.

"Who killed Bunny?" He looked deadly serious; Oleana had not seen him like this before.

"Is she dead?" Oleana was kind of relieved that he had chosen to talk about the cat and not Soltegov. She need not have worried. Harry was not planning to compromise the fact that he knew she had had a relationship with the dead Russian.

"Don't play games, Oleana – I know she's dead and I think you know who killed her."

"Harry, you don't know anything, and you know what, my dear?" She paused. "Your life might be easier if you keep it that way."

"Well, let me tell you what I do know." Harry reflected that the conversation was getting a bit aggressive and that sex was probably slipping off the menu with every sentence that now passed. "Someone found Bunny when she escaped and threatened Shaheen that they would kill her. On Tuesday night the cat's skin was delivered to Shaheen's place, and Farah and one of their kids discovered the grisly remains."

"That's terrible, Harry. It's very sad, but I don't know why you're angry with me."

"Because the stinking cat skin was delivered in a Carolina Herrera carrier bag." He paused; Oleana was starting to blush. "In that bag, there was this." He pulled the gift receipt from his pocket. Oleana had just realised that she had forgotten to check the carrier bag, or, if she had, she had certainly not noticed the damned receipt. Now her mind was racing for the second time in just over an hour, trying to find an alibi.

Harry continued. "This gift receipt was issued by the store to Natella Sultanova. I showed it to her; she has no idea why I have it, but she said it was a receipt for a gift that she bought for you." He gave Oleana no time to respond. "So the remains of the cat were delivered in a bag that was last known to be in your possession. That's why I'm betting you know the identity of the person that killed the cat, because they must have got the bag from you." He had unwittingly given Oleana her alibi and the twist that she would need in order to corner him.

"It's true – that is the gift certificate from Natella, but I gave one of my clients the bag. He wanted a bottle of vodka and I put it in a discreet CH bag." She had kept the lie as close to the police alibi, but just extended it a little. "Harry..." She put on her best vulnerable look. "Do you really think I would have left my gift receipt in a bag that was going to be used to deliver a dead cat?" She had Harry exactly where she wanted him.

"Well, put like that...I suppose not," he replied, and she knew what his next question would be. "So who did you give the bag to?"

"You don't know him Harry, but you once asked me about him and I denied knowing him because my client confidentiality is the key to my business here. His name's Ilyas Soltegov. He's a member of our Duma." She was careful to use his name in the present tense – she did not want Harry to know that she knew of her Controller's death.

Harry was by now on the back foot. He had thought that he would surprise her and that the lack of forewarning would cause her to compromise herself. Instead, she had admitted that she had lied to him for discretionary reasons and had dispelled his suspicions about the gift receipt at the same time. Harry knew that even the clumsiest cat-killer would not have missed that. He needed to think of another question quickly. "When did you give him the bag?"

"I'm not sure." She was starting to relax now. "I think it was Saturday, or Sunday maybe." She was purposely vague in order to give Harry the impression that the handover of the bag had been no big deal; it would also mean that the alleged cat-killer had had two days to do the dirty deed.

"Soltegov might have killed the cat, but he didn't deliver it." Harry's voice was steady. He knew what her next question would be.

"Why not?" She was going along with it.

"Because he was killed in an accident on Tuesday afternoon and the package was not delivered until Tuesday night." Harry looked for her reaction – she blushed again.

"Killed? My God. What kind of accident?" She was now enjoying this.

"Diving, drowning. I was there, in the water. He came to look at Moscow Island on the World. Shaheen had cut a deal for him. We went do a quick check for erosion of the sandbanks; one minute he was there, the next he was gone. We searched all over for him, but he just disappeared. They found his body the next day. The poor bloke must have lost sight of me and panicked or something." Harry was by now looking visibly upset.

"Oh Jesus, that's terrible." She appeared to look predictably moved. "Does his family know? Should I call them?"

"I have no idea, Oleana. I suppose the Russian Embassy will deal with it."

"You're right." She had this thing under complete control now. "I'll call his family in a day or two." She paused; now it was her turn to interrogate. "You said Shaheen was there – did he organise this?"

"Well, kind of; it was his property deal and I knew the guy who had the boat." Harry stuck as close to the truth as he could.

"Did Shaheen have anything to do with the diving?" she asked as she sipped her vodka.

"Only in as much as he was of no help because he was seasick. He was below decks the whole time, either puking or resting."

As Harry spoke, Oleana could picture the scene – Soroush had likely arranged for something to go wrong and faked being sick; that way, he would have been unavailable to help when it did, and he could not be implicated either. It was brilliant. She then asked the last question that Harry expected. "Are you sure it was an accident, Harry?"

"It's difficult to see how it could be anything else," Harry bluffed. "One minute he was behind me, the next he was gone."

"No, that's not what I mean, Harry." She liked using his name. "Could Shaheen have tampered with the diving equipment or anything?"

'Jesus Christ,' thought Harry; 'she's a bit too close to home on this one.'

"I suppose it is possible," he said, "but I don't think so. After all, how would he know who was going to use which diving apparatus?"

Oleana figured that a 50/50 chance of seeing Soltegov dead would be better than none for Soroush, and she would also bet that Harry was completely expendable in the Iranian's eyes.

"Do you trust Soroush?" she asked.

"I don't trust anyone," replied Harry. "The only thing you can rely on anyone to do is to let you down."

Oleana knew it was cynical but true. "There's something about Shaheen that unnerves me," she hinted. "I think he's cunning and ruthless; I don't think he cares what happens to you, Harry."

The seeds of doubt that Oleana was casting would not fall on stony ground. Harry was still inclined towards the idea that Shaheen had set him up on the night the two assassins had come calling. There were, however, still gaping holes in what he knew about Oleana.

"Did I see a police car outside your house earlier?" he said, changing the subject.

"I think it was," she said, knowing that she should not admit to the police encounter. "I think they went next door. Was there anyone else on the boat?"

Harry repeated that the boat belonged to a friend, Graham. Oleana would remember the name; perhaps he was in collusion with Shaheen. Moscow would want to know his name and background.

Oleana offered Harry some more vodka, but he refused, explaining that he had a lot to do. He had sensed sex was not on the table; perhaps that train had left the station for good, which, he silently mused, might not be such a bad thing.

As he left Oleana's house, Harry was already starting to regurgitate the conversation and think about what he should have said. He had lost control early on and never regained the initiative. The visit might well have caused more questions than answers and he had wanted to ask her why she was on the Palm on the day that the assassins disappeared. However, Harry had not wanted to put her guard up any more than it already was. At least she had been honest about why she had lied regarding her knowing Soltegov, and she had let Harry discover that Soltegov had had an accomplice in town. Whoever that was would more than likely be Bunny's killer. Given everything that was going on, Harry figured that *that* accomplice would surface sooner rather than later. It had been an exhausting few days. He went home, determined to sleep in over the weekend.

On the way back to the police station, Omar and the policewoman compared their observations of the meeting. They both agreed that the Russian woman was smart, in fact, frighteningly so. Everything she had said added up, except that she had lied about the cat; she had also not mentioned that Harry was a lover, but the policewoman pointed out that this was an acceptable omission for any self-respecting woman.

Omar had been dying to call Oleana's bluff over her involvement with the cat, but that would have betrayed the fact that her phone was being monitored, and he still needed that surveillance asset. He also wanted to figure out a way to bring up the number plate, but this woman was so savvy that she would immediately cease any dubious activities if she deduced that she was the focus of some undue attention. He needed her to stay active in whatever she was doing so that he could figure out what the hell was unfolding on his patch. He knew that she would make a blunder at some point – everyone always did.

Both Harry and Omar had actually come within a metre or two of opening the Pandora's box that Oleana's life had become, but neither had noticed the small traces of white fur on the cream-coloured carpet under the Russian beauty's desk. Nor had either of them thought to go through her garbage bin that sat in her tiny front yard. Had they looked in there, they would have found the remnants of a cheap, white, fur-skin rug that had been bought in Carrefour and likely come from a very young sheep or goat. The shape cut out of the rug resembled something like a small, headless cat, and the blood from the mincemeat that had been rubbed into the skin was now stinking and rancid, as was the skin that had been taken off the Carrefour butcher's leg of lamb and stuck onto the back of the rug by the congealed blood.

Inside her house, Oleana rinsed the vodka glasses and pondered over the two meetings; they had both gone as well as they could considering they had been impromptu. She reflected on how men were such pushovers for a healthily built blonde with an aesthetically matching combination of tits and arse.

She walked upstairs and opened the door to the spare bedroom. Bunny came trotting out, glad of some company. Oleana squatted down and made a fuss of her.

"How could anyone think I could kill you?" she asked the purring cat. "Although you are becoming a bit of a liability now, my baby, so we can't really become best of friends." She picked her up and went downstairs to vegetate in front of the TV. She would call the Russian Embassy in the morning, just to confirm that the news about Soltegov was true.

God only knew how the Godfather would react to this one.

CHAPTER TWENTY
Spooked

Delimkov remained stoic as Russia's SVR head of station in Abu Dhabi described Soltegov's demise via the secure link between the Embassy and the Godfather's Duma office. The officer had started the conversation with the basic details of the Dubai police report. He had dreaded making the call because he knew the reputation and the power of the man in Moscow. Mr Delimkov was not in the habit of treating bearers of bad news with respect, but in this case he let the SVR officer finish his report. He then went through the who, when, where, what and how of the matter.

By the time the questions had been answered, Delimkov was resigned to the fact that they had just thrown another inadequate asset at Shaheen Soroush and, in all likelihood, the bastard had managed to dispose of it. He asked the SVR officer what he knew about the other men on the boat.

"Not much," came the reply. "One is in the finance business, the other is a senior manager in a local security firm. The latter owned the boat. We're not aware of any direct link," he added, "other than they were helping Soroush show Soltegov the World Islands. The police said Soroush was transacting a deal; it is true that the case involving the

Moscow island has just been thrown out of the local courts after three years, so there was apparently an opportunity to assume the debt on the island. The police accepted this was their reason for being there."

Delimkov was trying to control his frustration. The Dubai police could well be right. On the other hand, they were unaware that Soroush had already killed two of the Russian team and Delimkov knew only too well that he owed a debt of gratitude to the SVR for cleaning up that unholy mess.

The SVR officer felt uncomfortable with the silence on the other end of the phone so he met the urge to talk. "We do know the local CID have been called in and, thus far, between them and the coastguard, they're saying it's a drowning accident. And they have seen a few," he added.

Delimkov responded with a rare opinion: "I'd like to think it was an accident, but we've seen what Shaheen Soroush is capable of, so I wouldn't be surprised if there's more to this than meets the eye. You need to check the other men thoroughly; let's find out if they're the type who could be involved." He changed tack. "When do we get the body and belongings?"

"I'm told the remains will be released tomorrow. The consular officer's contacted the deceased man's family. We'll ship the body out on the first available Aeroflot flight."

Delimkov knew that he was talking to a good man and he would get a better picture of the people involved within a week or two.

Once the phone call had ended, Delimkov leant back in his chair. Sadly, it was too early for him to slug a vodka – that would have to wait another couple of hours. The Controller was dead, their best money launderer incarcerated, the longest-serving and most up-and-coming of their hit men had been murdered, and he had fuck-all to show for any of it.

The cartel still held the title for the Ajman apartments in Vlad's name, but they were worthless, and it was clear that

Shaheen Soroush was willing to slaughter anyone who came too close and asked him for money.

Delimkov's world had been pretty much run on the doctrine of *'quitting while you are ahead is not quitting'*, but not only was he not ahead in this deal, he was so far behind that they were actually being lapped.

The principal decision now was whether he should simply walk away, or should he send Soroush a message that he would never forget? The only snag was that all the messages sent so far had resulted in Soroush getting the upper hand. To that end, Delimkov's instinct was to live to fight another day, but his primary concern was for his reputation. If word ever got out that Shaheen Soroush had embarrassed the Delimkov cartel dramatically and repeatedly, then his lucrative reign as Godfather would be over. He concluded to himself that it was not about the money anymore – this Soroush simply needed to be sent the final message that he could not intimidate Moscow and get away with it.

It was Sunday morning, the first day in the Arab workweek, when the report of a Russian's death in a diving accident off the World Islands appeared in the local newspapers. In keeping with the reluctance of the Dubai media to report bad news, the column-long story was on page four of both the *Gulf News* and the *Khaleej Times*. Abu Dhabi's *National*, however, put the piece at the bottom of page one and took the opportunity to attach safety advisory notices for divers.

The report caught the eye of Toby Sotheby, who was a keen diver and enjoyed pursuing this hobby off the sea life-rich eastern coastline of the Emirates. Toby was sitting in Costa Coffee, barely a mile from his office in the British Embassy in Abu Dhabi. He had worked for the Foreign Office for half a dozen years now, having been recruited after leaving the Army, where he had been a captain in the Queen's Royal Lancers.

All who knew Toby joked about his appalling dress sense, which invariably included lightweight, light-coloured suits, gaudy socks and Crocket & Jones Como driving shoes. His style, or lack thereof, had not changed a bit since his laconic days in the cavalry. To that end, the last thing that anyone would suspect was that this archetypal young aristocrat was actually a member of the Millbank Rowing Club – officially known as the Secret Intelligence Service, or by its more famous moniker, MI6.

Toby went by the rule that, without exception, every single story of which he had known the actual facts, when reported in the press, was reported incorrectly. To that end, whenever a particular article caught his eye, he would read between the lines by using a combination of cynicism and operational tradecraft.

The dead man was reported as Ilyas Soltegov, a member of the Duma. He was on a boat with an Iranian and two British nationals. "What the hell?" he whispered to himself as he sipped his coffee and finished the article.

In the first place, what was a member of the Duma doing messing around diving off the World Islands, and what were two British nationals doing with him, and a bloody Iranian? If these two Brits were hanging around in such circles, at worst they were hoods, at best he should recruit them as sources. He finished his coffee, stole the newspaper and drove to the Embassy; he needed a copy of that police report and he would have it by the end of the day.

Farah had noticed a change in Shaheen since the diving accident. During the initial two days he had been very despondent, but since the coroner's report had been released, his morale had noticeably changed for the better. Over the weekend he had even popped a bottle of his best champagne and they had drank it together, an event that had not happened in years, which resulted in them romping on the bed like teenagers. Farah was not really sure whether it was shock, stress or something else entirely that had caused the sudden increase in Shaheen's libido, but she had enjoyed the net result.

Farah was a 'the more I get, the more I want' kind of girl and she figured that Shaheen would be too wrapped up with lawyers and whatever else in the coming week for her needs, so she decided to call Oleana.

She was happy that the Russian seemed glad to hear from her, and suggested a late-morning coffee. Oleana suggested the day after tomorrow.

"How about I just come to your place?" Farah suggested

Oleana's response was instant. "No, that won't work, I have a house guest this week."

Farah gently coaxed the guest's gender out of Oleana and did not know whether or not to be relieved when Oleana revealed that the guest was female. By the end of the call, they had agreed to meet the next day at 1 pm in Café Bateel at the marina. Farah added that perhaps they should grab lunch too.

When Omar came to review this call to Oleana later, he would put it down as nothing more than a social meeting between two women.

Exceptionally, Harry willingly forewent sex that weekend. He knew that he was exhausted and simply needed seclusion, so spent the two days reading *Ask Forgiveness Not Permission*, a brilliantly written book by a former SF colleague. It held some real life lessons and parallels to Harry's current situation, as well as sound advice on getting the job done. Like the author, Harry had always considered himself fortunate to have never had to cope with Post Traumatic Stress Disorder (PTSD). However, he had to admit that killing three men in as many weeks was not a habit that he particularly wanted to indulge. He reasoned that the first two killings had been justified – the bastards had, after all, tried to kill him. Also, he reassured himself that, because the bodies had surreally disappeared, whoever had sent those men to Shaheen's house did not want their demise to reach judgement in law. He willed himself to the conclusion that if this represented an unholy truce, then that was good enough for him.

Soltegov's killing bothered him, however. He tried not to think about the hopelessness of the bound, weighted and gagged Russian trying to breathe seawater until his lungs gave out. He half-hoped that Soltegov had suffered a heart attack during the process, but, from the sounds of the police report, the Russian had undergone pure drowning. He knew that Graham was right to seek revenge for his BRIXMIS mates, and that this was probably the only time that the Russian had been served justice, but he could not get Soltegov's face out of his mind. He had even dreamt that the man had come alive while he had been dressing him underwater.

Harry figured that the immediacy of the 'operation' would fade given a few weeks, and until then he could bounce his doubts off Graham and gratify his sexual needs with Natella. Since his last meeting with Oleana, he had concluded that she now scared him somewhat. He had surmised that she could be as ruthless as she needed to be and just hoped that she did not know more about Bunny's death than she was admitting. For now, he knew that his only reason for keeping in contact with her was to find out the identity of the bastard that had skinned Bunny.

Unbeknownst to him, the SVR officer in the Russian Embassy had started his week in much the same way as his British counterpart, Toby Sotheby; the only difference being that he already had the identity of the British men that he was investigating.

The Russian was relieved to find that both men had LinkedIn and Facebook pages; the absence of one or both was always a clear indication that the individual was either an IT dinosaur – which he doubted these men were – or that they were staying offline for reasons of government or criminal concealment.

He noted that both men were from UK military backgrounds, but there was nothing here that raised any red flags. He also noted that Harry Linley, the diver, had a diving background, and there were photographs of him to prove it. He was interested that neither man had posted anything controversial or commented on anything that could be interpreted as such. There were no pictures of regular women. Their LinkedIn pages matched with the background information that was published elsewhere on the internet.

He went into the SVR database and entered the date-of-birth details that had been provided on Facebook. Harry Linley came up as a negative trace. He then entered Tree's details and leant back in his chair, watching as black and white photographs of a young man appeared on his screen.

Mr Graham Tree had been a soldier in BRIXMIS at the end of the Cold War and served in East Germany. He knew what it was to play cat-and-mouse with the Stasi and the KGB.

It was a tenuous link, and he thought it unlikely that Tree would have come across Soltegov given their difference in age and rank, but he needed to cover his own arse by letting Mr Delimkov figure that one out. He created a file for Linley on the SVR system and placed an 'active' tag on Tree's file. If either guy so much as farted online from here on in, then Russia's SVR would capture it.

★　★　★

Toby Sotheby would have been genuinely amused if he had known that, at the same time in the same town, he and his Russian counterpart were studying the same two British nationals. Fortunately for Toby, his database reached way beyond the Russian's with respect to the background available on both men. Clearly these guys were linked by the military, and Toby recognised the terminology used on their records and the type of medals held by each to quickly deduce that they were, in all likelihood, former Special Forces. A call to one of his London colleagues who was now in '6', but also former SF, would quickly confirm the men's standing with their respective regimental associations.

For some reason, Toby was not particularly interested in Linley; the man gave all the appearances of having been quite a capable adventurer, whether in military or civilian life, but was now entrenched in the murkiness and dullness of the financial sector. Graham Tree, however, was a different kettle of fish. He was former Intelligence Corps, also very likely former Special Forces, and now running a private security firm. Toby thought it likely that any immoral acts that these men might be involved in would be of a financial nature in Linley's case, but a physical one in Tree's.

It did not help that, as a former cavalry officer and now as an intelligence officer, Toby was instinctively resentful of the British Army's Intelligence Corps. In both roles he had seen the Corps derive significant influence, despite very dubious capability. He had no doubt that Tree would be some sort of cocky, over-confident, former senior non-commissioned officer, who himself had an inane resentment of commissioned officers and who probably spent his time taking the piss out of cavalry officers and spooks. There was very likely more to Graham Tree than met the eye, and Toby intended to manufacture a meeting to get the measure of the man.

★   ★   ★

The following morning in Moscow, Delimkov read the secure transmission from his man in Abu Dhabi. He too pondered over the BRIXMIS link, but due to his own country's security measures, he was unaware of the late-eighties plot to give the Brits a bloody nose in East Germany. The fact that the KGB had played such a major role in destroying the evidence of its own brutal history at the time of *perestroika* meant that Soltegov alone had held those secrets. Delimkov wondered what past deeds had passed through the Controller's mind before he sucked in his last breath of warm, salty water.

Delimkov did not believe in coincidences, but he also did not believe in mission creep – to go after Graham Tree solely on the basis that he had been some low-life corporal in BRIXMIS at the same time that Soltegov had been a major in the KGB would have been nuts.

He needed to concentrate on Soroush and send a message that the Iranian would never forget, but he was understandably reluctant to risk sending yet another Russian into Dubai. He had already lost enough good men to this deal.

He concluded that he would have to use someone in place, and there was only one sleeper already there of whom he was aware. She would have to do the job, then extract. He picked up his secure phone and waited for SVR in Abu Dhabi to answer. He issued his instruction and emphasised that conveying the message to the sleeper was the full extent of the officer's responsibility. "She'll take it from there."

The young SVR officer walked down the stairs to the cultural affairs office. He asked the young lady if he could borrow her mobile phone; she knew better than to refuse. He picked up the phone and texted, "*My Russian Kitchen House Cafeteria. Two for one Tuesday, 7 pm to 9 pm.*"

He waited about a minute and the phone bleeped; he read the reply – "*Thank you*" – and deleted the transmission from the cultural assistant's phone.

By seven the next evening, Oleana had parked her Mini at the back of Salam and Khalifa Street in Abu Dhabi and was sitting in the Russian Cafeteria, enjoying a cabbage salad. She recognised the man who entered the café at 7.20 pm as one of the men who had brought the ambulance to Shaheen's house and taken away Maxim and Boris. They did not acknowledge each other; she watched him as he selected cabbage rolls from the serving area, before sitting down and reading a magazine as he ate.

Oleana casually finished her salad and looked towards the counter, making eye contact with the young woman who was serving. "Thank you," she said to her in Russian, "that was very nice."

"Would you like anything else?" the young lady enquired.

"No, thank you," responded Oleana. "I'll just finish my drink and leave." She sipped her 7 Up, waiting for the man reading the magazine to move.

When he had finished his two rolls, he took a sip of his tea and stood up to leave. As he did so, he placed the magazine on the table while he checked his phone; he made a show of looking preoccupied and left the café.

Oleana waited for as long as she could – the seconds seemed interminably long. She had decided that her cue would be the young lady coming to clear the tables, but the little cow had not responded as expected. Oleana could not risk someone coming into the café and sitting at the reader's table. She made an exaggerated gesture to show that she had finished her drink and stood up to leave. As she approached the door, she brushed past the table where the man had left the magazine and swept it up into her hand before exiting.

The 'Moscow Rules' live-letterbox transfer was complete; her instructions would be in the magazine. Even if there had been knowing eyes in the café, they would only have had a fraction of a second to realise what had just happened. She would drive back to Dubai and examine the magazine when she was safely back home with Bunny.

Omar was frustrated. He had seen the message that had been sent to Oleana and traced it to a Russian Embassy employee. He had really not expected Oleana to go to some piece-of-shit cafeteria in Abu Dhabi just to sample some cheap Russian food, so he could have kicked himself when the ANPR system had shown that she had left Dubai for the capital. He was equally pissed off when he calculated that she must have only spent 45 minutes eating at most.

He had long ago learned that if a human being did something illogical, then it was normally for their own gain, and he would have to figure out what that was in this case. This woman was about as smart as anyone he had ever come across. He knew from the number plate and the eavesdropped conversation about the cat that she was far from innocent, but her movements, with only rare exception, gave no indication that she was anything other than ordinary. As the reality of the situation dawned on him, Omar understood that he should have taken a different view on the Russian from the outset. This profile did not only match that of a professional criminal, it also matched that of a well-trained spy. He smiled to himself – he may have missed the cafeteria trick but it was entirely possible that she had just fucked up, and this gave him a few options.

Oleana arrived home where she went straight to her desk and turned on her IKEA lamp. Whoever had put the sheet of writing paper in the magazine had stuck each corner to the page, with a handwritten message in Cyrillic script on the inside of the sheet. It was a simple but clever technique to ensure that the written instructions did not inadvertently drop out of the magazine during transit or transfer.

She gently peeled back each corner of the page, musing that the glue-stick that had been used was usefully useless at actually sticking anything for any amount of time. She turned the page over and read the text, which was in Russian:

From your boss: send the Iranian a painful message that he will never forget. On completion, Swordfish.

She had not expected this, but it was what it was and she would have to figure out a way to do it. She walked out into her small yard and lit the gas barbecue. She threw the paper onto it and let it burn to a cinder. It was time to re-organise her life.

It was noon the next day when Harry met Graham in the rear section of Costa Coffee in Dubai Marina. Harry had called the meeting just to seek some reassurance from Graham that he had heard nothing more about the drowning. Graham had not, but, with typical gusto, announced to Harry that it seemed his security company was going to bid on a local contract for the British Embassy. Harry asked how come, and Graham explained that one of the guys there had just called him to say that they were outsourcing some security aspects of the Embassy, and that their preference was to give the contract to a company with British management at the helm.

Graham chuckled as he told Harry, "This guy was a posh fucker. I managed to squeeze out of him that he was a former

Rupert in the donkey wallopers." Graham's slang for 'cavalry officer' was not lost on Harry.

"Anyway," continued Graham, "it sounds like the contract'll be money for old rope. I'll let you know how it goes."

"Nothing from the coastguard or police?" Harry wanted Graham back on the line of reassurance.

"Nothing, mate," replied Graham. "Look, they found the body, no foul play suspected, no links to you and me except for the unfortunate accident." He smiled. "Turned out to be the perfect crime, which is hardly surprising given the amount of money Her Majesty's Government spent on us. If they were going to nail anyone with this, it would've been your mate Shaheen, but we did him a massive favour by taking him out of the picture. Do you think he suspects?"

"I'm not sure, I've hardly spoken to him since. I've kind of been of keeping a low profile," replied Harry.

"Don't do that," Graham advised, "Domestic normality is the key – just keep living life the way you were doing in the weeks before all this. Go diving and shit like that." Graham was typically upbeat.

"Good idea," responded Harry, half-wishing that he could tell Graham that he had also snuffed another two guys just a few weeks previous to the drowning.

"The bastard put up a bit of a fight," said Graham with a smile. "We did a good job not to leave any marks, but thank fuck a few fish scoffed into him before the coastguard found him. Talk about reverse sushi!"

He had broken the tension and even in his sullen mood, Harry smiled. "Let's take a walk back to the car," he suggested.

The weather was perfect; they both walked slowly past the Marina Walk fountain and decided that, rather than go directly into the car park, they would meander along the paved 'boardwalk' to view the boats, the women and the scenery. This decision would eventually prove fate for one man and destiny for the other.

They were almost level with the Café Bateel when they spotted a flash of blonde hair sitting across the table from a woman with jet-black, voluptuous locks, enough to catch any man's eye – Harry recognised both women immediately. He was about to suggest to Graham that they turn back, but it was too late.

Farah had spotted him and blurted to Oleana, "Wow, look, there's Harry."

Oleana turned and both women smiled to reveal their perfectly enamelled teeth. Graham could not help himself and muttered, "Jesus Christ, Harry, they are essence."

Harry ignored the comment and made himself look relaxed and happy as he went up to the ladies and greeted them both with a kiss on each cheek.

"This is a nice surprise," Oleana lied. "So what are you doing up here, Harry?"

"I was just grabbing a quick coffee with my friend, Graham," he replied, gesturing towards the man next to him, "and we thought we'd take a stroll before heading back to work."

Oleana was as quick as a flash. "Graham with the boat? Harry told me about you."

"That's me, I'm Graham," he said, holding out his hand for each woman to shake in turn.

"I love boats," Oleana said, before turning to Farah. "What about you?"

"As long as they don't leave the marina," said Farah with a laugh. "I get motion sickness."

Oleana reflected that she had seen no sign of motion sickness when Farah had been writhing up and down on top of her body.

"You must take us out on your boat." Oleana was inviting herself. "Where is it? What's its name?"

"Just up at the Marina Yacht Club. Her name's *Luke's Lady*." Graham was loving the attention. This was, he reflected, the reason why he had bought a boat after all.

Harry wanted to shut him up – he was genuinely uncomfortable with Oleana knowing anything, but there was little he could do at that moment. He was also acutely aware that he needed at least one more meeting with the Russian bitch, so he rapidly cut in to change the subject. "How are you, Farah, and how's Shaheen?"

"We're fine, thank you, Harry." Farah was always so polite. "Shaheen's good – I haven't seen him so relaxed for as long as I can remember."

The hairs stuck up on the back of Oleana's neck. She surely knew why Shaheen was so relaxed – he had eradicated all the Russians to whom he had been financially or morally obliged.

"That's good," responded Harry. "Happy is healthy."

"So when will we see you again, Harry?" Farah asked.

"I'm not sure, whenever you invite me." Harry smiled.

"We'll do that soon, perhaps you can all come around together?" suggested Farah.

"Great!" gushed Graham.

"Perfect," said Oleana.

'No fucking way,' thought Harry.

The ladies invited Graham and Harry to join them for a salad but both men refused politely, though Harry did manage to slip in an invitation to Oleana: "Let's grab a coffee soon."

Unbeknownst to both of them, since her boss's note, this would more suit her needs than his.

The four said their goodbyes, and as the two men walked away, Harry analysed what had just gone on. Graham, meanwhile, was affirming the almost 10/10 rating that he had awarded each woman, each perfect in her own way. Harry did not want to burst Graham's bubble, so he decided not to mention that one was married to a treacherous man, the other was just plain treacherous all by herself. He did, however, concede that they were both very beautiful women.

As Farah watched the two men walk away, she commented on how nice they both were. She then felt encouraged when Oleana told her that the relationship with Harry had cooled somewhat.

"He's a nice guy, but he can be very moody. I'm not sure he doesn't have a bit of a dark side," Oleana said, purposely planting a seed in Farah's mind.

"Don't we all," replied Farah. "Which reminds me, when can we *really* see each other again?"

"Soon," encouraged Oleana, "but it'll have to be at your place or a hotel. I'm not sure how long my house guest is staying."

"I'll let you know something," said Farah with a smile. "Shaheen's probably going on a trip soon." She leant towards Oleana as if to impart a secret, and in a quiet voice told her, "We're leaving Dubai – Shaheen's relocating his business to Singapore. He'll leave first, then I'll follow with the kids. Shaheen wants to keep it quiet so this is just between you and me."

'The little shit,' thought Oleana, 'skipping town to dodge his responsibilities.' She had instantly assessed that the clock was running down for her to deliver the boss's message.

"When will he leave?" she asked.

"A week, maybe two," Farah replied. "He'll go as soon as he gets the all-clear from the lawyers. After that, you can come to the house anytime."

"And when will you leave?" Oleana needed to know.

"I think a couple of weeks after him. I just need to sell the furniture, pack the art and get rid of my car, then I can leave."

Oleana let the rest of lunch run its course, but all the time she was thinking about the 'message'; she would have to figure out some method of delivery and then move fast.

The following day Graham greeted Toby Sotheby in the reception of the company office. The red socks and the thick wavy hair could have belonged to no one else except a former cavalry officer.

The men quickly established common ground by comparing their military experience. Within three minutes, Graham had provided him with all the background information that would have otherwise taken multiple hours to research. The combination of Intelligence Corps and Special Reconnaissance Regiment indicated to Toby that Graham was a rare breed who was skilled in the collection and exploitation of information. The men of the SRR were considered by many to be the thinking man's SF; their job was to covertly infiltrate, sometimes for months, then extract themselves without detection. They were the surgeon's knife to the SAS's sledgehammer.

Toby explained that he worked in the Embassy's regional security office and that they needed to change the commercial guard force. He asked Graham if he would be interested in such a contract. When Graham proved receptive, Toby handed him a confidentiality agreement; Graham read it while the other man sat silently, before taking out a pen and signing it.

"Great,' said Toby, and handed him the fictitious bid document. "This will give you the technical and manpower requirements. Basically 10 men around the clock, all of whom must be vetted and fluent in English."

Graham looked over the document – it was typically governmental and verbose. Toby had wanted it that way in order to create a smokescreen for his real reason for being there.

"When do I need to bid by?" Graham asked.

"Two weeks will be fine, but I can meet you next week, after you've had time to study the requirements. We can then make sure you have a strong chance of success." Toby smiled.

"That kind of bid I can live with." Graham did not look up from the document.

"I'd like to see a former military man get this," Toby expanded. "We understand each other – trust, reliability and all that."

Graham nodded.

"If this works out, Graham, there might be the opportunity for you to carry out more elaborate work for HMG. Would that interest you?"

"Why not?" responded Graham. "I spent 22 years serving Her Majesty, why would I stop now?"

"Even if it meant individual commitment?" Toby knew the next answer would be critical.

"Is there any other kind?" Graham asked.

"Good point." Toby paused, knowing that he had pushed hard enough for one meeting. "So what does a single guy do around these parts at weekends?"

"Plenty," Graham replied. "Biking, boating, drinking." He paused before adding, "Shagging."

Toby nodded. "Indeed, this place is a lot livelier than Abu Dhabi. Do you have a boat?"

"I do." Graham loved talking about his big boy toys. "It's an Azimut 45, I picked it up for crumbs during the crisis."

"Very nice. Do you get to take it out much or do you keep it alongside?" Toby wondered whether Graham would take the bait.

"I use it quite a bit for entertaining and diving, especially this time of year." Graham considered telling him about the accident, then held back.

Toby tried again. "I'd love to go out around the Palm or the World at some juncture. Would you consider taking a few of my office out for a trip?"

"Why not? Just bring beer," Graham responded.

Toby had covered all the ground that he needed – this man was former Special Forces, and he was willing to indulge Her Majesty's Government from a corporate, individual or even maritime perspective. Toby knew that one more meeting would be all it took to recruit Graham Tree as a source; thereafter he could probe his links to the Iranian and the dead Russian.

The two former soldiers made their goodbyes and Toby commenced the drive back to Abu Dhabi. As he did so, Graham picked up his phone and called Harry.

"Mate, you will never guess what just happened to me."

"Go on," he heard from the other end of the phone.

"That contractor I told you about? I just met him. Mate, this guy was screaming out south of the river, he was going through the recruiting dance." It was slang, but Graham knew that Harry would immediately recognise precisely what he meant. There was only one renowned organisation that was south of the Thames and their most famous, though fictitious, member was a certain James Bond.

"No kidding." Harry was smiling as he spoke. "To join or tout?"

"It's got to be tout, mate. I'll meet him again next week, and rest assured, I'll try to get more information out of him than he ever gets out of me. He should have stuck to donkey walloping."

"Just take it easy, mate." Harry sounded serious. "The timing on this is spooky."

Graham realised that Harry had just made a good point. It could be a coincidence, but the Rupert had asked about the boat and not any other aspect of his life. "No worries, I'll take him up the garden path next time we meet."

The call ended; the transcript officer who was listening to Harry's calls would never be able to decipher the slang.

★   ★   ★

Shaheen was across town and moving fast. With Soltegov out of the way, he had told the lawyers to close all of his Dubai companies. He had an Indian buyer for his Roll Royce and the Ajman title would remain in his name for subsequent transfer to a Singaporean company; from there he would either sell it or dispose of it. The lawyers had told him, however, that he would need a signatory in the UAE. Shaheen had one in mind.

He actually still felt pangs of guilt over the two Russians that he had so effectively sent to jail, but reassured himself that there had been no other way.

He had also thought a lot about the sudden bout of seasickness during the boat trip, but reflected that it had actually transpired to be a real blessing. If he had been awake and on deck, he might have been able to help in the search for Soltegov and even save him – and that would have just been too ironic.

He did miss Bunny, though, and the fact that her remains had been delivered after Soltegov's death bothered him a lot; he would have liked to know who had done this. However, he knew that time was now his biggest enemy and he had to concentrate on his extraction so that it would not affect his distribution business or his freedom. Also, at the end of the day, Bunny was just a cat, and if her death was the price he had to pay in order to get the Ajman 'monkey' off his back, then it was actually no great sacrifice. He reflected that, if need be, he could always buy the kids a new Persian kitten in Singapore. He would be a lot happier, though, if he could just know who had delivered Bunny's skin.

Shaheen smiled as he logged on to his MacBook to reserve his flight to Singapore; he decided to book a flexible return flight in business class – this way, if he needed to return to Dubai within the year, he could do so. He could hardly wait to leave.

★　★　★

Omar and Oleana would have been surprised to know that both of them were sitting at their respective desks at exactly the same time, pondering their next move. The bombshell that Farah had dropped concerning Shaheen's imminent move to Singapore was not something that Oleana had expected. She knew that if she missed the boat in terms of delivering her boss's message, then the repercussions would be extreme; she did not want to think of the treatment she would have to endure. She jotted down some notes, searching for a break that could give her an avenue approach to inflicting physical pain on Shaheen. Her most obvious route in was through Farah, but she did not see how she could complete the mission without compromising herself.

Omar, meanwhile, had come to the conclusion that the only way in which he could draw Oleana out was to give her an indication that she was being monitored, and that that disclosure might be enough to expose her real dealings, which he was becoming increasingly convinced were linked to espionage. He picked up his phone and dialled her number, introducing himself when he heard Oleana's voice.

"I'm sorry to disturb you," he lied, "but we're just trying to tie up some loose ends regarding your deceased friend."

"He was not my friend, Officer Shamoon, he was my client," she corrected him.

"That may be," Omar replied, "but you had more telephone calls with him that anyone else."

Oleana felt a sudden rush of panic – had they been monitoring her calls? Clearly they had checked the Controller's phone records, but had they been listening too? She was aware that all calls and emails in the Emirates were captured by total collection metadata-mining, but could they have pulled and collated her conversations too? She would need to find out.

"He was here on business and I used to do a lot of his coordination, so that would make sense." She then added, "At least I earned my pay."

Omar knew he had sewn the seed of doubt, but he needed to slip in what would seem like an error and hope that she picked it up.

"Can you recall the last time you spoke to him?" he asked.

"No," she responded, "but no doubt you can tell me; you must have his phone records in front of you."

"That's true, Ms Katayeva, and my task is simply to ensure that the coroner's report corroborates the police report. You're not a suspect, and I do realise you're just a witness who happens to look after things as diverse as members of the Duma to cats." He hoped that she had taken the hint; he had one more ace up his sleeve.

Oleana's mind was racing – had he mentioned the cat because of the food in the cupboard, or had the bastards managed to eavesdrop on her calls regarding Bunny?

"I have to earn a living; it's not easy in Dubai. It's an expensive city." She was trying to defend herself yet steer him away. It did not work.

"I realise this, but at the end of the day, Ms Katayeva, every citizen breaks at least one law every single day. It's simply up to us to decide which ones we pursue and which ones we don't." He knew that this would put her on the back foot.

She knew he had a point; she needed to throttle back. "So how can I help?"

"Is there anything in any of the calls you had with him that would indicate that Mr Soltegov was worried by any particular individual? Had he wronged anyone since he'd been in Dubai?"

The path of least resistance had just become clear to Oleana; she wanted to thank the policeman, but that was never going to happen. She simply responded, "Not that I know of."

"Oh, just one more thing." Omar had been waiting to play his ace. "One of our young officers has been investigating the case of a stolen number plate."

Oleana felt like someone had just pole-axed her.

The detective continued. "He's somehow linked it with Mr Soltegov. Would you have any idea why your client would have been interested in a stolen number plate?"

"I have no idea," came the impulsive and expected reply.

Omar thanked her for her time and the call ended.

He knew that the combination of the cat and the number plate, even though not directly related, would be enough to ruffle the Russian's feathers. Hopefully she would assume that he knew a lot more than he really did and change her pattern of behaviour, enough to make a mistake and let him finally piece this mess together with useable evidence, rather than just subtle indications.

CHAPTER TWENTY-ONE
From Russia With Love

Oleana put down the phone with the realisation that the hunter might just have become the hunted. She was now under time pressure from Shaheen's exit schedule and she felt like the walls were closing in on her from all around. The mention of the cat and the number plate could not be coincidence. That idiot of a policeman might have got the facts muddled, but he did have the facts, and she knew it would only be a matter of time before he pieced together her involvement. She hoped to Christ that he had no idea why the plate had been stolen in the first place.

She took a deep breath, knowing better than to do anything on the spur of the moment. She would make a plan, sleep on it, then put it into action the following day. For now she would have to let things cool. She called Farah for a social chat; anyone listening would just hear girly talk. Once she had hung up, she waited 52 minutes and then rang Natella to catch up. She knew better that to call on a cardinal point or round number of the clock – everything she did from now on needed to look random and unplanned.

On the phone with Natella, she purposely brought up the subject of Harry and asked if Natella had seen him lately.

Oleana wondered whether Harry had spoken further to her about the gift receipt. If he had not, then this would give her plan a chance.

Little did Oleana know that, even if Harry had said anything to Natella, the very last person that *she* would tell was Oleana. Natella had no intention of letting the Russian know that she and Harry had reignited their relationship – instead she told her that she had not seen him in weeks.

The following day, Oleana picked her time carefully, figuring that exactly 3.37 pm would be a good time to call Harry. The timing would look random and if he was not in a meeting, then he would neither be rushing to finish his workday nor so engrossed in a post-lunch project that he would not have time to talk to her.

When he picked up, she asked him how he was and whether he had time to talk; he said that he did.

"Something's been bothering me a lot since we spoke, Harry, and I want put it right." She knew this opening line would have him intrigued. "You asked me about the bag with the gift receipt and who I had given the bag to? Well, when you asked me, I was totally surprised and I must admit a bit scared too, so I lied to you, and I wanted to call to tell you I'm sorry."

Harry was only half as surprised as Oleana thought he would be – he simply replied inquisitively, "Okay...?"

"I told you I gave the bag to Soltegov – I didn't. I gave it to someone else, but there was no way I thought you'd believe me if I told you who it was." She figured that she knew how to keep the gullible in suspense. "You see, I believe the man I gave the bag to has played us all to masterly effect, and especially you, Harry." She paused before dropping the bombshell. "I gave the bag to Shaheen Soroush."

"Shaheen?" Harry had not expected this. "I don't get it."

"Which is exactly the way Shaheen would plan it," she answered, reinforcing the opinion that she needed Harry to have. "Of late, I've started a new friendship with Farah. The weekend before your boating accident I went round their house and took them a bottle of booze. I took it in the Carolina Herrera bag and gave it to Shaheen, which is why it just never occurred to me to take the gift receipt out of the bag – I assumed he would throw it away. Instead, I believe he's used the disposal of the cat somehow to divert attention away from something, but I'm not sure what."

Harry was staggered as he put two and two together – it was brilliant. After they had snuffed Soltegov, Shaheen had sat in the boat, almost crying. He had bleated to Harry about how much he hated Soltegov because the Russian had taken Bunny and was threatening to kill her; but how had the cat then turned up on Shaheen's doorstep *after* Soltegov's death? Oleana had just provided the answer: Shaheen had fed Harry a load of bullshit about the threat and the cat because he wanted them to think that he was a complicit witness. In reality, Shaheen had then killed Bunny just to cover his own tracks and make himself look like an ally to Graham and Harry.

Not knowing which conclusions Harry was already reaching, Oleana continued. "For reasons of client confidentiality, Harry, you're going to have to trust me; there's some shit that I can't tell you for your own protection, but let me just say, in Shaheen's world we're all expendable. Mr Soltegov told me that Shaheen had caused the demise of two Russians in Dubai and was remorseless about it. Soltegov was acutely aware that Shaheen is a dangerous and ruthless man." She paused, before adding, "He's also been planning an exit from Dubai for weeks now, and unwinding all his assets and interests; there's no limit to what he'll do to expedite his leaving."

It was all making sense to Harry – Shaheen must have manufactured the attempt on his life; perhaps it was for as trivial a reason as being able to create a crime scene and exit the lease on the villa without penalty. The bastard had tried to throw him under the bus for an easy exit and then trumped up the alibi regarding Bunny. She had probably escaped in line with the side door being left open, but likely returned later, only to get swept up by Shaheen and slaughtered, so that she too would not impede his exit.

"You're shitting me, right?" He needed some sort of convincing.

"As you English would say, Harry, would I shit my favourite turd?" She smiled, enjoying her mastery of the English language, but rapidly turned serious again. "He took a lot from Soltegov, and other Russians, Harry – he never delivered. He's kept himself in the clear while trying to sacrifice everybody around him. I don't know what happened that day on the boat, but if it didn't happen exactly like you guys said it did, then you can be sure Shaheen will sacrifice you with it – he's done it before, he'll do it again." She was referring to the sacrifice of the dead Russians; Harry interpreted it as the attempt to sacrifice him. By now, he was also twitching about Oleana's boat comments.

"So what to do?" Harry asked the question that she had been begging for.

"I'm not a man, Harry" – she figured he had noticed – "so I can't do anything to Shaheen that he'll be afraid of. All I do know is that, given everything he's done, he has to be sent a very severe message indeed, and from what I can gather, the only emotion he'll ever understand is abject physical pain."

"How do you know?" asked Harry.

"I don't, but I imagine he reacts to little else." She paused. "He's a bully. I know for a fact that such men don't often have the ability to tolerate pain."

"Are you suggesting I hurt him, Oleana?" It was questioning the obvious but Harry had to know what she was suggesting.

"I'm suggesting, Harry, that this man will always be on the take until someone delivers a message; he'll sacrifice anything around him until he learns it doesn't pay, and then he'll use you and dispose of you if it suits his needs. He's caused the downfall of several men and even his own cat to cover his tracks. I'm sure the Russians are coming for him, but that might not be in time for you, Harry. If he perceives you or your friend Graham as weights around his neck, he'll eradicate you – it's his way."

Harry reflected that her use of "weights around his neck" was an unfortunate choice of phrase given her client's demise, but he certainly understood where she was coming from. The fact that he was a threat with regard to the boating alibi amounted to 'strike three' – Shaheen would have to be given a warning, and in no uncertain terms.

"I'll fix it," he said.

"I know I would if I were you, Harry; I don't want to see you or your friend come to any harm." Her tone grew more encouraging. "This is a one-shot deal – he might be out of here within a week or two and if that happens, then the only thing you can hope for is uncertainty."

Harry knew that she was right on all scores. "Leave it with me." He paused. "This goes no further."

"I have no idea what you're talking about," she assured him. "I've already forgotten this conversation."

As the call ended, Oleana almost wished that she had recorded it for posterity; she hoped that Harry would act on it and that Warrant Officer Shamoon would believe it.

Harry had a decision to make – should he involve Graham or not? He weighed the alternatives and decided that he would only bring him into it if there was absolutely no other choice; the less witnesses, the better. He also started to wonder if the killing thing had become a bit of a drug; was he about to make it four in four weeks? He wished that he could rely on the Russians to sort it out but knew that he could not count on something over which he had no control. For his own survival, he would have to piece together his plan within 24 hours, then entrap Shaheen; he just wished that they had not got rid of the Taser.

Two days passed and during that time, three significant events occurred of which Harry was unaware. The first was that Toby had invited Graham out for a "couple of beers"; the second was that Omar had listened to his and Oleana's call; the third was that Oleana had sold her Mini.

In the offices of the CID, Warrant Officer Omar Shamoon also had a decision to make. If he moved too soon, there would not be enough evidence to seal a case; if he moved too late, then he would not be able to convict this Russian Mata Hari. Frankly, he did not give a shit whether the Russians arranged for the Iranian to get a good thumping; he was sick to death of the Iranians in Dubai in any case. In his opinion they did little but grumble about their government, but unlike the heroes of the Arab Spring, they did nothing to correct the problem. He then reflected that it was actually better this way; if Iran ever became free, it would become Dubai's commercial competitor, except with more power, more resources and more wealth – the Emirates might empty overnight. 'Fuck them all,' he thought. Needless to say, he was not in a good mood.

He wanted to let the crime be committed, because 'conspiracy to commit' did not hold any water in the Arab world. However, he knew that this entire case could easily get way above his pay-grade if any of it leaked out, even within his own organisation. He would have to brief his colonel and let him make the call on the next decision; at least that way he would have absolved himself from any professional retribution.

The colonel listened carefully to Omar's brief. It was clear that they were onto something, but what? He had to make up his mind as to whether or not to commit time and resources, and to risk the Iranian's personal safety or try to prevent crime. Unwittingly, he had already become a victim of Carl von Clausewitz's observation that "*boldness becomes of rarer occurrence the higher an officer ascends the scale of rank*"; so he decided that prevention was better than cure.

"Tell the Iranian there's a credible threat against him," he told Omar.

"But to what extent should I explain?" Omar responded.

"No fucking extent at all, keep it simple and minimal." He paused. "Let's face it, if anyone gets the nod that they're about to get whacked, they should sit up and take notice – especially if it's from us!"

Omar knew that his colonel had a good point, and having heard his senior officer's wisdom, he recognised that objectivity was sometimes worth subjectivity many times over. He simply said, "I'll contact him and let him know."

"Do it," the colonel replied. "We have enough fucking problems without the Russians running amok committing violent crimes in our country."

Omar left the colonel's office feeling fully assured. It was a good decision.

Harry had already put his plan to beat the shit out of Shaheen into motion. The anger over the multiple deceits, the play-acting on the boat and the fact that the guy had skinned Bunny was enough to turn his stomach. Essentially Shaheen had completely screwed or tried to kill everything except his immediate family, and he actually deserved a good kicking.

The choice of weapon had not been particularly difficult – the objective was to inflict maximum amount of pain, get a complete confession, and leave minimum sign of injury. A half-metre length of smooth garden hose stuffed with heavy grade electrical cable would do it. A couple of blows around the head to the areas still covered by hair; then, once stunned, slam the genitals and the extremities; working into the ribs would then ensure pain would ensue for months. The Iranian piece of shit would not be able to properly sit, sleep, walk or shag for a few weeks at least. In fact, he might never piss properly again if Harry could exact a couple of decent kidney blows – and he would sure as hell try.

Shaheen, in the meantime, figured that he had about five more days to endure in Dubai before he could walk way free of shackles. Naturally, he would have to make damn sure that everything was cleared up before he returned, but for now, it was the exit that was important.

He reflected that he had loved Dubai since he had lived there, and the place had indeed been very kind to him, but now that he had decided to leave, in all honesty, he could not wait to get the hell out.

He was content that all was falling into place, and although he would dearly love to get rid of the *Burj Takseeb* deal, if he had to live with it, so be it. Then his phone rang.

"Mr Soroush?" he heard the voice ask on the other end of the phone.

"Yes," came the instinctive reply.

"My name is Warrant Officer Omar Shamoon of the Dubai Police. I need to communicate a very important message to you and we can either do it face-to-face or, if you're content for me to do so, I can brief you over the phone."

The very last thing that Shaheen needed was an extended meeting with a police officer so he made his decision quickly. "You can tell me over the phone."

"That's fine," came the reply, "but you must be aware that this call may be being recorded." Omar did not mention "by every prominent intelligence agency in the world"!

"Mr Soroush," he continued, "we have reason to believe there is a credible threat against your personal safety."

"Say what?" came the shocked reply. "From who?"

"Do you know of any reason why some Russian citizens might want to hurt you, Mr Soroush?"

'Probably plenty,' thought Shaheen, but instead he said, "No, I have no idea."

"Please take this as a credible threat, Mr Soroush," Omar explained. "We're not certain why, but we have credible information that there are Russian citizens who are arranging to hurt you. I must therefore advise that you ensure your personal safety becomes a foremost consideration. Please lock your doors; do not meet alone with any Russian citizens or anyone you believe might be associated with them or that you deem could inflict physical harm on you. Avoid keeping a regular commuting schedule and please call the police if you have the slightest suspicion that all is not well." He added, "For our part we are putting out additional patrols on your area of residence, and should you call, we'll have a car at your house within four minutes." It was a lie, but Omar knew that if such precise time-to-delivery statements worked for McDonald's, then they could sure as hell work for the police.

Shaheen listened carefully; he did feel reassured by the promise of additional patrols, but he had to ask: "Do you know who's made the threat?"

"We can't be sure, but we do think it very credible." Omar then probed further: "I was hoping you would know better than us."

Shaheen was feeling his world implode – he had thought that he was in the clear, and now this? He thanked Omar and took down the officer's mobile number.

Omar slipped in one last question: "Do you have a cat, Mr Soroush?"

"No, why?" Shaheen realised that it was a half-truth.

"Because the source of information mentioned an argument over a cat, and it made no sense to me," explained Omar.

"Hmm," Shaheen pretended to think. "That makes no sense to me either."

Omar asked Shaheen to call immediately if he noticed anything suspicious and the conversation ended, with one of them very worried and the other not worried at all.

Shaheen sat back in his chair. 'Holy shit,' he thought. What next?

The fact that Bunny's skin had been dumped after Soltegov's drowning meant that one of his Russian lunatics was loose in the city, and now the bastard was coming after him! It had been bad enough when he knew the identity of the protagonist, but now every swinging dick with a Russian accent could be the guy that was going to throttle him.

Shaheen's primary instinct, which was cowardice, started to kick in.

Whenever danger occurred, his first thought was to run away and he knew that in just five days, this could be achieved. He reasoned that perhaps the Russians would follow him to Singapore, but he quickly thought of a method to mitigate that risk. For now, he would need to protect himself in the short term. Hopefully the Russians had no clue that he would be out of Dubai within a week. He called Harry, asking him where he was.

"I'm at work." Harry did not know whether to be astounded or amused that Shaheen had called *him*.

"I'm on my way to speak to you – which coffee shop?"

"Starbucks," responded Harry, choosing one of the most discreet in the Financial Centre.

Forty-five minutes later, having ordered their coffees, the two men sat down at the back of the shop. Shaheen leant forward and began to speak, little guessing that what he was saying was making chills run all the way to Harry's nerve endings.

Shaheen confided in Harry about the call and its content from Dubai Police, and that the Russians were trying to kill him. He realised that the threat of harm was not the same as a death threat but reasoned that, at this juncture, in order to get what he needed, not letting the truth get in the way of a good story could only help.

"Why not leave town?" Harry asked, trying to appear calm and logical.

"I will," replied Shaheen, "but I need a week, and in that time I need protection. Can you get your friend Graham to help me? He has a security company, doesn't he?"

Harry's had to think fast. Clearly Oleana, or the person pulling her strings, had been compromised, and if that was the case, then he would also be implicated. He knew that if the police dug deep enough, they would inevitably discover the literal skeletons in the closet. If that happened, he would go to an Arab jail for a very long time. Perhaps, he reasoned, *he* should leave the country.

"Will Graham help?" Shaheen repeated, disrupting Harry's thoughts.

"Sure," Harry blurted, trying to conceal his panic. "I'm sure he'll be able to help." Harry had regained his composure. "But what's the cause of all this, Shaheen?" He needed to get Shaheen's side of the story.

Shaheen then explained to Harry the business altercation over the *Burj Takseeb* and the fact that the Russians claimed he owed them money because the project had failed through lack of water and electricity. He described how he had argued with them, that he had delivered his end of the deal and that it had been the authorities who were at fault. The Russians had not agreed and wanted their money.

Suddenly Harry started to wonder about the two men that he had killed in Shaheen's house. Perhaps they had come for Shaheen and not for him – but surely they would have known who their target was. Things had happened so quickly that night, that he still did not realise it had been the assassin's hesitation due to his recognition that Harry was not the target that had given Harry enough time to react and throw the knife. There was now, however, the first seed of doubt planted in his mind that he had not been set up by the man across the table.

"I'll talk to Graham."

Harry's new plan was already taking shape as both men walked out of the coffee shop into the afternoon sun and the warm breezes that made up Dubai's winter.

That evening, Harry sat with Graham and explained that a transaction between the Russians and the Iranian had gone south over a project called *Burj Takseeb*, and that the unexpected lack of power and water had caused the Russians to ask for a payment that the Iranian had refused. They had therefore ordered a hit on Shaheen, who had been fronting the deal. He required some immediate security measures.

This was Graham's business; he was already on the phone as Harry was talking, tasking one his most reliable team leaders, Richard, to organise an immediate discreet presence on Shaheen's street and the placement of one of their number in Shaheen's house. They would keep one team member close to Shaheen at all times, and put out an invisible barrier around Shaheen's movements of four counter-surveillance operatives, whose task it would be to detect anyone or any team watching Shaheen. It was the ultimate form of discreet protection.

If the team detected any suspicious activity, then they would deny access to the target by communicating with the minder, who would then change the pattern of Shaheen's activity in proportion to the extent of the threat. Graham told Harry that it would cost the client £12,500 a day.

Harry called Shaheen, told him the price and nodded to Graham.

Graham relayed his instructions to Richard: "It's a go, mate. Get one bloke out to the address. I'll text it over. Stand up the first team; expect 12-hour shifts for the next week. We'll brief the first team on the hoof."

Harry watched and listened to Graham with some envy. He knew that his own rewards in the financial sector were lucrative but he would have liked to be commanding, or even just part of this small team. He knew that within an hour, Shaheen would be as safe as he possibly could be, despite the fact that the team were not allowed to carry conventional weapons.

Graham finished the call with his team leader, content that, in keeping with Special Forces professionalism, instructions only had to be given once and they could be considered done. He looked at Harry. "Thanks for this, mate. Much appreciated business. I threw the extra 500 quid a day on there for you." Graham smiled. "Call it a commission."

Harry thanked Graham and thought better of telling him that Shaheen had specifically asked for his services, especially if meant an extra two or three thousand pounds in his account.

CHAPTER TWENTY-TWO
Chinese Whispers

Within two days of having his security detail around him Shaheen had got used to them and now enjoyed having them in tow. He had been introduced to each of the teams on first-name terms so that he knew who was on his side, and he had been genuinely surprised by the normality and diversity of their appearance.

Rather than being the big, burly black men favoured by so many film stars, all of these men were noticeable for not being noticeable. Two of them were from the Indian special forces, one of whom rode a food-delivery motorcycle; another two were described as former Philippines SEALS; the rest were mostly European in appearance; Shaheen guessed that they ranged in age from 30 to 55, and he concluded that the only thing these guys had in common from a physical perspective was that they had nothing in common. They were recruited, deployed and effective as an invisible shield.

Back in his office Harry continued to consider his options. He had to assume that the police had compromised his involvement. To that end, his choices were twofold. He could either complete Oleana's task to punish Shaheen and risk arrest or worse; or he could fabricate the 'message' in order to convince Oleana that it had been done. It was a no-brainer, but he would need to have another conversation with Shaheen first.

He made the call asking to meet. Omar would read the transcript some 12 hours later and hope that this meeting would be when the Brit would attempt the crime before the Russians did.

At about the same time as the policeman was reviewing the latest information, Graham was placing a call to Toby. "Something's come up," he explained. "Could be nothing, it could be something, but it might be of interest. When can we meet?"

Within an hour and a half, Toby was sitting in Graham's office, sipping tea, explaining truthfully how his firm had been tasked to protect the Iranian national against a credible Russian threat. He now had Toby's full attention. "There's been a big deal that's gone south," Graham expanded. "The Russians are claiming that the Iranians owe them tens of millions of dollars for a *Takseeb* project; there's a tower or two involved." Graham knew that '*Burj*' in Arabic meant 'tower'. "Somehow the Russians bought in, but as of yet, the Iranians haven't cooperated, and the Russians want their money back. They've put a contract out on Shaheen Soroush, who's presumably the front man. At the moment, we're passively protecting him."

Toby wanted to take notes – he had a memory like a sieve. He had even surprised himself on passing the various tests to get into MI6. However, he did not want to look unprofessional in front of this Special Forces source, so rather than pull his notebook from his pocket, he was desperately trying to commit every detail that Graham was providing to memory.

Following the meeting, he sat in his car recounting the conversation in his head and jotting down the details he could recall. He then exceeded the speed limit all the way back to Abu Dhabi.

Back in the Embassy he Google-translated '*Takseeb*' and nearly fell off his chair when he saw the English meaning of the Arabic word flash up on his screen:

Enrichment

"Holy shit," he said out loud to himself – the Russians had been trying to do some sort of deal with the Iranians on enrichment. "The bastards!" he exclaimed as he leant back in his chair. It all made sense. Russia's President vetoing the UN Security Council on peace initiatives to stop the carnage in Syria; his move in the Crimea and stance on Ukraine; Iran's President coming back to the nuclear negotiating table in order to deny enrichment, and their intransigence, despite the crisis in Iraq. Clearly Russia and Iran were making an unholy alliance while the world was focussed on Syria, the Crimea and Iraq, and, for their part, Russia would surely be accepting significant money for their nuclear know-how. Toby knew that this was big – really big.

He worked through the night, drafting and perfecting his report for the head of station meeting the following morning.

Source Report, HUMINT A-2, UK National

BACKGROUND
Dubai Police issued a personal safety warning to Iranian National, Shaheen Soroush.

Source is former UK Special Forces and has been contracted to provide close-protection security for Soroush for at least one week, at which time it is thought by the Source that Soroush will exit the UAE.

The threat has come from the Russians and is presumably captured by Metadata or SIGINT intercept by Dubai Authorities.

Source reports that Unknown Russians have put out a killing contract on Soroush as punishment for non-payment to the Russians for a co-funded 'Enrichment Tower'.

COMMENT

1. *It appears a uranium-enrichment facility has been provided but monies that were promised by the Iranians have not been forthcoming. Mr Soroush is reported as the front man and therefore the Russians who are owed tens of millions of US dollars have ordered his killing, presumably to send a stern message to the Iranian government.*

2. *It is not yet known the extent to which the Russians have provided knowledge or facilities to the Iranians.*

3. *It is not yet known if the information and facilities have been transferred to Iran, but the assumption must be that whatever the Russians have provided has already reached Iran.*

Toby placed the second-highest reliability grading permitted on a report from a human being; it took centre stage at the morning meeting the next day. Toby felt a glow of satisfaction as his colleagues around the table read it and waited for the head of station to speak.

"Who else knows about this?" asked the boss. "Has your source spoken to anyone else about it?"

"Not that I know of – he's former UKSF, hence he came to us rather than anyone else," replied Toby.

"How did you meet him?" came the next question from the head of the table.

"He was one of the Brits on board when that Russian Duma member drowned. In fact, the Iranian on the boat is the one he's now protecting." Toby paused. "He's obviously well in with these characters." He hoped that they would not question the A2 reliability grading.

"Do you think he knows any more about the enrichment program?" the boss asked.

"Again, I don't think so. He referred to it by the Arabic name the Iranians and Russians had used, '*Taksee b*'. I don't think he's given the real meaning a second thought." He paused again and joked, "You know these soldiers, they can't think beyond the next hedgerow."

A murmur of a chuckle went around the room; any snipe that these civil servants could make at the military was appreciated. Toby was playing the crowd.

"We need to run this one up the flagpole, Toby." The boss had made a decision. "Let's get London on the secure blower; you can brief them and we can await instructions from there. Is there anything else we should tell them?"

"Not immediately," Toby responded.

"Good work, Toby." The boss was clearly ready to end the meeting. "This could be just what we need to embarrass the Russians after the way they snubbed us and the Yanks over Syria, Crimea and Ukraine, the bastards."

Within an hour, the brief had not only been elevated to the top floor in Vauxhall Cross, it had made its way north of the river in time for the Prime Minister's 9.30 briefing. It was the PM who decided that Britain should inform the Americans, and at about 3.30 that afternoon, an MI6 officer strolled casually down Adam's Row in London's West End, just one block from the US Embassy in Grosvenor Square. He stopped outside the dull, worn door of number 48. He casually checked one last time that he had not been tailed before pushing the antiquated bell in the centre of the door three times. He paused for 10 seconds, then used the large lion's-head knocker and rapped three times. The opening buzzer sounded, the door opened, he took two steps in and he closed the door behind him. He was now confronted with a further iron door and a camera.

"Can I help?" came a woman's voice with an American accent.

"It's Pat to see John," the British spy replied.

About 30 seconds passed before the voice instructed, "Come on up." The agent walked up the stairs into what was the Central Intelligence Agency's real headquarters in the UK. A young woman in flat shoes, presumably the same who had greeted him on the intercom, met him at the top of the stairs. She showed him past several work stations where young men were reading their screens; only two of them bothered to glance up at Pat.

When they reached the modest corner office, his American counterpart was already out of his chair with his hand outstretched. "Good to see y'all again, Pat," he said in a southern drawl. "Tea, coffee, iced tea?" The last part was his idea of a joke. He had never understood why the Brits loved hot tea so much but hated the iced variety that was the staple refreshment of the southern states. Pat asked for a "white coffee", just to push home the British vernacular for ordering a 'coffee with cream', and both men sat down.

"What ya got?" the American asked. Pat quickly explained that their station in the UAE had recruited a reliable source who was close to the Iranian subject involved, and that the Russians had put out a death threat against the Iranian because he had failed to make the payment on the 'Enrichment Programme'. He explained that the source was one of the elements guarding the potential victim, hence why he was in the circle of knowledge. "However,"

Pat clarified, "we don't think the source is aware that the kill is over an enrichment programme, because the Russians and Iranians have been using Arabic to communicate. The threat was picked up by the Emiratis, presumably over a phone-tap."

"Son of a bitch!" the American exclaimed. "You mean that the goddamn Russians have been playing us like a flute all this time over Crimea, Ukraine and Syria, and all the while they're busy doing an enrichment deal with the latest regime in Iran?"

"Certainly appears that way," Pat confirmed. "And worse still, the Iranians are back at the world's negotiating table, not agreeing to previously proposed levels and saying that they're not enriching uranium to weapons-grade, when the whole time it seems they've been paying the Russians for the capability."

"So why did they stop paying?" the American asked.

"Not sure, but our source did say it was some sort of argument over power and water. We don't know whether that refers to the centrifuge needing more power than the Russians said it would, or if 'water' has something to do with heavy water. We just don't know at this stage." Pat sipped his milky coffee.

"What are the Brits doing with this?" John asked directly.

Pat put on his best British accent for the amusement of his American colleagues. "Giving it to you, old boy. Like we always do. We collect and collate, then leave it to the elephant that is the State Department to exploit."

"Well it won't be a Republican elephant!" joked John, referring to the GOP's mascot.

"That's fine, John." Pat flashed him a smiled. "After all, it was the Democrats' donkey that kicked bin Laden and droned the hell out of his hierarchy."

"Good point, my friend!" John laughed. "So let's see what Big Ears does with this."

The two men shook hands and promised to get together for a beer in the not-too-distant future. Pat left Adam's Row and made his way to Bond Street, where he merged with the shoppers; from there he crossed down to South Kensington and then doubled back to Victoria, before finally heading towards his own annex in Vauxhall Cross, where he would make a full report on his meeting with the CIA.

The following morning in Washington DC, the Director of the Central Intelligence Agency left his office in Langley and travelled towards the Naval Observatory. Today, while the President was visiting the Far East, he would be giving his line-item intelligence brief to the Vice President.

The director enjoyed briefing the VP; this man had headed up the Joint Intelligence Committee for years before he had become the President's running mate. The VP appreciated how difficult it was to get good intelligence, and even more so, how difficult it was to exploit information in the right time or space.

The emergence of the Russians in the UAE assisting the Iranians with a uranium-enrichment programme was item three on the briefing agenda. The director passed on the information as he had received it and added that their own people in Dubai had confirmed at colonel-level with the Emirati CID that a credible threat by the Russians against the Iranian target had been intercepted. He went on to say that the Iranian had been told of the threat and that the individual had put his own personal protective services in place; this was how the Agency, via the Brits, had managed to get the information.

The Vice President's reaction was much the same as his CIA man in London's had been. He cussed out the Russian President and the double-dealings of the Iranians. He turned to his Chief of Staff. "Get me the Secretary of State on the phone."

Within 10 minutes he was briefing the Secretary of State, a former naval officer and winner of the Distinguished Service Cross in Vietnam. "Oh shit," were the Secretary's first words as the VP described the intelligence. "This corroborates an Iranian media report this morning that up to 230 Iranian MPs have signed a draft law to oblige the government to increase uranium enrichment to a level of 60 percent. The chairman of their parliament's Foreign Committee's stated that the vote's a warning to the US and Western governments, and that by pursuing the plan, the parliament's trying to support the Iranian negotiating team in their talks with the West."

"Oh shit," echoed the Director of the CIA. "The difference between producing 60 percent enriched uranium and 90 percent for weapons-grade is tiny; it's not a straight-line curve – the process gets a whole lot easier as the percentage increases. This is real. How do you want to play it, gentlemen?" He paused, looking at the VP and then specifically at the Secretary of State. "It is you, after all, that's been looking the Iranians and the Russians in the eye while they've been lying to you."

"I'll tell you how I'm going to play it," the Secretary replied. "I'm going to confront both of their foreign ministers head on. I know they'll deny everything, they always fucking do, but at least they'll know that we know the full extent of what they're up to, and for that we can withhold any further easing of sanctions until the bastards come clean. I'll call them both into Geneva on 'an immediate'; if they don't come, our reprisal will be to brief the media on what we know. But a congressional sanction threat on its own should bring at least one of them to the table."

It would be 48 hours before 'America's Secretary' would look his troublesome counterparts in the eye to tell them what he knew. He could hardly wait to fire a rocket up their respective arses and tell them that he had caught them with their pants down around their ankles.

★ ★ ★

In Dubai, Oleana was making her final preparations. She so wanted to call Harry to get an update on whether he had beat the shit out of Shaheen yet, but she knew better than to ask, and especially over the phone. She decided instead to call Farah and invite her for 'coffee'.

Farah was delighted and turned on in equal measure to hear Oleana's voice. She was hoping that Oleana had in mind the same variant of coffee as she wanted.

As it turned out, she did.

Oleana met Farah, wearing business attire, at the coffee shop in the rear of the Fairmont Hotel, where she had booked a day room in case the coffee progressed – it did. The two women enjoyed full use of the facilities that the suite offered; over the course of about three hours, they enjoyed the champagne, the bed and the shower, the whole time exploring every inch of each other's body with their fingers or tongue. Both women walked back to the valet-parking feeling refreshed from multiple orgasms and the cleanliness of woman-to-woman lust.

Farah drove home to resume her motherly and spousal duties; Oleana drove home a worried woman. Farah had confided to her that the Dubai Police had warned Shaheen he was in physical danger from the Russians. She had told Oleana that they had a permanent bodyguard in the house, and that one of them accompanied Shaheen wherever he went. There were others about as well, but she never saw them. She had added that Shaheen thought he would be able to leave Dubai within four days.

Oleana knew that that bastard policeman must have warned Shaheen; perhaps he was in cahoots with the Iranian. She had expected them to monitor her calls, and for the conversation with Harry to throw them off her tail, but she had not expected them to act on them like this. She realised that she may have underestimated Omar. She wondered if Shaheen was close to one of the ruling sheikhs; perhaps it was one of them who had insisted he be protected.

She would have to warn Harry that, if he tried to hurt Shaheen at this point, he could end up walking into an ambush of bodyguards – or even the police. She would have to call him off.

Across town, Harry had been contemplating an escape route by which he could avoid attacking Shaheen. It was obvious that the police were onto him, but he would have to give Oleana the impression that the job was done by the time Shaheen left Dubai. When his phone rang and it came up as Oleana, he could not have been more surprised.

"Harry, darling, I have to see you." Oleana poured on the sexiness.

"Okay," Harry answered cautiously.

"Come to Mall of the Emirates after work. Meet me at 5.45 in the Cheesecake Factory." She knew that the place was huge and that they could position themselves well away from prying eyes and ears.

Later that afternoon Shaheen emerged from his lawyers' offices with a pile of papers. He walked to his car with Graham's man and texted Harry, simply asking, "*Please come round to the house tomorrow morning, I have something for you*".

Harry read the message, not knowing what the hell it meant, but knowing he needed to find out.

It was just past 5.42 pm when Harry strolled into the huge restaurant and scanned for Oleana. He saw her sitting at a table in plain view; he walked towards it and smiled. When he reached the table, she simply stood up and said, "Follow me." She led him away from where she had been sitting and around the corner to another, empty, seating area. Any watcher or listener would now have to move with her.

The CID officer who had been observing from an adjacent table cursed to himself as he lost sight of them both. He knew that he would compromise himself if he also changed tables. He decided that, if push came to shove, in order to save face, he would have to make up a report.

"Harry, the police are onto us," she said, as soon as they had sat down. "Shaheen has bodyguards — there's no way you can deliver the message, the goalposts have moved. We both have to be very careful."

There was no way that Harry was going to let her know that he already knew what was going on. "How the fuck did that happen?"

"I'm not sure," Oleana replied, "but I'm guessing it's something to do with Soltegov; I think they might be listening to your calls." She wanted to make him think that he was in the shit and that she was in the clear.

Harry played along. "Shit, that's not good. What shall we do about Shaheen?"

"Nothing, Harry. Leave it for now. Hopefully you'll get your chance another day. He's a very bad man; I don't know who's protecting him or why, but we need to break off and pretend the whole thing never happened."

"Whole thing?" Harry smiled.

She smiled back. "Don't be naughty, Harry — that was a fling and we both know it. We're in a new game now, and you, my friend, need to get yourself off the playing field."

The waitress came to take their orders, but Oleana closed the menus and stood up, telling her, "We've changed our minds. We're leaving."

Harry took the cue and followed her. As she passed by where the lone CID watcher was sitting, she dropped the menus down onto his table, smiled and simply said, "Enjoy your meal."

The man decided that he would definitely need to fabricate his report of the meeting:

Harry left the mall with a smile so wide that his teeth were dry. This was perfect – he had got himself an out, and even though he thought that Shaheen was a complete slimeball, he had already concluded that he would never be able to carry out the punishment. Now that he was off the hook with Oleana, he could get his life back, stop killing people, and try to nurture his relationship with Natella.

About the same time that Harry arrived home, the CID watcher was walking into Omar's desk space.

"How did it go?" came the inevitable question, as Omar spun around in his chair.

"You know they're lovers, right?" the watcher replied – it was as much a question as it was a statement.

"Are you surprised?" Omar smiled. "Any man with half a chance would be her lover. She's beautiful. But the big question is, is it still in play?"

"All the indications are that it's still in play. They had a detailed conversation. I couldn't hear very much because of the background noise," he embellished, "but judging from the intensity of the conversation, I'd say they're still going for it."

The Watcher left the office, knowing that if the hit did happen, then he would get credit; if it did not, he could blame it on a subsequent event. His career was safe, even if he had just lied through his back teeth to his superior and fellow officer.

Omar wanted to question his watcher further, but then decided that there was little point; he had to trust his man on the ground, even though, in reality, he knew he could not. If his officer said that it was in play, he would have to let it run. Omar would feel slightly reassured the following day, however, when he noted that Soroush had placed a call to Harry. At least the two men were still in contact.

On Friday morning, the first day of the Arab weekend, Harry went to find out what Shaheen had for him. As he walked into the villa on the Palm, he did not know why he felt so surprised to see packing boxes littered around the house – he knew that Shaheen really was leaving.

The two men sat in the living room and drank tea while one of Graham's team sat 'minding' in the hallway. Harry asked how it was going with the security team and Shaheen joked that he could easily get used to it. He then got around to letting Harry know the reason for the invitation.

"Look, Harry, we haven't known each other for very long, but in that time you took care of Bunny without any fuss or asking for reward, you were a reassuring force during the Soltegov accident, and you've made sure I'm well cared for now by Graham's team. I'd like to help you as you've helped me and I've been thinking perhaps there's an opportunity for some business continuation that would be to your advantage."

"Shaheen, you don't owe me anything," Harry cut in.

Shaheen ignored him and continued. "I own two tower blocks in Ajman; I called them *Burj Takseeb*. The idea was to create low-cost but quality accommodations in Ajman that could enrich the lives and lifestyles of those who couldn't afford Dubai." He sipped his tea. "But it didn't go as planned. I completed the tower and got shafted by bad timing and the previous owner, who hadn't obtained clearance from the authorities in Ajman for power and water to the complex. Essentially I didn't get any, so the whole project fell into disrepair. The Russians owned more than half the apartments in the complex, hence the position I'm in today."

"Is there a way out?" Harry prompted.

"To be honest, I don't know," replied Shaheen. "But I have a feeling that Dubai's economy has turned, and now that it's hosting Expo 2020, it's well and truly back to good times. If this trend continues, then Ajman might tag along and give me the power and water that I need to bring the project back to life – and profitability."

"So what do you want from me?" Harry urged him on.

Shaheen leant forward and picked up some documents from the coffee table. "Harry, these are power of attorney documents, assigning you full signature authority over the property. To develop, to sell, to lease; whatever you can do, as the opportunity arises. If you do this for me, I'll pay you 40 percent of my gain from the property. You're in the financial industry, I know you'll find a way. And in the meantime, I retain full legal liability."

"Why can't you do it yourself?" Harry asked.

"Because, Harry, I'm out of here in 48 hours and I'll never be back. All my businesses except this one have been moved; all my employees have either been offered relocation or redundancy. I've tried to be kind to everyone who I've done business with out here, but it's almost cost me my freedom and my life. I've had enough of the environment, Harry." Shaheen was close to tears. "I worked my way up from nothing in Iran, but because I chose an industry as old as the human race itself, I've spent my whole life running away. In Singapore I won't need to run anymore. Their laws are just and based on precedent, not religion. I need this for my business, my family and my life."

It was profound and Harry recognised that Shaheen was being genuine. He wondered if he had misjudged the man, and as he read the documents that Shaheen had handed him, he could not help but wonder if this was not some kind of trick.

"Can I think about it?" Harry asked.

"Not really, Harry," Shaheen responded quickly. "I need this sorted and I can't have anyone else knowing about it until I'm out of the country, in case I get blocked from leaving. As soon as I've left, my lawyers have been instructed to inform the relevant authorities. You'll note there are full permissions for you to rescind the power of attorney at any time, and that you have no financial liability if the property continues to lie dormant or lose money. There is no downside, Harry – you'll have to trust me on this one."

Harry had lived his life managing risk, and the fact that he still had a pulse and had successfully transitioned professional sectors was proof enough that he was good at it. He read the three-page contract once more, then looked Shaheen in the eye. "Do you have a pen?"

Shaheen handed him a Mont Blanc pen with which Harry signed three sets of the documents, all of which had already been signed by Shaheen's lawyers and stamped with the relevant UAE official stamps. Harry decided not to ask how that had been achieved. He offered the pen back to Shaheen.

"Keep it, Harry. Let it bring you luck and us good fortune."

"I could drink to that." Harry answered with a smile.

Shaheen offered his hand to shake. "I'm glad you're doing this, Harry. If it succeeds, I could not think of a more worthy man with whom I should share profit."

Harry felt pangs of guilt. Not 24 hours earlier he had been planning to beat the shit out of Shaheen for his deceit over Bunny *et al*. Now he was his business partner. He reflected on how Oleana would shit herself if she ever found out.

★   ★   ★

An hour previous to Harry's arrival at Shaheen's house, three business jets arrived at Geneva International Airport: one from Tehran, one from Moscow and one from Andrews Air Force Base, in Maryland. Their respective occupants made their way to the city's Intercontinental Hotel, already reinforced with a phalanx of police and military security.

Two hours later the US Secretary of State sat in a suite on the hotel's sixteenth floor, facing the Russian and Iranian foreign ministers. He had decided to cut to the chase after a curt greeting – he would not mention Crimea, Ukraine, Iraq or Syria. "Thank you for coming at such short notice, gentlemen. As you could probably tell from our communiqué, we believe the urgency is justified." Each of the men opposite were confused by the presence of the other – the Secretary had decided to ambush them with his reason for being there. "We have received credible and corroborated intelligence in the form of technical and human intelligence that your country, sir" – he looked at Russia – "and your country, sir" – he moved his stare to Iran – "have been colluding in an enrichment programme that is being run jointly out of the UAE." He did not wait for them to deny the accusation. "We are aware that payments have been made and that there has recently been a dispute over such payments and programme resources, to such an extent that Russia has pushed out a death threat to the Iranian front man." He decided to throw in a curve-ball. "We have known about this programme for some time," he lied, "but given the magnitude of the Iranian Parliament's vote to enrich up to 60 percent –which, as you know, is at odds with the previously agreed 20 percent – it seems there's some explaining to do."

The American then sat patiently as both men predictably protested and denied that their countries were cooperating on any enrichment programme.

After each man had had his say, the Secretary leant forward, his tone steady and without emotion. "Gentlemen, whatever has been going on between your countries with regard to enrichment needs to stop right now, otherwise it will become public knowledge, and the talks that have provided the opportunity for Iran to be welcomed back into the international community will collapse. The United States needs quick and credible proof from both of your countries that the illicit enrichment programme being run out of the UAE has ceased. Until that time, there will be no easing of sanctions, no monies released to Iran and" – here he looked pointedly once more at Russia – "no leeway whatsoever given over Russia's position in the Crimea, Ukraine or Syria, which we believe is linked to all of this."

The Secretary of State stood up, signifying that the meeting was over. "Shall we say one week to clear up this mess?" Both men nodded and he left the room. When he reached the hallway he turned to his Secret Service close-protection detail.

"Now let's get the fuck out of here."

Back in the sixteenth-floor suite, the Russian and Iranian foreign ministers looked at each other. "What was that all about?" Russia asked.

"I haven't a clue," responded Iran. "To be honest, I know nothing about anything he was talking about."

"Me neither." replied the Russian, "which makes me think that either our governments are deceiving both of us at the same time, which is possible but unlikely; or the Americans have reverse-engineered this to make it seem as if we're misbehaving, to show themselves once more to be the world's policemen, and to gain leverage at the negotiating table over everything from Ukraine to lifting your sanctions."

His counterpart nodded, and both men agreed that they would get to the bottom of what was going on and report any progress within 48 hours.

On their separate journeys back to Geneva Airport, both foreign ministers were wondering whether they had in fact been sidelined or undermined by their leaders. Perhaps they had not been told about the enrichment programme so that they could not be accused of lying during negotiations; or perhaps it was because neither of their respective leaders trusted them. This was not a good situation for either of them – they were well aware that retirement homes for out-of-favour politicians in their countries most often took the form of a prison cell.

Encrypted conversations back to Moscow and Teh-ran commenced as soon as the wheels of each govern-ment-owned business jet had left the ground. Before either minister had reached their home country, their briefs on the enrichment programme had already been walked in to the Russian President and the Iranian Supreme Leader.

Both leaders went berserk on being given the informa-tion. Both gave similar orders: "Find out who organised this and arrest them."

The SPV officer in Dubai almost shit himself when his director's office in Moscow contacted him. He had no clue about any threat issued by any Russian against any Iranian in Dubai and certainly none about any enrichment pro-gramme. He knew that if he did not find answers fast, this whole thing could cost him his job.

He immediately called his closest link in the Dubai police. Two hours later he was sitting in a shitty coffee shop on the Deira side of Dubai Creek listening to the police captain recount what he knew – that a CID colonel had confirmed that a credible threat had been made by a Russian group against an Iranian-born businessman who also held Saint Kitts and Nevis citizenship. The warning had been made under the crime prevention initiative; however, the colonel believed that the threat was still in play. The police were not aware of the American-generated intelligence regarding a joint enrichment programme, and they were now investigating this line of inquiry. They did know that the recently deceased Soltegov was somehow linked to all these events, but were not sure how.

The SPV officer now had a name; this was a start and would placate his superior, and perhaps his president. He asked the police captain if there was anything else.

"Not at the moment."

The officer thanked him and, before leaving the café, told him that he and his family would enjoy an all-expenses-paid holiday to any part of Russia that they chose.

In Moscow, the SPV director smiled as he heard Soltegov's name. He was not sorry that this bastard was dead – the man had always been a renegade, hence why he had not been promoted beyond the rank of colonel while in the KGB. The director knew that Soltegov worked for one man only, one godfather. He picked up the direct line to the President's office and spoke this name to his leader.

"Arrest him," the President ordered. "Then we'll throw away the key."

At 3 am, the police breaching team smashed in the door of Alexei Delimkov's Moscow apartment. He and his wife had not taken one step out of their bed before they found themselves pushed back by the black-clad assault team. They saw the barrels of the specialised AK-47-6 rifles pointed at them by each of the assault team. Delimkov was handcuffed and told that he was being charged with treason.

He was thrown into the waiting police van, from where he could hear his wife sobbing as she was pushed into a separate vehicle. Delimkov knew that he must have mightily pissed off someone on high – he just hoped that it was not the President.

By 9 am that day, bloodied, beaten and bruised, Delimkov had admitted to diverting money from government departments and laundering the funds through various international projects, including in Dubai. He vehemently denied, however, any knowledge of technology in any nuclear enrichment programmes, or indeed the transfer thereof. He pleaded with the interrogating brutes, insisting that he was telling the truth, and such were his protestations that they believed him. They reasoned that, in any case, his confession alone was enough to condemn him to a gulag for the next 10 years.

Iran's links into Dubai were several-fold more efficient than any Western power's. The lineage of the Emiratis had been literally impregnated with the combination of Arab sperm and Persian eggs over the course of countless generations. Hence, when the Iranian intelligence officers called in favours, they got answers.

They quickly learned that Shaheen Soroush was the Russian's target and that the reason for this was a monetary dispute over real estate. Soroush was a wanted man in Iran for un-Islamic business practices, and in particular for his involvement with satellite TV broadcasts of pornography. The Dubai station head reported back to Tehran that they could find no trace of anything that would link Soroush to an enrichment programme, and in their assessment, Soroush was far more likely to work against the Islamic Republic of Iran than for it.

The intelligence assessment that then went to the President before finally reaching the ears of the Supreme Leader concluded that the report was, in all likelihood, an American-manufactured ruse to buy time or leverage in their ongoing negotiations. The report added that the Iranian Ambassador had requested that the Emiratis arrest Shaheen Soroush pending further investigation. However, the fact that Soroush was a citizen of a country other than Iran was complicating the process somewhat..

The Russians and Iranians communicated to each other that no evidence of any joint government-sponsored enrichment programme had been evidenced in the UAE, and together they concluded that the accusation was some sort of play for time by the Americans. They separately communicated with the US Department of State, requesting a meeting.

CHAPTER TWENTY-THREE
Cat And Mouse

Harry sat at his desk staring at the papers that Shaheen had given him. He could not decide whether they were a blessing or a curse. He could not comprehend what had happened in his life over the past few weeks either.

He had joined the financial sector to make some serious money and to get away from the security sector, where so many of his former military colleagues like Graham now worked. He had yet to make big bucks, and although he knew that he would never be in the hedge fund manager league of earnings, he had always hoped that a single big deal would one day set him free.

Harry had once chuckled at the comment of American billionaire, Ted Turner, who had responded to a question about when enough was enough by saying, "*No one in this world needs more than 22 million dollars.*"

Harry had initially viewed the comment as billionaire arrogance epitomised, but then he had pondered that Turner was precisely right. The 22 million was not enough to buy huge jets and yachts, but it was more than enough to travel the world first-class, and never have to work again. $22 million represented the metaphoric market bulls that he needed to catch. He hoped that these papers in front of him might represent a significant part of that ambition.

The ringing of his mobile phone interrupted his thoughts; he smiled when he saw Natella's name on the caller ID. He knew that he had not given her enough time of late but vowed that that would change. Harry greeted her in the kindest tone he could exude. "How are you? I was just thinking about you." He was lying but he hoped that she would be pleased by it.

"You were?" She was clearly delighted and they exchanged a few pleasantries before she revealed the real reason for her call.

"Something weird just happened," she explained. "I just got a call from a landline number I didn't recognise and it was Oleana. She wanted to know how we were getting on and if I had heard from you lately. I told her we were friendly but that I hadn't seen you very much recently because you'd been so busy. I suggested that she and I meet for a coffee but she said she was tied up for the next few days and that she would call me next week. She also said she had lost her mobile phone so she would call me with a new number when she had bought one."

Harry quickly deduced that Oleana was trying to send him a message not to call her on her phone, and that perhaps he should do the same thing. He needed to go along with Natella's confusion, however, so simply replied, "Hmm, that is all a bit strange, but she must have her reasons."

Natella agreed and lingered on the phone in order to give Harry the chance to arrange their next date. He did not let her down and gave her Thursday evening to look forward to.

Harry arrived home that night, half-expecting Oleana to be waiting for him – she was not. He poured himself a bottle of

Old Speckled Hen beer and decided to vegetate in front of the television.

He must have dozed off on his sofa, because when his home phone rang at 10.30 pm, he woke with a start. It was the Indian concierge on his tower block's reception. "Sir, we have a package that has been hand-delivered for you. Is it okay to bring it up?" Harry told him that it was – he knew that this last-leg delivery was their favoured method of getting a small tip for their services. Harry pulled a 10-dirham note from his pocket in anticipation of the doorbell ringing.

The Indian concierge handed Harry a plain cardboard box that was about half a metre cubed; he then smiled broadly as the 10-dirham note hit his palm.

Harry noted that the only writing on the box was the number of his apartment; he asked the concierge who had made the delivery and was told that it was the driver of a private taxi.

Harry carried the box to his dining room table and retrieved a sharp kitchen knife to cut through the tape. Like most people, Harry liked surprises, but in this case he did not know what to expect as he opened the box.

Inside was a blue and black vented holdall bag. Harry did not bother to lift the bag out of the box, but rather grabbed the zipper and pulled it open. He physically jumped as Bunny's head popped out of the bag. "Jesus Christ!" he blasphemed out loud, smiling broadly. "You scared the shit out of me, Bunny! Where the fuck did you come from? Everybody thought you'd been skinned."

He picked her up and held her, as much to check that it really was her as to pet her and make sure that she was okay. Her purring was a strong indication that she was *the* Bunny, and he could see that her being confined in the package had not affected her in any way.

He put her down onto his kitchen floor and she weaved in and out of his legs characteristically. He put a small bowl of water down to see whether she would drink it – she did not, so he assumed that she had not been packaged up for long. He concluded that wherever she had been, she had been well cared for.

He trimmed down the box in which she had been delivered and tore up strips of newspaper to make an *ad hoc* litter-box, before opening a tin of sardines. He got ready for bed and was totally pleased to see that she had somehow found her way to him. For her part, Bunny chose to soak up his body heat by spending the night sleeping between his legs.

By 8.00 am the following day, Brigadier General Mabkhoot, the head of operations for Dubai's police, was viewing the Iranian Ambassador's request that they detain Shaheen Soroush on suspicion of espionage. By any measure, the brigadier had worked his way to the top by application of professional toil, intellect and achieving results. He was an honest, hard-working policeman who was justifiably proud of everything that his force achieved. His role now, as it had always been, was to implement the law to create one of the most secure societies that the modern world had to offer. He had always flown under the radar and avoided publicity – it was not he, after all, who wrote or interpreted the laws of his visionary country. His job was to ensure adherence to them while concurrently protecting and serving his leader *and* the community.

The brigadier immediately noted that there was very little hard evidence on which to arrest Soroush, and he instinctively held no favour whatsoever for radicals, whether governmental or independent. He had realised, however, that in order to become a general, he was on occasion required to trade in his pure police logic for the sake of regional politics. He ordered Soroush to be detained for questioning in the hope that he might have fulfilled a regional favour, but the suspect would be quickly released thereafter.

★   ★   ★

While the Dubai police commenced the detainment process, the private secretaries of the Russian and Iranian foreign ministers made a secure call between Moscow and Tehran. The dearth of credible information surrounding a rogue nuclear enrichment programme was obvious to both senior civil servants, who had made sure their respective bosses match their own opinion.

The Russian then suggested a proposal on behalf of his senior. "My minister thinks we should cooperate and be united in our response to America." He knew that this would gain the Iranian representative's full attention. "America has either manufactured this entire situation or it has been misinformed. Either way, it has tried to put our backs to the wall over this intelligence report in order to undermine both our countries, in your case over the negotiations on enrichment levels, and perhaps over our common stance on Syria."

"Go on," urged the Iranian.

"We propose that, instead of denying the erroneous intelligence report, we confirm the existence of the rogue programme in the UAE, and blame it on a mafia cartel in our case and on an extremist element in yours, both of which operated without the permission of our governments. The protagonists were motivated by misguided loyalty to their countries, and by money. The opportunity was taken because of the US's intransigence over sanctions against Iran, and her continuous negative PR against Russia. For our part, we've arrested the head of the Moscow cartel."

"We have persuaded the Emiratis to arrest the Iranian," exaggerated the voice in Tehran.

"Perfect." The Russian smiled on the other end of the phone. "We believe the US will respond to our 'admission' in three ways: the first, of course, will be one of smugness;

the second will be for them to run around in ever-decreasing investigative circles until they disappear up their own arses; but the third will be agreement – that their procrastination and hostility is playing into the hands of the radicals. We believe it'll soften them to the idea of a deal." He paused. "Especially given the soft negotiation stance of the current administration. We believe we have nothing to lose by leading them up the garden path."

"One might say the ultimate practical joke," the Iranian summarised.

"Indeed – the dislocation of expectation by the appearance of cooperation and admission," the Russian answered. He paused before asking, "Will your minister go for it?"

"There's no doubt in my mind," came the reply.

On the M-Frond of Dubai's Palm, a police Land Cruiser followed the unmarked Chevrolet Escalade. Only the Dubai-savvy would have recognised the latter's four-figure registration with the initial 'B' followed by an '8' as a government registration.

Outside Villa 132, the two cars pulled up short of the driveway; two policemen got out of the Escalade and walked around the side of the house. The others went to the front door and rang the doorbell.

A young boy, clearly Soroush's son, answered the door and the policeman asked him in Arabic if his father was in.

"I don't think so, but he could be upstairs," the son replied.

Farah appeared from the kitchen area to see who was at the door; she suddenly noticed the two policemen in the garden and screamed.

"Please, madam," calmed the policeman at the door. "We're here to make sure your husband's safe. Is he at home?"

"No, he's not here," Farah answered. "Is there a problem?"

"No problem," the policeman lied. "We just wanted to make sure he was okay and ask him a couple of questions." He paused. "When will he be back?"

"I don't know," Farah replied truthfully. "He didn't say."

The policeman handed Farah a business card. "Please could you have him call me when he comes home?"

She looked at the card and said she would.

The arrest team smiled as they climbed back into their vehicles; they would have to wait another few hours for the day's fun. As they drove off the Palm, they radioed in that the suspect had not been in place, but that he would call them when he returned.

The CID policewoman who worked with Omar walked over to his desk and repeated the arrest team's message. As she did so, she watched Omar studying his computer screen. He did not look round as she spoke; instead he seemed riveted by what the displayed information was telling him. He gradually broke into a broad smile, leant back in his chair and started to laugh out loud. The policewoman asked him what was so funny.

In the baggage-collection area of Terminal 1 in Singapore Changi Airport, the passengers from Emirates flight EK354 were instructed to proceed to Carousel 6. As the passengers clustered around the designated belt, the expensive-looking suitcases bearing first- and business-class coloured tags fell off the conveyor onto the carousel, reaching their prioritised rendezvous with their owners.

Shaheen recognised the first of his oversized bags, grateful that Emirates offered such generous baggage allowance for its business-class passengers. He had been relieved that no one on the upper deck of the business-class section of the

Airbus 380 had recognised him, and even more so when the giant airliner had been pushed back from its stand at 3.15 that morning.

As he reached forward to pull his second bag from the carousel, he glanced up, and his roving eye noticed a tall, slim, attractive, but slightly dishevelled woman. He reflected that she looked as if she had just got out of bed – or economy class. She had her blonde hair in a loose bun and held by a clip and was wearing black Juicy sweatpants with a matching top and a pair of Aviators sunglasses.

He felt chills as the realisation hit that he knew her. She looked like the Russian chick that Harry had dated, but he could not be sure. Had she seen him? If so, she had not acknowledged his presence. What the fuck was she doing here? Shaheen was starting to panic. Could it be coincidence? Surely the world was not that small.

He hurriedly arranged his bags onto the baggage cart and scurried away towards customs, and then to the Raffles hotel limo waiting for him. He hoped to hell that she had not seen him.

Oleana hated flying economy, but in this case it was her own money funding the flight, so it was necessary suffering. She had grudgingly paid the excess baggage charges but was grateful to be out of reach of the CID policeman that had made her whole life an uncertain mess. Back in Dubai, she had half-expected to be stopped by the police or immigration at any juncture, but she had purposely not cancelled her UAE residency so as not to attract undue attention – it would be valid for another six months. Her flirting with the passport-control officer seemed to have worked perfectly, and her claim to be visiting friends in Singapore was only half a lie.

As the aircraft had taxied towards the runway in Dubai, she had sent what was intended to be her last text from her

UAE mobile phone to Alexei Delimkov's mobile number in Moscow; it simply read:

No delivery, Swordfish.

Oleana had no idea that the Godfather would never see the message, nor that it would be another week before his wife would be released from jail and able to read it. She would never understand that '*Swordfish*' meant the Fixer had exited the country.

Oleana breezed through Singapore's customs and made her way to the MRT metro for the half-hour ride into the city centre. As she rode the train, she hoped that her stay in the three-star Grand Blue Wave Hotel would not be extended any longer than necessary, and that Bunny had been safely delivered to Harry.

Back in Dubai, Omar had gone to the cafeteria with the policewoman; he placed the tray of tea and a wrapped chicken shawarma on the table where she was sitting.

"How did she know he was leaving?" she asked, as Omar sat down.

"I can't be sure," replied Omar; the irony was still amusing him. "But I can't help but laugh. Soroush thought he'd done everything right to make a clean and quiet exit from Dubai – and he had. But the very person who's out to harm him not only got inside his circle of knowledge, but she was also on the same damn plane as him." He took a bite from his shawarma and spoke as he ate. "He's now in for a world of hurt. We won't warn him she's there – we can't compromise how we know it's her who's the threat. The Iranians also want him disposed of, and the Singapore authorities are blissfully unaware of any of this."

"Surely we should warn them?" the policewoman insisted.

"That's way above my pay-grade, but if I were a betting man, I'd say we need to leave this well alone. It's complicated enough as it is, and now the operations boss needs to explain to the Iranians that their man exited Dubai before the detainment was effected. They're sure to think it was orchestrated." Omar pondered in silence for a couple of moments. "The Russian woman is very special – clearly well trained. Her only mistake was to throw the registration plate in the dumpster and she got unlucky with that. For everything else, whatever she was doing, and I suspect we'll never fully know, she covered her tracks. If she has gone to Singapore to kill Soroush for sure, and I can't think of another reason, my guess is he's a dead man walking."

"Do you think she'll come back to Dubai?" the policewoman asked.

"I doubt it, but I hope beyond all measure that she does," the veteran detective replied.

"To arrest her?" came the obvious question.

"You must be joking – I want her to come back so that I can figure out what she is and what she does." Omar smiled. "You see, after a few years in CID you'll find it becomes less about arrests and enforcement, and more about who can outfox whom. We have all the technical resources money can buy, but if someone knows the extent of our surveillance and they go low-tech, then it all comes down to our tradecraft verses their guile. That's when we have to become good detectives, and I actually end up smiling when I drive to work." He could see that the policewoman was intrigued by what he was saying. "I thought we had the better of Ms Katayeva, but it seems like that was far from the case." He sighed. "But all I can do is keep a watching alert on her passport and hope to hell that one day she decides it's safe to come back here. After all, she hasn't committed any detected crime as yet."

* * *

Later that week in Geneva, the full negotiating committee had gathered, in order to move to the next level of agreement regarding the restriction of Iran's production of weapons-grade enriched uranium. Two hours before the main committee convened, America's Secretary of State was once again sat opposite his Russian and Iranian counterparts for a 'private' discussion.

The eloquent Russian minister took the lead and humbly admitted from the Russian side that rogue criminal elements, motivated by money, had been behind the UAE enrichment debacle that had so ably been discovered by the Americans. He added that, by order of the President, the Russian organiser had been arrested and was to be charged with treason.

The Iranian minister then took up the confessional. He told the American how their investigations had revealed that the Russians were in contact with a renegade element of Iranian heritage – their aim was to procure or achieve the capability to produce weapons-grade uranium while the Geneva conferences sat around and pontificated over percentages. He added that, while 20 percent enrichment had been approved in the negotiations, this was probably not enough to placate the rogue elements in Iran. If the overweight statesmen and post-menopausal women of the Geneva conference could not come up with the permissions required for increased levels, then it was likely that even the Iranian government would not be able to contain these elements – including those that had been uncovered by the CIA.

The Secretary was extremely content that the men in front of him had come clean. They had surely realised that believing WMDs to exist where there were none was not a mistake the might of America's intelligence resources wanted to make twice.

The voice of America paused for an unusually long period of time after Iran had stopped talking; he wanted to make absolutely sure that neither man felt compelled to say anything else. They did not.

He then lifted his head and spoke. "The admission of involvement, even by rogue elements, is deeply appreciated, gentlemen. I think we all know that such action is important to restore mutual trust." Both men nodded as he spoke. "Clearly America has to be confident that both your countries are capable of controlling these rogue elements, not least because, though we are often accused of being the world's policeman, that is not our intent, nor our aspiration."

'Yeah, right,' was the sarcastic thought from across the table.

The Secretary continued. "However, the United States is acutely aware that we must help you help yourselves. To that end I can certainly see how a token increase in permitted enrichment levels could put your rogue elements out of business. I will therefore propose to my president that the US endorse permitted enrichment of up to 40 percent. I realise this isn't the 60 percent voted for by your parliament," he said, looking at Iran. "However, it's twice the previous level we agreed and it meets you halfway. I would point out that we do realise permitting you to reach 40 percent does make it easier for you to achieve weapons-grade enrichment levels. As part of the agreement, therefore, you would have to agree to increased levels of monitoring."

The Iranian minister nodded and put on his best poker-face. "I think my leadership could live with that." The meeting ended shortly thereafter.

Within two days, the world's media had announced a monumental agreement between the West and Iran; despite the tantrum-level of protest from Israel, it was unanimously agreed that Iran would be permitted by the world's powers to enrich uranium up to 40 percent, but that, in turn, they would implement an open-door policy with regard to inspections and monitoring.

Iran declared a victory in negotiation; the West declared it was a fair compromise and the beginning of the Islamic Republic rejoining the international community.

Behind closed doors, the foreign ministers of Russia and Iran high-fived on the unofficial agreement that, in return for Russia's assistance in duping the Americans, all equipment relating to the newly permitted enrichment levels would be purchased from Russia. The deal was worth billions of dollars.

Israel viewed the West's concessions to Iran as absolute folly, comparable even to the second Gulf War cock-up. The Prime Minister took a respite from his ongoing battle against Hamas and flew to Washington DC to sit in the Oval Office as its most frequently visiting foreign leader. He animatedly warned the President and Secretary of State that, thanks to the West's naive agreements and with the Russians' help, Iran was now within a stone's throw of producing WMDs – and if it could, it would achieve the ultimate doomsday capability. He had not yet left back through the White House gates before the two American statesmen had reassured one other that the Prime Minister had been typically verbose, sensationalist and aggressive in his rhetoric – after all, "He would say that, wouldn't he?"

They agreed between themselves that the CIA had been all over this from start to finish and that, in any case, the UN inspection teams would demonstrate their efficiency by monitoring and controlling the enrichment levels.

Neither felt so reassured the following week, however, when the wise and credible prince who headed Saudi Arabia's Intelligence Agency, visited them with a stern message, unwittingly echoing precisely what the Israeli leader had said in the very same chair only a week before.

The prince explained that the enrichment agreement threatened to shift the entire power base in the Middle East from Sunni to Shia. He sternly informed the two Americans that they had very likely allowed for the creation of an Iranian nuclear powder keg, capable of causing a financial, political and physical crisis. This, he explained, could be enough to provide Israel with justification for a pre-emptive first strike. If that were to happen, the entire region would descend into war – which was why Saudi Arabia would now increase its own capability to ensure the kingdom's protection against both a nuclear Iran *and* Israel.

As the Saudi prince exited the Oval Office, the President's expression was one of a deer caught in headlamps. He looked across to his Secretary of State.

"Did we fuck this up?"

"Maybe, Mr President," monotoned the older and more pragmatic politician. "But if we can keep a lid on it until after the next election, it'll be some other poor bastard's problem to sort out."

CHAPTER TWENTY-FOUR
The Cat's Whiskers

It was about six weeks after the Iran enrichment agreement that Harry's mobile rang and Shaheen's lawyers greeted him. They informed him that, due to the awarding of Expo 2020 to Dubai, the Ajman authorities had had an increase in infrastructure funding from Abu Dhabi. This additional financial support would permit the completion of pumping houses and power generation, and, on a first-come-first-served basis, the *Burj Takseeb* could be connected to the utilities.

The lawyers told Harry that Shaheen, now living in Singapore, had been informed, and sufficient funds had been transferred to the bank account over which Harry had power of attorney in order to bring the tower up to habitable standards. Within another six weeks the first apartments could be rented or resold.

Harry enquired after Shaheen's welfare, to which the lawyer replied, "He's absolutely fine – his business is booming out there; he's even taken control of another six television channels." He paused. "Sadly the same can't be said for his married life."

"Why? What happened?" Harry asked predictably.

"It's all a bit bizarre really," the lawyer responded, "but a good bit of scandal."

"Go on," Harry urged.

"Well, I'm not sure whether you're aware of this, but Shaheen's wife followed him out to Singapore about two weeks after he left Dubai. Anyway, clearly Shaheen wasn't expecting her for another week, and she walks into his hotel room to find him doing a sixty-niner with a Singapore escort girl. So no sooner has she arrived than she announces she wants to separate, and she moves into a separate residential suite in a separate hotel, pending her renting a permanent place where the kids can easily switch between their mother and father."

"Blimey," said Harry.

"But that's not the best part of it." The lawyer could hardly wait to get the words out. "Shaheen's wife's taken a lover and she's been very public about it – but the shocker is that the lover's another woman!" The lawyer laughed. "Apparently some drop-dead-gorgeous Russian chick who's moved in with Shaheen's wife – they seem like a permanent item."

"Hot Russian chicks. They get everywhere." Harry laughed. "Shaheen's wife's also beautiful, so that would be worth watching, if you know what I mean."

"It's nearly *ex*-wife now, Harry, and I know exactly what you mean." The lawyer then reverted to being serious. "I suggest we, and by that I mean you, put the Ajman tower on the market. I'll try and track down the Russian investors."

Vlad, the imprisoned Russian money launderer, had lost 15 kilos since he had been incarcerated in one of Dubai's desert prisons. He had also lost his treasured anal virginity, which by any measure was a high price to pay for the glass and a half of red wine that he had drunk with his sidekick and Shaheen Soroush in the JW Marriot's steakhouse. Vlad had reflected of late that if he did not have bad luck, he would not have any luck at all, so it was very much to his surprise when his lawyer turned up at the jail seeking a meeting.

The lawyer sat opposite Vlad and explained that Shaheen Soroush's lawyers had been trying to find him, but had eventually figured out that he was in jail. They had contacted Vlad's lawyer to explain how the apartments that Vlad owned in Ajman had now been connected to the utilities, and were currently worth in excess of the original estimated valuation. Shaheen's lawyers had stated that they would like the tower to be populated, so, because Vlad was the sole signatory on the title deed to half of the apartments in the complex, they wanted to know if he would like to rent them out or sell them.

Vlad was taken aback. After all this trouble and shit, the place now had water and electricity? "Why couldn't this have happened a year ago?" he said out loud.

The lawyer shrugged his shoulders. "Welcome to the Middle East."

Vlad gestured around him. "Tell me about it." He then gave his lawyer Soltegov's and Delimkov's telephone numbers. "Call them and ask them what they want me to do." The lawyer told him that he would return in a week.

In Singapore, Farah had finished shopping for designer clothes in the Orchard Road area and returned to her residence in the aptly-named Shangri La Hotel. As she walked through the door, Oleana appeared from the kitchen and greeted her with a kiss. They proceeded to prepare dinner for themselves, discussing how the decision they had made while making love in Dubai's Fairmont Hotel had turned out to be the best one they had made in a long time. For Farah, the turmoil of having her cat murdered and leaving her precious villa and friends in Dubai, all because of her husband's fucked-up lifestyle, had been the last straw. For Oleana, the alibi of eloping to Singapore in order to escape the closing net of Dubai was as good as it was going to get. Shaheen had to pay Farah a small fortune in support and Oleana could parasite on that. In return, she would give Farah physical and emotional love and be kind to the children – she did also enjoy going out in public with Farah and watching the heads turn wherever they went. She had decided that this would be her life from now on – until she was once again forced to change.

Shaheen was barely two miles across town from Farah and Oleana when, a week later, his lawyers called. They reported that the Vlad's lawyer had been unable to contact any of the man's superiors, but that he was willing to sell his entire share in the apartment block. Shaheen smiled and simply said, "Tell Harry to sell it all."

The transaction with the Saudi buyer was neither long nor complicated. He was fuelled by the attraction of Dubai's Expo 2020 and the property price rises; he also had the cash and was looking for the excuse to dine out in Dubai as the owner of two apartment blocks, which in Ajman were affordable. He paid $38 million, plus all closing fees for the entire complex.

At closing, the lawyers dispensed $15.2 million into Vlad's account, $9.12 million into Harry's account and $13.68 million into Shaheen's account. For diverse and differing reasons, the profit for each man was absolute.

In the British Embassy in Abu Dhabi, Toby Sotheby was thinking about the upcoming weekend's polo match when his phone rang. It was the Ambassador's executive assistant, asking him to come to the Ambassador's office right away. This was a first for Toby since his welcoming interview, so he went upstairs, wondering if they had uncovered any of his cock-ups.

When he arrived at the office, the assistant told him to go right in. Inside, the Ambassador came out from behind his desk, shook his hand and asked him to take a seat.

"I have some very good news for you, Toby." The Ambassador smiled broadly. "Your exemplary work and discovery of the rogue Iranian and Russian enrichment programme in the UAE prevented enormous embarrassment for the UAE and Western governments. It also enabled the West to undermine such rogue elements by re-negotiating enrichment levels and taking criminals and extremists out of the market, all without permitting Iran to get the weapons-grade uranium it might have otherwise sought."

'Where is he going with this?' thought Toby.

"The Americans are wholly aware that it was the hard work and, may I say, brilliance of British intelligence that gained them the upper hand, and it's been assessed that our favour to the US will represent a significant bargaining chip when next we need one." The Ambassador paused for effect. "To that end head of your service has made certain recommendations, and Her Majesty the Queen has seen fit to invest you as an Officer of the Most Excellent Order of the British Empire – an OBE! The announcement will be official from Monday," he added, "at which time you'll be able to disclose the award to your friends and use the letters after your name." He handed Toby an envelope bearing the Buckingham Palace crest. "The Palace will be in touch in due course to arrange your date with the Queen, and let me be the first to congratulate you. I'm sure this award will precipitate a meteoric rise within MI6."

Toby accepted the congratulations and firm handshake, and left the Ambassador's office feeling stunned. He returned to his own basement office, slumped down in his chair, and read the letter from the Palace. He was elated to have the award – it would undoubtedly be worth many bottles of champagne in Piccadilly's Cavalry and Guards Club. His dilemma, however, was whether he should tell Graham Tree, who had, after all, gone out of his way in recognising the value of the intelligence and delivering it in such a way that placed Great Britain in high standing and ensured that no one other than the culprits would be embarrassed. As he googled '*OBE*' and saw the ornate gold medal in the shape of a cross appear on his screen, he decided it was more prudent that Graham not know. Toby reassured himself that 'OBE' might just as well stand for 'Other Buggers' Efforts' and, in any case, such awards were wasted on those Special Forces types – *they* would never dine out on them.

Upon his early and brokered release from jail, Vlad neglected to tell his partner in crime Luka of his windfall. He figured that he was the one who had paid the penance, and although he was shocked that the Controller was dead and that Delimkov had been incarcerated, it was none of his concern. Vlad was deported from the UAE to Russia, where he quietly remained and invested the $100,000 necessary to acquire a Dominican passport and nationality. He then flew to Costa Rica, where his newfound fortune allowed him to settle, and enjoy the low cost of living that this paradise offered. His intent was never again to return to Russia – or, for that matter, the UAE.

Harry remained in Dubai and enjoyed the lifestyle that being a millionaire in a tax-free environment afforded. He banked some 50 percent and invested in a charming apartment on Richmond Hill in London. The remainder he placed in a new and dynamic hedge fund being run by a group of young Zuckerberg-type geniuses out of Dubai's International

Financial Centre. The former gave him the family nest-egg and marital home that he had yearned for in the UK; the interest on the latter would provide him with more income than he earned from his day job. He calculated that within three years, he should be earning over $1 million a year from both his salary and the investment. Harry decided that he would continue to work out of Dubai, but planned to marry Natella and fund her qualifications through British law school. In return, he hoped that she would give him a son.

Bunny remained with Harry and was content to share him with Natella, provided that the sleeping arrangement in the bed continued to afford her a space on his warm spots. When Harry took her on a special road trip to meet another white Persian cat – almost identical to her, except bigger and male – she found herself receptive to this newcomer's advances. Sixty-four days later, she gave birth to four balls of meow-ing fur. One of her daughters, Soraya, would remain with Bunny and Harry for life.

Across the Gulf, in the land from which Bunny's breed had originated, the Iranians picked up the 40 percent enrich-ment ball and ran with it. They opened their doors to the inspectors, but concealed the ongoing development of their nuclear weapons under the guise of space research towards the production of rockets. Simultaneously, they continued preparations to enrich beyond the agreed level of percent, which could relatively easily be achieved.

At the same time, the West eased their sanctions, unfroze Iran's financial assets, and re-opened the SWIFT bank-transfer codes – all the measures that had brought the country to the negotiating table in the first place. The coun-try's currency regained strength, and neither the President nor his ministers could believe that they had had such luck. They had achieved everything that they wanted for essentially no concessions at all, and it was all down to this one man. Shaheen Soroush, who had been unknown to all of them – except for his pornographic films, which, of course, they had all enjoyed at some juncture or other. They were jovial whenever talk arose of his staying one step ahead of the Emirati authorities, vainly joking that it must be due to his genetic Iranian guile. They also agreed that, were it not for him being a wanted man for un-Islamic activities, he would likely be a recipient of the country's highest award, the Islamic Republic Medal.

This, as opposed to the execution by stoning he would in all likelihood face if he ever again dared to enter the country of his birth.

EPILOGUE
Hell Hath No Fury

In Moscow, Ivanna Delimkova, the Godfather's wife, had assumed total and savage control of his cartel.

She would not be so resigned to let the *Takseeb* matter rest, and her Russian revenge on all those she believed to have caused the downfall of her husband would not be a dish served cold.

It's not over yet!

Harry and Bunny will return in...

OSCAR KING's

MOSCOW PAYBACK

The second Harry Linley adventure

Read the first chapter now…

F arah and Sohar Soroush waited patiently at Amsterdam's Schiphol Airport. They had arrived a little too early for their flight as Farah had not wanted to misjudge the protracted taxi ride from the city to the terminal.

Sohar, just 12 years old, was still excited about the entire trip. Her visit to the Anne Frank Museum had brought her summer term's project on the young German Jew to life, and now she was leafing through the brochures that she had gathered during the visit showing the house in which her ill-fated heroine had hidden from the Nazis during World War 2.

She was sad her dad wasn't with them and even sadder that he had cancelled at the last moment, but she knew he worked hard, and it was some consolation that her incessantly teasing brother had decided to stay with his father. She had missed her dad since her parents' separation and her mother had moved in with Oleana, but she was acutely aware that her mum was about as happy as she had ever seen her.

Farah checked her watch and pressed a 'favourite' on her Galaxy S5. She heard Oleana's voice on the other end. "Just letting you know we're at the airport and we'll be boarding in a couple of hours."

"Great," replied Oleana. "I've really missed you guys; it's been so quiet here with you away and Aryan at his father's. What time do you get into Kuala Lumpur?"

"Seven in the morning, then a quick transfer to the commuter flight and an hour back to Singapore; we'll land at 9.45." The thought of the transfer made Farah feel even more exhausted, but she quickly reflected how much cheaper it had been than a direct flight.

"Okay, babe." Oleana was genuinely excited. "I'll have a lovely salad lunch and some Frascatti on ice ready for you when you get home."

Farah smiled as she thanked her and they said a fond goodbye. Sadly, it wouldn't be long before Oleana wished she'd kept her lover on the phone a little longer.

As mother and daughter made their way to departure gate G03, Farah reflected that 'coming out' with Oleana had been just about the best decision she'd ever made. The tenderness and genuine caring in their relationship was something she truly appreciated, and of course it didn't do any harm that Shaheen funded their entire lavish lifestyle. If good for little else, he was at least a generous ex-husband.

They were greeted at the end of the walkway by a petite, beautiful flight attendant, looking resplendent in her figure-hugging but traditionally coloured uniform.

"Is the flight full?" Farah asked, hoping there would be some gaps in the seating.

"I'm afraid it is," was the disappointing response from the beauty from Banting. "We have many people transiting to a medical conference in Australia, so it will be full for you and busy for us."

The jam-packed passenger load made the flight some 14 minutes late for its pushback from the gate, but the captain assured the passengers they could make this time up on the 13-hour flight to Kuala Lumpur. The aircraft climbed to its cruising altitude of Flight Level 330 and like the other passengers Farah and Sohar settled down to watch films and relax with the first round of drinks and lunch.

Sohar was engrossed in *Up*, which she had already seen multiple times. Farah had just finished watching a forgettable romantic comedy when she glanced at her rose gold Rolex Daytona – they had been airborne for nearly three hours. She slipped the watch from her wrist and pulled out the winder while she tried to calculate the time in Singapore.

She needn't have bothered; this was the end of her life.

The 'Snowdrift' acquisition radar had picked up its target about 80 kilometres out. The SA-11 missile battery's temporary commander – a Russian 'advisor' – leant over the Ukrainian separatist's shoulder; he spoke quietly: "That's your target; it's a Ukrainian transport, let's take it out."

The young separatist officer just hoped the advisor would talk him though it but he needn't have worried. This was the aircraft that the advisor had come for, and he knew it was no military target.

At just under 70 kilometres the radar offered acquisition – they took it.

At 30 kilometres the guidance and tracking radar activated. The advisor said just one word: "*Strelyat!*"

Without hesitation the Ukrainian separatist released the missile, which would now accelerate to three times the speed of sound in the direction of its target. Just 15 metres below the Boeing 777, the missile's 70 kilos of high explosive detonated.

Farah felt a massive and shocking convulsion as her seat pushed upward against her spine when the multiple G-force from the explosion penetrated the belly of the plane. She felt acute pain as her spinal discs compressed and ruptured, before the air was sucked out of her lungs at the same moment the aircraft instantly decompressed from a cabin pressure of 8,000 feet to 33,000 feet. She tried to gasp as the air hit her face at -63°C; she had never felt anything so stunningly cold in her life. She reached for Sohar's hand, found it and wanted to look over at her daughter, but she couldn't move, she couldn't see. There was no more pain, no more fear, as their unconscious, hypoxic bodies hurtled with the aircraft towards a God-forsaken field on the outskirts of a village in eastern Ukraine; a place so insignificant, no animal would ever bother fighting for it, let alone civilised human beings.

More quality fiction from
Nine Elms Books

www.bene-factum.co.uk/fiction

THE MERCHANTS OF LIGHT

Marta Maretich

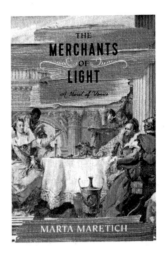

Nine Elms Books 2015
Paperback and e-book
ISBN: 978-1-910533-06-2
£9.99

A Novel of Venice

In May 1945, a beleaguered Monuments Man arrives in the bombed-out German city of Würzburg. His mission: to rescue vulnerable art treasures from the ravages of war. But surrounded by utter devastation, he wonders if there will be anything left to save...

What he finds will uncover the story of Tiepolo, the vibrant and prolific Venetian artist, and most successful painter of his day, and of Cecilia, mother to their tribe of talented children and model for the sublime beauties that appear throughout her husband's works.

This family's dramatic saga interweaves with the 20th-century struggle to rescue their most spectacular masterpiece, creating a bridge between old world and new, and asking: can human creativity triumph over human destruction?

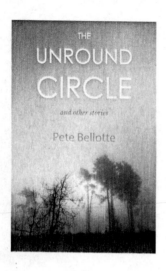

THE UNROUND CIRCLE

Pete Bellotte

Nine Elms Books 2015
Paperback and e-book
ISBN: 978-1-910533-09-3
£9.99

Just because I made it up, doesn't mean it isn't true.

Master of the written word Pete Bellotte presents twenty-two short stories exploring the limitless range of behaviour that people are capable of.

Amusing, perplexing, dark-minded, or even hilarious, the characters inhabiting this universe have just one thing in common: a determination to challenge expectations and upset the norm. You'll never see them coming.

In their own way, all of them – liars and murderers, heroes and romantics – fight back against the forces, right or wrong, that work against them. They defy convention... Break the bonds... Unround the circle.

BODYLINE

Simon Rae

Nine Elms Books 2015
Paperback and e-book
ISBN: 978-1-910533-03-1
£7.99

Murder stopped play.

The villagers of Little Bolton gather on the green one glorious Sunday afternoon for their weekly cricket match. With the game underway nobody suspects that among the men in whites stands a killer.

But when one of their number mysteriously collapses out on the field, Inspector Dalliance is sent in to investigate foul play. Soon enough he realises that the rural idyll in which he finds himself is in fact a viper's nest of bitter feelings and intense rivalries.

With the modern world encroaching on their traditional way of life, the stakes are higher for these people than Dalliance can imagine. He must root out the wrongdoers and heal this community in quiet turmoil, before it takes justice into its own hands once more.